D1159672

THE BEST OF
FREDERIK POHL

THE BEST OF FREDERIK POHL

Introduction by
LESTER DEL REY

Afterword by
FREDERIK POHL

NELSON DOUBLEDAY, Inc.
Garden City, New York

Published by arrangement with Ballantine Books
A Division of Random House, Inc.
201 East 50th Street
New York, New York 10022

ACKNOWLEDGMENTS

"The Tunnel Under the World," copyright © 1954 by Galaxy Publishing Corp. for *Galaxy* Magazine, January 1954.
"Punch," copyright © 1961 by H.M.H. Publishing Co., Inc., for *Playboy* Magazine.
"Three Portraits and a Prayer," copyright © 1962 by Galaxy Publishing Corp. for *Galaxy* Magazine, August 1962.
"Day Million," copyright © 1966 by Rogue Magazine for *Rogue* Magazine.
"Happy Birthday, Dear Jesus," copyright © 1956 Ballantine Books, Inc., for *Alternating Currents.*
"We Never Mention Aunt Nora," copyright © 1958 by Galaxy Publishing Corp. for *Galaxy* Magazine, July 1958.
"Father of the Stars," copyright © 1964 by Galaxy Publishing Corp. for *If* Magazine, November 1964.
"The Day the Martians Came" copyright © 1967 by Harlan Ellison for *Dangerous Visions.*
"The Midas Plague" copyright © 1954 by Galaxy Publishing Corp. for *Galaxy* Magazine, April 1954.
"The Snowmen," copyright © 1959 by Galaxy Publishing Corp. for *Galaxy* Magazine, December 1959.
"How to Count on Your Fingers" copyright © 1956 by Columbia Publications for *Science Fiction Stories,* September 1956.
"Grandy Devil," copyright © 1955 by Galaxy Publishing Corp. for *Galaxy* Magazine, June 1955.
"Speed Trap," copyright © 1967 by H.M.H. Publishing Corp. for *Playboy* Magazine.
"The Richest Man in Levittown" (orig. published as "The Bitterest Pill"), copyright © 1959 by Galaxy Publishing Corp. for *Galaxy* Magazine, April 1959.
"The Day the Icicle Works Closed," copyright © 1959 by Galaxy Publishing Corp. for *Galaxy* Magazine, February 1960.
"The Hated," copyright © 1961 by Ballantine Books, Inc., for *Turn Left at Thursday*.
"The Martian in the Attic," copyright © 1960 by Digest Productions Corp. for *If* Magazine, July 1960.
"The Census Takers," copyright © 1955 by Fantasy House, Inc., for *Fantasy & Science Fiction,* February 1956.
"The Children of Night," copyright © 1964 by Galaxy Publishing Corp. for *Galaxy* Magazine, October 1964.

CONTENTS

A Variety of Excellence

NOTHING IS EASY to categorize about the life and works of Frederik Pohl. His stories vary more in length, attitude, type and treatment than those of any other writer I know. About the only point of similarity is the high level of excellence to be found in everything from his short-shorts to his novels. To make things more difficult for a biographer, he has been one of the leaders in almost every activity that in any way relates to the broad field of science fiction.

Even his career as a writer falls into two widely separated periods which seem totally unrelated to each other.

He began writing professionally in the very early forties, when he was just out of his teens. A large number of his stories, under a host of pen names, were written in collaboration with one or more other authors, and nobody seems entirely sure of exactly how many people or stories were involved. There were also twelve stories under the name of James McCreigh. The work produced during this period was generally quite competent—good enough to win him welcome from a number of markets—but there was nothing about it to distinguish him from many other young writers of the period.

The second phase of his writing career began eleven years later, after a long hiatus; and his reputation was established from the first story, a serial by Frederik Pohl and C. M. Kornbluth—called *Gravy Planet* in the magazine version, but retitled *The Space Merchants* for book publication. This was unquestionably the most important novel published in 1952. It was favorably reviewed by publications that ranged from *The Wall Street Journal* to organs of the extreme political left, none of which normally gave any space to science fiction.

Pohl and Kornbluth brought the art of satire back to science fiction and were soon being widely imitated by other writers; in fact, the influence of this work reshaped much of the field during the next two decades.

This novel was soon followed by two other collaborations with

Kornbluth. Some of the self-proclaimed critics in the field, who remembered Pohl's earlier stories and esteemed the independent work of Kornbluth, immediately decided that Pohl was largely dependent on Kornbluth for the high quality of their novels. They proceeded to pick the works apart, deciding who had done what—and the parts they admired were always ascribed to Kornbluth.

Kornbluth agreed with Pohl that these critics were amazingly consistent in being wrong about it, so far as could be remembered. But this didn't quiet the part-pickers. Even the publication of Pohl's first independent novel, *Slave Ship,* wasn't enough to convince them, though it certainly should have done so. However, as other works by Pohl appeared, even the most severe critics were forced to concede that he was one of the major novelists of the field.

Meantime, among the readers, he was developing a high reputation as a writer of shorter fiction, in which he had no collaborator. His novelette, "The Midas Plague," was the first of his independent stories to appear in *Galaxy* Magazine, in April, 1954. This is a brilliant example of satirical writing, with the shocking bite of its main assumption muted nicely by an element of humor. It is also an extrapolation of one trend, carried just a bit further than any other writer would dare to go with it, and then justified by the other well-developed details of such a society.

I recently had an excellent chance to discover just how good Pohl is as a writer of shorter fiction. In making the selections that appear in this book, I read through every word of eight collections of Pohl's shorter works. That comes to about half a million words!

Generally I've found that reading all of any one collection of shorts and novelettes by a single writer is not to be done at a single stretch. After all, shorter works are never meant to be read together, but rather to be separated by many months in magazine publication. Most writers tend to stick to certain themes, or do certain types of stories much better than others. When read at one sitting, these become too obvious, too repetitive—boring, in fact, in such an unfair way of reading them.

For that reason, I approached the task rather reluctantly. I planned to read one book at a time, then wait a week, and try another.

It didn't work that way. I read all eight books in less than a week—and found that I thoroughly enjoyed them. I not only didn't find that the reading grew monotonous, but I began to look forward to each new volume with anticipation.

The works in this collection all appeared between 1954 and 1967;

there have been outstanding stories since, but I agree with Frederik Pohl that we need more time to determine which of those should endure as his best. Meantime, these are the ones I consider his best, chosen from a rich production that can often be honestly termed memorable. Probably other readers would have made other choices —there are too many good stories to make selection simple. But I have chosen these after a great deal of consideration.

As I read, I kept a list of the stories I felt mandatory for inclusion, planning to fill the remainder with "next-best" stories. Again, it didn't work out that way. My list of "must" stories was twice as long as the limits of the book permitted. So I had to go back and weed out stories, hating to eliminate even one, to reach a manageable length.

There seems to be no limit to the variety to be found in the shorter works of Frederik Pohl, in fact. They vary in length from 1,500 to 21,000 words, and that is the smallest element of their variety. Some of them, like "The Midas Plague," might be called satirical—but not with the cold sardonic contrivance so common to this much-abused form of literature. Pohl is involved in the cultures he shows; he may be sardonic or amused, but he feels himself a part of that which he holds up to the distorting mirror of reality.

Some stories depend on a twist at the end; usually this occurs in the shorter pieces, as should be the case. However, the twist is not to surprise the reader, but to bring the idea to a quick and pointed conclusion that is completely satisfactory. And there is always more than the twist. "Grandy Devil" is based on a marvelous character in a family that is strangely immortal; "Punch" tells us more about ourselves and all intelligent life than is conveyed in many novels, short as the story is.

"Tunnel Under the World" is a story of terror and of pathos—an odd blend of emotions, indeed. It is also a fine suspense-action story. "The Hated" could have been a simple action story, but the heroes it presents to us are engaging in a different kind of conflict with their environment.

There are stories that would simply be sentimental in the hands of a lesser writer. "Father of the Stars" tells of a man who felt he had to go to the ends of explored space, and how he succeeded; we've all read that story a dozen times, but not in this form! "Three Portraits and a Prayer" tells of an old scientist who learned he was wrong. There's sentiment there for those who can empathize—but no sentimentality.

Some might be called "idea" stories. (All are built around ideas, of course; but some ideas tend to obtrude beyond the story, except in the hands of a very skillful craftsman.) "The Day the Martians Came" is one of the oldest ideas, first given acceptable form in Wells' *War of the Worlds*. The title gives it all away—or does it? All the ingredients are familiar—except the way we see it, and what we realize from Pohl's view. "Speed Trap," on the other hand, is a totally new idea, so far as I can determine, beautifully turned into excellent fiction. "The Day the Icicle Works Closed" gives us a new service for tourists, another idea that makes me wonder why no one thought of it before.

It's hard to say whether there's a new idea in "Day Million"—Pohl says it's a love story, the oldest idea in literature. It is a love story, but I find nothing old in it.

And finally, skipping over a few other selections you can discover for yourself, there is an article, as a sample of several excellent pieces of science non-fiction authored by Pohl. In this day of computers, we should all master arithmetic to the base two, but most of us still cling to the decimal rut. Pohl teaches us how natural and simple the new system is—and shows us that it's the only way to master some of the ordinary problems of daily life.

There was also no problem of balancing the book to insure sufficient variety. That took care of itself.

Pohl's career in science fiction is at least as varied and complex as his writing.

Like so many of us, he began his public life as a "fan," a reader of science fiction who became so enamored of the literature that he had to join with others in discussing and proselytizing it. In those days, there was a small number of such fans who were so well known that many became more famous in science fiction than some of the writers. Pohl rapidly joined this number, and became a leader among the others.

He was part of the movement that led to the formation of the first great fan tradition—the annual World Science Fiction Convention. As much as any single person could be, he was a moving force in the organization of the very first one, held in 1939. (He didn't attend. There were feuds in those days that seemed earthshaking then, and he was too strong a fan not to take sides. Happily, those feuds are now dead, and ancient enemies are now the best of friends.)

Almost at once, he graduated to editing his own magazines. This came about before he was twenty-one. Somehow, despite a very low budget for his magazines, he managed to become a major editor, with magazines second only to the acknowledged and established leader. And when I visited New York City in those days to see John

W. Campbell, the only other editor it occurred to me to see was Frederik Pohl.

He might have gone on with the magazines, but the war interrupted his career. And when he returned, he turned to another field. He opened an agency to handle the stories of other writers, and rapidly became one of the leading agents in science fiction, perhaps the leading one. His roster of clients read like a *Who's Who* of science fiction, from long-established professionals to beginners who were quickly promoted to stardom under his handling. I couldn't have issued the four magazines I was then editing without his service; his help to Horace L. Gold in the launching of *Galaxy* must have been beyond value.

It was partly as a result of his work as an agent that he returned to writing. He made a strong effort to bring back many of the writers who had dropped out of the field, among them his close friend, Cyril Kornbluth, who had begun under a number of pen names and had been one of the better young writers before the war, but had since abandoned all writing efforts. In persuading him to return to writing, Pohl discussed many ideas for stories with him. It was during these discussions that the idea of collaborating again came up, resulting in the novel, *The Space Merchants*.

As an agent, Pohl was also instrumental in steering many writers into the book field, where publishers were then just becoming interested in science fiction. Among the writers steered into this new market was Isaac Asimov. And Asimov benefited in this partly by the fact that Pohl was also still an active and important fan! There was an organization in New York called the Hydra Club which had been founded by Frederik Pohl and me in 1947, and the monthly meetings of this club were attended by most of the major writers and editors in the field at the time. It was at such a meeting that Pohl brought Isaac Asimov together with Walter Bradbury, editor for Doubleday; the result was a contract for the first of an incredible number of books by Asimov.

Eventually, the lure of writing proved more compelling than the work as an agent, and Pohl gave up his agency to become a full-time writer. He continued to collaborate with Kornbluth, but he began to work a great deal on his own. He also collaborated on two projects with me. I can't speak for other collaborators, but in my own case, Pohl contributed fully half of the writing and all the basic ideas, while taking only half the credit. But our work was so much rewritten back and forth, and so completely the result of constant rethinking that I can't even guess who was responsible for what, in most instances.

But our methods were so dissimilar that we both decided after the second attempt to abandon working together, financially successful though it had been. One lasting result, however, was that my wife Evelyn and I moved out to Red Bank, where we were always the closest of friends with Fred Pohl and his wife Carol during the next two decades.

Pohl also began a series of collaborations with Jack Williamson. It seemed an unlikely combination; Pohl's writing was accepted as somewhat sardonic and cynical (though that was an unfair judgment), while Williamson was noted for his extreme romantic euphoria about man in the future. Yet the collaboration worked well through three juvenile books and many adult serials.

Nothing ever went in a straight line in his career, however. Now that he was a successful author, it wasn't too surprising that he resumed his career as an editor. Horace L. Gold resigned as editor of *Galaxy* and *If,* and Pohl was immediately chosen as his successor.

Now he was editing two of the leading magazines in the field, with a competitive budget, quite different from his previous experience.

He proceeded to demonstrate just how good an editor he really was, and the results were quickly apparent, as he began discovering new talent and making full use of the old. Many of the leading authors today first appeared in his magazines–Niven and Tiptree, to name two quite dissimilar ones from a large group. The stories he printed won a majority of the Hugo awards in the succeeding years, and *If* was picked for the Hugo three successive years!

Then the magazines were sold to Universal Publishing and Distributing Corporation. Pohl was offered the chance to continue editing the magazines, but it would have meant full-time commuting to New York City, and he decided to go back to writing without editing. He felt there were rewards enough in that; rightly so, as it proved, since he was named as Guest of Honor by the World Science Fiction Convention in 1972 and won a Hugo for his writing in 1973–the only man to win that honor both for his writing and his editing.

There were a few other contributions during all this time, of course. He became one of the most sought lecturers on science fiction and the world of the future, addressing all sorts of groups and crusading for what science fiction had long been, but which was just being discovered by a wider audience. He helped enlarge that audience. He taught science fiction in schools for young writers. And he traveled widely (to both Russia and Japan, for instance) to deepen the international flavor of science fiction.

As I write this, he is again serving as an editor, this time as science fiction consultant for a large soft-cover book publishing house. And, happily, he is still writing some of the best science fiction to be found in books or magazines.

Lester del Rey
August 11, 1974

The Tunnel Under the World

ON THE MORNING of June 15th, Guy Burckhardt woke up screaming out of a dream.

It was more real than any dream he had ever had in his life. He could still hear and feel the sharp, ripping-metal explosion, the violent heave that had tossed him furiously out of bed, the searing wave of heat.

He sat up convulsively and stared, not believing what he saw, at the quiet room and the bright sunlight coming in the window.

He croaked, "Mary?"

His wife was not in the bed next to him. The covers were tumbled and awry, as though she had just left it, and the memory of the dream was so strong that instinctively he found himself searching the floor to see if the dream explosion had thrown her down.

But she wasn't there. Of course she wasn't, he told himself, looking at the familiar vanity and slipper chair, the uncracked window, the unbuckled wall. It had only been a dream.

"Guy?" His wife was calling him querulously from the foot of the stairs. "Guy, dear, are you all right?"

He called weakly, "Sure."

There was a pause. Then Mary said doubtfully, "Breakfast is ready. Are you sure you're all right? I thought I heard you yelling."

Burckhardt said more confidently, "I had a bad dream, honey. Be right down."

In the shower, punching the lukewarm-and-cologne he favored, he told himself that it had been a beaut of a dream. Still bad dreams weren't unusual, especially bad dreams about explosions. In the past thirty years of H-bomb jitters, who had not dreamed of explosions?

Even Mary had dreamed of them, it turned out, for he started to tell her about the dream, but she cut him off. "You *did?*" Her voice was astonished. "Why, dear, I dreamed the same thing! Well, almost the same thing. I didn't actually *hear* anything. I dreamed that something woke me up, and then there was a sort of quick bang, and then something hit me on the head. And that was all. Was yours like that?"

Burckhardt coughed. "Well, no," he said. Mary was not one of the strong-as-a-man, brave-as-a-tiger women. It was not necessary, he thought, to tell her all the little details of the dream that made it seem so real. No need to mention the splintered ribs, and the salt bubble in his throat, and the agonized knowledge that this was death. He said, "Maybe there really was some kind of explosion downtown. Maybe we heard it and it started us dreaming."

Mary reached over and patted his hand absently. "Maybe," she agreed. "It's almost half-past eight, dear. Shouldn't you hurry? You don't want to be late to the office."

He gulped his food, kissed her and rushed out—not so much to be on time as to see if his guess had been right.

But downtown Tylerton looked as it always had. Coming in on the bus, Burckhardt watched critically out the window, seeking evidence of an explosion. There wasn't any. If anything, Tylerton looked better than it ever had before. It was a beautiful crisp day, the sky was cloudless, the buildings were clean and inviting. They had, he observed, steam-blasted the Power & Light Building, the town's only skyscraper—that was the penalty of having Contro Chemicals' main plant on the outskirts of town; the fumes from the cascade stills left their mark on stone buildings.

None of the usual crowd were on the bus, so there wasn't anyone Burckhardt could ask about the explosion. And by the time he got out at the corner of Fifth and Lehigh and the bus rolled away with a muted diesel moan, he had pretty well convinced himself that it was all imagination.

He stopped at the cigar stand in the lobby of his office building, but Ralph wasn't behind the counter. The man who sold him his pack of cigarettes was a stranger.

"Where's Mr. Stebbins?" Burckhardt asked.

The man said politely, "Sick, sir. He'll be in tomorrow. A pack of Marlins today?"

"Chesterfields," Burckhardt corrected.

"Certainly, sir," the man said. But what he took from the rack and slid across the counter was an unfamiliar green-and-yellow pack.

"Do try these, sir," he suggested. "They contain an anti-cough factor. Ever notice how ordinary cigarettes make you choke every once in a while?"

Burckhardt said suspiciously, "I never heard of this brand."

"Of course not. They're something new." Burckhardt hesitated, and the man said persuasively, "Look, try them out at my risk. If you don't like them, bring back the empty pack and I'll refund your money. Fair enough?"

Burckhardt shrugged. "How can I lose? But give me a pack of Chesterfields, too, will you?"

He opened the pack and lit one while he waited for the elevator. They weren't bad, he decided, though he was suspicious of cigarettes that had the tobacco chemically treated in any way. But he didn't think much of Ralph's stand-in; it would raise hell with the trade at the cigar stand if the man tried to give every customer the same high-pressure sales talk.

The elevator door opened with a low-pitched sound of music. Burckhardt and two or three others got in and he nodded to them as the door closed. The thread of music switched off and the speaker in the ceiling of the cab began its usual commercials.

No, not the *usual* commercials, Burckhardt realized. He had been exposed to the captive-audience commercials so long that they hardly registered on the outer ear any more, but what was coming from the recorded program in the basement of the building caught his attention. It wasn't merely that the brands were mostly unfamiliar; it was a difference in pattern.

There were jingles with an insistent, bouncy rhythm, about soft drinks he had never tasted. There was a rapid patter dialogue between what sounded like two ten-year-old boys about a candy bar, followed by an authoritative bass rumble: "Go right out and get a DELICIOUS Choco-Bite and eat your TANGY Choco-Bite *all up*. That's *Choco-Bite!*" There was a sobbing female whine: "I *wish* I had a Feckle Freezer! I'd do *anything* for a Feckle Freezer!" Burckhardt reached his floor and left the elevator in the middle of the last one. It left him a little uneasy. The commercials were not for familiar brands; there was no feeling of use and custom to them.

But the office was happily normal—except that Mr. Barth wasn't in. Miss Mitkin, yawning at the reception desk, didn't know exactly why. "His home phoned, that's all. He'll be in tomorrow."

"Maybe he went to the plant. It's right near his house."

She looked indifferent. "Yeah."

A thought struck Burckhardt. "But today is June 15th! It's quarterly tax return day—he has to sign the return!"

Miss Mitkin shrugged to indicate that that was Burckhardt's problem, not hers. She returned to her nails.

Thoroughly exasperated, Burckhardt went to his desk. It wasn't that he couldn't sign the tax returns as well as Barth, he thought resentfully. It simply wasn't his job, that was all; it was a responsibility that Barth, as office manager for Contro Chemicals' downtown office, should have taken.

He thought briefly of calling Barth at his home or trying to reach him at the factory, but he gave up the idea quickly enough. He didn't really care much for the people at the factory and the less contact he had with them, the better. He had been to the factory once, with Barth; it had been a confusing and, in a way, a frightening experience. Barring a handful of executives and engineers, there wasn't a soul in the factory—that is, Burckhardt corrected himself, remembering what Barth had told him, not a *living* soul—just the machines.

According to Barth, each machine was controlled by a sort of computer which reproduced, in its electronic snarl, the actual memory and mind of a human being. It was an unpleasant thought. Barth, laughing, had assured him that there was no Frankenstein business of robbing graveyards and implanting brains in machines. It was only a matter, he said, of transferring a man's habit patterns from brain cells to vacuum-tube cells. It didn't hurt the man and it didn't make the machine into a monster.

But they made Burckhardt uncomfortable all the same.

He put Barth and the factory and all his other little irritations out of his mind and tackled the tax returns. It took him until noon to verify the figures—which Barth could have done out of his memory and his private ledger in ten minutes, Burckhardt resentfully reminded himself.

He sealed them in an envelope and walked out to Miss Mitkin. "Since Mr. Barth isn't here, we'd better go to lunch in shifts," he said. "You can go first."

"Thanks." Miss Mitkin languidly took her bag out of the desk drawer and began to apply makeup.

Burckhardt offered her the envelope. "Drop this in the mail for me, will you? Uh—wait a minute. I wonder if I ought to phone Mr. Barth to make sure. Did his wife say whether he was able to take phone calls?"

"Didn't say." Miss Mitkin blotted her lips carefully with a Kleenex. "Wasn't his wife, anyway. It was his daughter who called and left the message."

"The kid?" Burckhardt frowned. "I thought she was away at school."

"She called, that's all I know."

Burckhardt went back to his own office and stared distastefully at the unopened mail on his desk. He didn't like nightmares; they spoiled his whole day. He should have stayed in bed, like Barth.

A funny thing happened on his way home. There was a disturbance at the corner where he usually caught his bus–someone was screaming something about a new kind of deep-freeze–so he walked an extra block. He saw the bus coming and started to trot. But behind him, someone was calling his name. He looked over his shoulder; a small harried-looking man was hurrying toward him.

Burckhardt hesitated, and then recognized him. It was a casual acquaintance named Swanson. Burckhardt sourly observed that he had already missed the bus.

He said, "Hello."

Swanson's face was desperately eager. "Burckhardt?" he asked inquiringly, with an odd intensity. And then he just stood there silently, watching Burckhardt's face, with a burning eagerness that dwindled to a faint hope and died to a regret. He was searching for something, waiting for something, Burckhardt thought. But whatever it was he wanted, Burckhardt didn't know how to supply it.

Burckhardt coughed and said again, "Hello, Swanson."

Swanson didn't even acknowledge the greeting. He merely sighed a very deep sigh.

"Nothing doing," he mumbled, apparently to himself. He nodded abstractedly to Burckhardt and turned away.

Burckhardt watched the slumped shoulders disappear in the crowd. It was an *odd* sort of day, he thought, and one he didn't much like. Things weren't going right.

Riding home on the next bus, he brooded about it. It wasn't anything terrible or disastrous; it was something out of his experience entirely. You live your life, like any man, and you form a network of impressions and reactions. You *expect* things. When you open your medicine chest, your razor is expected to be on the second shelf; when you lock your front door, you expect to have to give it a slight extra tug to make it latch.

It isn't the things that are right and perfect in your life that make it familiar. It is the things that are just a little bit wrong–the sticking latch, the light switch at the head of the stairs that needs an extra push because the spring is old and weak, the rug that unfailingly skids underfoot.

It wasn't just that things were wrong with the pattern of Burckhardt's life; it was that the *wrong* things were wrong. For instance, Barth hadn't come into the office, yet Barth *always* came in.

Burckhardt brooded about it through dinner. He brooded about it, despite his wife's attempt to interest him in a game of bridge with the neighbors, all through the evening. The neighbors were people he liked—Anne and Farley Dennerman. He had known them all their lives. But they were odd and brooding, too, this night and he barely listened to Dennerman's complaints about not being able to get good phone service or his wife's comments on the disgusting variety of television commercials they had these days.

Burckhardt was well on the way to setting an all-time record for continuous abstraction when, around midnight, with a suddenness that surprised him—he was strangely *aware* of it happening—he turned over in his bed and, quickly and completely, fell asleep.

On the morning of June 15th, Burckhardt woke up screaming.

It was more real than any dream he had ever had in his life. He could still hear the explosion, feel the blast that crushed him against a wall. It did not seem right that he should be sitting bolt upright in bed in an undisturbed room.

His wife came pattering up the stairs. "Darling!" she cried. "What's the matter?"

He mumbled, "Nothing. Bad dream."

She relaxed, hand on heart. In an angry tone, she started to say: "You gave me such a shock——"

But a noise from outside interrupted her. There was a wail of sirens and a clang of bells; it was loud and shocking.

The Burckhardts stared at each other for a heartbeat, then hurried fearfully to the window.

There were no rumbling fire engines in the street, only a small panel truck, cruising slowly along. Flaring loud-speaker horns crowned its top. From them issued the screaming sound of sirens, growing in intensity, mixed with the rumble of heavy-duty engines and the sound of bells. It was a perfect record of fire engines arriving at a four-alarm blaze.

Burckhardt said in amazement, "Mary, that's against the law! Do you know what they're doing? They're playing records of a fire. What are they up to?"

"Maybe it's a practical joke," his wife offered.

"Joke? Waking up the whole neighborhood at six o'clock in the morning?" He shook his head. "The police will be here in ten minutes," he predicted. "Wait and see."

But the police weren't—not in ten minutes, or at all. Whoever the pranksters in the car were, they apparently had a police permit for their games.

The car took a position in the middle of the block and stood silent for a few minutes. Then there was a crackle from the speaker, and a giant voice chanted:

Feckle Freezers!
Feckle Freezers!
Gotta have a
Feckle Freezer!
Feckle, Feckle, Feckle,
Feckle, Feckle, Feckle–

It went on and on. Every house on the block had faces staring out of windows by then. The voice was not merely loud; it was nearly deafening.

Burckhardt shouted to his wife, over the uproar, "What the hell is a Feckle Freezer?"

"Some kind of a freezer, I guess, dear," she shrieked back unhelpfully.

Abruptly the noise stopped and the truck stood silent. It was still misty morning; the sun's rays came horizontally across the rooftops. It was impossible to believe that, a moment ago, the silent block had been bellowing the name of a freezer.

"A crazy advertising trick," Burckhardt said bitterly. He yawned and turned away from the window. "Might as well get dressed. I guess that's the end of—"

The bellow caught him from behind; it was almost like a hard slap on the ears. A harsh, sneering voice, louder than the archangel's trumpet, howled:

"Have you got a freezer? *It stinks!* If it isn't a Feckle Freezer, *it stinks!* If it's a last year's Feckle Freezer, *it stinks!* Only this year's Feckle Freezer is any good at all! You know who owns an Ajax Freezer? Fairies own Ajax Freezers! You know who owns a Triplecold Freezer? Commies own Triplecold Freezers! Every freezer but a brand-new Feckle Freezer *stinks!*"

The voice screamed inarticulately with rage. "I'm warning you! Get out and buy a Feckle Freezer right away! Hurry up! Hurry for Feckle! Hurry for Feckle! Hurry, hurry, hurry, Feckle, Feckle, Feckle, Feckle, Feckle, Feckle . . ."

It stopped eventually. Burckhardt licked his lips. He started to say to his wife, "Maybe we ought to call the police about—" when the speakers erupted again. It caught him off guard; it was intended to catch him off guard. It screamed:

"Feckle, Feckle, Feckle, Feckle, Feckle, Feckle, Feckle, Feckle.

Cheap freezers ruin your food. You'll get sick and throw up. You'll get sick and die. Buy a Feckle, Feckle, Feckle, Feckle! Ever take a piece of meat out of the freezer you've got and see how rotten and moldy it is? Buy a Feckle, Feckle, Feckle, Feckle, Feckle. Do you want to eat rotten, stinking food? Or do you want to wise up and buy a Feckle, Feckle, Feckle——"

That did it. With fingers that kept stabbing the wrong holes, Burckhardt finally managed to dial the local police station. He got a busy signal–it was apparent that he was not the only one with the same idea–and while he was shakily dialing again, the noise outside stopped.

He looked out the window. The truck was gone.

Burckhardt loosened his tie and ordered another Frosty-Flip from the waiter. If only they wouldn't keep the Crystal Cafe so *hot!* The new paint job–searing reds and blinding yellows–was bad enough, but someone seemed to have the delusion that this was January instead of June; the place was a good ten degrees warmer than outside.

He swallowed the Frosty-Flip in two gulps. It had a kind of peculiar flavor, he thought, but not bad. It certainly cooled you off, just as the waiter had promised. He reminded himself to pick up a carton of them on the way home; Mary might like them. She was always interested in something new.

He stood up awkwardly as the girl came across the restaurant toward him. She was the most beautiful thing he had ever seen in Tylerton. Chin-height, honey-blond hair and a figure that–well, it was all hers. There was no doubt in the world that the dress that clung to her was the only thing she wore. He felt as if he were blushing as she greeted him.

"Mr. Burckhardt." The voice was like distant tomtoms. "It's wonderful of you to let me see you, after this morning."

He cleared his throat. "Not at all. Won't you sit down, Miss——"

"April Horn," she murmured, sitting down–beside him, not where he had pointed on the other side of the table. "Call me April, won't you?"

She was wearing some kind of perfume, Burckhardt noted with what little of his mind was functioning at all. It didn't seem fair that she should be using perfume as well as everything else. He came to with a start and realized that the waiter was leaving with an order for *filets mignon* for two.

"Hey!" he objected.

"Please, Mr. Burckhardt." Her shoulder was against his, her face was turned to him, her breath was warm, her expression was tender and solicitous. "This is all on the Feckle Corporation. Please let them —it's the *least* they can do."

He felt her hand burrowing into his pocket.

"I put the price of the meal into your pocket," she whispered conspiratorially. "Please do that for me, won't you? I mean I'd appreciate it if you'd pay the waiter—I'm old-fashioned about things like that."

She smiled meltingly, then became mock-businesslike. "But you must take the money," she insisted. "Why, you're letting Feckle off lightly if you do! You could sue them for every nickel they've got, disturbing your sleep like that."

With a dizzy feeling, as though he had just seen someone make a rabbit disappear into a top hat, he said, "Why, it really wasn't so bad, uh, April. A little noisy, maybe, but——"

"Oh, Mr. Burckhardt!" The blue eyes were wide and admiring. "I *knew* you'd understand. It's just that—well, it's such a *wonderful* freezer that some of the outside men get carried away, so to speak. As soon as the main office found out about what happened, they sent representatives around to every house on the block to apologize. Your wife told us where we could phone you—and I'm so very pleased that you were willing to let me have lunch with you, so that I could apologize, too. Because truly, Mr. Burckhardt, it is a *fine* freezer.

"I shouldn't tell you this, but—" The blue eyes were shyly lowered— "I'd do almost anything for Feckle Freezers. It's more than a job to me." She looked up. She was enchanting. "I bet you think I'm silly, don't you?"

Burckhardt coughed. "Well, I——"

"Oh, you don't want to be unkind!" She shook her head. "No, don't pretend. You think it's silly. But really, Mr. Burckhardt, you wouldn't think so if you knew more about the Feckle. Let me show you this little booklet——"

Burckhardt got back from lunch a full hour late. It wasn't only the girl who delayed him. There had been a curious interview with a little man named Swanson, whom he barely knew, who had stopped him with desperate urgency on the street—and then left him cold.

But it didn't matter much. Mr. Barth, for the first time since Burckhardt had worked there, was out for the day—leaving Burckhardt stuck with the quarterly tax returns.

What did matter, though, was that somehow he had signed a purchase order for a twelve-cubic-foot Feckle Freezer, upright model, self-defrosting, list price $625, with a ten per cent "courtesy" discount—"Because of that *horrid* affair this morning, Mr. Burckhardt," she had said.

And he wasn't sure how he could explain it to his wife.

He needn't have worried. As he walked in the front door, his wife said almost immediately, "I wonder if we can't afford a new freezer, dear. There was a man here to apologize about that noise and—well, we got to talking and——"

She had signed a purchase order, too.

It had been the damnedest day, Burckhardt thought later, on his way up to bed. But the day wasn't done with him yet. At the head of the stairs, the weakened spring in the electric light switch refused to click at all. He snapped it back and forth angrily and, of course, succeeded in jarring the tumbler out of its pins. The wires shorted and every light in the house went out.

"Damn!" said Guy Burckhardt.

"Fuse?" His wife shrugged sleepily. "Let it go till the morning, dear."

Burckhardt shook his head. "You go back to bed. I'll be right along."

It wasn't so much that he cared about fixing the fuse, but he was too restless for sleep. He disconnected the bad switch with a screwdriver, tumbled down into the black kitchen, found the flashlight and climbed gingerly down the cellar stairs. He located a spare fuse, pushed an empty trunk over to the fuse box to stand on and twisted out the old fuse.

When the new one was in, he heard the starting click and steady drone of the refrigerator in the kitchen overhead.

He headed back to the steps, and stopped.

Where the old trunk had been, the cellar floor gleamed oddly bright. He inspected it in the flashlight beam. It was metal!

"Son of a gun," said Guy Burckhardt. He shook his head unbelievingly. He peered closer, rubbed the edges of the metallic patch with his thumb and acquired an annoying cut—the edges were *sharp*.

The stained cement floor of the cellar was a thin shell. He found a hammer and cracked it off in a dozen spots—everywhere was metal.

The whole cellar was a copper box. Even the cement-brick walls were false fronts over a metal sheath!

Baffled, he attacked one of the foundation beams. That, at least, was real wood. The glass in the cellar windows was real glass.

He sucked his bleeding thumb and tried the base of the cellar stairs. Real wood. He chipped at the bricks under the oil burner. Real bricks. The retaining walls, the floor—they were faked.

It was as though someone had shored up the house with a frame of metal and then laboriously concealed the evidence.

The biggest surprise was the upside-down boat hull that blocked the rear half of the cellar, relic of a brief home-workshop period that Burckhardt had gone through a couple of years before. From above, it looked perfectly normal. Inside, though, where there should have been thwarts and seats and lockers, there was a mere tangle of braces, rough and unfinished.

"But I *built* that!" Burckhardt exclaimed, forgetting his thumb. He leaned against the hull dizzily, trying to think this thing through. For reasons beyond his comprehension, someone had taken his boat and his cellar away, maybe his whole house, and replaced them with a clever mock-up of the real thing.

"That's crazy," he said to the empty cellar. He stared around in the light of the flash. He whispered, "What in the name of Heaven would anybody do that for?"

Reason refused an answer; there wasn't any reasonable answer. For long minutes, Burckhardt contemplated the uncertain picture of his own sanity.

He peered under the boat again, hoping to reassure himself that it was a mistake, just his imagination. But the sloppy, unfinished bracing was unchanged. He crawled under for a better look, feeling the rough wood incredulously. Utterly impossible!

He switched off the flashlight and started to wriggle out. But he didn't make it. In the moment between the command to his legs to move and the crawling out, he felt a sudden draining weariness flooding through him.

Consciousness went—not easily, but as though it were being taken away, and Guy Burckhardt was asleep.

On the morning of June 16th, Guy Burckhardt woke up in a cramped position huddled under the hull of the boat in his basement—and raced upstairs to find it was June 15th.

The first thing he had done was to make a frantic, hasty inspection of the boat hull, the faked cellar floor, the imitation stone. They were all as he had remembered them, all completely unbelievable.

The kitchen was its placid, unexciting self. The electric clock was purring soberly around the dial. Almost six o'clock, it said. His wife would be waking at any moment.

Burckhardt flung open the front door and stared out into the quiet street. The morning paper was tossed carelessly against the steps, and as he retrieved it, he noticed that this was the 15th day of June.

But that was impossible. *Yesterday* was the 15th of June. It was not a date one would forget, it was quarterly tax-return day.

He went back into the hall and picked up the telephone; he dailed for Weather Information, and got a well-modulated chant: "—and cooler, some showers. Barometric pressure thirty point zero four, rising . . . United States Weather Bureau forecast for June 15th. Warm and sunny, with high around—"

He hung the phone up. June 15th.

"Holy Heaven!" Burckhardt said prayerfully. Things were very odd indeed. He heard the ring of his wife's alarm and bounded up the stairs.

Mary Burckhardt was sitting upright in bed with the terrified, uncomprehending stare of someone just waking out of a nightmare.

"Oh!" she gasped, as her husband came in the room. "Darling, I just had the most *terrible* dream! It was like an explosion and—"

"Again?" Burckhardt asked, not very sympathetically. "Mary, something's funny! I *knew* there was something wrong all day yesterday and—"

He went on to tell her about the copper box that was the cellar, and the odd mock-up someone had made of his boat. Mary looked astonished, then alarmed, then placatory and uneasy.

She said, "Dear, are you *sure?* Because I was cleaning that old trunk out just last week and I didn't notice anything."

"Positive!" said Guy Burckhardt. "I dragged it over to the wall to step on it to put a new fuse in after we blew the lights out and—"

"After we what?" Mary was looking more than merely alarmed.

"After we blew the lights out. You know, when the switch at the head of the stairs stuck. I went down to the cellar and—"

Mary sat up in bed. "Guy, the switch didn't stick. I turned out the lights myself last night."

Burckhardt glared at his wife. "Now I *know* you didn't! Come here and take a look!"

He stalked out to the landing and dramatically pointed to the bad switch, the one that he had unscrewed and left hanging the night before . . .

Only it wasn't. It was as it had always been. Unbelieving, Burckhardt pressed it and the lights sprang up in both halls.

Mary, looking pale and worried, left him to go down to the kitchen and start breakfast. Burckhardt stood staring at the switch for a long time. His mental processes were gone beyond the point of disbelief and shock; they simply were not functioning.

He shaved and dressed and ate his breakfast in a state of numb introspection. Mary didn't disturb him; she was apprehensive and soothing. She kissed him good-by as he hurried out to the bus without another word.

Miss Mitkin, at the reception desk, greeted him with a yawn. "Morning," she said drowsily. "Mr. Barth won't be in today."

Burckhardt started to say something, but checked himself. She would not know that Barth hadn't been in yesterday, either, because she was tearing a June 14th pad off her calendar to make way for the "new" June 15th sheet.

He staggered to his own desk and stared unseeingly at the morning's mail. It had not even been opened yet, but he knew that the Factory Distributors envelope contained an order for twenty thousand feet of the new acoustic tile, and the one from Finebeck & Sons was a complaint.

After a long while, he forced himself to open them. They were.

By lunchtime, driven by a desperate sense of urgency, Burckhardt made Miss Mitkin take her lunch hour first—the June-fifteenth-that-was-yesterday, *he* had gone first. She went, looking vaguely worried about his strained insistence, but it made no difference to Burckhardt's mood.

The phone rang and Burckhardt picked it up abstractedly. "Contro Chemicals Downtown, Burckhardt speaking."

The voice said, "This is Swanson," and stopped.

Burckhardt waited expectantly, but that was all. He said, "Hello?"

Again the pause. Then Swanson asked in sad resignation, "Still nothing, eh?"

"Nothing what? Swanson, is there something you want? You came up to me yesterday and went through this routine. You——"

The voice crackled: "Burckhardt! Oh, my good heavens, *you remember!* Stay right there—I'll be down in half an hour!"

"What's this all about?"

"Never mind," the little man said exultantly. "Tell you about it when I see you. Don't say any more over the phone—somebody may be listening. Just wait there. Say, hold on a minute. Will you be alone in the office?"

"Well, no. Miss Mitkin will probably——"

"Hell. Look, Burckhardt, where do you eat lunch? Is it good and noisy?"

"Why, I suppose so. The Crystal Cafe. It's just about a block——"

"I know where it is. Meet you in half an hour!" And the receiver clicked.

The Crystal Cafe was no longer painted red, but the temperature was still up. And they had added piped-in music interspersed with commercials. The advertisements were for Frosty-Flip, Marlin Cigarettes–"They're sanitized," the announcer purred–and something called Choco-Bite candy bars that Burckhardt couldn't remember ever having heard of before. But he heard more about them quickly enough.

While he was waiting for Swanson to show up, a girl in the cellophane skirt of a nightclub cigarette vendor came through the restaurant with a tray of tiny scarlet-wrapped candies.

"Choco-Bites are *tangy,"* she was murmuring as she came close to his table. "Choco-Bites are *tangier* than tangy!"

Burckhardt, intent on watching for the strange little man who had phoned him, paid little attention. But as she scattered a handful of the confections over the table next to his, smiling at the occupants, he caught a glimpse of her and turned to stare.

"Why, Miss Horn!" he said.

The girl dropped her tray of candies.

Burckhardt rose, concerned over the girl. "Is something wrong?"

But she fled.

The manager of the restaurant was staring suspiciously at Burckhardt, who sank back in his seat and tried to look inconspicuous. He hadn't insulted the girl! Maybe she was just a very strictly reared young lady, he thought–in spite of the long bare legs under the cellophane skirt–and when he addressed her, she thought he was a masher.

Ridiculous idea. Burckhardt scowled uneasily and picked up his menu.

"Burckhardt!" It was a shrill whisper.

Burckhardt looked up over the top of his menu, startled. In the seat across from him, the little man named Swanson was sitting, tensely poised.

"Burckhardt!" the little man whispered again. "Let's get out of here! They're on to you now. If you want to stay alive, come on!

There was no arguing with the man. Burckhardt gave the hovering manager a sick, apologetic smile and followed Swanson out. The little man seemed to know where he was going. In the street, he clutched Burckhardt by the elbow and hurried him off down the block.

"Did you see her?" he demanded. "That Horn woman, in the phone booth? She'll have them here in five minutes, believe me, so hurry it up!"

Although the street was full of people and cars, nobody was paying any attention to Burckhardt and Swanson. The air had a nip in it—more like October than June, Burckhardt thought, in spite of the weather bureau. And he felt like a fool, following this mad little man down the street, running away from some "them" toward—toward what? The little man might be crazy, but he was afraid. And the fear was infectious.

"In here!" panted the little man.

It was another restaurant—more of a bar, really, and a sort of second-rate place that Burckhardt had never patronized.

"Right straight through," Swanson whispered; and Burckhardt, like a biddable boy, sidestepped through the mass of tables to the far end of the restaurant.

It was L-shaped, with a front on two streets at right angles to each other. They came out on the side street, Swanson staring coldly back at the question-looking cashier, and crossed to the opposite sidewalk.

They were under the marquee of a movie theater. Swanson's expression began to relax.

"Lost them!" he crowed softly. "We're almost there."

He stepped up to the window and bought two tickets. Burckhardt trailed him into the theater. It was a weekday matinee and the place was almost empty. From the screen came sounds of gunfire and horses' hoofs. A solitary usher, leaning against a bright brass rail, looked briefly at them and went back to staring boredly at the picture as Swanson led Burckhardt down a flight of carpeted marble steps.

They were in the lounge and it was empty. There was a door for men and one for ladies; and there was a third door, marked "MANAGER" in gold letters. Swanson listened at the door, and gently opened it and peered inside.

"Okay," he said, gesturing.

Burckhardt followed him through an empty office, to another door—a closet, probably, because it was unmarked.

But it was no closet. Swanson opened it warily, looked inside, then motioned Burckhardt to follow.

It was a tunnel, metal-walled, brightly lit. Empty, it stretched vacantly away in both directions from them.

Burckhardt looked wondering around. One thing he knew and knew full well:

No such tunnel belonged under Tylerton.

There was a room off the tunnel with chairs and a desk and what looked like television screens. Swanson slumped in a chair, panting.

"We're all right for a while here," he wheezed. "They don't come here much any more. If they do, we'll hear them and we can hide."

"Who?" demanded Burckhardt.

The little man said, "Martians!" His voice cracked on the word and the life seemed to go out of him. In morose tones, he went on: "Well, I think they're Martians. Although you could be right, you know; I've had plenty of time to think it over these last few weeks, after they got you, and it's possible they're Russians after all. Still—"

"Start from the beginning. Who got me when?"

Swanson sighed. "So we have to go through the whole thing again. All right. It was about two months ago that you banged on my door, late at night. You were all beat up–scared silly. You begged me to help you—"

"*I* did?"

"Naturally you don't remember any of this. Listen and you'll understand. You were talking a blue streak about being captured and threatened, and your wife being dead and coming back to life, and all kinds of mixed-up nonsense. I thought you were crazy. But–well, I've always had a lot of respect for you. And you begged me to hide you and I have this darkroom, you know. It locks from the inside only. I put the lock on myself. So we went in there–just to humor you–and along about midnight, which was only fifteen or twenty minutes after, we passed out."

"Passed out?"

Swanson nodded. "Both of us. It was like being hit with a sandbag. Look, didn't that happen to you again last night?"

"I guess it did." Burckhardt shook his head uncertainly.

"Sure. And then all of a sudden we were awake again, and you said you were going to show me something funny, and we went out and bought a paper. And the date on it was June 15th."

"June 15th? But that's today! I mean—"

"You got it, friend. It's *always* today!"

It took time to penetrate.

Burckhardt said wonderingly, "You've hidden out in that darkroom for how many weeks?"

"How can I tell? Four or five, maybe, I lost count. And every day the same–always the 15th of June, always my landlady, Mrs. Keefer, is sweeping the front steps, always the same headline in the papers at the corner. It gets monotonous, friend."

It was Burckhardt's idea and Swanson despised it, but he went along. He was the type who always went along.

"It's dangerous," he grumbled worriedly. "Suppose somebody comes by? They'll spot us and——"

"What have we got to lose?"

Swanson shrugged. "It's dangerous," he said again. But he went along.

Burckhardt's idea was very simple. He was sure of only one thing—the tunnel went somewhere. Martians or Russians, fantastic plot or crazy hallucination, whatever was wrong with Tylerton had an explanation, and the place to look for it was at the end of the tunnel.

They jogged along. It was more than a mile before they began to see an end. They were in luck—at least no one came through the tunnel to spot them. But Swanson had said that it was only at certain hours that the tunnel seemed to be in use.

Always the fifteenth of June. Why? Burckhardt asked himself. Never mind the how. *Why?*

And falling asleep, completely involuntarily—everyone at the same time, it seemed. And not remembering, never remembering anything—Swanson had said how eagerly he saw Burckhardt again, the morning after Burckhardt had incautiously waited five minutes too many before retreating into the darkroom. When Swanson had come to, Burckhardt was gone. Swanson had seen him in the street that afternoon, but Burckhardt had remembered nothing.

And Swanson had lived his mouse's existence for weeks, hiding in the woodwork at night, stealing out by day to search for Burckhardt in pitiful hope, scurrying around the fringe of life, trying to keep from the deadly eyes of *them.*

Them. One of "them" was the girl named April Horn. It was by seeing her walk carelessly into a telephone booth and never come out that Swanson had found the tunnel. Another was the man at the cigar stand in Burckhardt's office building. There were more, at least a dozen that Swanson knew of or suspected.

They were easy enough to spot, once you knew where to look, for they alone in Tylerton changed their roles from day to day. Burckhardt was on that 8:51 bus, every morning of every day-that-was-June-15th, never different by a hair or a moment. But April Horn was sometimes gaudy in the cellophane skirt, giving away candy or cigarettes; sometimes plainly dressed; sometimes not seen by Swanson at all.

Russians? Martians? Whatever they were, what could they be hoping to gain from this mad masquerade?

Burckhardt didn't know the answer, but perhaps it lay beyond the door at the end of the tunnel. They listened carefully and heard distant sounds that could not quite be made out, but nothing that seemed dangerous. They slipped through.

And, through a wide chamber and up a flight of steps, they found they were in what Burckhardt recognized as the Contro Chemicals plant.

Nobody was in sight. By itself, that was not so very odd; the automatized factory had never had very many persons in it. But Burckhardt remembered, from his single visit, the endless, ceaseless busyness of the plant, the valves that opened and closed, the vats that emptied themselves and filled themselves and stirred and cooked and chemically tasted the bubbling liquids they held inside themselves. The plant was never populated, but it was never still.

Only now it *was* still. Except for the distant sounds, there was no breath of life in it. The captive electronic minds were sending out no commands; the coils and relays were at rest.

Burckhardt said, "Come on." Swanson reluctantly followed him through the tangled aisles of stainless steel columns and tanks.

They walked as though they were in the presence of the dead. In a way, they were, for what were the automatons that once had run the factory, if not corpses? The machines were controlled by computers that were really not computers at all, but the electronic analogues of living brains. And if they were turned off, were they not dead? For each had once been a human mind.

Take a master petroleum chemist, infinitely skilled in the separation of crude oil into its fractions. Strap him down, probe into his brain with searching electronic needles. The machine scans the patterns of the mind, translates what it sees into charts and sine waves. Impress these same waves on a robot computer and you have your chemist. Or a thousand copies of your chemist, if you wish, with all of his knowledge and skill, and no human limitations at all.

Put a dozen copies of him into a plant and they will run it all, twenty-four hours a day, seven days of every week, never tiring, never overlooking anything, never forgetting.

Swanson stepped up closer to Burckhardt. "I'm scared," he said.

They were across the room now and the sounds were louder. They were not machine sounds, but voices; Burckhardt moved cautiously up to a door and dared to peer around it.

It was a smaller room, lined with television screens, each one—a dozen or more, at least—with a man or woman sitting before it, staring into the screen and dictating notes into a recorder. The viewers dialed from scene to scene; no two screens ever showed the same picture.

The pictures seemed to have little in common. One was a store, where a girl dressed like April Horn was demonstrating home freezers. One was a series of shots of kitchens. Burckhardt caught a glimpse of what looked like the cigar stand in his office building.

It was baffling and Burckhardt would have loved to stand there and puzzle it out, but it was too busy a place. There was the chance that someone would look their way or walk out and find them.

They found another room. This one was empty. It was an office, large and sumptuous. It had a desk, littered with papers. Burckhardt stared at them, briefly at first—then, as the words on one of them caught his attention, with incredulous fascination.

He snatched up the topmost sheet, scanned it, and another, while Swanson was frenziedly searching through the drawers.

Burckhardt swore unbelievingly and dropped the papers to the desk.

Swanson, hardly noticing, yelped with delight: "Look!" He dragged a gun from the desk. "And it's loaded, too!"

Burckhardt stared at him blankly, trying to assimilate what he had read. Then, as he realized what Swanson had said, Burckhardt's eyes sparked. "Good man!" he cried. "We'll take it. We're getting out of here with that gun, Swanson. And we're not going to the police! Not the cops in Tylerton, but the F.B.I., maybe. Take a look at this!"

The sheaf he handed Swanson was headed: "Test Area Progress Report. Subject: Marlin Cigarettes Campaign." It was mostly tabulated figures that made little sense to Burckhardt and Swanson, but at the end was a summary that said:

> Although Test 47-K3 pulled nearly double the number of new users of any of the other tests conducted, it probably cannot be used in the field because of local sound-truck control ordinances.
>
> The tests in the 47-K12 group were second best and our recommendation is that retests be conducted in this appeal, testing each of the three best campaigns with and without the addition of sampling techniques.
>
> An alternative suggestion might be to proceed directly with the top appeal in the K12 series, if the client is unwilling to go to the expense of additional tests.
>
> All of these forecast expectations have an 80% probability of being within one-half of one per cent of results forecast, and more than 99% probability of coming within 5%.

Swanson looked up from the paper into Burckhardt's eyes. "I don't get it," he complained.

Burckhardt said, "I don't blame you. It's crazy, but it fits the facts, Swanson, *it fits the facts*. They aren't Russians and they aren't Martians. These people are advertising men! Somehow–heaven knows how they did it–they've taken Tylerton over. They've got us, all of us, you and me and twenty or thirty thousand other people, right under their thumbs.

"Maybe they hypnotize us and maybe it's something else; but however they do it, what happens is that they let us live a day at a time. They pour advertising into us the whole damned day long. And at the end of the day, they see what happened–and then they wash the day out of our minds and start again the next day with different advertising."

Swanson's jaw was hanging. He managed to close it and swallow. "Nuts!" he said flatly.

Burckhardt shook his head. "Sure, it sounds crazy, but this whole thing is crazy. How else would you explain it? You can't deny that most of Tylerton lives the same day over and over again. You've *seen* it! And that's the crazy part and we have to admit that that's true–unless *we* are the crazy ones. And once you admit that somebody, somehow, knows how to accomplish that, the rest of it makes all kinds of sense.

"Think of it, Swanson! They test every last detail before they spend a nickel on advertising! Do you have any idea what that means? Lord knows how much money is involved, but I know for a fact that some companies spend twenty or thirty million dollars a year on advertising. Multiply it, say, by a hundred companies. Say that every one of them learns how to cut its advertising cost by only ten per cent. And that's peanuts, believe me!

"If they know in advance what's going to work, they can cut their costs in half–maybe to less than half, I don't know. But that's saving two or three hundred million dollars a year–and if they pay only ten or twenty per cent of that for the use of Tylerton, it's still dirt cheap for them and a fortune for whoever took over Tylerton."

Swanson licked his lips. "You mean," he offered hesitantly, "that we're a–well, a kind of captive audience?"

Burckhardt frowned. "Not exactly." He thought for a minute. "You know how a doctor tests something like penicillin? He sets up a series of little colonies of germs on gelatin disks and he tries the stuff on one after another, changing it a little each time. Well, that's us–we're the germs, Swanson. Only it's even more efficient than that.

They don't have to test more than one colony, because they can use it over and over again."

It was too hard for Swanson to take in. He only said, "What do we do about it?"

"We go to the police. They can't use human beings for guinea pigs!"

"How do we get to the police?"

Burckhardt hesitated. "I think–" he began slowly. "Sure. This is the office of somebody important. We've got a gun. We'll stay right here until he comes along. And he'll get us out of here."

Simple and direct. Swanson subsided and found a place to sit, against the wall, out of sight of the door. Burckhardt took up a position behind the door itself——

And waited.

The wait was not as long as it might have been. Half an hour, perhaps. Then Burckhardt heard approaching voices and had time for a swift whisper to Swanson before he flattened himself against the wall.

It was a man's voice, and a girl's. The man was saying, "–reason why you couldn't report on the phone? You're ruining your whole day's tests! What the devil's the matter with you, Janet?"

"I'm sorry, Mr. Dorchin," she said in a sweet, clear tone. "I thought it was important."

The man grumbled, "Important! One lousy unit out of twenty-one thousand."

"But it's the Burckhardt one, Mr. Dorchin. Again. And the way he got out of sight, he must have had some help."

"All right, all right. It doesn't matter, Janet; the Choco-Bite program is ahead of schedule anyhow. As long as you're this far, come on in the office and make out your worksheet. And don't worry about the Burckhardt business. He's probably just wandering around. We'll pick him up tonight and——"

They were inside the door. Burckhardt kicked it shut and pointed the gun.

"That's what you think," he said triumphantly.

It was worth the terrified hours, the bewildered sense of insanity, the confusion and fear. It was the most satisfying sensation Burckhardt had ever had in his life. The expression on the man's face was one he had read about but never actually seen: Dorchin's mouth fell open and his eyes went wide, and though he managed to make a sound that might have been a question, it was not in words.

The girl was almost as surprised. And Burckhardt, looking at her, knew why her voice had been so familiar. The girl was the one who had introduced herself to him as April Horn.

Dorchin recovered himself quickly. "Is this the one?" he asked sharply.

The girl said, "Yes."

Dorchin nodded. "I take it back. You were right. Uh, you–Burckhardt. What do you want?"

Swanson piped up, "Watch him! He might have another gun."

"Search him then," Burckhardt said. "I'll tell you what we want, Dorchin. We want you to come along with us to the FBI and explain to them how you can get away with kidnaping twenty thousand people."

"Kidnaping?" Dorchin snorted. "That's ridiculous, man! Put that gun away; you can't get away with this!"

Burckhardt hefted the gun grimly. "I think I can."

Dorchin looked furious and sick–but oddly, not afraid. "Damn it–" he started to bellow, then closed his mouth and swallowed. "Listen," he said persuasively, "you're making a big mistake. I haven't kidnaped anybody, believe me!"

"I don't believe you," said Burckhardt bluntly. "Why should I?"

"But it's true! Take my word for it!"

Burckhardt shook his head. "The FBI can take your word if they like. We'll find out. Now how do we get out of here?"

Dorchin opened his mouth to argue.

Burckhardt blazed, "Don't get in my way! I'm willing to kill you if I have to. Don't you understand that? I've gone through two days of hell and every second of it I blame on you. Kill you? It would be a pleasure and I don't have a thing in the world to lose! Get us out of here!"

Dorchin's face went suddenly opaque. He seemed about to move; but the blond girl he had called Janet slipped between him and the gun.

"Please!" she begged Burckhardt. "You don't understand. You mustn't shoot!"

"Get out of my way!"

"But, Mr. Burckhardt—"

She never finished. Dorchin, his face unreadable, headed for the door. Burckhardt had been pushed one degree too far. He swung the gun, bellowing. The girl called out sharply. He pulled the trigger. Closing on him with pity and pleading in her eyes, she came again between the gun and the man.

Burckhardt aimed low instinctively, to cripple, not to kill. But his aim was not good.

The pistol bullet caught her in the pit of the stomach.

Dorchin was out and away, the door slamming behind him, his footsteps racing into the distance.

Burckhardt hurled the gun across the room and jumped to the girl.

Swanson was moaning. "That finishes us, Burckhardt. Oh, why did you do it? We could have got away. We could have gone to the police. We were practically out of here! We—"

Burckhardt wasn't listening. He was kneeling beside the girl. She lay flat on her back, arms helterskelter. There was no blood, hardly any sign of the wound; but the position in which she lay was one that no living human being could have held.

Yet she wasn't dead.

She wasn't dead—and Burckhardt, frozen beside her, thought: *She isn't alive, either.*

There was no pulse, but there was a rhythmic ticking of the outstretched fingers of one hand.

There was no sound of breathing, but there was a hissing, sizzling noise.

The eyes were open and they were looking at Burckhardt. There was neither fear nor pain in them, only a pity deeper than the Pit.

She said, through lips that writhed erratically, "Don't—worry, Mr. Burckhardt. I'm—all right."

Burckhardt rocked back on his haunches, staring. Where there should have been blood, there was a clean break of a substance that was not flesh; and a curl of thin golden-copper wire.

Burckhardt moistened his lips.

"You're a robot," he said.

The girl tried to nod. The twitching lips said, "I am. And so are you."

Swanson, after a single inarticulate sound, walked over to the desk and sat staring at the wall. Burckhardt rocked back and forth beside the shattered puppet on the floor. He had no words.

The girl managed to say, "I'm—sorry all this happened." The lovely lips twisted into a rictus sneer, frightening on that smooth young face, until she got them under control. "Sorry," she said again. "The—nerve center was right about where the bullet hit. Makes it difficult to—control this body."

Burckhardt nodded automatically, accepting the apology. Robots.

It was obvious, now that he knew it. In hindsight, it was inevitable. He thought of his mystic notions of hypnosis or Martians or something stranger still–idiotic, for the simple fact of created robots fitted the facts better and more economically.

All the evidence had been before him. The automatized factory, with its transplanted minds–why not transplant a mind into a humanoid robot, give it its original owner's features and form?

Could it know that it was a robot?

"All of us," Burckhardt said, hardly aware that he spoke out loud. "My wife and my secretary and you and the neighbors. All of us the same."

"No." The voice was stronger. "Not exactly the same, all of us. I chose it, you see. I–" This time the convulsed lips were not a random contortion of the nerves–"I was an ugly woman, Mr. Burckhardt, and nearly sixty years old. Life had passed me. And when Mr. Dorchin offered me the chance to live again as a beautiful girl, I jumped at the opportunity. Believe me, I *jumped,* in spite of its disadvantages. My flesh body is still alive–it is sleeping, while I am here. I could go back to it. But I never do."

"And the rest of us?"

"Different, Mr. Burckhardt. I work here. I'm carrying out Mr. Dorchin's orders, mapping the results of the advertising tests, watching you and the others live as he makes you live. I do it by choice, but you have no choice. Because, you see, you are dead."

"Dead?" cried Burckhardt; it was almost a scream.

The blue eyes looked at him unwinkingly and he knew that it was no lie. He swallowed, marveling at the intricate mechanisms that let him swallow, and sweat, and eat.

He said: "Oh. The explosion in my dream."

"It was no dream. You are right–the explosion. That was real and this plant was the cause of it. The storage tanks let go and what the blast didn't get, the fumes killed a little later. But almost everyone died in the blast, twenty-one thousand persons. You died with them and that was Dorchin's chance."

"The damned ghoul!" said Burckhardt.

The twisted shoulders shrugged with an odd grace. "Why? You were gone. And you and all the others were what Dorchin wanted–a whole town, a perfect slice of America. It's as easy to transfer a pattern from a dead brain as a living one. Easier–the dead can't say no. Oh, it took work and money–the town was a wreck–but it was possible to rebuild it entirely, especially because it wasn't necessary to have all the details exact.

"There were the homes where even the brain had been utterly destroyed, and those are empty inside, and the cellars that needn't be too perfect, and the streets that hardly matter. And anyway, it only has to last for one day. The same day–June 15th–over and over again; and if someone finds something a little wrong, somehow, the discovery won't have time to snowball, wreck the validity of the tests, because all errors are canceled out at midnight."

The face tried to smile. "That's the dream, Mr. Burckhardt, that day of June 15th, because you never really lived it. It's a present from Mr. Dorchin, a dream that he gives you and then takes back at the end of the day, when he has all his figures on how many of you respond to what variation of which appeal, and the maintenance crews go down the tunnel to go through the whole city, washing out the new dream with their little electronic drains, and then the dream starts all over again. On June 15th.

"Always June 15th, because June 14th is the last day any of you can remember alive. Sometimes the crews miss someone–as they missed you, because you were under your boat. But it doesn't matter. The ones who are missed give themselves away if they show it–and if they don't, it doesn't affect the test. But they don't drain us, the ones of us who work for Dorchin. We sleep when the power is turned off, just as you do. When we wake up, though, we remember." The face contorted wildly. "If I could only forget!"

Burckhardt said unbelievingly, "All this to sell merchandise! It must have cost millions!"

The robot called April Horn said, "It did. But it has made millions for Dorchin, too. And that's not the end of it. Once he finds the master words that make people act, do you suppose he will stop with that? Do you suppose——"

The door opened, interrupting her. Burckhardt whirled. Belatedly remembering Dorchin's flight, he raised the gun.

"Don't shoot," ordered the voice calmly. It was not Dorchin; it was another robot, this one not disguised with the clever plastics and cosmetics, but shining plain. It said metallically, "Forget it, Burckhardt. You're not accomplishing anything. Give me that gun before you do any more damage. Give it to me *now*."

Burckhardt bellowed angrily. The gleam on this robot torso was steel; Burckhardt was not at all sure that his bullets would pierce it, or do much harm if they did. He would have put it to the test——

But from behind him came a whimpering, scurrying whirlwind: its name was Swanson, hysterical with fear. He catapulted into Burckhardt and sent him sprawling, the gun flying free.

"Please!" begged Swanson incoherently, prostrate before the steel robot. "He would have shot you–please don't hurt me! Let me work for you, like that girl. I'll do anything, anything you tell me—"

The robot voice said, "We don't need your help." It took two precise steps and stood over the gun–and spurned it, left it lying on the floor.

The wrecked blond robot said, without emotion, "I doubt that I can hold out much longer, Mr. Dorchin."

"Disconnect if you have to," replied the steel robot.

Burckhardt blinked. "But you're not Dorchin!"

The steel robot turned deep eyes on him. "I am," it said. "Not in the flesh–but this is the body I am using at the moment. I doubt that you can damage this one with the gun. The other robot body was more vulnerable. Now will you stop this nonsense? I don't want to have to damage you; you're too expensive for that. Will you just sit down and let the maintenance crews adjust you?"

Swanson groveled. "You–you won't punish us?"

The steel robot had no expression, but its voice was almost surprised. "Punish you?" it repeated on a rising note. "How?"

Swanson quivered as though the word had been a whip; but Burckhardt flared: "Adjust *him,* if he'll let you–but not me! You're going to have to do me a lot of damage, Dorchin. I don't care what I cost or how much trouble it's going to be to put me back together again. But I'm going out of that door! If you want to stop me, you'll have to kill me. You won't stop me any other way!"

The steel robot took a half-step toward him, and Burckhardt involuntarily checked his stride. He stood poised and shaking, ready for death, ready for attack, ready for anything that might happen.

Ready for anything except what did happen. For Dorchin's steel body merely stepped aside, between Burckhardt and the gun, but leaving the door free.

"Go ahead," invited the steel robot. "Nobody's stopping you."

Outside the door, Burckhardt brought up sharp. It was insane of Dorchin to let him go! Robot or flesh, victim or beneficiary, there was nothing to stop him from going to the FBI or whatever law he could find away from Dorchin's sympathetic empire, and telling his story. Surely the corporations who paid Dorchin for test results had no notion of the ghoul's technique he used; Dorchin would have to keep it from them, for the breath of publicity would put a stop to it. Walking out meant death, perhaps, but at that moment in his pseudo-life, death was no terror for Burckhardt.

There was no one in the corridor. He found a window and stared out of it. There was Tylerton—an ersatz city, but looking so real and familiar that Burckhardt almost imagined the whole episode a dream. It was no dream, though. He was certain of that in his heart and equally certain that nothing in Tylerton could help him now.

It had to be the other direction.

It took him a quarter of an hour to find a way, but he found it—skulking through the corridors, dodging the suspicion of footsteps, knowing for certain that his hiding was in vain, for Dorchin was undoubtedly aware of every move he made. But no one stopped him, and he found another door.

It was a simple enough door from the inside. But when he opened it and stepped out, it was like nothing he had ever seen.

First there was light—brilliant, incredible, blinding light. Burckhardt blinked upward, unbelieving and afraid.

He was standing on a ledge of smooth, finished metal. Not a dozen yards from his feet, the ledge dropped sharply away; he hardly dared approach the brink, but even from where he stood he could see no bottom to the chasm before him. And the gulf extended out of sight into the glare on either side of him.

No wonder Dorchin could so easily give him his freedom! From the factory there was nowhere to go. But how incredible this fantastic gulf, how impossible the hundred white and blinding suns that hung above!

A voice by his side said inquiringly, "Burckhardt?" And thunder rolled the name, mutteringly soft, back and forth in the abyss before him.

Burckhardt wet his lips. "Y-yes?" he croaked.

"This is Dorchin. Not a robot this time, but Dorchin in the flesh, talking to you on a hand mike. Now you have seen, Burckhardt. Now will you be reasonable and let the maintenance crews take over?"

Burckhardt stood paralyzed. One of the moving mountains in the blinding glare came toward him.

It towered hundreds of feet over his head; he stared up at its top, squinting helplessly into the light.

It looked like——

Impossible!

The voice in the loudspeaker at the door said, "Burckhardt?" But he was unable to answer.

A heavy rumbling sigh. "I see," said the voice. "You finally understand. There's no place to go. You know it now. I could have told you, but you might not have believed me, so it was better for you to see it yourself. And after all, Burckhardt, why would I reconstruct a city just the way it was before? I'm a businessman; I count costs. If a thing has to be full-scale, I build it that way. But there wasn't any need to in this case."

From the mountain before him, Burckhardt helplessly saw a lesser cliff descend carefully toward him. It was long and dark, and at the end of it was whiteness, five-fingered whiteness . . .

"Poor little Burckhardt," crooned the loudspeaker, while the echoes rumbled through the enormous chasm that was only a workshop. "It must have been quite a shock for you to find out you were living in a town built on a table top."

It was the morning of June 15th, and Guy Burckhardt woke up screaming out of a dream.

It had been a monstrous and incomprehensible dream, of explosions and shadowy figures that were not men and terror beyond words.

He shuddered and opened his eyes.

Outside his bedroom window, a hugely amplified voice was howling.

Burckhardt stumbled over to the window and stared outside. There was an out-of-season chill to the air, more like October than June; but the scene was normal enough—except for a sound-truck that squatted at curbside halfway down the block. Its speaker horns blared:

"Are you a coward? Are you a fool? Are you going to let crooked politicians steal the country from you? NO! Are you going to put up with four more years of graft and crime? NO! Are you going to vote straight Federal Party all up and down the ballot? YES! *You just bet you are!*"

Sometimes he screams, sometimes he wheedles, threatens, begs, cajoles . . . but his voice goes on and on through one June 15th after another.

Punch

THE FELLOW was over seven feet tall and when he stepped on Buffie's flagstone walk one of the stones split with a dust of crushed rock. "Too bad," he said sadly, "I apologize very much. Wait."

Buffie was glad to wait, because Buffie recognized his visitor at once. The fellow flickered, disappeared and in a moment was there again, now about five feet two. He blinked with pink eyes. "I materialize so badly," he apologized. "But I will make amends. May I? Let me see. Would you like the secret of transmutation? A cure for simple virus diseases? A list of twelve growth stocks with spectacular growth certainties inherent in our development program for your planet, that is, the Earth?"

Buffie said he would take the list of growth stocks, hugging himself and fighting terribly to keep a straight face. "My name is Charlton Buffie," he said, extending a hand gladly. The alien took it curiously, and shook it, and it was like shaking hands with a shadow.

"You will call me 'Punch,' please," he said. "It is not my name but it will do, because after all this projection of my real self is only a sort of puppet. Have you a pencil?" And he rattled off the names of twelve issues Buffie had never heard of.

That did not matter in the least. Buffie knew that when the aliens gave you something it was money in the bank. Look what they had given the human race. Faster-than-light space ships, power sources from hitherto non-radioactive elements like silicon, weapons of great force and metalworking processes of great suppleness. His wife's aunt's brother-in-law, the colonel, was even now off in space somewhere in a highly armed space ship built according to their plans.

Buffie thought of ducking into the house for a quick phone call to his broker, but instead he invited Punch to look around his apple orchard. Make the most of every moment, he said to himself, every moment with one of these guys is worth ten thousand dollars. "I would enjoy your apples awfully," said Punch, but he seemed disappointed. "Do I have it wrong? Don't you and certain friends plan a sporting day, as Senator Wenzel advised me?"

"Oh, sure! Certainly. Good old Walt told you about it, did he? Yes." That was the thing about the aliens, they liked to poke around in human affairs. They said when they came to Earth that they wanted to help us, and all they asked of us in return was that they be permitted to study our ways. It was nice of them to be so interested, and it was nice of Walt Wenzel, Buffie thought, to send the alien along to him. "We're going after mallard, down to Little Egg, some of the boys and me. There's Chuck–he's the mayor here, and Jer–Second National Bank, you know, and Padre–"

"That is it!" cried Punch. "To see you shoot the mallard." He pulled out an Esso road map, overtraced with golden raised lines, and asked Buffie to point out where Little Egg was. "I cannot focus well enough to stay in a moving vehicle," he said, blinking in a regretful way. "Still, I can meet you there. If, that is, you wish–"

"I do! I do! I do!" Buffie was painfully exact in pointing out the place. Punch's lips moved silently, translating the golden lines into polar space-time coordinates, and he vanished just as the station wagon with the rest of the boys came roaring into the carriage drive with a hydromatic spatter of gravel.

The boys were extremely impressed. Padre had seen one of the aliens once, at a distance, drawing pictures of the skaters in Rockefeller Center, but that was the closest any of them had come. "God! What luck." "Did you get a super-hairpin from him, Buffie?" "Or a recipe for a nyew, smyooth Martini with dust on it?" "Not Buffie, fellows! He probably held out for something *real* good, like six new ways to– Oh, excuse me, Padre." "But seriously, Buffie, these people are unpredictably generous. Look how they built that dam in Egypt! Has this Punch given you anything?"

Buffie grinned wisely as they drove along, their shotguns firmly held between their knees. "Damn it," he said mildly, "I forgot to bring cigarettes. Let's stop at the Blue Jay Diner for a minute." The cigarette machine at the Blue Jay was out of sight of the parking lot, and so was the phone booth.

It was too bad, he reflected, to have to share everything with the boys, but on the other hand he already had his growth stocks. Anyway there was plenty for everyone. Every nation on Earth had its silicon-drive space ships now, fleets of them milling about on maneuvers all over the Solar System. With help from the star-people, an American expedition had staked out enormous radium beds on Callisto, the Venezuelans had a diamond mountain on Mercury, the

Soviets owned a swamp of purest penicillin near the South Pole of Venus. And individuals had done very well too. A ticket-taker at Steeplechase Park explained to them the reason why the air jets blew up ladies' skirts, and they tipped him with a design for a springless safety pin that was earning him a million dollars a month in royalties. An usherette at La Scala became the cosmetic queen of Europe for showing three of them to their seats. They gave her a simple painless eye dye, and now 99% of Milan's women had bright blue eyes from her salon.

All they wanted to do was help. They said they came from a planet very far away and they were lonely and they wanted to help us make the jump into space. It would be fun, they promised, and would help to end poverty and war between nations, and they would have company in the void between the stars. Politely and deferentially they gave away secrets worth trillions, and humanity burst with a shower of gold into the age of plenty.

Punch was there before them, inspecting the case of bourbon hidden in their blind. "I am delighted to meet you, Chuck, Jer, Bud, Padre and of course Buffie," he said. "It is kind of you to take a stranger along on your fun. I regret I have only some eleven minutes to stay."

Eleven minutes! The boys scowled apprehensively at Buffie. Punch said, in his wistful voice, "If you will allow me to give you a memento, perhaps you would like to know that three grams of common table salt in a quart of Crisco, exposed for nine minutes to the radiations from one of our silicon reactors, will infallibly remove warts." They all scribbled, silently planning a partnership corporation, and Punch pointed out to the bay where some tiny dots rose and fell with the waves. "Are those not the mallards you wish to shoot?"

"That's right," said Buffie glumly. "Say, you know what I was thinking? I was thinking–that transmutation you mentioned before–I wonder–"

"And are these the weapons with which you kill the birds?" He examined Padre's ancient over-and-under with the silver chasing. "Extremely lovely," he said. "Will you shoot?"

"Oh, not *now,*" said Buffie, scandalized. "We can't do that. That transmutation–"

"It is extremely fascinating," said the star-man, looking at them with his mild pink eyes and returning the gun. "Well. I may tell you, I think, what we have not announced. A surprise. We are soon to be present in the flesh, or near at any rate."

"Near?" Buffie looked at the boys and the boys looked at him; there had been no suggestion of this in the papers and it almost took their minds off the fact that Punch was leaving. He nodded violently, like the flickering of a bad fluorescent lamp.

"Near indeed, in a relative way," he said. "Perhaps some hundreds of millions of miles. My true body, of which this is only a projection, is at present in one of our own interstellar ships now approaching the orbit of Pluto. The American fleet, together with those of Chile, New Zealand and Costa Rica, is there practicing with its silicon-ray weapons and we will shortly make contact with them for the first time in a physical way." He beamed. "But only six minutes remain," he said sadly.

"That transmutation secret you mentioned–" Buffie began, recovering his voice.

"Please," said Punch, "may I not watch you hunt? It is a link between us."

"Oh, do you shoot?" asked Padre.

The star-man said modestly, "We have but little game. But we love it. Won't you show me your ways?"

Buffie scowled. He could not help thinking that twelve growth stocks and a wart-cure were small pickings from the star-men, who had given wealth, weapons and the secret of interstellar travel. "We can't," he growled, his voice harsher than he intended. "We don't shoot sitting birds."

Punch gasped with delight. "Another bond between us! But now I must go to our fleet for the–hum. For the surprise." He began to shimmer like a candle. "Neither do we," he said, and went out.

Three Portraits and a Prayer

Howard Chandler Christy: The Lovely Young Girl

When Dr. Rhine Cooperstock was put under my care I was enlarged with pride. Dr. Cooperstock was a hero to me. I don't mean a George Washington, all virtue and no fire. I mean he was a dragon killer. He had carried human knowledge far into the tiny spaces of an atomic nucleus. He was a very great man. And I was his doctor and he was dying.

Dr. Cooperstock was dying in the finest suite in the Morgan Pavilion and with all the best doctors. (I am not modest.) We couldn't keep him alive for more than a matter of months, and we couldn't cure him at all. But we could make him comfortable. If round-the-clock nurses and color television constitute comfort.

I don't ask you to understand technical medical terms. He was an old man, his blood vessels deteriorating, and clots formed, impeding the circulation. One day a clot would form in heart, brain or lungs and he would die. If it was in the lung it would be painful and slow. In the heart, painful and fast. In the brain most painful of all, but so fast that it would be a mercy.

Meanwhile we fed him heparin and sometimes coumarol and attempted by massages and heat and diet to stave off the end. Although, in fact, he was all but dead anyway, so little freedom of movement we allowed him.

"Martin, the leg hurts. You'd better leave a pill," he would say to me once or twice a week, and I would hesitate. "I don't know if I can make it to the bathroom tonight, Martin," he would say, his tone cheerfully resigned. Then he would call for the bedpan while I was there, or mention casually that some invisible wrinkle in the sheet caused him pain and stand by bravely while the bed was remade, and say at last, self-deprecating, "I think I will need that pill, Martin." So I would allow myself to be persuaded and let him have a red-and-white capsule and in the morning it would be gone. I never told him that they contained only aspirin and he never admitted to me that he did not take the pills at all but was laboriously building up a hoard against the day when the pain would be really serious and he would take them all at once.

Dr. Cooperstock knew the lethal dose as well as I did. As he knew the names of all his veins and arteries and the chemistry of his disease. A man like Rhine Cooperstock, even at seventy, can learn enough medicine for that in a week.

He acquired eleven of the little capsules in one month at the Pavilion; I know, because I counted them after he left. That would have been enough for suicide, if they had not been aspirin. I suppose he would have stopped there, perhaps beginning to take a few, now and then, both to keep me from getting suspicious and for the relief of the real pain he must have felt. But he did leave. Nan Halloran came and got him.

She invaded the Pavilion like a queen. Expensive, celebrated hospital, we were used to the famous; but this was Nan Halloran, blue-eyed, black-haired, a face like a lovely child and a voice like the sway of hips. She was a most remarkable woman. I called her a queen, but she was not that; she was a goddess, virgin and fertile. I speak subjectively, of course, for in medical fact she was surely not one and may not have been either. She breezed into the room, wrinkling her nose. "Coopie," she said, "what is that awful smell? Will you do me a favor, dear? I need it very much."

You would not think that a man like Dr. Cooperstock would have much to do with a television star; but he knew her; years before, when he was still teaching sometimes, she had somehow wandered into his class. "Hello, Nan," he said, looking quite astonished and pleased. "I'll do anything I can for you, of course. That smell," he apologized, touching the leg with its bright spots of color and degenerated tissues, "is me."

"Poor Coopie." She looked around at me and smiled. Although I am fat and not attractive and know in my heart that, whatever long-term wonders I may work with the brilliance of my mind and the cleverness of my speech, no woman will ever lust for me on sight, I tingled. I looked away. She said sweetly, "It's about that fusion power thing, Coopie. You know Wayne Donner, of course? He and I are good friends. He has these utility company interests, and he wants to convert them to fusion power, and I told him you were the only man who could help him."

Dr. Cooperstock began to laugh, and laughed until he was choking and gagging. I laughed too, although I think that in all the world Dr. Cooperstock and I must be two of the very few men who would laugh at the name of Wayne Donner. "Nan," he said when he could, "you're amazing. It's utterly impossible, I'm afraid."

She sat on the edge of his bed with a rustle of petticoats. She had lovely legs. "Oh, did that hurt you? But I didn't even touch your leg, dear. Would you please get up and come now, because the driver's waiting?"

"Nan!" he cried. "Security regulations. Death. Lack of proper engineering! Did you ever think of any of those things? And they're only a beginning."

"If you're going to make objections we'll be here all day, darling. As far as security is concerned," she said, "this is for the peaceful use of atomic power, isn't it? I promise you that Wayne has enough friends in the Senate that there will be no problem. And the engineering's all right, because Wayne has all those people already, of course. This isn't any little Manhattan Project, honey. Wayne spends *money*."

Dr. Cooperstock shook his head and, although he was smiling, he was interested, too. "What about death, Nan?" he said gently.

"Oh, I know, Coopie. It's terrible. But you can't lick this thing. So won't you do it for me? Wayne only needs you for a few weeks and he already talked to some doctors. They said it would be all right."

"Miss Halloran," I said. I admit I was furious. "Dr. Cooperstock is my patient. As long as that is so, I will decide what is or is not all right."

She looked at me again, sweetly and attentively.

I have now and had then no doubt at all; I was absolutely right in my position. Yet I felt as though I had committed the act of a clumsy fool. She was clean and lovely, her neck so slim that the dress she wore seemed too large for her, like an adorable child's. She was no child; I knew that she had had a hundred lovers because everyone knows that, even doctors who are fat and a little ugly and take it all out in intelligence. Yet she possessed an innocence I could not withstand. I wanted to take her sweetly by the hand and shelter her, and walk with her beside a brook and then that night crush her and caress her again and again with such violence and snorting passion that she would Awaken and then, with growing abandon, Respond. I did know it was all foolishness. I did. But when she mentioned the names of five or six doctors on Donner's payroll who would care for Dr. Cooperstock and suggested like a child that with them in charge it would really be all right, I agreed. I even apologized. Truth to tell, they were excellent men, those doctors. But if she had named six chiropractors and an unfrocked abortionist I still would have shrugged and shuffled and stammered, "Oh, well, I suppose, Miss Halloran, yes, it will be all right."

So we called the nurses in and very carefully dressed the old man and wheeled him out into the hall. I said something else that was foolish in the elevator. I said, because I had assumed that it was so, that she probably had a cab waiting and a cab would not do to transport a man as sick as Dr. Cooperstock. But she had been more sure of herself than that. The driver who was waiting was at the wheel of a private ambulance.

A TIME cover,
attributed to Artzybasheff,
with mosaic of dollar signs.

I did not again hear of Dr. Cooperstock for five weeks. Then I was telephoned to come and get him, for he was ready to return to the Pavilion to die. It was Wayne Donner himself who called me.

I agreed to come to one of Donner's New York offices to meet him, for in truth I was curious. I knew all about him, of course—rather, I knew as much as he wished anyone to know. I have seen enough of the world's household names in the Pavilion to know what their public-relations men can do. The facts that were on record about Wayne Donner were that he was very rich. He had gone from a lucky strike in oil and the twenty-seven and a half per cent depletion allowance to aluminum. And thence to electric power. He was almost the wealthiest man in the world, and I know his secret.

He could afford anything, anything at all, because he had schooled himself to purchase only bargains. For example, I knew that he was Nan Halloran's lover and, although I do not know her price, I know that it was what he was willing to pay. Otherwise he would have given her that thin, bright smile that meant the parley was over, there would be no contract signed that day, and gone on to another incredible beauty more modest in her bargaining. Donner allowed himself to want only what he could get. I think he was the only terrible man I have ever seen. And he had nearly been President of the United

States! Except that Governor Hewlett of Ohio spoke so honestly and so truthfully about him in the primaries that not all of Donner's newspapers could get him the vote; what was terrible was not that he then destroyed Hewlett, but that Hewlett was not destroyed for revenge. Donner hated too deeply to be satisfied with revenge, I think; he was too contemptuous of his enemies to trouble to crush them. He would not give them that satisfaction. Hewlett was blotted out only incidentally. Because Donner's papers had built the campaign against him to such a pitch that it was actually selling papers, and thus it was profitable to go on to ruin the man. When I saw Donner he had Hewlett's picture framed in gilt in his waiting room. I wondered how many of his visitors understood the message. For that matter I wondered how many needed it.

When I was admitted, Dr. Cooperstock was on a relaxing couch. "Hello, Martin," he said over the little drone of its motor. "This is Wayne Donner. Dr. Finneman. Dr. Grace."

I shook hands with the doctors first, pettishly enough but I felt obliged to show where I stood, and then with Donner. He was very courteous. He had discovered what bargains could be bought with that coin too. He said, "Dr. Finneman here has a good deal of respect for you, Doctor. I'm sure you're well placed at the Pavilion. But if you ever consider leaving I'd like to talk to you."

I thanked him and refused. I was flattered, though. I thought of how his fusion-power nonsense might have killed Dr. Cooperstock before he was ready to die, and I thought of him with Nan Halloran, sweat on that perfect face. And I am not impressed by money.

Yet I was flattered that he would take the trouble and time, and God knows how much an hour of his time was worth, to himself offer me a job. I was flattered even though I knew that the courtesy was for his benefit, not mine. He wanted the best he chose to afford—in the way of a doctor, in my case, but the best of anything else too. If he hired a gardener he would want the man to be a very good gardener. Aware as he was of the dignities assumed by a professional man, he had budgeted the time to give me a personal invitation instead of letting his housekeeper or general manager attend to it. It was only another installment of expense he chose to afford and yet I was glad to get out of there. I was almost afraid I would reconsider and say yes, and I hated that man very much.

When we got Dr. Cooperstock back and bedded and checked over I examined the records Dr. Finneman had sent. He had furnished complete tests and a politely guarded prognosis, and of course he was right; Cooperstock was sinking, but not fast; he was good for another month or two with luck. I told him as much, snappishly. "Don't be angry with me, Martin," he said, "you'd have done the same thing for Nan if she asked you."

"Probably, but I'm not dying."

"Don't be vulgar, Martin."

"I'm not a nuclear physicist, either."

"It's only to make a few dollars for the man, Martin. Heavens. What difference can another billion or two make to Donner? Besides," he said strongly, "you know I've always opposed this fetish of security. Think of Oppenheimer, not allowed to read his own papers! Think of the waste, the same work done in a dozen different places, because in Irkutsk they aren't allowed to know what's going on in Denver and in Omaha somebody forgot to tell them."

"Think of Wayne Donner with all the power in the world," I said.

He said, "I guess Nan hit you harder than I thought, to make you so mad."

Although I watched the papers I did not see anything about converting Donner's power stations to fusion energy. In fact, I didn't see much of Donner's name at all, which caused me to wonder. Normally he would have been spotted in the Stork or cruising off Bimini or in some other way photographed and written about a couple of times a week. His publicity men must have been laboring extra hard.

Nan Halloran came to see Dr. Cooperstock but I did not join them. I spent my time with him when there was no one else, after my evening rounds. Sometimes we played cards but more often I listened to him talk. The physics of the atomic nucleus was poetry when he talked of it. He told me about Gamow's primordial atom from which all the stars and dust clouds had exploded. He explained Fred Hoyle to me, and Heisenberg. But he was tiring early now.

Behind the drawer of his night table, in a used cigarette package thumbtacked to the wood, his store of red-and-white capsules was growing again. They were still aspirin. But I think I would not have denied him the real thing if he had known the deception and asked. We took off two toes in March and it was only a miracle that we saved the leg.

By Gilbert Stuart.
His late period.
Size 9' x 5'; heroic.

In the beginning of May newspaper stories again began to appear about Donner, but I could not understand them. The stories were datelined Washington. Donner was reported in top-level conferences, deeply classified. There were no leaks, no one knew what the talks were about. But the presidential press secretary was irritable with the reporters who asked questions, and the cabinet members were either visibly worried or visibly under orders to keep their mouths shut. *And* worried. I showed one or two of the stories to Dr. Cooperstock, but he was too tired to guess at implications.

He was hanging on, but it would not be for long. Any night I expected the call from his nurses, and we would not be able to save him again.

Then I was called to my office. I was lecturing to fourth-year men when the annunciator spoke my name; and when I got to my office Governor Hewlett was there.

"I need to see Dr. Cooperstock," he said. "I'm afraid it may excite him. The resident thought you should be present."

I said, "I suppose you know that any shock may kill him. I hope it's important."

"It is important. Yes." The Governor limped ahead of me to the elevator, his bald head gleaming, smiling at the nurses with his bad teeth and his wonderful eyes. Dr. Cooperstock was a hero to me. Governor Hewlett was something less, perhaps a saint or a martyr. He was what St. George would have been if in the battle he had been killed as well as the dragon; Hewlett had spent himself against Donner in the campaign and now he lingered on to serve out his punishment for his daring, the weasels always chipping away at him, a constant witness before commissions and committees with slanders thick in the air, a subject for jokes and political cartoons. A few senators and others of his own party still listened to him, but they could not save him from the committees.

The Governor did not waste words. "Dr. Cooperstock, what have you done? What is Wayne Donner up to?"

Cooperstock had been dozing. Elaborately he sat up. "I don't see, sir, that it is–"

"Will you answer me, please? I'm afraid this is quite serious. The Secretary of Defense, who was with me in the House fifteen years ago, told me something I did not suspect. Do you know that he may be asked to resign and that Wayne Donner may get his job?"

Dr. Cooperstock said angrily, "That's nonsense. Donner's just a businessman now. Anyway, what conceivable difference can–"

"It makes a difference, Dr. Cooperstock, because the rest of the cabinet is to be changed around at the same time. Every post of importance is to go to a man of Donner's. You recall that he wanted to be President. Perhaps this time he does not want to bother with a vote. What weapon have you given him to make him so strong, Dr. Cooperstock?"

"Weapon? Weapon?" Cooperstock stopped and began to gasp, lying back on his pillow, but he thrust me away when I came to him. "I didn't give him any weapon," he said thoughtfully, after staring at the Governor's face for a moment, forcing his lungs to work more easily. "At least, I don't think I did. It was only a commercial matter. You see, Governor, I have never believed in over-classification. Knowledge should be free. The basic theory–"

"Donner doesn't intend to make it free, Dr. Cooperstock, he plans to keep it for himself. Please tell me what you know."

"Well, it's fusion power," Cooperstock said.

"The hydrogen bomb?"

"Oh, for God's sake, Governor! It is fusion of hydrogen, yes, but not in any sense a bomb. The self-supporting reaction takes place in a magnetic bottle. It will not explode, even if the bottle fails; you would have to coax it to make it blow up. Only heat comes out, with which Donner is going to drive steam generators, perfectly normal. I assure you there is no danger of accident."

"I was not thinking of an accident," said the Governor after a moment.

"Well– In that event–I mean, it is true," said Cooperstock with some difficulty, "that, yes, as the reactor is set up, it would be possible to remove the safeguards. This is only the pilot model. The thing *could* be done."

"By remote control, as I understand," said Hewlett wearily. "And in that event each of Donner's power stations would become a hydrogen bomb. Did you know that he has twenty-four of them under construction, all over the nation?"

Cooperstock said indignantly, "He could not possibly have twenty-four installations completed in this time. I can hardly believe he has even one! In the New York plant on the river we designed only the fusion chamber itself. The hardware involved in generating power will take months."

"But I don't think he bothered with the hardware for generating power, you see," said the Governor.

Dr. Cooperstock began to gasp again. The Governor sat watching him for a moment, his face sagging with a painful fatigue, and then he roused himself and said at last, "Well, you shouldn't have done this, Dr. Cooperstock, but God bless you, you're a great man. We all owe you a debt. Only we'll have to do something about this now."

In my office the Governor took me aside. "I am sorry to have disturbed your patient. But it was important, as you see."

"Donner is a terrible man."

"Yes, I think that describes him. Well. It's all up to us now," said the Governor, looking very gray. "I confess I don't know what we can do."

"Surely the government can handle—"

"Doctor," he said, "I apologize for troubling you with my reflections. I've not much chance to talk them out with anyone, but I assure you I have thought of everything the government can do. Donner has eight oil senators in his pocket, you know. They would be delighted to filibuster any legislation. For more direct action, I'm afraid we can't get what we need without a greater risk than I can lightly contemplate. Donner has threatened to blow up every city of over eight hundred thousand, you see. I now find that this threat is not empty. Thank you, Doctor," he said, getting up. "I hope I haven't distressed your patient as much as he has distressed me."

He limped to the door, shook hands and was gone.

Half an hour later it was time for my rounds. I had spent the time sitting, doing nothing, almost not even thinking.

But I managed to go around, and then Dr. Cooperstock's nurse signaled me. He had asked her to phone Nan Halloran for him, and should she do it? There was a message: "I have something else for Wayne."

I found that puzzling but, as you will understand, I was in an emotionally numb state; it was difficult to guess at what it meant. I told the nurse she could transmit the message. But when Nan Halloran arrived, an hour or two later, I waited in the hall outside Dr. Cooperstock's room until she came out.

"Why, Doctor," she said, looking very lovely.

I took her by the arm. It was the first time I had touched that flesh; we had not even shaken hands before. I took her to my office. She seemed eager to go along with me. She asked no questions.

In the office, the door closed, I was extremely conscious of being alone in a room with her. She knew that, of course. She took a cigarette out of her purse, sat down and crossed her legs. Gallant, I stumbled to my desk and found a match to light her cigarette.

"You've been worrying Coopie," she said reproachfully. "You and that Hewlett. Can't he stay out of a simple business matter?"

She surprised me; it was such a foolish thing to say and she was not foolish. I told her very briefly what Hewlett had said. No one had told me to be silent. She touched my hand, laughing. "Would it make so very much difference . . . Martin? (May I?) Donner's not a monster."

"I don't know that."

She said impishly, "I do. He's a man like other men, Martin. And really he's not so young, even with all the treatments. What would you give him, with all his treatments? Twenty more years, tops?"

"A dictatorship even for twenty minutes is an evil thing, Miss Halloran," I said, wondering if I had always sounded so completely pompous.

"Oh, but bad words don't make bad things. Sakes! Think what they could call *me,* dear! Donner's only throwing his weight around, and doesn't everyone? As much weight as he has?"

"Treason—" I began, but she hardly let me get even the one word out.

"No bad words, Martin. You'd be astonished if you knew what wonderful things Wayne wants to do. It takes a man like him to take care of some problems. He'll get rid of slums, juvenile delinquents, gangsters . . ."

"Some problems are better not solved. Hitler solved the Jewish question in Europe."

She said sweetly, "I respect you, Martin. So does Wayne. You have no idea how much he and Dr. Cooperstock think of you, and so do I, so please don't do anything impulsive."

She walked out the room and left it very empty.

I felt turgid, drained and a little bit stupid. I had never wanted anything as much as I had wanted her.

It was several minutes before I began to wonder why she had taken the trouble to entice me in a pointless conversation. I knew that Nan Halloran was her own bank account, spent as thriftily as Donner's billions. I wondered what it was that I had had that she was willing to purchase with the small change of a few words and a glimpse of her knees and the scent of her perfume.

Before I had quite come to puzzle the question through, while I was still regretting I had had no higher-priced commodity for her, my phone rang. It was Dr. Cooperstock's nurse, hysterical.

Nan Halloran's conversation had not been pointless. While we were talking two ambulance attendants had come to assist Dr. Cooperstock into a wheelchair, and he was gone.

To Whom
all things concern

On the fourth of May Dr. Cooperstock defected and in the morning of the fifth Governor Hewlett telephoned me. "He's not back?" he said, and I said he wasn't, and Hewlett, pausing only a second, said, "Well. We can't wait any longer. The Army is moving in."

I went from my office to the operating room and I was shaking as I scrubbed in.

It was a splenectomy, but the woman was grossly fat, with a mild myocarditis that required external circulation. It took all of my attention, for which I was grateful. We were five hours in the room, but it was successful and it was not until I was smoking a cigarette in the little O.R. lounge that I began to shake.

Twenty-four nuclear bombs in twenty-four cities. And of course one of them, the one that we knew was ready to go off, was in the city I was in. I remembered the power plant, off in the Hudson River under the bridge, yellow brick and green glass. It was not more than a mile away.

And yet I was alive. The city was not destroyed. There had been no awful blast of heat and concussion.

I walked into the recovery room to look at the splenectomy. She was all right, but the nurse stared at me, so I went back to my office, realizing that I was crying.

And Nan Halloran was there waiting for me, looking like a drunken doll.

She pulled herself together as I came in. Her lipstick was smeared, and she shook. "You win, Martin," she said, with a little laugh. "Who would have thought old Coopie was such a lion? He gave me something for you."

I poured her a drink. "What happened?"

"Oh," said she. She drank the whiskey, politely enough, but showing she needed it. "Coopie came to Wayne and made a deal. Politics, he said, is out of my line, but you owe me something, I've helped you, I'll help you more, only you must promise that research will be free and well endowed. He had it very carefully worked out, the man is a genius." She giggled and held out her glass. "Funny. Of course he's a genius. So Wayne took the hook and said it was a deal, what was

Coopie going to do for him next? And Coopie offered to show him how to convert the power plant to a different kind of bomb. Neutrons, he said." So Dr. Cooperstock had taken the billionaire down into the guarded room and, explaining how it was possible to change the type of nuclear reaction from a simple hot explosion to a cold, killing flood of rays that would leave the city unharmed, if dead, he had diverted the hydrogen fuel supply, starved the reaction and shut off the magnetic field that contained it.

And then he had told Donner all deals were off.

There was nothing hard about rebuilding the field and restarting the reaction, of course. It only took a few days; but Donner no longer had days. "I told Wayne," said Nan Halloran gravely, draining her glass, "I told him he should wait until he had all the bombs ready, but he's—he was—he's still, but I think not for long, hard-headed. I have to go now, my plump friend, and I do thank you for the drink. I believe they're going to arrest me." She got up and picked up her white gloves, and at the door she paused and said, "Did I tell you? I've got so many things on my mind. Coopie's dead. He wouldn't let Wayne's doctors touch him."

They did arrest her, of course. But by and by, everything calming down, they let her go again. She's even starring in the movies again; you can see her whenever you like. I've never gone.

The letter in the envelope was from Dr. Cooperstock and it said:

> I've pulled their fuses, Martin, for you and the Governor, and if it kills me, as you should know it must, please don't think that I mind dying. Or that I am afraid to live, either. This is not suicide. Though I confess that I cannot choose between the fear of living in this world and the fear of what may lie beyond it.
>
> The leg is very bad. You would not even let me wear elastic socks, and for the past hour I have been crawling around the inside of Donner's stainless-steel plumbing. It was really a job for a younger man, but I couldn't find one in time.
>
> So I suppose these are my last words, and I wish I could make them meaningful. I expect there is a meaning to this. Science, as one of my predecessors once said—Teller, was it?—has become simpler and more beautiful. And surely it has become more wonderful and strange. If gravity itself grows old and thin, so that the straggling galaxies themselves weaken as they clutch each other, it seems somehow a much lesser thing that we too should grow feeble. Yet I do hate it. I am able to bear it at all, indeed, only

through a Hope which I never dared confess even to you, Martin, before this.

When I was young I went to church and dreaded dying for the fear of hellfire. When I was older I dreaded nothing; and when I was older still I began to dread again. The hours, my friend, in which I held imaginary conversations with the God I denied—proving to Him, Martin, that He did not exist—were endless. And then, past Jehovah and prophets, I found another God, harsher, more awful and more remote. I could not pray to Him, Creator of the Big Bang, He Who Came Before the Monobloc. But I could fear Him.

Now I am not afraid of Him. A galaxy twenty billion years old has given me courage. If there was no monobloc there can have been no God Who made it. I live in the hope of the glorious steady state!

It was weak and wicked of me to give Donner a gun to point at the world, therefore, and I expect it is fair if I die taking it back; but it is not to save the world that I do it but to save my own soul in the galaxies yet to be born. For if the steady state is true there is no end to time. And infinity is not bounded, in any way. Everything must happen in infinity. Everything must happen . . . an infinity of times.

So Martin, in those times to come, when these atoms that compose us come together again, under what cis-Andromedan star I cannot imagine, we will meet—if there is infinity it is sure—and I can hope. In that day may we be put together more cleanly, Martin. And may we meet again, all of us, in shapes of pleasing strength and health, members of a race that is, I pray, a little wiser and more kind.

That was the letter from Dr. Rhine Cooperstock. I folded it away. I called my secretary on the intercom to tell her that his suite would now be free for another patient; and I went out into the spring day, to the great black headlines with Donner's name over all the papers and to the life that Copperstock had given back to us all.

Day Million

ON THIS DAY I want to tell you about, which will be about a thousand years from now, there were a boy, a girl and a love story.

Now although I haven't said much so far, none of it is true. The boy was not what you and I would normally think of as a boy, because he was a hundred and eighty-seven years old. Nor was the girl a girl, for other reasons; and the love story did not entail that sublimation of the urge to rape and concurrent postponement of the instinct to submit which we at present understand in such matters. You won't care much for this story if you don't grasp these facts at once. If, however, you will make the effort, you'll likely enough find it jam-packed, chockfull and tiptop-crammed with laughter, tears and poignant sentiment which may, or may not, be worth while. The reason the girl was not a girl was that she was a boy.

How angrily you recoil from the page! You say, who the hell wants to read about a pair of queers? Calm yourself. Here are no hot-breathing secrets of perversion for the coterie trade. In fact, if you were to see this girl, you would not guess that she was in any sense a boy. Breasts, two; vagina, one. Hips, Callipygean; face, hairless; supra-orbital lobes, non-existent. You would term her female at once, although it is true that you might wonder just what species she was a female of, being confused by the tail, the silky pelt or the gill slits behind each ear.

Now you recoil again. Cripes, man, take my word for it. This is a sweet kid, and if you, as a normal male, spent as much as an hour in a room with her, you would bend heaven and earth to get her in the sack. Dora (we will call her that; her "name" was omicron-Dibase seven-group-totter-oot S Doradus 5314, the last part of which is a color specification corresponding to a shade of green)—Dora, I say, was feminine, charming and cute. I admit she doesn't sound that way. She was, as you might put it, a dancer. Her art involved qualities of intellection and expertise of a very high order, requiring both tremendous natural capacities and endless practice; it was performed in null-gravity and I can best describe it by saying that it was something like the performance of a contortionist and something like classical ballet, maybe resembling Danilova's dying swan. It was also pretty damned sexy. In a symbolic way, to be sure; but face it, most of the things we call "sexy" are symbolic, you know, except perhaps an exhibitionist's open fly. On Day Million when Dora danced, the people who saw her panted; and you would too.

About this business of her being a boy. It didn't matter to her audiences that genetically she was male. It wouldn't matter to you, if you were among them, because you wouldn't know it–not unless you took a biopsy cutting of her flesh and put it under an electron-microscope to find the XY chromosome–and it didn't matter to them because they didn't care. Through techniques which are not only complex but haven't yet been discovered, these people were able to determine a great deal about the aptitudes and easements of babies quite a long time before they were born–at about the second horizon of cell-division, to be exact, when the segmenting egg is becoming a free blastocyst–and then they naturally helped those aptitudes along. Wouldn't we? If we find a child with an aptitude for music we give him a scholarship to Juilliard. If they found a child whose aptitudes were for being a woman, they made him one. As sex had long been dissociated from reproduction this was relatively easy to do and caused no trouble and no, or at least very little, comment.

How much is "very little"? Oh, about as much as would be caused by our own tampering with Divine Will by filling a tooth. Less than would be caused by wearing a hearing aid. Does it still sound awful? Then look closely at the next busty babe you meet and reflect that she may be a Dora, for adults who are genetically male but somatically female are far from unknown even in our own time. An accident of environment in the womb overwhelms the blueprints of heredity. The difference is that with us it happens only by accident and we don't know about it except rarely, after close study; whereas the people of Day Million did it often, on purpose, because they wanted to.

Well, that's enough to tell you about Dora. It would only confuse you to add that she was seven feet tall and smelled of peanut butter. Let us begin our story.

On Day Million Dora swam out of her house, entered a transportation tube, was sucked briskly to the surface in its flow of water and ejected in its plume of spray to an elastic platform in front of her –ah–call it her rehearsal hall. "Oh, shit!" she cried in pretty confusion, reaching out to catch her balance and find herself tumbled against a total stranger, whom we will call Don.

They met cute. Don was on his way to have his legs renewed. Love was the farthest thing from his mind; but when, absent-mindedly taking a short cut across the landing platform for submarinites and finding himself drenched, he discovered his arms full of the loveliest girl he had ever seen, he knew at once they were meant for each other. "Will you marry me?" he asked. She said softly, "Wednesday," and the promise was like a caress.

Don was tall, muscular, bronze and exciting. His name was no more Don than Dora's was Dora, but the personal part of it was Adonis in tribute to his vibrant maleness, and so we will call him Don for short. His personality color-code, in Ångstrom units, was 5290, or only a few degrees bluer than Dora's 5314, a measure of what they had intuitively discovered at first sight, that they possessed many affinities of taste and interest.

I despair of telling you exactly what it was that Don did for a living—I don't mean for the sake of making money, I mean for the sake of giving purpose and meaning to his life, to keep him from going off his nut with boredom—except to say that it involved a lot of traveling. He traveled in interstellar spaceships. In order to make a spaceship go really fast about thirty-one male and seven genetically female human beings had to do certain things, and Don was one of the thirty-one. Actually he contemplated options. This involved a lot of exposure to radiation flux—not so much from his own station in the propulsive system as in the spillover from the next stage, where a genetic female preferred selections and the subnuclear particles making the selections she preferred demolished themselves in a shower of quanta. Well, you don't give a rat's ass for that, but it meant that Don had to be clad at all times in a skin of light, resilient, extremely strong copper-colored metal. I have already mentioned this, but you probably thought I meant he was sunburned.

More than that, he was a cybernetic man. Most of his ruder parts had been long since replaced with mechanisms of vastly more permanence and use. A cadmium centrifuge, not a heart, pumped his blood. His lungs moved only when he wanted to speak out loud, for a cascade of osmotic filters rebreathed oxygen out of his own wastes. In a way, he probably would have looked peculiar to a man from the twentieth century, with his glowing eyes and seven-fingered hands; but to himself, and of course to Dora, he looked mighty manly and grand. In the course of his voyages Don had circled Proxima Centauri, Procyon and the puzzling worlds of Mira Ceti; he had carried agricultural templates to the planets of Canopus and brought back warm, witty pets from the pale companion of Aldebaran. Blue-hot or red-cool, he had seen a thousand stars and their ten thousand planets. He had, in fact, been traveling the starlanes with only brief leaves on Earth for pushing two centuries. But you don't care about that, either. It is people that make stories, not the circumstances they find themselves in, and you want to hear about these two people. Well, they made it. The great thing they had for each other grew and flowered and burst into fruition on Wednesday, just as Dora had promised. They met at the encoding room, with a couple of well-wishing friends apiece to cheer them on, and while their identities were being taped and stored they smiled and whispered to each other and bore the jokes of their friends with blushing repartee. Then they exchanged their mathematical analogues and went away, Dora to her dwelling beneath the surface of the sea and Don to his ship.

It was an idyll, really. They lived happily ever after—or anyway, until they decided not to bother any more and died.

Of course, they never set eyes on each other again.

Oh, I can see you now, you eaters of charcoal-broiled steak, scratching an incipient bunion with one hand and holding this story with the other, while the stereo plays d'Indy or Monk. You don't believe a word of it, do you? Not for one minute. People wouldn't live like that, you say with an irritated and not amused grunt as you get up to put fresh ice in a stale drink.

And yet there's Dora, hurrying back through the flushing commuter pipes toward her underwater home (she prefers it there; has had herself somatically altered to breathe the stuff). If I tell you with what sweet fulfillment she fits the recorded analogue of Don into the symbol manipulator, hooks herself in and turns herself on . . . if I try to tell you any of that you will simply stare. Or glare; and grumble, what the hell kind of love-making is this? And yet I assure you, friend, I really do assure you that Dora's ecstasies are as creamy and passionate as any of James Bond's lady spies, and one hell of a lot more so than anything you are going to find in "real life." Go ahead, glare and grumble. Dora doesn't care. If she thinks of you at all, her thirty-times-great-great-grandfather, she thinks you're a pretty primordial sort of brute. You are. Why, Dora is farther removed from you than you are from the australopithecines of five thousand centuries ago. You could not swim a second in the strong currents of her life. You don't think progress goes in a straight line, do you? Do you recognize that it is an ascending, accelerating, maybe even exponential curve? It takes hell's own time to get started, but when it goes it goes like a bomb. And you, you Scotch-drinking steak-eater in your Relaxacizer chair, you've just barely lighted the primacord of the fuse. What is it now, the six or seven hundred thousandth day after Christ? Dora lives in Day Million. A thousand years from now. Her body fats are polyunsaturated, like Crisco. Her wastes are hemodialyzed out of her bloodstream while she sleeps—that means she doesn't have to go to the bathroom. On whim, to pass a slow half-hour, she can command more energy than the entire nation of Portugal can spend today, and use it to launch a weekend satellite or remold a crater on the Moon. She loves Don very much. She keeps his every gesture, mannerism, nuance, touch of hand, thrill of intercourse, passion of kiss stored in symbolic-mathematical form. And when she wants him, all she has to do is turn the machine on and she has him.

And Don, of course, has Dora. Adrift on a sponson city a few hundred yards over her head or orbiting Arcturus, fifty light-years away, Don has only to command his own symbol-manipulator to rescue Dora from the ferrite files and bring her to life for him, and there she is; and rapturously, tirelessly they ball all night. Not in the flesh, of course; but then his flesh has been extensively altered and it wouldn't really be much fun. He doesn't need the flesh for pleasure. Genital organs feel nothing. Neither do hands, nor breasts, nor lips; they are only receptors, accepting and transmitting impulses. It is the brain that feels, it is the interpretation of those impulses that makes agony or orgasm; and Don's symbol-manipulator gives him the analogue of cuddling, the analogue of kissing, the analogue of wildest, most ardent hours with the eternal, exquisite and incorruptible analogue of Dora. Or Diane. Or sweet Rose, or laughing Alicia; for to be sure, they have each of them exchanged analogues before, and will again.

Balls, you say, it looks crazy to me. And you—with your aftershave lotion and your little red car, pushing papers across a desk all day and chasing tail all night—tell me, just how the hell do you think you would look to Tiglath-Pileser, say, or Attila the Hun?

Happy Birthday, Dear Jesus

It was the craziest Christmas I ever spent. Partly it was Heinemann's fault–he came up with a new wrinkle in gift-wrapping that looked good but like every other idea that comes out of the front office meant plenty of headaches for the rest of us. But what really messed up Christmas for me was the girl.

Personnel sent her down–after I'd gone up there myself three times and banged my fist on the table. It was the height of the season and when she told me that she had had her application in *three weeks* before they called her, I excused myself and got Personnel on the store phone from my private office. "Martin here," I said. "What the devil's the matter with you people? This girl is the Emporium type if I ever saw one, and you've been letting her sit around nearly a month while——"

Crawford, the Personnel head, interrupted me. "Have you talked to her very much?" he wanted to know.

"Well, no. But——"

"Call me back when you do," he advised, and clicked off.

I went back to the stockroom where she was standing patiently, and looked her over a little thoughtfully. But she looked all right to me. She was blond-haired and blue-eyed and not very big; she had a sweet, slow smile. She wasn't exactly beautiful, but she looked like a girl you'd want to know. She wasn't bold, and she wasn't too shy; and that's a perfect description of what we call "The Emporium Type."

So what in the world was the matter with Personnel?

Her name was Lilymary Hargreave. I put her to work on the gift-wrap spraying machine while I got busy with my paper work. I have a hundred forty-one persons in the department and at the height of the Christmas season I could use twice as many. But we do get the work done. For instance, Saul & Capell, the next biggest store in town, has a hundred and sixty in their gift and counseling department, and their sales run easily twenty-five per cent less than ours. And in the four years that I've headed the department we've yet to fail to get an order delivered when it was promised.

All through that morning I kept getting glimpses of the new girl. She was a quick learner–smart, too smart to be stuck with the sprayer for very long. I needed someone like her around, and right there on the spot I made up my mind that if she was as good as she looked I'd put her in a counseling booth within a week, and the devil with what Personnel thought.

The store was packed with last-minute shoppers. I suppose I'm sentimental, but I love to watch the thousands of people bustling in and out, with all the displays going at once, and the lights on the trees, and the loudspeakers playing *White Christmas* and *The Eighth Candle* and *Jingle Bells* and all the other traditional old favorites. Christmas is more than a mere selling season of the year to me; it *means* something.

The girl called me over near closing time. She looked distressed and with some reason. There was a dolly filled with gift-wrapped packages, and a man from Shipping looking annoyed. She said, "I'm sorry, Mr. Martin, but I seem to have done something wrong."

The Shipping man snorted. "Look for yourself, Mr. Martin," he said, handing me one of the packages.

I looked. It was wrong, all right. Heinemann's new wrinkle that year was a special attached gift card–a simple Yule scene and the printed message:

The very Merriest of Season's Greetings

From ....

To ....

$8.50

The price varied with the item, of course. Heinemann's idea was for the customer to fill it out and mail it, ahead of time, to the person it was intended for. That way, the person who got it would know just about how much he ought to spend on a present for the first person. It was smart, I admit, and maybe the smartest thing about it was rounding the price off to the nearest fifty cents instead of giving it exactly. Heinemann said it was bad-mannered to be too precise–and the way the customers were going for the idea, it had to be right.

But the trouble was that the gift-wrapping machines were geared to only a plain card; it was necessary for the operator to put the price in by hand.

I said, "That's all right, Joe; I'll take care of it." As Joe went satisfied back to Shipping, I told the girl: "It's my fault. I should have explained to you, but I guess I've just been a little too rushed."

She looked downcast. "I'm sorry," she said.

"Nothing to be sorry about." I showed her the routing slip attached to each one, which the Shipping Department kept for its records once the package was on its way. "All we have to do is go through these; the price is on every one. We'll just fill out the cards and get them out. I guess——" I looked at my watch—"I guess you'll be a little late tonight, but I'll see that you get overtime and dinner money for it. It wasn't your mistake, after all."

She said hesitantly, "Mr. Martin, couldn't it—well, can I let it go for tonight? It isn't that I mind working, but I keep house for my father and if I don't get there on time he just won't remember to eat dinner. Please?"

I suppose I frowned a little, because her expression was a little worried. But, after all, it was her first day. I said, "Miss Hargreave, don't give it a thought. I'll take care of it."

The way I took care of it, it turned out, was to do it myself; it was late when I got through, and I ate quickly and went home to bed. But I didn't mind, for oh! the sweetness of the smile she gave me as she left.

I looked forward to the next morning, because I was looking forward to seeing Lilymary Hargreave again. But my luck was out—for she was.

My number-two man, Johnny Furness, reported that she hadn't phoned either. I called Personnel to get her phone number, but they didn't have it; I got the address, but the phone company had no phone listed under her name. So I stewed around until the coffee break, and then I put my hat on and headed out of the store. It wasn't merely that I was interested in seeing her, I told myself; she was just too good a worker to get off on the wrong foot this way, and it was only simple justice for me to go to her home and set her straight.

Her house was in a nondescript neighborhood—not too good, not too bad. A gang of kids were playing under a fire hydrant at the corner—but, on the other hand, the houses were neat and nearly new. Middle-class, you'd have to say.

I found the address, and knocked on the door of a second-floor apartment.

It was opened by a tall, leathery man of fifty or so—Lilymary's father, I judged. "Good morning," I said. "Is Miss Hargreave at home?"

He smiled; his teeth were bright in a very sun-bronzed face. "Which one?"

"Blond girl, medium height, blue eyes. Is there more than one?"

"There are four. But you mean Lilymary; won't you come in?"

I followed him, and a six-year-old edition of Lilymary took my hat and gravely hung it on a rack made of bamboo pegs. The leathery man said, "I'm Morton Hargreave, Lily's father. She's in the kitchen."

"George Martin," I said. He nodded and left me, for the kitchen, I presumed. I sat down on an old-fashioned studio couch in the living room, and the six-year-old sat on the edge of a straight-backed chair across from me, making sure I didn't pocket any of the souvenirs on the mantel. The room was full of curiosities—what looked like a cloth of beaten bark hanging on one wall, with a throwing-spear slung over the cloth. Everything looked vaguely South-Seas, though I am no expert.

The six-year-old said seriously, "This is the man, Lilymary," and I got up.

"Good morning," said Lilymary Hargreave, with a smudge of flour and an expression of concern on her face.

I said, floundering, "I, uh, noticed you hadn't come in and, well, since you were new to the Emporium, I thought——"

"I *am* sorry, Mr. Martin," she said. "Didn't Personnel tell you about Sundays?"

"What about Sundays?"

"I must have my Sundays off," she explained. "Mr. Crawford said it was very unusual, but I really can't accept the job any other way."

"Sundays off?" I repeated. "But—but, Miss Hargreave, don't you see what that does to my schedule? Sunday's our busiest day! The Emporium isn't a rich man's shop; our customers work during the week. If we aren't staffed to serve them when they can come in, we just aren't doing the job they expect of us!"

She said sincerely, "I'm terribly sorry, Mr. Martin."

The six-year-old was already reaching for my hat. From the doorway her father said heartily, "Come back again, Mr. Martin. We'll be glad to see you."

He escorted me to the door, as Lilymary smiled and nodded and headed back to the kitchen. I said, "Mr. Hargreave, won't you ask Lilymary to come in for the afternoon, at least? I hate to sound like a boss, but I'm really short-handed on weekends, right now at the peak of the season."

"Season?"

"The Christmas season," I explained. "Nearly ninety per cent of our annual business is done in the Christmas season, and a good half of it on weekends. So won't you ask her?"

He shook his head. "Six days the Lord labored, Mr. Martin," he boomed, "and the seventh was the day of rest. I'm sorry."

And there I was, outside the apartment and the door closing politely but implacably behind me.

Crazy people. I rode the subway back to the store in an irritable mood; I bought a paper, but I didn't read it, because every time I looked at it all I saw was the date that showed me how far the Christmas season already had advanced, how little time we had left to make our quotas and beat last year's record: the eighth of September.

I would have something to say to Miss Lilymary Hargreave when she had the kindness to show up at her job. I promised myself. But, as it turned out, I didn't. Because that night, checking through the day's manifolds when everyone else had gone home, I fell in love with Lilymary Hargreave.

Possibly that sounds silly to you. She wasn't even there, and I'd only known her for a few hours, and when a man begins to push thirty without ever being married, you begin to think he's a hard case and not likely to fall slambang, impetuously in love like a teenager after his first divorce. But it's true, all the same.

I almost called her up. I trembled on the brink of it, with my hand on the phone. But it was close to midnight, and if she wasn't home getting ready for bed I didn't want to know it, so I went home to my own bed. I reached under the pillow and turned off my dreamster before I went to sleep; I had a full library for it, a de luxe model with five hundred dreams that had been a present from the firm the Christmas before. I had Haroun al Rashid's harem and three of Charles Second's favorites on tape, and I had rocketing around the moon and diving to Atlantis and winning a sweepstakes and getting elected king of the world; but what I wanted to dream about was not on anybody's tape, and its name was Lilymary Hargreave.

Monday lasted forever. But at the end of forever, when the tip of the nightingale's wing had brushed away the mountain of steel and the Shipping personnel were putting on their hats and coats and powdering their noses or combing their hair, I stepped right up to Lilymary Hargreave and asked her to go to dinner with me.

She looked astonished, but only for a moment. Then she smiled. . . . I have mentioned the sweetness of her smile. "It's wonderful of you to ask me, Mr. Martin," she said earnestly, "and I do appreciate it. But I can't."

"Please," I said.

"I *am* sorry."

I might have said please again, and I might have fallen to my knees at her feet, it was that important to me. But the staff was still in the shop, and how would it look for the head of the department to fall at the feet of his newest employee? I said woodenly, "That's too bad." And I nodded and turned away, leaving her frowning after me. I cleared my desk sloppily, chucking the invoices in a drawer, and I was halfway out the door when I heard her calling after me:

"Mr. Martin, Mr. Martin!"

She was hurrying toward me, breathless. "I'm sorry," she said, "I didn't mean to scream at you. But I just phoned my father, and——"

"I thought you didn't have a phone," I said accusingly.

She blinked at me. "At the rectory," she explained. "Anyway, I just phoned him, and–well, we'd both be delighted if you would come and have dinner with us at home."

Wonderful words! The whole complexion of the shipping room changed in a moment. I beamed foolishly at her, with a soft surge at my heart; I felt happy enough to endow a home, strong enough to kill a cave bear or give up smoking or any crazy, mixed-up thing. I wanted to shout and sing; but all I said was: "That sounds great." We headed for the subway, and although I must have talked to her on the ride I cannot remember a word we said, only that she looked like the angel at the top of our tallest Christmas tree.

Dinner was good, and there was plenty of it, cooked by Lilymary herself, and I think I must have seemed a perfect idiot. I sat there, with the six-year-old on one side of me and Lilymary on the other, across from the ten-year-old and the twelve-year-old. The father of them all was at the head of the table, but he was the only other male. I understood there were a couple of brothers, but they didn't live with the others. I suppose there had been a mother at some time, unless Morton Hargreave stamped the girls out with a kind of cookie-cutter; but whatever she had been she appeared to be deceased. I felt overwhelmed. I wasn't used to being surrounded by young females, particularly as young as the median in that gathering.

Lilymary made an attempt to talk to me, but it wasn't altogether successful. The younger girls were given to fits of giggling, which she had to put a stop to, and to making what were evidently personal remarks in some kind of a peculiar foreign tongue–it sounded like a weird aboriginal dialect, and I later found out that it was. But it was disconcerting, especially from the lips of a six-year-old with the giggles. So I didn't make any very intelligent responses to Lilymary's overtures.

But all things end, even eating dinner with giggling girls. And then Mr. Hargreave and I sat in the little parlor, waiting for the girls to–finish doing the dishes? I said, shocked, "Mr. Hargreave, do you mean they *wash* them?"

"Certainly they wash them," he boomed mildly. "How else would they get them clean, Mr. Martin?"

"Why, *dishwashers,* Mr. Hargreave." I looked at him in a different way. Business is business. I said, "After all, this is the Christmas season. At the Emporium we put a very high emphasis on dishwashers as a Christmas gift, you know. We—"

He interrupted good-humoredly. "I already have my gifts, Mr. Martin. Four of them, and very fine dishwashers they are."

"But Mr. Hargreave—"

"Not Mister Hargreave." The six-year-old was standing beside me, looking disapproving. "*Doctor* Hargreave."

"Corinne!" said her father. "Forgive her, Mr. Martin. But you see we're not very used to the–uh, civilized way of doing things. We've been a long time with the Dyaks."

The girls were all back from the kitchen, and Lilymary was out of her apron and looking–unbelievable. "Entertainment," she said brightly. "Mr. Martin, would you like to hear Corinne play?"

There was a piano in the corner. I said hastily, "I'm crazy about piano music. But—"

Lilymary laughed. "She's good," she told me seriously. "Even if I do have to say it to her face. But we'll let you off that if you like. Gretchen and I sing a little bit, if you'd prefer it?"

Wasn't there any TV in this place? I felt as out of place as an Easterbunny-helper in the Santa Claus line, but Lilymary was still looking unbelievable. So I sat through Lilymary and the twelve-year-old named Gretchen singing ancient songs while the six-year-old named Corinne accompanied them on the piano. It was pretty thick. Then the ten-year-old, whose name I never did catch, did recitations; and then they all looked expectantly at me.

I cleared my throat, slightly embarrassed. Lilymary said quickly,

"Oh, you don't have to do anything, Mr. Martin. It's just our custom, but we don't expect strangers to conform to it!"

I didn't want that word "stranger" to stick. I said, "Oh, but I'd like to. I mean, I'm not much good at public entertaining, but—" I hesitated, because that was the truest thing I had ever said. I had no more voice than a goat, and of course the only instrument I had ever learned to play was a TV set. But then I remembered something from my childhood.

"I'll tell you what," I said enthusiastically. "How would you like something appropriate to the season? 'A Visit from Santa Claus,' for instance?"

Gretchen said snappishly, "What season? *We* don't start celebrating—"

Her father cut her off. "Please do, Mr. Martin," he said politely. "We'd enjoy that very much."

I cleared my throat and started:

'Tis the season of Christmas, and all through the house
St. Nick and his helpers begin their carouse.
The closets are stuffed and the drawers overflowing
With gift-wrapped remembrances, coming and going.
What a joyous abandon of Christmastime glow!
What a making of lists! What a spending of dough!
So much for—

"Hey!" said Gretchen, looking revolted. "Daddy, *that* isn't how—"

"Hush!" said Dr. Hargreave grimly. His own expression wasn't very delighted either, but he said, "Please go on."

I began to wish I'd kept my face shut. They were all looking at me very peculiarly, except for Lilymary, who was conscientiously studying the floor. But it was too late to back out; I went on:

So much for the bedroom, so much for the bath,
So much for the kitchen–too little by half!
Come Westinghouse, Philco! Come Hotpoint, G.E.!
Come Sunbeam! Come Mixmaster! Come to the Tree!
So much for the wardrobe–how shine Daddy's eyes
As he reaps his Yule harvest of slippers and ties.
So much for the family, so much for the friends,
So much for the neighbors–the list never ends.
A contingency fund for the givers belated
Whose gifts must be hastily reciprocated.
And out of—

Gretchen stood up. "It's our bedtime," she said. "Good night, everybody."

Lilymary flared, "It is not! Now be still!" And she looked at me for the first time. "Please go on," she said, with a furrowed brow.

I said hoarsely:

And out of the shops, how they spring with a clatter,
The gifts and appliances words cannot flatter!
The robot dishwasher, the new Frigidaire,
The doll with the didy and curlable hair!
The electrified hairbrush, the black lingerie,
The full-color stereoscopic TV!
Come, Credit Department! Come, Personal Loan!
Come, Mortgage, come Christmas Club, come——

Lilymary turned her face away. I stopped and licked my lips.

"That's all I remember," I lied. "I–I'm sorry if——"

Dr. Hargreave shook himself like a man waking from a nightmare. "It's getting rather late," he said to Lilymary. "Perhaps–perhaps our guest would enjoy some coffee before he goes."

I declined the coffee and Lilymary walked me to the subway. We didn't talk much.

At the subway entrance she firmly took my hand and shook it. "It's been a pleasant evening," she said.

A wandering group of carolers came by; I gave my contribution to the guitarist. Suddenly angry, I said, "Doesn't that *mean* anything to you?"

"What?"

I gestured after the carolers. "That. Christmas. The whole sentimental, lovable, warmhearted business of Christmas. Lilymary, we've only known each other a short time, but——"

She interrupted: "Please, Mr. Martin. I–I know what you're going to say." She looked terribly appealing there in the Christmassy light of the red and green lights from the Tree that marked the subway entrance. Her pale, straight legs, hardly concealed by the shorts, picked up chromatic highlights; her eyes sparkled. She said, "You see, as Daddy says, we've been away from–civilization. Daddy is a missionary, and we've been with the Dyaks since I was a little girl. Gretch and Marlene and Corinne were born there. We–we do things differently on Borneo." She looked up at the Tree over us, and sighed. "It's very hard to get used to," she said. "Sometimes I wish we had stayed with the Dyaks."

Then she looked at me. She smiled. "But sometimes," she said, "I am very glad we're here." And she was gone.

Ambiguous? Call it merely ladylike. At any rate, that's what I called it; I took it to be the beginning of the kind of feeling I so desperately wanted her to have; and for the second night in a row I let Haroun's harem beauties remain silent on their tapes.

Calamity struck. My number-two man, Furness, turned up one morning with a dismal expression and a letter in a government-franked envelope. "Greeting!" it began. "You are summoned to serve with a jury of citizens for the term——"

"Jury duty!" I groaned. "At a time like this! Wait a minute, Johnny, I'll call up Mr. Heinemann. He might be able to fix it if——"

Furness was shaking his head. "Sorry, Mr. Martin. I already asked him and he tried; but no go. It's a big case–blindfold sampling of twelve brands of filter cigarettes–and Mr. Heinemann says it wouldn't look right to try to evade it."

So there was breaking another man in, to add to my troubles.

It meant overtime, and that meant that I didn't have as much time as I would like for Lilymary. Lunch together, a couple of times; odd moments between runs of the gift-wrapping machines; that was about it.

But she was never out of my thoughts. There was something about her that appealed to me. A square, yes. Unworldly, yes. Her family? A Victorian horror; but they were *her* family. I determined to get them on my side, and by and by I began to see how.

"Miss Hargreave," I said formally, coming out of my office. We stepped to one side, in a corner under the delivery chutes. The rumble of goods overhead gave us privacy. I said, "Lilymary, you're taking this Sunday off, as usual? May I come to visit you?"

She hesitated only a second. "Why, of course," she said firmly. "We'd be delighted. For dinner?"

I shook my head: "I have a little surprise for you," I whispered. She looked alarmed. "Not for you, exactly. For the kids. Trust me, Lilymary. About four o'clock in the afternoon?"

I winked at her and went back to my office to make arrangements. It wasn't the easiest thing in the world–it was our busy season, as I say–but what's the use of being the boss if you can't pull rank once in a while? So I made it as strong as I could, and Special Services hemmed and hawed and finally agreed that they would work in a special Visit from Santa Claus at the Hargreave home that Sunday afternoon.

Once the kids were on my side, I plotted craftily, it would be easy enough to work the old man around, and what kid could resist a Visit from Santa Claus?

I rang the bell and walked into the queer South-Seas living room as though I belonged there. "Merry Christmas!" I said genially to the six-year-old who let me in. "I hope you kiddies are ready for a treat!" treat!"

She looked at me incredulously, and disappeared. I heard her say something shrill and protesting in the next room, and Lilymary's voice being firm and low-toned. Then Lilymary appeared. "Hello, Mr. Martin," she said.

"George."

"Hello, George." She sat down and patted the sofa beside her. "Would you like some lemonade?" she asked.

"Thank you," I said. It was pretty hot for the end of September, and the place didn't appear to be air-conditioned. She called, and the twelve-year-old, Gretchen, turned up with a pitcher and some cookies. I said warningly:

"Mustn't get too full, little girl! There's a surprise coming."

Lilymary cleared her throat, as her sister set the tray down with a clatter and stamped out of the room. "I–I wish you'd tell me about this surprise, George," she said. "You know, we're a little, well, set in our ways, and I wonder——"

"Nothing to worry about, Lilymary," I reassured her. "What is it, a couple of minutes before four? They'll be here any minute."

"They?"

I looked around; the kids were out of sight. "Santa Claus and his helpers," I whispered.

She began piercingly: "Santa Cl——"

"Ssh!" I nodded toward the door. "I want it to be a surprise for the kids. Please don't spoil it for them, Lilymary."

Well, she opened her mouth; but she didn't get a chance to say anything. The bell rang; Santa Claus and his helpers were right on time.

"Lilymary!" shrieked the twelve-year-old, opening the door. "Look!"

You couldn't blame the kid for being excited. "Ho-ho-ho," boomed Santa, rolling inside. "Oh, hello, Mr. Martin. This the place?"

"Certainly, Santa," I said, beaming. "Bring it in, boys."

The twelve-year-old cried, "Corinne! Marlene! This you got to see!" There was an odd tone to her voice, but I didn't pay much attention. It wasn't my party any more. I retired, smiling, to a corner of the room while the Santa Claus helpers began coming in with their sacks of gear on their shoulders. It was "Ho-ho-ho, little girl!" and "Merry Christmas, everybody!" until you couldn't hear yourself think.

Lilymary was biting her lip, staring at me. The Santa tapped her on the shoulder. "Where's the kitchen, lady?" he asked. "That door? Okay, Wynken–go on in and get set up. Nod, you go down and hurry up the sound truck, then you can handle the door. The rest of you helpers–" he surveyed the room briefly– "start lining up your Christmas Goodies there, and there. Now hop to it, boys! We got four more Visits to make this afternoon yet."

You never saw a crew of Christmas Gnomes move as fast as them. Snap, and the Tree was up, complete with its tinsel stars and gray colored Order Forms and Credit Application Blanks. Snip, and two of the helpers were stringing the red and green lights that led from the Hargreave living room to the sound truck outside. Snip-snap, and you could hear the sound truck pealing the joyous strains of *All I Want for Christmas Is Two of Everything* in the street, and twos and threes of the neighborhood children were beginning to appear at the door, blinking and ready for the fun. The kitchen helpers were ladling out mugs of cocoa and colored-sugar Christmas cookies and collecting the dimes and quarters from the kids; the demonstrator helpers were showing the kids the toys and trinkets from their sacks; and Santa himself was seated on his glittering throne. "Ho-ho-ho, my boy," he was saying. "And where does your daddy work this merry Christmas season?"

I was proud of them. There wasn't a helper there who couldn't have walked into Saul & Cappell or any other store in town, and walked out a Santa with a crew of his own. But that's the way we do things at the Emporium, skilled hands and high paychecks, and you only have to look at our sales records to see that it pays off.

Well, I wanted to stay and watch the fun, but Sunday's a bad day to take the afternoon off; I slipped out and headed back to the store. I put in a hard four hours, but I made it a point to be down at the Special Services division when the crews came straggling in for their checkout. The crew I was interested in was the last to report, naturally–isn't that always the way? Santa was obviously tired; I let him shuck his uniform and turn his sales slips in to the cashier before I tackled him. "How did it go?" I asked anxiously. "Did Miss Hargreave–I mean the grown-up Miss Hargreave–did she say anything?"

He looked at me accusingly. "You," he whined. "Mr. Martin, you shouldn't have run out on us like that. How we supposed to keep up a schedule when you throw us that kind of a curve, Mr. Martin?"

It was no way for a Santa to be talking to a department head, but I overlooked it. The man was obviously upset. "What are you talking about?" I demanded.

"Those Hargreaves! Honestly, Mr. Martin, you'd think they didn't want us there, the way they acted! The kids were bad enough. But when the old man came home–wow! I tell you, Mr. Martin, I been eleven Christmases in the Department, and I never saw a family with less Christmas spirit than those Hargreaves!"

The cashier was yelling for the cash receipts so he could lock up his ledgers for the night, so I let the Santa go. But I had plenty to think about as I went back to my own department, wondering about what he had said.

I didn't have to wonder long. Just before closing, one of the office girls waved me in from where I was checking out a new Counselor, and I answered the phone call. It was Lilymary's father. Mad? He was blazing. I could hardly make sense out of most of what he said. It was words like "perverting the Christian festival" and "selling out the Saviour" and a lot of stuff I just couldn't follow at all. But the part he finished up with, that I could understand. "I want you to know, Mr. Martin," he said in clear, crisp, emphatic tones, "that you are no longer a welcome caller at our home. It pains me to have to say this, sir. As for Lilymary, you may consider this her resignation, to be effective at once!"

"But," I said, "but——"

But I was talking to a dead line; he had hung up. And that was the end of that.

Personnel called up after a couple of days and wanted to know what to do with Lilymary's severance pay. I told them to mail her the check; then I had a second thought and asked them to send it up to me. I mailed it to her myself, with a little note apologizing for what I'd done wrong–whatever it was. But she didn't even answer.

October began, and the pace stepped up. Every night I crawled home, bone-weary, turned on my dreamster and slept like a log. I gave the machine a real workout; I even had the buyer in the Sleep Shoppe get me rare, out-of-print tapes on special order–Last Days of Petronius Arbiter, and Casanova's Diary, and The Polly Adler Story, and so on–until the buyer began to leer when she saw me coming. But it didn't do any good. While I slept I was surrounded with the loveliest of them all; but when I woke the face of Lilymary Hargreave was in my mind's eye.

October. The store was buzzing. National cost of living was up .00013, but our rate of sale was up .00021 over the previous year. The store bosses were beaming, and bonuses were in the air for everybody. November. The tide was at its full, and little wavelets began to ebb backward. Housewares was picked clean, and the manufacturers only laughed as we implored them for deliveries; but Home Appliances was as dead as the January lull. Our overall rate of sale slowed down microscopically, but it didn't slow down the press of work. It made things tougher, in fact, because we were pushing twice as hard on the items we could supply, coaxing the customers off the ones that were running short.

Bad management? No. Looking at my shipment figures, we'd actually emptied the store four times in seven weeks—better than fifty per cent turnover a week. Our July purchase estimates had been off only slightly—two persons fewer out of each hundred bought air-conditioners than we had expected, one and a half persons more out of each hundred bought kitchenware. Saul & Cappell had been out of kitchenware except for spot deliveries, sold the day they arrived, ever since late September!

Heinemann called me into his office. "George," he said, "I just checked your backlog. The unfilled order list runs a little over eleven thousand. I want to tell you that I'm surprised at the way you and your department have——"

"Now, Mr. Heinemann!" I burst out. "That isn't fair! We've been putting in overtime every night, every blasted one of us! Eleven thousand's pretty good, if you ask me!"

He looked surprised. "My point exactly, George," he said. "I was about to compliment you."

I felt *so* high. I swallowed. "Uh, thanks," I said. "I mean, I'm sorry I——"

"Forget it, George." Heinemann was looking at me thoughtfully. "You've got something on your mind, don't you?"

"Well——"

"Is it that girl?"

"Girl?" I stared at him. "Who said anything about a girl?"

"Come off it," he said genially. "You think it isn't all over the store?" He glanced at his watch. "George," he said, "I never interfere in employees' private lives. You know that. But if it's that girl that's bothering you, why don't you marry her for a while? It might be just the thing you need. Come on now, George, confess. When were you married last? Three years? Five years ago?"

I looked away. "I never was," I admitted.

That jolted him. "Never?" He studied me thoughtfully for a second. "You aren't—?"

"No, no, no!" I said hastily. "Nothing like that. It's just that, well, it's always seemed like a pretty big step to take."

He relaxed again. "Ah, you kids," he said genially. "Always afraid of getting hurt, eh? Well, I'll mind my own business, if that's the way you want it. But if I were you, George, I'd go get her."

That was that. I went back to work; but I kept right on thinking about what Heinemann had said.

After all . . . why not?

I called, "Lilymary!"

She faltered and half-turned. I had counted on that. You could tell she wasn't brought up in this country; from the age of six on, our girls learn Lesson One: When you're walking alone at night, *don't stop*.

She didn't stop long. She peered into the doorway and saw me, and her expression changed as though I had hit her with a club. "George," she said, and hesitated, and walked on. Her hair was a shimmering rainbow in the Christmas lights.

We were only a few doors from her house. I glanced, half-apprehensive, at the door, but no Father Hargreave was there to scowl. I followed her and said, "Please, Lilymary. Can't we just talk for a moment?"

She faced me. "Why?"

"To—" I swallowed. "To let me apologize."

She said gently, "No apology is necessary, George. We're different breeds of cats. No need to apologize for that."

"Please."

"Well," she said. And then, "Why not?"

We found a bench in the little park across from the subway entrance. It was late; enormous half-tracks from the Sanitation Department were emptying trash cans, sprinkler trucks came by and we had to raise our feet off the ground. She said once, "I really ought to get back. I was only going to the store." But she stayed.

Well, I apologized, and she listened like a lady. And like a lady she said, again, "There's nothing to apologize for." And that was that, and I still hadn't said what I had come for. I didn't know how.

I brooded over the problem. With the rumble of the trash trucks and the roar of their burners, conversation was difficult enough anyhow. But even under those handicaps, I caught a phrase from Lilymary. "–back to the jungle," she was saying. "It's home for us, George. Father can't wait to get back, and neither can the girls."

I interruped her. "Get back?"

She glanced at me. "That's what I said." She nodded at the Sanitation workers, baling up the enormous drifts of Christmas cards, thrusting them into the site burners. "As soon as the mails open up," she said, "and Father gets his visa. It was mailed a week ago, they say. They tell me that in the Christmas rush it might take two or three weeks more to get to us, though."

Something was clogging up my throat. All I could say was, "Why?"

Lilymary sighed. "It's where we live, George," she explained. "This isn't right for us. We're mission brats and we belong out in the field, spreading the Good News. . . . Though Father says you people need it more than the Dyaks." She looked quickly into my eyes. "I mean—"

I waved it aside. I took a deep breath. "Lilymary," I said, all in a rush, "will you marry me?"

Silence, while Lilymary looked at me.

"Oh, George," she said, after a moment. And that was all; but I was able to translate it; the answer was no.

Still, proposing marriage is something like buying a lottery ticket; you may not win the grand award, but there are consolation prizes. Mine was a date.

Lilymary stood up to her father, and I was allowed in the house. I wouldn't say I was welcomed, but Dr. Hargreave was polite–distant, but polite. He offered me coffee, he spoke of the dream superstitions of the Dyaks and old days in the Long House, and when Lilymary was ready to go he shook my hand at the door.

We had dinner. . . . I asked her–but as a piece of conversation, not a begging plea from the heart–I asked her why they had to go back. The Dyaks, she said; they were Father's people; they needed him. After Mother's death, Father had wanted to come back to America . . . but it was wrong for them. He was going back. The girls, naturally, were going with him.

We danced. . . . I kissed her, in the shadows, when it was growing late. She hesitated, but she kissed me back.

I resolved to destroy my dreamster; its ersatz ecstasies were pale.

"There," she said, as she drew back, and her voice was gentle, with a note of laughter. "I just wanted to show you. It isn't all hymn-singing back on Borneo, you know."

I reached out for her again, but she drew back, and the laughter was gone. She glanced at her watch.

"Time for me to go, George," she said. "We start packing tomorrow."

"But—"

"It's time to go, George," she said. And she kissed me at her door; but she didn't invite me in.

I stripped the tapes off my dreamster and threw them away. But hours later, after the fiftieth attempt to get to sleep, and the twentieth solitary cigarette, I got up and turned on the light and looked for them again.

They were pale; but they were all I had.

Party Week! The store was nearly bare. A messenger from the Credit Department came staggering in with a load of files just as the closing gong sounded.

He dropped them on my desk. "Thank God!" he said fervently. "Guess you won't be bothering with these tonight, eh, Mr. Martin?"

But I searched through them all the same. He looked at me wonderingly, but the clerks were breaking out the bottles and the runners from the lunchroom were bringing up sandwiches, and he drifted away.

I found the credit check I had requested. *"Co-Maker Required!"* was stamped at the top, and triply underlined in red, but that wasn't what I was looking for. I hunted through the text until I found what I wanted to know: "Subject is expected to leave this country within forty-eight hours. Subject's employer is organized and incorporated under laws of State of New York as a religious mission group. No earnings record on file. *Caution:* Subject would appear a bad credit risk, due to—"

I read no farther. Forty-eight hours!

There was a scrawl at the bottom of the page, in the Credit Manager's own handwriting: "George, what the devil are you up to? This is the fourth check we made on these people!"

It was true enough; but it would be the last. In forty-eight hours they would be gone.

I was dull at the Christmas Party. But it had been a splendid Christmas for the store, and in an hour everyone was too drunk to notice.

I decided to skip Party Week. I stayed at home the next morning, staring out the window. It had begun to snow, and the cleaners were dragging away old Christmas trees. It's always a letdown when Christmas is over; but my mood had nothing to do with the season, only with Lilymary and the numbers of miles from here to Borneo.

I circled the date in red on my calendar: December 25th. By the 26th they would be gone. . . .

But I couldn't, repeat couldn't, let her go so easily. It wasn't that I wanted to try again, and be rebuffed again; it was not a matter of choice. I had to see her. Nothing else, suddenly, had any meaning. So I made the long subway trek out there, knowing it was a fool's errand. But what kind of an errand could have been more appropriate for me?

They weren't home, but I wasn't going to let that stop me. I banged on the door of the next apartment, and got a surly, suspicious, what-do-you-want-with-*them?* inspection from the woman who lived there. But she thought they might possibly be down at the Community Center on the next block.

And they were.

The Community Center was a big yellow-brick recreation hall; it had swimming pools and pingpong tables and all kinds of odds and ends to keep the kids off the streets. It was that kind of a neighborhood. It also had a meeting hall in the basement, and there were the Hargreaves, all of them, along with a couple of dozen other people. None of them were young, except the Hargreave girls. The hall had a dusty, storeroom quality to it, as though it wasn't used much—and in fact, I saw, it still had a small Christmas tree standing in it. Whatever else they had, they did not have a very efficient cleanup squad.

I came to the door to the hall and stood there, looking around. Someone was playing a piano, and they were having a singing party. The music sounded familiar, but I couldn't recognize the words——

Adeste fideles,
Laeti triumphantes.
Venite, venite in Bethlehem.

The girls were sitting together, in the front row; their father wasn't with them, but I saw why. He was standing at a little lectern in the front of the hall.

Natum videte, regem angelorum.
Venite adoremus, venite adoremus——

I recognized the tune then; it was a slow, draggy-beat steal from that old-time favorite, *Christmas-Tree Mambo.* It didn't sound too bad, though, as they finished with a big major chord from the piano and all fifteen or twenty voices going. Then Hargreave started to talk.

I didn't listen. I was too busy watching the back of Lilymary's head. I've always had pretty low psi, though, and she didn't turn around.

Something was bothering me. There was a sort of glow from up front. I took my eyes off Lilymary's blond head, and there was Dr. Hargreave, radiant; I blinked and looked again, and it was not so radiant. A trick of the light, coming through the basement windows onto his own blond hair, I suppose, but it gave me a curious feeling for a moment. I must have moved, because he caught sight of me. He stumbled over a word, but then he went on. But that was enough. After a moment Lilymary's head turned, and her eyes met mine.

She knew I was there. I backed away from the door and sat down on the steps coming down from the entrance.

Sooner or later she would be out.

It wasn't long at all. She came toward me with a question in her eye. She was all by herself; inside the hall, her father was still talking.

I stood up straight and said it all. "Lilymary," I said, "I can't help it, I want to marry you. I've done everything wrong, but I didn't mean to. I–I don't even want it conditional, Lilymary, I want it for life. Here or Borneo, I don't care which. I only care about one thing, and that's you." It was funny–I was trying to tell her I loved her, and I was standing stiff and awkward, talking in about the same tone of voice I'd use to tell a stock boy he was fired.

But she understood. I probably didn't have to say a word, she would have understood anyhow. She started to speak, and changed her mind, and started again, and finally got out, "What would you do in Borneo?" And then, so soft that I hardly knew I was hearing it, she added, "Dear."

Dear! It was like the first time Heinemann came in and called me "Department Head!" I felt nine feet tall.

I didn't answer her. I reached out and I kissed her, and it wasn't any wonder that I didn't know we weren't alone until I heard her father cough, not more than a yard away.

I jumped, but Lilymary turned and looked at him, perfectly calm. "You ought to be conducting the service, Father!" she scolded him.

He nodded his big fair head. "Doctor Mausner can pronounce the Benediction without me," he said. "I should be there but–well, He has plenty of things to forgive all of us already; one more isn't going to bother Him. Now, what's this?"

"George has asked me to marry him."

"And?"

She looked at me. "I—" she began, and stopped. I said, "I love her."

He looked at me too, and then he sighed. "George," he said after a moment, "I don't know what's right and what's wrong, for the first time in my life. Maybe I've been selfish when I asked Lilymary to go back with me and the girls. I didn't mean it that way, but I don't deny I wanted it. I don't know. But—" He smiled, and it was a big, warm smile. "But there's something I do know. I know Lilymary; and I can trust her to make up her own mind." He patted her lightly.

"I'll see you after the service," he said to me, and left us. Back in the hall, through the door he opened, I could hear all the voices going at once.

"Let's go inside and pray, George," said Lilymary, and her whole heart and soul was on her face as she looked at me, with love and anxiousness.

I only hesitated a moment. Pray? But it meant Lilymary, and that meant–well, everything.

So I went in. And we were all kneeling, and Lilymary coached me through the words; and I prayed. And, do you know?–I've never regretted it.

We Never Mention Aunt Nora

MARY LYNNE EDKIN brought the man home to meet her brother.

It was uncomfortable for everyone. Mary Lynne's brother Alden looked up from his chair. He snapped his fingers and the sound on the trivision obediently diminished to a merely obtrusive level.

He held out his hand. "Pleased to meet you," he said, but it was obviously a lie.

Mary Lynne got that expression on her face.

"Al," she said dangerously.

Her brother shrugged and snapped his fingers twice more. The set shut itself off.

Mary Lynne's expression cleared. She was not a pretty girl, but she was a pleasant-looking one. The no-midriff fashion was kind to her; she still had a nice figure.

"Al," she said, but smiling now, "Al, guess what! Jimmy and I want to get married!"

"Oh-ho," said her brother, and he stood up in order to take a better look.

Even standing, he had to look up at this man James Croy. Croy was *big.* Six feet ten or eleven at the least, and his hair was snow white. Still, thought Alden Edkin, the man's face didn't look old. Maybe he was platinum blond. Al snorted, for he didn't hold with men dyeing their hair, common though the practice was.

He asked accusingly, "How come I never met him before?"

"Now, Al–"

"How come?"

Mary Lynne blushed. "Well, Al, there hasn't been much chance for you to meet."

"Oh-ho," said her brother again. "You just met him yourself."

"But I love him, Al!" cried Mary Lynne, clutching at the tall man's arm. "He's–he–oh, I can't explain it. But I love him!"

"Sure you do," said her brother. "You love him. But what do you know about him?"

"I know enough!"

Alden said sternly, "Family, Mary Lynne! Marriage isn't just between two people. We come of good stock and we can't marry just anybody. Think of the children you may have! Our family—"

"Our family!" echoed his sister. "What's so special about our family? How many times have you said that Aunt Nora—"

"Mary Lynne!" Alden warned. She paused. He said, "No offense, Mr. Croy. But what do we know? You may be after her money, for all we can tell."

The large man cleared his throat and straightened the crease in his Bermudas. He said modestly, "I assure you, Mr. Edkin, I am not interested in money."

"But you'd say that anyhow. Wouldn't you? Not that there's much *cash*. But there's this big house—Mary Lynne's and mine. And, Mary, you have to think of what Mother and Dad would want. They didn't leave you this big house—it will be yours when I'm gone—so that some adventurer could come along and—"

"Alden!" Mary Lynne was furious. She turned to the man she loved apologetically, but he was merely looking politely concerned. She whirled on her brother. "Apologize to Jimmy!"

There was a marked silence.

"Well," said her brother at last, talking to the wall, "there's one good thing. Being that she's under age, she can't—"

He stopped and waited.

They all waited. The big house that Mother and Dad had left them happened to be on the lip of the takeoff pits for the Moon rocket. The screeching howl of the night rocket's takeoff rattled the windows and made the trivision set moan shrilly in resonance.

But it only lasted for a few seconds.

"—can't get married without my consent," Alden Edkin finished.

"Alden!" cried his sister again, but it was more a sob than a protest.

Alden Edkin merely looked obstinate. He was good at it.

James Croy cleared his throat. "Sir," he said, "I know that what you say is true. We cannot marry without your consent. I hope that you'll give it."

"Don't hold your breath." Edkin sat down and glanced longingly at the trivision set. "As I say, we don't know anything about you."

"That's easily taken care of, Mr. Edkin," said Croy, smiling. "I'm an orphan. No ties, no family. Until recently, I was a draftsman for Amalgamated Luna, in the rocket engine department."

"Until recently? You don't even have a job?"

"Not exactly, sir. But I was fortunate enough to design a rather good firing chamber. They've adopted it for the Mars rocket."

Edkin nodded thoughtfully. "You sold them the design?"

Croy shook his head. "Not outright. But the royalties are—well, ample. I assure you that I can support Mary Lynne in adequate style. And I should mention that the royalty contract runs for thirty years, with cost-of-living increases."

"Um." Alden Edkin found that he was beginning to relax slightly. This Croy was, in his way, not without a certain charm.

Edkin said in a warmer tone, "Well, money isn't the only consideration. Still . . . Say, what about making some coffee, Mary Lynne? I'm sure our guest would enjoy it."

She looked at him in some surprise, shrugged, patted her proposed fiancé's arm and left the room.

Edkin said, "I hope you won't pay any attention to what Mary Lynne said about Aunt Nora."

"Of course not," said Croy and smiled. He had a very nice smile. His eyes were deep-set, somber and serious, and the smile beneath them was like sunlight bursting out from under a cloud.

Edkin was momentarily dazzled. He shook his head to clear it; for a second, he had almost thought he could see *through* the man. But that was nonsense.

Croy was saying, "I don't drink coffee, Mr. Edkin, but I'm glad Mary Lynne's out of the room. I hope we can get better acquainted."

"Sure," said Edkin testily. "Well, sit down and tell me something about yourself. Where was your family when you had one?"

"We're originally from Portland, Mr. Edkin."

"Portland, Maine? Say, I was stationed near Presq'Isle when I was in the Army."

"No," said Croy regretfully, "Portland, Oregon. After my parents passed away, I attended several schools, graduating from the University of California."

"Oh, we know lots of people there!" exclaimed Edkin. "Our cousins on my mother's side have some friends who teach at Berkeley. Perhaps you know them—Harold Sizeland and—"

"Sorry," Croy apologized. "I was at the Los Angeles campus. But let's not talk about *me,* Mr. Edkin. Mary Lynne tells me you're in credit maintenance."

"That's right." Actually he was a loan collector; it was close enough.

Croy leaned confidentially closer. "You can help me, Mr. Edkin. I'm planning a sort of surprise for Mary Lynne."

"Surprise?"

"Here," said Croy, reaching into his pocket. Hs pulled out several sheets of legal cap, stapled into a blue folder. "Since you're in the financial line," he said, "you'll know if this is all right. What it is, it's a kind of trust agreement for Mary Lynne."

Edkin scowled. "You're taking a lot for granted, Croy. I haven't agreed to anything."

"Of course not. But won't you look this over for me? You see, it puts all the royalties from my firing chamber in her name. Irrevocably. So that if anything happened to me, or there was, well, anything serious–" he didn't say the word "divorce," but he shrugged it–"she'll be well provided for. I'd appreciate your opinion of the contract."

Edkin glanced at the papers suspiciously.

He was ready to stand up and order from the house this brash young giant who interrupted his trivision programs and proposed to carry off his sister. But something hit him in the eye. And what that something happened to be was a neatly typed line specifying Mary Lynne's guaranteed minimum annual income from the trust agreement.

Thirty-five thousand dollars a year.

Edkin swallowed.

Attached to the certificate of agreement was a notarized copy of the Amalgamated Luna royalty contract. Unless it was a fake, the thirty-five-thousand-dollar figure was exactly right.

Mary Lynne came back into the room, and nearly dropped the coffee tray.

"Hi there, Mary Lynne!" greeted her brother, looking up from where he was patting Croy on the shoulder. "Coffee, eh? Good!"

She stared at him unbelievingly. He bobbed his head, winked conspiratorially at Croy, jammed the papers in his pocket and stood up.

"Coffee, eh?" he repeated, carrying chairs toward the table. "Your young man won't drink it, Mary Lynne. But surely he'll have some cake, eh? Or a drink? Some tea? Perhaps a glass of chocolate milk–Mary Lynne will be glad to warm it. No?"

He shrugged and sat down, smiling. "No matter," he observed.

"Now tell me. When would you two lovebirds like the happy event to take place?"

Three days later, the marriage was performed. It was the minimum legal waiting period.

Alden Edkin, as it happened, was a bachelor who believed that every man who glanced at his sister was a prospective rapist–and that those who proposed marriage were after her money besides. Still, he was not an idiot.

He had taken certain precautions.

First, he took a copy of the trust agreement to Mr. Senutovitch in his company's legal department. Mr. Senutovitch read the papers over with real enjoyment.

"Ah, bully stuff, Edkin," he said sentimentally. He leaned back and gazed at the ceiling while the arms of his reclining chair sighed faintly and adjusted to his position. "It's a pleasure to read the work of a master."

"You think it's all legal, Mr. Senutovitch?"

"Legal?" Mr. Senutovitch coughed gently. "Did you notice the classic language of the operative clause? That's Paragraph Three: 'Does hereby devise, grant, give, bestow and convey, without let or distraint, absolutely.' Oh, it's a grand piece of work."

"And irrevocable?"

Mr. Senutovitch smiled. "Quite irrevocable."

"You're sure, Mr. Senutovitch?"

The lawyer said mildly, "Edkin, I wrote this company's Chattel Lien Form. I'm sure."

The other precaution Edkin took was to drop into his company's Credit Reference Library and put through the name of Croy, James T., for a report.

It would take a few days for the credit report to come through, and meanwhile the ceremony would be performed and the couple off on their honeymoon. But at least, Edkin consoled himself, when it did come through, it would be a comprehensive document. The company took an expansive view of what a credit report should cover.

The company, moreover, was not to be deceived by any such paltry devices as a change of name–or, for that matter, of fingerprints, retinal patterns or blood type. If a man could change his basic genetic construction, he might fool the company, but not with anything less; the Credit Reference Library was hooked in by direct wire with the F.B.I. office in Washington–for the convenience of the

F.B.I., not of the company. There would be no secrets left to Mr. Croy. And therefore no secret worries for Alden Edkin.

And then Edkin stood by, fighting a manly urge to weep, as his sweet young sister gave herself in wedlock to this white-haired giant with the deep, penetrating eyes. The ceremony was performed before Father Hanover at Trinity Episcopal Church. There were few witnesses, though Mr. Senutovitch showed up, wrung the bridegroom's hand warmly and left without a word.

In the empty house, Alden Edkin took a deep breath, let it out, and put through a phone call to their only surviving relative. It was the least he could do.

A plump face over the fur collar of a lounging robe peered out of the phone's screen at him.

"Aunt Nora?" said Edkin tentatively. "My, you're looking well."

"You lie," she said shrilly. "I look *old*. What do you want? If it's money, I won't give you a—"

"No, nothing like that, Aunt Nora."

"Then what? You sorry you threw me out of the house twenty years ago? Is that what you called up to say?"

"Aunt Nora," said Edkin boldly, "I say let bygones be bygones. I called you up to tell you the news about Mary Lynne—my sister—your niece."

"Well? Well? What about her?"

"She just got married, Aunt Nora," said Edkin, beaming.

"What about it? People do, you know. There's nothing strange."

Edkin was shocked. Such a lack of family feeling! And from *her,* who should feel herself lucky beyond imagining that anyone in the family called her up at all. He was angry enough to say what he had vowed he would never refer to.

"At least," he said icily, "she got *married*."

Pause.

Thinly: "What do you mean by that?"

"You know perfectly well, Aunt Nora."

In the tiny screen, her face was a doll's face, an angry doll; it flushed red. She must have been shaking the phone, Edkin thought distractedly; rings of color haloed the edge of the screen.

She cried, "You're a sanctimonious jerk, Alden Edkin! You forbade me to associate with your sister—my own niece!—so I wouldn't corrupt her . . . when she was three months old and the good Lord Himself couldn't corrupt her, because she didn't so much as know which end was up! And now, just because she's getting married, you call me up. Hoping, no doubt, that because I'm getting old and absent-minded, I'll send along a little check for ten thousand dollars or so as a wedding present. Well, you're wrong! If Mary Lynne wants to call me up, I'll talk to her—but not to you! Understand?"

And the little screen flashed red and orange as she hung up.

Edkin pushed down the off button and shrugged. Aunt Nora! Who could account for her moods? A product of her sordid past, of course, but— It had been a mistake to call her up. Definitely.

Virtuously, Alden Edkin went to bed.

The following morning, he got the report from the Credit Reference Library. It had received special priority. The paper it was typed on flamed with warning red.

Alden Edkin was waiting at the airfield when the honeymooners returned from their Grand Tour.

He had been champing at the bit for six weeks—six long weeks and not a word from them, six weeks when they were out of touch with the world. Because they *wanted* it that way!

It was Alden Edkin's conviction that he knew *why* James Croy wanted it that way. He stood there by the customs gate, grinding his teeth, a plump angry man with a face that was rapidly turning purple.

He saw them coming down the wheeled steps from the plane and he bawled, "Mary Lynne! Mary Lynne, come down here this minute! Get away from that monster Croy!"

Mary Lynne, her arm adoringly on the arm of her husband, shuddered. "Oh-oh," she muttered. "Storm clouds rising. Batten down all hatches."

Croy tsked solicitously. "Poor man, he's upset, isn't he? But you mustn't worry."

"I'm not worried, darling."

"Of course not, of course not. Trust me." Croy nodded approvingly. "I've got to stop off for a second. A little errand— But I'll be right back and then I'm sure we can straighten out whatever's troubling your brother." Gently he kissed her ear. "My darling," he whispered, soft as a moth's wing.

And then that perfect gentleman, James Croy, bowed to the brother-in-law who was raging impotently across the customs gate, turned on his heel and disappeared into the men's room.

The men's room had a North Entrance, a South Entrance, a Mezzanine Entrance and a Service Entrance to the floor below. It is not a matter of record which door Croy used to come out, but it was not the one by which he had gone in.

The policemen finally went away. "Sorry," said the sergeant, curt and somewhat bored—he had been with Missing Persons for a good long time. "Probably he'll turn up."

But it wasn't true, and both he and Alden Edkin knew it. And when he had left, Edkin told his sister what the red-bordered credit report had shown.

Across the top was printed in bold letters *Zero Credit Rating Zero.*

"You can't fool Consolidated Credit," snapped Edkin. "They know. And this man Croy—why, he's a monster, Mary Lynne! He preys on women."

"Oh, no," wept his sister. But she was already in her heart convinced.

"Oh, yes! He is! Listen to this! Four years ago, in Miami, he married a girl named Doris L. Cockingham. There's no record of a divorce! He just married her—set up a trust for her with the royalties from an electric underwater lung, left her pregnant and disappeared. Eh?"

"I don't believe you," sobbed his sister.

"Then listen to this! Eleven months later, in Troy, New York, he married Marsha Gutknecht. Revolting! Can you *understand* a man like that? Loose morals, bigamy—why, he'd *never* get credit with a record like that."

"There must be some perfectly simple explanation," whimpered Mary Lynne. "When Jim comes back—"

"He won't be back!" said her brother brutally. "Get used to that idea, Mary Lynne! The Gutknecht woman never saw him again, and she was pregnant, too. He *meant* to run away! He used false names. Told different stories to each of them. But he couldn't fool Consolidated Credit. He put four hundred thousand dollars in trust for this woman and took off and never gave her another thought. How do you like that, Mary Lynne?"

"Jim wouldn't—"

"Jim did! And again the following year. Whitefish Bay, Wisconsin—a girl named Deloris Bennyhoff. Then in Jim Thorpe, Pennsylvania—" He crumpled the paper in rage. "Ah, what's the use? Five women! He married them, runs off, leaves them pregnant. And what do you have to say to that, Mary Lynne?"

Mary Lynne looked at her brother through blurred eyes.

In a faint, faint voice, she said, "Well, at least he runs true to form, Alden."

Oh, they looked for him. But they couldn't find him. The police couldn't find him, private detectives couldn't find him, even Consolidated Credit couldn't find him. Jim Croy was gone—probably forever, at least under that name. And while they were looking, events took their natural course, and Mary Lynne made reservations at the hospital and began to pack a little bag.

And Aunt Nora phoned.

Her plump face peered somberly out of the phone screen. "I'm coming east," she announced.

"You're not!" croaked Alden, wincing already. "I mean—"

"Thursday," she said. "On the six o'clock plane."

"But, Aunt Nora—" It was the last thing he wanted! So many years of cutting her out of the family circle because of the indiscretion of her youth, and now—

"Meet me," she said, and hung up.

There was nothing to be done about it. Aunt Nora showed up at the house her sister had left the children just as Mary Lynne gasped, checked her wristwatch, gasped again and reached for her ready-packed bag.

"Hello, Aunt Nora," said Alden distractedly. "Mary Lynne, aren't you ready yet? Good-by, Aunt Nora. Make yourself at home."

"Wait!" cried Aunt Nora, but she was talking to a closed door.

She sighed, shook her head irritably and took off her coat. Men were so foolish about babies! There would be plenty of time; she would unpack her bag, get settled in, and then, with full leisure, proceed to the hospital. And she was willing to bet that she would be there well before the baby arrived.

She was right—though what she found in the upper bureau drawer of her room made her hurry to the hospital sooner than she'd planned.

"Alden!" she gasped. "The picture! I saw the picture—"

"Hello, Aunt Nora," said Edkin gloomily. "Lord, but this takes a long time!"

"It just seems long," snapped Nora and waved a picture under his nose. It was inscribed in white ink: *For Mary Lynne, from Jimmy, with love*. "Who's this?"

Edkin said guiltily, "Mary's—ah—husband. He's away just now."

"I bet he is! That's not any Jimmy! That's Sam!"

"Sam?"

"*My* Sam. The one who left me in a delicate condition years ago! And the only difference is, now he marries them!"

Alden, hardly listening, said soothingly, "That was a long time ago, Aunt Nora. We don't worry about it now. Besides, you gave the baby up for adoption, didn't you? I never even saw him—or her? What was it, a boy?"

She said shortly, "No."

"A girl, then."

"Guess again," said Aunt Nora in a more peculiar tone. "And it wasn't exactly adoption."

Her tone was peculiar enough to attract his full attention. He looked at her queerly, but she didn't seem to be joking. Funny. He didn't have the faintest idea of what she meant—

Until an endless twenty minutes later.

Until the white-faced nurse came out of the delivery room wheeling a bassinet; until, without a word, the nurse pointed a shaking finger, and Edkin saw what it was that his sister had—with the help of what called itself James Croy—brought into an unsuspecting world.

Father of the Stars

I

NORMAN MARCHAND sat in the wings of the ballroom's small stage, on a leather hassock someone had found for him. There were 1,500 people outside in the ballroom, waiting to do him honor.

Marchand remembered the ballroom very well. He had once owned it. Forty . . . no, it wasn't forty. Not even fifty. Sixty years ago it had been, sixty and more years ago that he and Joyce had danced in that ballroom. Then the hotel was the newest on Earth, and he was the newly married son of the man who had built it, and the party was the reception for his wedding to Joyce. Of course, none of these people would know about that. But Marchand remembered . . . *Oh, Joyce, my very dear!* But she had been dead a long time now.

It was a noisy crowd. He peered out through the wings and could see the head table filling up. There was the Vice-President of the United States shaking hands with the Governor of Ontario as though, for the moment, they had forgotten they were of different parties. There was Linfox, from the Institute, obligingly helping a chimpanzee into the chair next to what, judging by the microphones ranked before it, would probably be Marchand's own. Linfox seemed a little ill at ease with the chimp. The chimpanzee had no doubt been smithed, but the imposition of human intelligence did not lengthen its ape's legs.

Then Dan Fleury appeared, up the steps from the floor of the ballroom where the rest of the 1,500 diners were taking their places.

Fleury didn't look well at all, Marchand thought—not without a small touch of satisfaction, since Fleury was fifteen years younger than himself. Still, Marchand wasn't jealous. Not even of the young bellhop who had brought him the hassock, twenty years old at the most and built like a fullback. One life was enough for a man to live.

Especially when you had accomplished the dream you had set out to bring to fruition. Or almost.

Of course, it had cost him everything his father left. But what else was money for?

"It's time to go in, sir. May I help you!" It was the young fullback nearly bursting his bellhop's uniform with the huge, hard muscles of youth. He was very solicitous. One of the nice things about having this testimonial dinner in a Marchand hotel was that the staff was as deferential to him as though he still owned the place. Probably that was why the committee had picked it, Marchand ruminated, quaint and old-fashioned as the hotel must seem now. Though at one time–

He recollected himself. "I'm sorry, young man. I was–woolgathering. Thank you."

He stood up, slowly but not very painfully, considering that it had been a long day. As the fullback walked him onto the stage, the applause was enough to drive down the automatic volume control on his hearing aid.

For that reason he missed the first words from Dan Fleury. No doubt they were complimentary. Very carefully he lowered himself into his chair, and as the clapping eased off, he was able to begin to hear the words.

Dan Fleury was still a tall man, built like a barrel, with bushy eyebrows and a huge mane of hair. He had helped Marchand's mad project for thrusting Man into space from its very beginnings. He said as much now. "Man's grandest dream!" he roared. "The conquering of the stars themselves! And here is the one man who taught us how to dream it, Norman Marchand!"

Marchand bowed to the storm of applause.

Again his hearing aid saved his ears and cost him the next few words: "–and now that we are on the threshold of success," Fleury was booming, "it is altogether fitting that we should gather here tonight . . . to join in fellowship and in the expression of that grand hope . . . to rededicate ourselves to its fulfillment . . . and to pay our respects and give of our love to the man who first showed us what dream to have!"

While the AVC registered the power of Dan Fleury's oratory, Marchand smiled out on the foggy sea of faces. It was, he thought, almost cruel of Fleury to put it like that. The threshold of success indeed! How many years now had they waited on it patiently?–and the door still locked in their faces. Of course, he thought wryly, they must have calculated that the testimonial dinner would have to be held soon unless they wanted a cadaver for a guest. But still . . . He turned painfully and looked at Fleury, half perplexed. There was something in his tone. Was there—Could there be—

There could not, he told himself firmly. There was no news, no breakthrough, no report from one of the wandering ships, no dream come true at last. He would have been the first to know. Not for anything would they have kept a thing like that from him. And he did not know that thing.

"—and now," Fleury was saying, "I won't keep you from your dinners. There will be many a long, strong speech to help your digestions afterward, I promise you! But now let's eat!"

Laughter. Applause. A buzz and clash of forks.

The injunction to eat did not, of course, include Norman Marchand. He sat with his hands in his lap, watching them dig in, smiling and feeling just a touch deprived, with the wry regret of the very old. He didn't envy the young people anything *really,* he told himself. Not their health, their youth, or their life expectancy. But he envied them the bowls of ice.

He tried to pretend he enjoyed his wine and the huge pink shrimp in crackers and milk. According to Asa Czerny, who ought to know since he had kept Marchand alive this long, he had a clear choice. He could eat whatever he chose, or he could stay alive. For a while. And ever since Czerny had been good enough, or despairing enough, to give him a maximum date for his life expectancy, Marchand had in idle moments tried to calculate just how much of those remaining months he was willing to give up for one really good meal. He rather believed that when Czerny looked up at him after the weekly medical checkup and said that only days were left, that he would take those last days and trade them in for a sauerbraten with potato pancakes and sweet-sour red cabbage on the side. But that time was not yet. With any kind of luck he still had a month. Perhaps as much as two . . .

"I beg your—pardon," he said, half-turning to the chimpanzee. Even smithed, the animal spoke so poorly that Marchand had not at first known that he was being addressed.

He should not have turned.

His wrist had lost its suppleness; the spoon in his hand tilted; the soggy crackers fell. He made the mistake of trying to move his knee out of the way—it was bad enough to be old; he did not want to be sloppy—and he moved too quickly.

The chair was at the very edge of the little platform. He felt himself going over.

Ninety-six is too old to be falling on your head, he thought; if I was going to do this sort of thing, I might just as well have eaten some of those shrimp. . . . But he did not kill himself.

He only knocked himself unconscious. And not for very long at that, because he began to wake up while they were still carrying him back to his dressing room behind the stage.

Once upon a time, Norman Marchand had given his life to a hope.

Rich, intelligent, married to a girl of beauty and tenderness, he had taken everything he owned and given it to the Institute for Colonizing Extra-Solar Planets. He had, to begin with, given away several million dollars.

That was the whole of the personal fortune his father had left him, and it was nowhere near enough to do the job. It was only a catalyst. He had used it to hire publicity men, fund raisers, investment counselors, foundation managers. He had spent it on documentary films and on TV commercials. With it he had financed cocktail parties for United States Senators, and prize contests for the nation's sixth grades, and he had done what he set out to do.

He had raised money. A very great deal of money.

He had taken all the money he had begged and teased out of the pockets of the world and used it to finance the building of twenty-six great ships, each the size of a dozen ocean liners, and he had cast them into space like a farmer sowing wheat upon the wind.

I tried, he whispered to himself, returning from the darkest place he had ever seen. I wanted to see Man reach out and touch a new home . . . and I wanted to be the one to guide him there. . . .

And someone was saying: "–he knew about it, did he? But we were trying to keep it quiet–" Someone else told the first person to shut his mouth. Marchand opened his eyes.

Czerny was there, unsmiling. He saw that Marchand was conscious. "You're all right," he said, and Marchand knew that it was true, since Czerny was scowling angrily at him. If the news had been bad, he would have smiled– "No, you don't!" cried Czerny, catching him by the shoulder. "You stay right there. You're going home to bed."

"But you said I was all right."

"I meant you were still breathing. Don't push it, Norm."

Marchand protested, "But the dinner–I ought to be there–"

Asa Czerny had cared for Marchand for thirty years. They had gone fishing together, and once or twice they had gotten drunk. Czerny would not have refused for nothing. He only shook his head.

Marchand slumped back. Behind Czerny the chimpanzee was squatting silently on the edge of a chair, watching. He's worried,

Marchand thought. Worried because he feels it's his fault, what happened to me. The thought gave him enough strength to say: "Stupid of me to fall like that, Mr.– I'm sorry."

Czerny supplied the introduction. "This is Duane Ferguson, Norman. He was supernumerary on the Copernicus. Smithed. He's attending the dinner in costume, as it were." The chimpanzee nodded but did not speak. He was watching that silver-tongued orator, Dan Fleury, who seemed upset. "Where is that ambulance?" demanded Czerny, with a doctor's impatience with interns, and the fullback in bellhop's uniform hurried silently away to find out.

The chimpanzee made a barking sound, clearing his throat. "Ghwadd"–he said–more or less: the German *ich* sound followed by the word "what." "Ghwadd did jou mee-an aboud evdial, Midda Vleury?"

Dan Fleury turned and looked at the chimp blankly. But not, Marchand thought suddenly, as though he didn't know what the chimp was talking about. Only as if he didn't intend to answer.

Marchand rasped, "What's this 'evdial,' Dan?"

"Search me. Look, Mr. Ferguson, perhaps we'd better go outside."

"Ghwadd?" The harsh barking voice struggled against the simian body it occupied, and came closer to the sounds it meant to emit. "*What* did you bean–did you *mean?*"

He was a rude young man, Marchand thought irritably. The fellow was tiring him.

Although there was something about that insistent question–

Marchand winced and felt for a moment as though he were going to throw up. It passed, leaving him wobbly. It wasn't possible he had broken anything, he told himself. Czerny would not lie about that. But he felt as if he had.

He lost interest in the chimp-man, did not even turn his head as Fleury hurried him out of the room, whispering to him in an agitated and low-pitched chirrup like the scratching of a cricket's legs.

If a man wanted to abandon his God-given human body and put his mind, thoughts, and–yes–soul into the corpus of an anthropoid, there was nothing in that to entitle him to any special consideration from Norman Marchand.

Of course not! Marchand rehearsed the familiar argument as he waited for the ambulance. Men who volunteered for the interstellar flights he had done so much to bring about knew what they were getting into. Until some super-Batman invented the mythical FTL drive, it would always be so. At possible speeds–less than light's 186,000 m.p.s. crawl–it was a matter of decades to reach almost every worthwhile planet that was known.

The smith process allowed these men to use their minds to control chimpanzee bodies–easily bred, utterly expendable–while their own bodies rested in the deep-freeze for all the long years between the stars.

It took brave men, naturally. They were entitled to courtesy and consideration.

But so was he, and it was not courteous to blather about "evdial," whatever that was, while the man who had made their trip possible was seriously injured. . . .

Unless . . .

Marchand opened his eyes again.

"Evdial." Unless "evdial" was the closest chimpanzee vocal chords and chimpanzee lips could come to–to–unless what they had been talking about, while he was unconscious, was that utterly impossible, hopeless, and fantastic dream that he, Marchand, had turned his back upon when he began organizing the colonization campaign.

Unless someone had really found the way to FTL travel.

II

As soon as he was able the next day, Marchand got himself into a wheelchair–all by himself; he didn't want any help in this–and rolled it out into the chart room of the home the Institute had given him, rent free, for all of his life. (He had, of course, given it in the first place to the Institute.)

The Institute had put $300,000 into the chart room. Stayed and guy-wired stars flecked the volume of a forty-foot ballroom, representing in scale all the space within fifty-five light-years of Sol. Every star was mapped and tagged. They had even moved a few of them slightly, a year ago, to correct for proper motion. It was that carefully done.

The twenty-six great starships the Institute had financed were there, too, or such of them as were still in space. They were out of scale, of course, but Marchand understood what they represented. He rolled his chair down the marked path to the center of the room and sat there, looking around, just under yellow Sol.

There was blue-white Sirius dominating them all, Procyon hanging just above. The two of them together were incomparably the brightest objects in the room, though red Altair was brighter in its own right than Procyon. In the center of the chamber Sol and Alpha Centauri A made a brilliant pair.

He gazed with rheuming eyes at the greatest disappointment of his life, Alpha Centauri B. So close. So right. So sterile. It was an ironic blunder of creation that the nearest and best chance of another home had never formed planets . . . or had formed them and swept them into the Bode-area traps set by itself and its two companions.

But there were other hopes. . . .

Marchand sought and found Tau Ceti, yellow and pale. Only eleven light-years away, the colony should be definitely established by now. In another decade or less they should have an answer . . . if, of course, it had planets Man could live on.

That was the big question, to which they had already received so many noes. But Tau Ceti was still a good bet, Marchand told himself stoutly. It was a dimmer, cooler sun than Sol. But it was Type G, and according to spectropolarimetry, almost certainly planetiferous. And if it was another disappointment–

Marchand turned his eyes to 40 Eridani A, even dimmer, even farther away. The expedition to 40 Eridani A had been, he remembered, the fifth ship he had launched. It ought to be reaching its destination soon–this year or perhaps next. There was no sure way of estimating time when the top velocity was so close to light's own. . . .

But now, of course, the top velocity was more.

The sudden wash of failure almost made him physically ill. Faster than light travel–why, how dared they!

But he didn't have time to waste on that particular emotion, or indeed on any emotion at all. He felt time draining away from him and sat up straight again, looking around. At 96, you dare not do anything slowly, not even daydream.

He glanced at and dismissed Procyon. They had tried Procyon lately–the ship would not be even halfway. They had tried almost everything. Even Epsilon Eridani and Groombridge 1618; even, far down past the probable good bets among the spectroscopic classes, 61 Cygni A and Epsilon Indi, a late and despairing try at Proxima Centauri (though they were very nearly sure it was wasted; the Alpha Centauri expedition had detected nothing like viable planets).

There had been twenty-six of them in all. Three ships lost, three returned, one still Earthbound. Nineteen were still out there.

Marchand looked for comfort at the bright green arrow that marked where the *Tycho Brahe* rode its jets of ionized gas, the biggest of his ships, three thousand men and women. It seemed to him that someone had mentioned the *Tycho Brahe* recently. When? Why? He was not sure, but the name stuck in his mind.

The door opened and Dan Fleury walked in, glancing at the arrayed stars and ships and not seeing them. The chart room had never meant anything to Fleury. He scolded, "Damn it, Norman, you scared us witless! Why you're not in the hospital now–"

"I was in the hospital, Dan. I wouldn't stay. And finally I got it through Asa Czerny's head that I meant it, so he said I could come home if I would stay quiet and let him look in. Well, as you see, I'm quiet. And I don't care if he looks in. I only care about finding out the truth about FTL."

"Oh, cripes, Norm! Honestly, you shouldn't worry yourself–"

"Dan, for thirty years you've never used the word 'honestly' except when you were lying to me. Now give. I sent for you this morning because you know the answer. I want it.

"For God's sake, Dan!"

Fleury glanced around the room, as though he were seeing the glowing points of light for the first time . . . perhaps he was, Marchand thought.

He said at last, "Well, there is something."

Marchand waited. He had had a great deal of practice at waiting.

"There's a young fellow," said Fleury, starting over again. "He's named Eisele. A mathematician, would you believe it? He's got an idea."

Fleury pulled over a chair and sat down.

"It's far from perfect," he added.

"In fact," he said, "a lot of people think it won't work at all. You know the theory, of course. Einstein, Lorentz-Fitzgerald, the whole roster–they're all against it. It's called–get this!–polynomiation."

He waited for a laugh, hopelessly. Then he said, "Although I must say he appears to have something, since the tests–"

Marchand said gently and with enormous restraint: "Dan, will you please spit it out? Let's see what you said so far. There's this fellow named Eisele, and he has something, and it's crazy, but it works."

"Well–yes."

Marchand slowly leaned back and closed his eyes. "So that means that we were all wrong. Especially me. And all our work–"

"Look, Norman! Don't *ever* think like that. Your work has made all the difference. If it weren't for you, people like Eisele never would have had the chance. Don't you know he was working under one of our grants?"

"No. I didn't know that." Marchand's eyes went out to the *Tycho*

Brahe for a moment. "But it doesn't help much. I wonder if fifty-odd thousand men and women who have given most of their lives to the deep freeze because of—my work—will feel the way you do. But thanks. You've told me what I want to know."

When Czerny entered the chart room an hour later, Marchand said at once, "Am I in good enough shape to stand a smith?"

The doctor put down his bag and took a chair before he answered. "We don't have anyone available, Norman. There hasn't been a volunteer for years."

"No. I don't mean smithed into a human body. I don't want any would-be suicide volunteer donors—you said yourself the smithed bodies sometimes suicided, anyway. I'll settle for a chimp. Why should I be any better than that young fellow—what's his name?"

"You mean Duane Ferguson."

"Sure. Why should I be any better than he is?"

"Oh, cut it out, Norman. You're too old. Your phospholipids—"

"I'm not too old to die, am I? And that's the worst that could happen."

"It wouldn't be stable! Not at your age; you just don't understand the chemistry. I couldn't promise you more than a few weeks."

Marchand said joyously, "Really! I didn't expect that much. That's more than you can promise me now."

The doctor argued, but Marchand had held up his end of many a hard-fought battle in ninety-six years, and besides, he had an advantage over Czerny. The doctor knew even better than Marchand himself that getting into a passion would kill him. At the moment when Czerny gauged the risk of a smith translation less than the risk of going on arguing about it, he frowned, shook his head grudgingly, and left.

Slowly Marchand wheeled after him.

He did not have to hurry to what might be the last act of his life. There was plenty of time. In the Institute they kept a supply of breeding chimpanzees, but it would take several hours to prepare one.

One mind had to be sacrificed in the smith imposition. The man would ultimately be able to return to his own body, his risk less than one chance in 50 of failure. But the chimp would never be the same. Marchand submitted to the beginnings of the irradiation, the delicate titration of his body fluids, the endless strapping and patching and clamping. He had seen it done, and there were no surprises in the procedure. . . . He had not known, however, that it would hurt so much.

III

Trying not to walk on his knuckles (but it was hard; the ape body was meant to crouch, the arms were too long to hang comfortably along his sides), Marchand waddled out into the pad area and bent his rigid chimp's spine back in order to look up at the hated thing. Dan Fleury came toward him. "Norm?" he asked tentatively. Marchand attempted to nod; it was not a success, but Fleury understood. "Norman," he said, "this is Sigmund Eisele. He invented the FTL drive."

Marchand raised one long arm and extended a hand that resisted being opened: it was used to being clawed into a fist. "Congradulazhuns," he said, as clearly as he could. Virtuously he did not squeeze the hand of the young dark-eyed man who was being introduced to him. He had been warned that chimpanzee strength maimed human beings. He was not likely to forget, but it was tempting to allow himself to consider it for a moment.

He dropped the hand and winced as pain flooded through him.

Czerny had warned him to expect it. "Unstable, dangerous, won't last," had rumbled through his conversation, "and don't forget, Norman, the sensory equipment is set high for you; you're not used to so much input: it will hurt."

But Marchand had assured the doctor he would not mind that, and indeed he didn't. He looked at the ship again. "Zo thads id," he grumbled, and again bent the backbone, the whole barrel chest of the brute he occupied, to stare at the ship on the pad. It was perhaps a hundred feet tall. "Nod mudge," he said scornfully. "De *Zirian,* dad was our firzd, zdood nine hoonderd feed dall and garried a dousand beople to Alpha Zendauri."

"And it brought a hundred and fifty back alive," said Eisele. He didn't emphasize the words in any way, but he said it quite clearly. "I want to tell you I've always admired you, Dr. Marchand. I hope you won't mind my company. I understand you want to go along with me out to the *Tycho Brahe.*"

"Why zhould I mind?" He did, of course. With the best will in the world, this young fellow had thrown seventy years of dedication, plus a handsome fortune—eight million dollars of his own, countless hundreds of millions that Marchand had begged from millionaires, from government handouts, from the pennies of schoolchildren—tossed them all into the chamber pot and flushed them into history. They would say: "A nonce figure of the early twenty-first century, Norman

Marchand, or Marquand, attempted stellar colonization with primitive rocket-propelled craft. He was, of course, unsuccessful, and the toll of life and wealth in his ill-conceived venture enormous. However, after Eisele's faster-than-light became practicable . . ." They would say that he was a failure. And he was.

When *Tycho Brahe* blasted off to the stars, massed bands of five hundred pieces played it to its countdown, and television audiences all over the world watched it through their orbiting satellites. A President, a Governor, and half the Senate were on hand.

When Eisele's little ship took off to catch it and tell its people their efforts had been all in vain, it was like the departure of the 7:17 ferry for Jersey City. To that extent, thought Marchand, had Eisele degraded the majesty of starflight. Yet he would not have missed it for anything. Not though it meant forcing himself as super-cargo on Eisele, who had destroyed his life, and on the other smithed chimpanzee, Duane Ferguson, who was for some reason deemed to have special privileges in regard to the *Brahe*.

They shipped an extra FTL unit–Marchand heard one of the men call it a polyflecter, but he would not do it the honor of asking anyone what that meant–for some reason. Because it was likely to break down, so spares were needed? Marchand dismissed the question, realizing that it had not been a fear but a hope. Whatever the reason, he didn't care; he didn't want even to be here; he only regarded it as his inescapable duty.

And he entered Eisele's ship.

The interior of Eisele's damned ship was built to human scale, nine-foot ceilings and broad acceleration couches, but they had brought hammocks scaled to a chimpanzee torso for himself and Duane Ferguson. Doubtless they had looted the hammocks from the new ship. The one that would never fly–or at least not on streams of ionized gas. And doubtless this was almost the last time that a man's mind would have to leave Earth in an ape's body.

What Eisele's damned ship rode to the stars on in place of ionized gas Marchand did not understand. The whatcha-flecter, whatever the damned thing was named, was so tiny. The whole ship was a pigmy.

There was no room for reaction mass, or at least only for enough to get it off-Earth. Then the little black box–it was not really little, since it was the size of a grand piano, and it was not black, but gray, but it was a box, all right–would work its magic. They called that magic "polynomiation." What polynomiation was Marchand did not try to understand, beyond listening, or seeming to listen, to Eisele's brief, crude attempt to translate mathematics into English. He heard just enough to recognize a few words. Space was N-dimensional. All right, that answered the whole question, as far as he was concerned, and he did not hear Eisele's tortuous efforts to explain how one jacked oneself up, so to speak, into a polynomial dimension–or no, not that, but translated the existing polynomial extensions of a standard four-space mass into higher orders–he didn't hear. He didn't hear any of it. What he was listening to was the deep liquid thump of the great ape's heart that now was sustaining his brain.

Duane Ferguson appeared, in the ape's body that he would never leave now. That was one more count of Marchand's self-indictment; he had heard them say that the odds had worked against Ferguson, and his body had died in the imposition.

As soon as he had heard what Eisele was up to, Marchand had seized on it as a chance for expiation. The project was very simple. A good test for Eisele's drive, and a mission of mercy, too. They intended to fleet after the plodding, long-gone *Tycho Brahe* and catch it in mid-space . . . for even now, thirty years after it had left Port Kennedy, it was still decelerating to begin its search orbit around Groombridge 1618. As Marchand strapped himself in, Eisele was explaining it all over again. He was making tests on his black box and talking at the same time. "You see, sir, we'll try to match course and velocity, but, frankly, that's the hard part. Catching them's nothing: we've got the speed. Then we'll transfer the extra polyflecter to the *Tycho Brahe*–"

"Yez, thanggs," said Marchand politely, but he still did not listen to the talk about the machine. As long as it existed, he would use it –his conscience would not let him off that–but he didn't want details.

Because the thing was, there were all those wasted lives.

Every year in the *Tycho Brahe's* deep freeze means a month off the life of the body that lay there. Respiration was slowed, but it was not stopped. The heart did not beat, but blood was perfused through a pump; tubes dripped sugar and minerals into the torpid blood; catheters carried wastes away. And Groombridge 1618 was a flight of ninety years.

The best a forty-year-old man could hope for on arriving was to be restored into a body whose biological age was nearly fifty–while behind him on the Earth was nothing but a family long dead, friends turned into dust.

It had been worth it. Or so the colonists had thought. Driven by the worm that wriggled in the spine of the explorer, the itch that drove him on; because of the wealth and the power and the freedom that a new world could give them, and because of the place they would have in the history books–not Washington's place, or even Christ's. They would have the place of an Adam and an Eve.

It had been worth it, all those thousands had thought when they volunteered and set out. But what would they think when they landed!

If they landed without knowing the truth, if some ship like Eisele's did not reach and tell them in mid-space, they would find the greatest disappointment any man had ever borne. The Groombridge 1618 expedition aboard the *Tycho Brahe* still had forty years to go on its original trip plan. With Eisele's invention driving faster-than-light commerce, there would be a planet populated by hundreds of thousands of people, factories at work, roads built, the best land taken, the history books already into their fifth chapter . . . and what would the three thousand aging adventurers think then?

Marchand moaned and shook, not entirely because the ship was taking off and the acceleration squeezed his rib cage down against his spine.

When they were in the polyflecter's grip, he floated across the pilot room to join the others. "I vas never in zpaze bevore," he said.

Eisele said with great deference, "Your work was on the Earth."

"Vas, yez." But Marchand left it at that. A man whose whole life was a failure owed something to humanity, and one of the things he owed was the privilege of allowing them to overlook it.

He watched carefully while Eisele and Ferguson read their instruments and made micrometric settings on the polyflecter. He did not understand anything about the faster-than-light drive, but he understood that a chart was a chart. Here there was a doubly profiled representation of the course line of the Groombridge 1618 expedition. The *Tycho Brahe* was a point of light, some nine-tenths of the way from Sol to the Groombridge star in distance, which meant something under three-quarters of the way in time.

"Mass detectors, Dr. Marchand," said Eisele cheerfully pointing to the charts. "Good thing they're not much closer, or they wouldn't have mass enough to show." Marchand understood: the same detectors that would show a sun or a planet would also show a mere million-ton ship if its speed was great enough to add sufficient mass. "And a good thing," added Eisele, looking worried, "that they're not much farther away. We're going to have trouble matching their velocity now, even though they've been decelerating for nine years. . . . Let's get strapped in."

From the hammock Marchand braced himself for another surge of acceleration. But it was not that; it was something different and far worse.

It was a sausage-grinder, chewing his heart and sinews and spitting them out in strange crippled shapes.

It was a wine-press, squeezing his throat, collapsing his heart.

It was the giddy nausea of a roller coaster, or a small craft in a typhoon. Wherever it took them, the stars on the profile charts slipped and slid and flowed into new positions.

Marchand, absorbed in the most crushing migraine of all but a century, hardly knew what was happening, but he knew that in the hours they found the *Tycho Brahe,* after giving it a thirty-year start.

IV

The captain of the *Tycho Brahe* was a graying, yellow-fanged chimp named Lafcadio, his brown animal eyes hooded with shock, his long, stringy arms still quivering with the reaction of seeing a ship–a ship–and human beings.

He could not take his eyes off Eisele, Marchand noted. It had been thirty years in an ape's body for the captain. The ape was old now. Lafcadio would be thinking himself more than half chimp already, the human frame only a memory that blurred against the everyday reminders of furry-backed hands and splayed prehensile feet. Marchand himself could feel the ape's mind stealing back, though he knew it was only imagination.

Or was it imagination? Asa Czerny had said the imposition would not be stable–something to do with the phospholipids–he could not remember. He could not, in fact, remember anything with the clarity and certainty he could wish, and it was not merely because his mind was ninety-six years old.

Without emotion, Marchand realized that his measured months or weeks had dwindled to a few days.

It could, of course, be the throbbing pain between his temples that was robbing him of reason. But Marchand only entertained that thought to dismiss it; if he had courage enough to realize that his life's work was wasted, he could face the fact that pain was only a second-order derivative of the killer that stalked his ape's body. But it made it hard for him to concentrate. It was through a haze that he heard the talk of the captain and his crew–the twenty-two smithed chimpanzees who superintended the running of the *Tycho Brahe* and watched over the three thousand frozen bodies in its hold. It was over a deep, confusing roar that he heard Eisele instruct them in the transfer of the FTL unit from his tiny ship to the great, lumbering ark that his box could make fleet enough to span the stars in a day's journey.

He was aware that they looked on him, from time to time, with pity.

He did not mind their pity. He only asked that they allow him to live with them until he died, knowing as he knew that that would be no long time; and he passed, while they were still talking, into a painful, dizzying reverie that lasted until—he did not know the measure of the time—until he found himself strapped in a hammock in the control room of the ship and felt the added crushing agony that told him they were once again slipping through the space of other dimensions.

"Are you all right?" said a familiar thick, slurred voice.

It was the other, last victim of his blundering, the one called Ferguson. Marchand managed to say that he was.

"We're almost there," said Ferguson. "I thought you'd like to know. There's a planet. Inhabitable, they think."

From Earth the star called Groombridge 1618 was not even visible to the naked eye. Binoculars might make it a tiny flicker of light, lost among countless thousands of farther but brighter stars. From Groombridge 1618 Sol was not much more.

Marchand remembered struggling out of his hammock, overruling the worry on Ferguson's simian face, to look back at the view that showed Sol. Ferguson had picked it out for him, and Marchand looked at light that had been 15 years journeying from his home. The photons that impinged on his eyes now had paused to drench the Earth in the colors of sunset when he was in his seventies and his wife only a few years mourned. He did not remember getting back to his hammock.

He did not remember, either, at what moment of time someone told him about the planet they hoped to own. It hung low around the little orange disk of Groombridge 1618—by solar standards, at least. The captain's first approximation made its orbit quite irregular, but at its nearest approach it would be less than ten million miles from the glowing fire-coal of its primary. Near enough. Warm enough. Telescopes showed it a planet with oceans and forests, removing the lingering doubts of the captain, for its orbit could not freeze it even at greatest remove from its star, or char it at closest—or else the forest could not have grown. Spectroscopes, thermocouples, filarometers showed more, the instruments racing ahead of the ship, now in orbit and compelled to creep at rocket speeds the last little inch of its journey. The atmosphere could be breathed, for the ferny woods had flushed out the poisons and filled it with oxygen. The gravity was more than Earth's–a drag on the first generation, to be sure, and an expense in foot troubles and lumbar aches for many more–but nothing that could not be borne. The world was fair.

Marchand remembered nothing of how he learned this or of the landing or of the hurried, joyful opening of the freezing crypts, the awakening of the colonists, the beginning of life on the planet . . . he only knew that there was a time when he found himself curled on a soft, warm hummock, and he looked up and saw sky.

V

The protuberant hairy lip and sloping brows of a chimpanzee were hovering over him. Marchand recognized that young fellow Ferguson. "Hello," he said. "How long have I been unconscious?"

The chimp said, with embarrassment, "Well–you haven't been unconscious at all, exactly. You've been–" His voice trailed off.

"I see," said Marchand, and struggled up. He was grateful for the strength of the slope-shouldered, short-legged body he had borrowed, for this world he had come to had an uncomfortably powerful grip. The effort made him dizzy. A pale sky and thin clouds spiraled around him; he felt queer flashes of pain and pleasure, remembered tastes he had never experienced, felt joys he had never known. . . . With an effort he repressed the vestigial ape and said, "You mean I've been –what would you call it? Unstable? The smithing didn't quite take." But he didn't need confirmation from Ferguson. He knew–and knew that the next time he slipped away would be the last. Czerny had warned him. The phospholipids, wasn't that it? It was almost time to go home. . . .

Off to one side, he saw men and women, human men and women, on various errands, and it made him ask: "You're still an ape?"

"I will be for a while, Dr. Marchand. My body's gone, you know."

Marchand puzzled over that for a while. His attention wandering, he caught himself licking his forearm and grooming his round belly. "No!" he shouted, and tried to stand up.

Ferguson helped him, and Marchand was grateful for the ape's strong arm. He remembered what had been bothering him. "Why?" he asked.

"Why what, Dr. Marchand?"

"Why did you come?"

Ferguson said anxiously, "I wish you'd sit down till the doctor gets here. I came because there's someone on the *Tycho Brahe* I wanted to see."

A girl?–thought Marchand wonderingly. "And did you see her?"

"Not her–them. Yes, I saw them. My parents. You see, I was two years old when the *Tycho Brahe* left. My parents were good breeding stock–volunteers were hard to get then, they tell me–oh, of course, you'd know better than I. Anyway they–I was adopted by an aunt. They left me a letter to read when I was old enough. . . . Dr. Marchand! What's the matter?"

Marchand reeled and fell; he could not help it; he knew he was a spectacle, could feel the incongruous tears rheuming out of his beast eyes, but this last and unexpected blow was too harsh. He had faced the fact of fifty thousand damaged lives and accepted guilt for them, but one abandoned baby, left to an aunt and the apology of a letter, broke his heart.

"I wonder why you don't kill me," he said.

"Dr. Marchand! I don't know what you're talking about."

"If only–" said Marchand carefully. "I don't expect any favors, but if only there were some way I could *pay*. But I can't. I have nothing left, not even enough life to matter. But I'm sorry, Mr. Ferguson, and that will have to do."

Ferguson said, "Dr. Marchand, if I'm not mistaken, you're saying that you apologize for the Institute." Marchand nodded. "But–oh, I'm not the one to say this, but there's no one else. Look. Let me try to make it clear. The first thing the colonists did yesterday was choose a name for the planet. The vote was unanimous. Do you know what they called it?"

Marchand only looked at him dully.

"Please listen, Dr. Marchand. They named it after the man who inspired all their lives. Their greatest hero. They named it Marchand."

Marchand stared at him, and stared longer, and then without changing expression closed his eyes. "Dr. Marchand!" said Ferguson tentatively, and then, seriously worried at last, turned and scuttled ape-like, legs and knuckles bearing him rapidly across the ground, to get the ship's doctor, who had left him with strict orders to call him as soon as the patient showed any signs of life.

When they got back, the chimp was gone. They looked at the fronded forest and at each other.

"Wandered off, I expect," said the doctor. "It may be just as well."

"But the nights are cold! He'll get pneumonia. He'll die."

"Not any more," said the doctor, as kindly as he could. "He's already dead in every way that matters."

He bent and rubbed his aching thighs, worn already from the struggle against this new Eden's gravity, then straightened and looked at the stars in the darkening western sky. A bright green one was another planet of Groombridge 1618's, farther out, all ice and copper salts. One of the very faintest ones, perhaps, was Sol. "He gave us these planets," said the doctor, and turned back toward the city. "Do you know what being a good man means, Ferguson? It means being better than you really are–so that even your failures carry someone a little farther to success–and that's what he did for us. I hope he heard what you were trying to tell him. I hope he remembers it when he dies," the doctor said.

"If he doesn't," said Ferguson very clearly, "the rest of us always will."

The next day they found the curled-up body.

It was the first funeral ever held on the planet, and the one that the history books describe. That is why, on the planet called Marchand, the statue at the spaceport has a small bas-relief carved over the legend:

THE FATHER OF THE STARS

The bas-relief is in the shape of a chimpanzee, curled on itself and looking out with blind, frightened eyes upon the world, for it was the chimpanzee's body that they found, and the chimpanzee's body that they buried under the monument. The bas-relief and the body, they are ape. But the statue that rises above them is a god's.

The Day the Martians Came

THERE WERE two cots in every room of the motel, besides the usual number of beds, and Mr. Mandala, the manager, had converted the rear section of the lobby into a men's dormitory. Nevertheless he was not satisfied and was trying to persuade his colored bellmen to clean out the trunk room and put cots in that too. "Now, please, Mr. Mandala," the bell captain said, speaking loudly over the noise in the lounge, "you know we'd do it for you if we could. But it cannot be, because first we don't have any other place to put those old TV sets you want to save and because second we don't *have* any more cots."

"You're arguing with me, Ernest. I told you to quit arguing with me," said Mr. Mandala. He drummed his fingers on the registration desk and looked angrily around the lobby. There were at least forty people in it, talking, playing cards and dozing. The television set was mumbling away in a recap of the NASA releases, and on the screen Mr. Mandala could see a picture of one of the Martians, gazing into the camera and weeping large, gelatinous tears.

"Quit that," ordered Mr. Mandala, turning in time to catch his bellman looking at the screen. "I don't pay you to watch TV. Go see if you can help out in the kitchen."

"We been in the kitchen, Mr. Mandala. They don't need us."

"Go when I tell you to go, Ernest! You too, Berzie." He watched them go through the service hall and wished he could get rid of some of the crowd in the lounge as easily. They filled every seat and the overflow sat on the arms of the chairs, leaned against the walls and filled the booths in the bar, which had been closed for the past two hours because of the law. According to the registration slips they were nearly all from newspapers, wire services, radio and television networks and so on, waiting to go to the morning briefing at Cape Kennedy. Mr. Mandala wished morning would come. He didn't like so many of them cluttering up his lounge, especially since he was pretty sure a lot of them were not even registered guests.

On the television screen a hastily edited tape was now showing the return of the Algonquin Nine space probe to Mars but no one was watching it. It was the third time that particular tape had been repeated since midnight and everybody had seen it at least once; but when it changed to another shot of one of the Martians, looking like a sad dachshund with elongated seal-flippers for limbs, one of the poker players stirred and cried: "I got a Martian joke! Why doesn't a Martian swim in the Atlantic Ocean?"

"It's your bet," said the dealer.

"Because he'd leave a ring around it," said the reporter, folding his cards. No one laughed, not even Mr. Mandala, although some of the jokes had been pretty good. Everybody was beginning to get tired of them, or perhaps just tired.

Mr. Mandala had missed the first excitement about the Martians, because he had been asleep. When the day manager phoned him, waking him up, Mr. Mandala had thought, first, that it was a joke and, second, that the day man was out of his mind; after all, who would care if the Mars probe had come back with some kind of animals? Or even if they weren't animals, exactly. When he found out how many reservations were coming in over the teletype he realized that some people did in fact care. However, Mr. Mandala didn't take much interest in things like that. It was nice the Martians had come, since they had filled his motel, and every other motel within a hundred miles of Cape Kennedy, but when you had said that you had said everything about the Martians that mattered to Mr. Mandala.

On the television screen the picture went to black and was replaced by the legend *Bulletin from NBC News*. The poker game paused momentarily.

The lounge was almost quiet as an invisible announcer read a new release from NASA: "Dr. Hugo Bache, the Fort Worth, Texas, veterinarian who arrived late this evening to examine the Martians at the Patrick Air Force Base reception center, has issued a preliminary report which has just been released by Colonel Eric T. 'Happy' Wingerter, speaking for the National Aeronautics and Space Administration."

A wire-service man yelled, "Turn it up!" There was a convulsive movement around the set. The sound vanished entirely for a moment, then blasted out:

". . . Martians are vertebrate, warm-blooded and apparently mammalian. A superficial examination indicates a generally low level of metabolism, although Dr. Bache states that it is possible that this is in some measure the result of their difficult and confined voyage through 137,000,000 miles of space in the specimen chamber of the Algonquin Nine spacecraft. There is no, repeat no, evidence of communicable disease, although standing sterilization precautions are . . ."

"Hell he says," cried somebody, probably a stringer from CBS. "Walter Cronkite had an interview with the Mayo Clinic that . . ."

"Shut up!" bellowed a dozen voices, and the TV became audible again:

". . . completes the full text of the report from Dr. Hugo Bache as released at this hour by Colonel 'Happy' Wingerter." There was a pause; then the announcer's voice, weary but game, found its place and went on with a recap of the previous half-dozen stories. The poker game began again as the announcer was describing the news conference with Dr. Sam Sullivan of the Linguistic Institute of the University of Indiana, and his conclusions that the sounds made by the Martians were indeed some sort of a language.

What nonsense, thought Mr. Mandala, drugged and drowsy. He pulled a stool over and sat down, half asleep.

Then the noise of laughter woke him and he straightened up belligerently. He tapped his call bell for attention. "Gentlemen! Ladies! Please!" he cried. "It's four o'clock in the morning. Our other guests are trying to sleep."

"Yeah, sure," said the CBS man, holding up one hand impatiently, "but wait a minute. I got one. What's a Martian high-rise? You give up?"

"Go ahead," said a red-haired girl, a staffer from *Life.*

"Twenty-seven floors of basement apartments!"

The girl said, "All right, I got one too. What is a Martian female's religious injunction requiring her to keep her eyes closed during intercourse?" She waited a beat. "God forbid she should see her husband having a good time!"

"Are we playing poker or not?" groaned one of the players, but they were too many for him. "Who won the Martian beauty contest? . . . Nobody won!" How do you get a Martian female to give up sex? . . . Marry her!" Mr. Mandala laughed out loud at that one, and when one of the reporters came to him and asked for a book of matches he gave it to him. "Ta," said the man, puffing his pipe alight. "Long night, eh?"

"You bet," said Mr. Mandala genially. On the television screen the tape was running again, for the fourth time. Mr. Mandala yawned, staring vacantly at it; it was not much to see but, really, it was all that anyone had seen or was likely to see of the Martians. All these reporters and cameramen and columnists and sound men, thought Mr. Mandala with pleasure, all of them waiting here for the ten A.M. briefing at the Cape would have a forty-mile drive through the palmetto swamps for nothing. Because what they would see when they got there would be just about what they were seeing now.

One of the poker players was telling a long, involved joke about Martians wearing fur coats at Miami Beach. Mr. Mandala looked at them with dislike. If only some of them would go to their rooms and go to sleep he might try asking the others if they were registered in the motel. Although actually he couldn't squeeze anyone else in anyway, with all the rooms doubly occupied already. He gave up the thought and stared vacantly at the Martians on the screen, trying to imagine people all over the world looking at that picture on their television sets, reading about them in their newspapers, *caring* about them. They did not look worth caring about as they sluggishly crawled about on their long, weak limbs, like a stretched seal's flippers, gasping heavily in the drag of Earth's gravity, their great long eyes dull.

"Stupid-looking little bastards," one of the reporters said to the pipe smoker. "You know what I heard? I heard the reason the astronauts kept them locked in the back was the stink."

"They probably don't notice it on Mars," said the pipe smoker judiciously. "Thin air."

"Notice it? They love it." He dropped a dollar bill on the desk in front of Mr. Mandala. "Can I have change for the Coke machine?" Mr. Mandala counted out dimes silently. It had not occurred to him that the Martians would smell, but that was only because he hadn't given it much of a thought. If he had thought about it at all, that was what he would have thought.

Mr. Mandala fished out a dime for himself and followed the two men over to the Coke machine. The picture on the TV changed to some rather poorly photographed shots brought back by the astronauts, of low, irregular sand-colored buildings on a bright sand floor. These were what NASA was calling "the largest Martian city," altogether about a hundred of the flat, windowless structures. "I dunno," said the second reporter at last, tilting his Coke bottle. "You think they're what you'd call intelligent?"

"Difficult to say, exactly," said the pipe smoker. He was from Reuter's and looked it, with a red, broad English squire's face. "They do build houses," he pointed out.

"So does a bull gorilla."

"No doubt. No doubt." The Reuter's man brightened. "Oh, just a moment. That makes me think of one. There once was—let me see, at home we tell it about the Irish—yes, I have it. The next spaceship goes to Mars, you see, and they find that some dread Terrestrial disease has wiped out the whole race, all but one female. These fellows too, gone. All gone except this one she. Well, they're terribly upset, and they debate it at the UN and start an anti-genocide pact and America votes two hundred million dollars for reparations and, well, the long and short of it is, in order to keep the race from dying out entirely they decide to breed a non-human man to this one surviving Martian female."

"Cripes!"

"Yes, exactly. Well, then they find Paddy O'Shaughnessy, down on his luck and they say to him, 'See here, just go in that cage there, Paddy, and you'll find this female. And all you've got to do is render her pregnant, do you see?' And O'Shaughnessy says, 'What's in it for me?' and they offer him, oh, thousands of pounds. And of course he agrees. But then he opens the door of the cage and he sees what the female looks like. And he backs out." The Reuter's man replaced his empty Coke bottle in the rack and grimaced, showing Paddy's expression of revulsion. "'Holy saints,' he says, 'I never counted on anything like this.' 'Thousands of pounds, Paddy!' they say to him, urging him on. 'Oh, very well, then,' he says, 'but on one condition.' 'And what may that be?' they ask him. 'You've got to promise me,' he says, 'that the children'll be raised in the Church.'"

"Yeah, I heard that," said the other reporter. And he moved to put his bottle back, and as he did his foot caught in the rack and four cases of empty Coke bottles bounced and clattered across the floor.

Well, that was just about more than Mr. Mandala could stand and he gasped, stuttered, dinged his bell and shouted, "Ernest! Berzie! On the double!" And when Ernest showed up, poking his dark plum-colored head out of the service door with an expression that revealed an anticipation of disaster, Mr. Mandala shouted: "Oh, curse your thick heads, I told you a hundred times, keep those racks cleaned out." And he stood over the two bellmen, fuming, as they bent to the litter of whole bottles and broken glass, their faces glancing up at him sidewise, worried, dark plum and Arabian sand. He knew that all the reporters were looking at him and that they disapproved.

And then he went out into the late night to cool off, because he was sorry and knew he might make himself still sorrier.

The grass was wet. Condensing dew was dripping from the fittings of the diving board into the pool. The motel was not as quiet as it should be so close to dawn, but it was quiet enough. There was only an occasional distant laugh, and the noise from the lounge. To Mr. Mandala it was reassuring. He replenished his soul by walking all the galleries around the rooms, checking the ice makers and the cigarette machines, and finding that all was well.

A military jet from McCoy was screaming overhead. Beyond it the stars were still bright, in spite of the beginnings of dawn in the east. Mr. Mandala yawned, glanced mildly up and wondered which of them was Mars, and returned to his desk; and shortly he was too busy with the long, exhausting round of room calls and check-outs to think about Martians. Then, when most of the guests were getting noisily into their cars and limo-buses and the day men were coming on, Mr. Mandala uncapped two cold Cokes and carried one back through the service door to Ernest.

"Rough night," he said, and Ernest, accepting both the Coke and the intention, nodded and drank it down. They leaned against the wall that screened the pool from the access road and watched the newsmen and newsgirls taking off down the road toward the highway and the ten o'clock briefing. Most of them had had no sleep. Mr. Mandala shook his head, disapproving so much commotion for so little cause.

And Ernest snapped his fingers, grinned and said, "I got a Martian joke, Mr. Mandala. What do you call a seven-foot Martian when he's comin' at you with a spear?"

"Oh, hell, Ernest," said Mr. Mandala, "you call him sir. Everybody knows that one." He yawned and stretched and said reflectively, "You'd think there'd be some new jokes. All I heard was the old ones, only instead of picking on the Jews and the Catholics and—and everybody, they were telling them about the Martians."

"Yeah, I noticed that, Mr. Mandala," said Ernest.

Mr. Mandala stood up. "Better get some sleep," he advised, "because they might all be back again tonight. I don't know what for. . . . Know what I think, Ernest? Outside of the jokes, I don't think that six months from now anybody's going to remember there ever were such things as Martians. I don't believe their coming here is going to make a nickel's worth of difference to anybody."

"Hate to disagree with you, Mr. Mandala," said Ernest mildly, "but I don't think so. Going to make a difference to some people. Going to make a *damn* big difference to me."

The Midas Plague

AND SO THEY WERE MARRIED.

The bride and groom made a beautiful couple, she in her twenty-yard frill of immaculate white, he in his formal gray ruffled blouse and pleated pantaloons.

It was a small wedding—the best he could afford. For guests, they had only the immediate family and a few close friends. And when the minister had performed the ceremony, Morey Fry kissed his bride and they drove off to the reception. There were twenty-eight limousines in all (though it is true that twenty of them contained only the caterer's robots) and three flower cars.

"Bless you both," said old man Elon sentimentally. "You've got a fine girl in our Cherry, Morey." He blew his nose on a ragged square of cambric.

The old folks behaved very well, Morey thought. At the reception, surrounded by the enormous stacks of wedding gifts, they drank the champagne and ate a great many of the tiny, delicious canapés. They listened politely to the fifteen-piece orchestra, and Cherry's mother even danced one dance with Morey for sentiment's sake, though it was clear that dancing was far from the usual pattern of her life. They tried as hard as they could to blend into the gathering, but all the same, the two elderly figures in severely simple and probably rented garments were dismayingly conspicuous in the quarter-acre of tapestries and tinkling fountains that was the main ballroom of Morey's country home.

When it was time for the guests to go home and let the newlyweds begin their life together Cherry's father shook Morey by the hand and Cherry's mother kissed him. But as they drove away in their tiny runabout their faces were full of foreboding.

It was nothing against Morey as a person, of course. But poor people should not marry wealth.

Morey and Cherry loved each other, certainly. That helped. They told each other so, a dozen times an hour, all of the long hours they were together, for all of the first months of their marriage. Morey even took time off to go shopping with his bride, which endeared him to her enormously. They drove their shopping carts through the immense vaulted corridors of the supermarket, Morey checking off the items on the shopping list as Cherry picked out the goods. It was fun.

For a while.

Their first fight started in the supermarket, between Breakfast Foods and Floor Furnishings, just where the new Precious Stones department was being opened.

Morey called off from the list, "Diamond lavaliere, costume rings, earbobs."

Cherry said rebelliously, "Morey, I *have* a lavaliere. Please, dear!"

Morey folded back the pages of the list uncertainly. The lavaliere was on there, all right, and no alternative selection was shown.

"How about a bracelet?" he coaxed. "Look, they have some nice ruby ones there. See how beautifully they go with your hair, darling!" He beckoned a robot clerk, who bustled up and handed Cherry the bracelet tray. "Lovely," Morey exclaimed as Cherry slipped the largest of the lot on her wrist.

"And I don't have to have a lavaliere?" Cherry asked.

"Of course not." He peeked at the tag. "Same number of ration points exactly!" Since Cherry looked only dubious, not convinced, he said briskly, "And now we'd better be getting along to the shoe department. I've got to pick up some dancing pumps."

Cherry made no objection, neither then nor throughout the rest of their shopping tour. At the end, while they were sitting in the supermarket's ground-floor lounge waiting for the robot accountants to tote up their bill and the robot cashiers to stamp their ration books, Morey remembered to have the shipping department save out the bracelet.

"I don't want that sent with the other stuff, darling," he explained. "I want you to wear it right now. Honestly, I don't think I ever saw anything looking so *right* for you."

Cherry looked flustered and pleased. Morey was delighted with himself; it wasn't everybody who knew how to handle these little domestic problems just right!

He stayed self-satisfied all the way home, while Henry, their companion-robot, regaled them with funny stories of the factory in which it had been built and trained. Cherry wasn't used to Henry by a long shot, but it was hard not to like the robot. Jokes and funny stories when you needed amusement, sympathy when you were depressed, a never-failing supply of news and information on any subject you cared to name–Henry was easy enough to take. Cherry even made a special point of asking Henry to keep them company through dinner, and she laughed as thoroughly as Morey himself at its droll anecdotes.

But later, in the conservatory, when Henry had considerately left them alone, the laughter dried up.

Morey didn't notice. He was very conscientiously making the rounds: turning on the tri-D, selecting their afterdinner liqueurs, scanning the evening newspapers.

Cherry cleared her throat self-consciously, and Morey stopped what he was doing. "Dear," she said tentatively, "I'm feeling kind of restless tonight. Could we–I mean do you think we could just sort of stay home and–well, relax?"

Morey looked at her with a touch of concern. She lay back wearily, eyes half closed. "Are you feeling all right?" he asked.

"Perfectly. I just don't want to go out tonight, dear. I don't feel up to it."

He sat down and automatically lit a cigarette. "I see," he said. The tri-D was beginning a comedy show; he got up to turn it off, snapping on the tape-player. Muted strings filled the room.

"We had reservations at the club tonight," he reminded her.

Cherry shifted uncomfortably. "I know."

"And we have the opera tickets that I turned last week's in for. I hate to nag, darling, but we haven't used *any* of our opera tickets."

"We can see them right here on the tri-D," she said in a small voice.

"That has nothing to do with it, sweetheart. I–I didn't want to tell you about it, but Wainwright, down at the office, said something to me yesterday. He told me he would be at the circus last night and as much as said he'd be looking to see if we were there, too. Well, we weren't there. Heaven knows what I'll tell him next week."

He waited for Cherry to answer, but she was silent.

He went on reasonably, "So if you *could* see your way clear to going out tonight–"

He stopped, slack-jawed. Cherry was crying, silently and in quantity.

"Darling!" he said inarticulately.

He hurried to her, but she fended him off. He stood helpless over her, watching her cry.

"Dear, what's the matter?" he asked.

She turned her head away.

Morey rocked back on his heels. It wasn't exactly the first time he'd seen Cherry cry–there had been that poignant scene when they Gave Each Other Up, realizing that their backgrounds were too far apart for happiness, before the realization that they *had* to have each other, no matter what. . . . But it was the first time her tears had made him feel guilty.

And he did feel guilty. He stood there staring at her.

Then he turned his back on her and walked over to the bar. He ignored the ready liqueurs and poured two stiff highballs, brought them back to her. He set one down beside her, took a long drink from the other.

In quite a different tone, he said, "Dear, what's the *matter?*"

No answer.

"Come on. What is it?"

She looked up at him and rubbed at her eyes. Almost sullenly, she said, "Sorry."

"I know you're sorry. Look, we love each other. Let's talk this thing out."

She picked up her drink and held it for a moment, before setting it down untasted. "What's the use, Morey?"

"Please. Let's try."

She shrugged.

He went on remorselessly, "You aren't happy, are you? And it's because of–well, all this." His gesture took in the richly furnished conservatory, the thick-piled carpet, the host of machines and contrivances for their comfort and entertainment that waited for their touch. By implication it took in twenty-six rooms, five cars, nine robots. Morey said, with an effort, "It isn't what you're used to, is it?"

"I can't help it," Cherry said. "Morey, you know I've tried. But back home–"

"Dammit," he flared, "*this* is your home. You don't live with your father any more in that five-room cottage; you don't spend your evenings hoeing the garden or playing cards for matchsticks. You live here, with me, your husband! You knew what you were getting into. We talked all this out long before we were married–"

The words stopped, because words were useless. Cherry was crying again, but not silently.

Through her tears, she wailed: "Darling, I've tried. You don't *know* how I've tried! I've worn all those silly clothes and I've played all those silly games and I've gone out with you as much as I *possibly* could and–I've eaten all that terrible food until I'm actually getting fa-fa-*fat!* I thought I could stand it. But I just can't go on like this;

I'm not used to it. I–I love you, Morey, but I'm going crazy, living like this. I can't help it, Morey–*I'm tired of being poor!*"

Eventually the tears dried up, and the quarrel healed, and the lovers kissed and made up. But Morey lay awake that night, listening to his wife's gentle breathing from the suite next to his own, staring into the darkness as tragically as any pauper before him had ever done.

Blessed are the poor, for they shall inherit the Earth.

Blessed Morey, heir to more worldly goods than he could possibly consume.

Morey Fry, steeped in grinding poverty, had never gone hungry a day in his life, never lacked for anything his heart could desire in the way of food, or clothing, or a place to sleep. In Morey's world, no one lacked for these things; no one could.

Malthus was right–for a civilization without machines, automatic factories, hydroponics and food synthesis, nuclear breeder plants, ocean-mining for metals and minerals . . .

And a vastly increasing supply of labor . . .

And architecture that rose high in the air and dug deep in the ground and floated far out on the water on piers and pontoons . . . architecture that could be poured one day and lived in the next . . .

And robots.

Above all, robots . . . robots to burrow and haul and smelt and fabricate, to build and farm and weave and sew.

What the land lacked in wealth, the sea was made to yield and the laboratory invented the rest . . . and the factories became a pipeline of plenty, churning out enough to feed and clothe and house a dozen worlds.

Limitless discovery, infinite power in the atom, tireless labor of humanity and robots, mechanization that drove jungle and swamp and ice off the Earth, and put up office buildings and manufacturing centers and rocket ports in their place . . .

The pipeline of production spewed out riches that no king in the time of Malthus could have known.

But a pipeline has two ends. The invention and power and labor pouring in at one end must somehow be drained out at the other . . .

Lucky Morey, blessed economic-consuming unit, drowning in the pipeline's flood, striving manfully to eat and drink and wear and wear out his share of the ceaseless tide of wealth.

Morey felt far from blessed, for the blessings of the poor are always best appreciated from afar.

Quotas worried his sleep until he awoke at eight o'clock the next morning, red-eyed and haggard, but inwardly resolved. He had reached a decision. He was starting a new life.

There was trouble in the morning mail. Under the letterhead of the National Ration Board, it said:

"We regret to advise you that the following items returned by you in connection with your August quotas as used and no longer serviceable have been inspected and found insufficiently worn." The list followed—a long one, Morey saw to his sick disappointment. "Credit is hereby disallowed for these and you are therefore given an additional consuming quota for the current month in the amount of 435 points, at least 350 points of which must be in the textile and home-furnishing categories."

Morey dashed the letter to the floor. The valet picked it up emotionlessly, creased it and set it on his desk.

It wasn't fair! All right, maybe the bathing trunks and beach umbrellas hadn't been *really* used very much—though how the devil, he asked himself bitterly, did you go about using up swimming gear when you didn't have time for such leisurely pursuits as swimming? But certainly the hiking slacks were used! He'd worn them for three whole days and part of a fourth; what did they expect him to do, go around in *rags?*

Morey looked belligerently at the coffee and toast that the valet-robot had brought in with the mail, and then steeled his resolve. Unfair or not, he had to play the game according to the rules. It was for Cherry, more than for himself, and the way to begin a new way of life was to begin it.

Morey was going to consume for two.

He told the valet-robot, "Take that stuff back. I want cream and sugar with the coffee—*lots* of cream and sugar. And besides the toast, scrambled eggs, fried potatoes, orange juice—no, make it half a grapefruit. *And* orange juice, come to think of it."

"Right away, sir," said the valet. "You won't be having breakfast at nine then, will you, sir?"

"I certainly will," said Morey virtuously. "Double portions!" As the robot was closing the door, he called after it, "Butter and marmalade with the toast!"

He went to the bath; he had a full schedule and no time to waste. In the shower, he carefully sprayed himself with lather three times. When he had rinsed the soap off, he went through the whole assortment of taps in order: three lotions, plain talcum, scented talcum and thirty seconds of ultra-violet. Then he lathered and rinsed again, and dried himself with a towel instead of using the hot-air drying jet. Most of the miscellaneous scents went down the drain with the rinse water, but if the Ration Board accused him of waste, he could claim he was experimenting. The effect, as a matter of fact, wasn't bad at all.

He stepped out, full of exuberance. Cherry was awake, staring in dismay at the tray the valet had brought. "Good morning, dear," she said faintly. "Ugh."

Morey kissed her and patted her hand. "Well!" he said, looking at the tray with a big, hollow smile. "Food!"

"Isn't that a *lot* for just the two of us?"

"Two of us?" repeated Morey masterfully. "Nonsense, my dear, I'm going to eat it all by myself!"

"Oh, Morey!" gasped Cherry, and the adoring look she gave him was enough to pay for a dozen such meals.

Which, he thought as he finished his morning exercises with the sparring-robot and sat down to his *real* breakfast, it just about had to be, day in and day out, for a long, long time.

Still, Morey had made up his mind. As he worked his way through the kippered herring, tea and crumpets, he ran over his plans with Henry. He swallowed a mouthful and said, "I want you to line up some appointments for me right away. Three hours a week in an exercise gym—pick one with lots of reducing equipment, Henry. I think I'm going to need it. And fittings for some new clothes—I've had these for weeks. And, let's see, doctor, dentist—say, Henry, don't I have a psychiatrist's date coming up?"

"Indeed you do, sir!" it said warmly. "This morning, in fact. I've already instructed the chauffeur and notified your office."

"Fine! Well, get started on the other things, Henry."

"Yes, sir," said Henry, and assumed the curious absent look of a robot talking on its TBR circuits—the "Talk Between Robots" radio—as it arranged the appointments for its master.

Morey finished his breakfast in silence, pleased with his own virtue, at peace with the world. It wasn't so hard to be a proper, industrious consumer if you *worked* at it, he reflected. It was only the malcontents, the ne'er-do-wells and the incompetents who simply could not adjust to the world around them. Well, he thought with distant pity, someone had to suffer; you couldn't break eggs without making an omelet. And his proper duty was not to be some sort of wild-eyed crank, challenging the social order and beating his breast about injustice, but to take care of his wife and his home.

It was too bad he couldn't really get right down to work on consuming today. But this was his one day a week to hold a *job*—four of the other six days were devoted to solid consuming—and, besides, he had a group therapy session scheduled as well. His analysis, Morey told himself, would certainly take a sharp turn for the better, now that he had faced up to his problems.

Morey was immersed in a glow of self-righteousness as he kissed Cherry good-by (she had finally got up, all in a confusion of delight at the new regime) and walked out the door to his car. He hardly noticed the little man in enormous floppy hat and garishly ruffled trousers who was standing almost hidden in the shrubs.

"Hey, Mac." The man's voice was almost a whisper.

"Huh? Oh—what is it?"

The man looked around furtively. "Listen, friend," he said rapidly, "you look like an intelligent man who could use a little help. Times are tough; you help me, I'll help you. Want to make a deal on ration stamps? Six for one. One of yours for six of mine, the best deal you'll get anywhere in town. Naturally, my stamps aren't exactly the real McCoy, but they'll pass, friend, they'll pass—"

Morey blinked at him. "No!" he said violently, and pushed the man aside. Now it's racketeers, he thought bitterly. Slums and endless sordid preoccupation with rations weren't enough to inflict on Cherry; now the neighborhood was becoming a hangout for people on the shady side of the law. It was not, of course, the first time he had ever been approached by a counterfeit ration-stamp hoodlum, but never at his own front door!

Morey thought briefly, as he climbed into his car, of calling the police. But certainly the man would be gone before they could get there; and, after all, he had handled it pretty well as it was.

Of course, it would be nice to get six stamps for one.

But very far from nice if he got caught.

"Good morning, Mr. Fry," tinkled the robot receptionist. "Won't you go right in?" With a steel-tipped finger, it pointed to the door marked GROUP THERAPY.

Someday, Morey vowed to himself as he nodded and complied, he would be in a position to afford a private analyst of his own. Group therapy helped relieve the infinite stresses of modern living, and without it he might find himself as badly off as the hysterical mobs in the ration riots, or as dangerously anti-social as the counterfeiters. But it lacked the personal touch. It was, he thought, too public a performance of what should be a private affair, like trying to live a happy married life with an interfering, ever-present crowd of robots in the house–

Morey brought himself up in panic. How had *that* thought crept in? He was shaken visibly as he entered the room and greeted the group to which he was assigned.

There were eleven of them: four Freudians, two Reichians, two Jungians, a Gestalter, a shock therapist and the elderly and rather quiet Sullivanite. Even the members of the majority groups had their own individual differences in technique and creed, but, despite four years with this particular group of analysts, Morey hadn't quite been able to keep them separate in his mind. Their names, though, he knew well enough.

"Morning, Doctors," he said. "What is it today?"

"Morning," said Semmelweiss morosely. "Today you come into the room for the first time looking as if something is really bothering you, and yet the schedule calls for psychodrama. Dr. Fairless," he appealed, "can't we change the schedule a little bit? Fry here is obviously under a strain; *that's* the time to start digging and see what he can find. We can do your psychodrama next time, can't we?"

Fairless shook his gracefully bald old head. "Sorry, Doctor. If it were up to me, of course–but you know the rules."

"Rules, rules," jeered Semmelweiss. "Ah, what's the use? Here's a patient in an acute anxiety state if I ever saw one–and believe me, I saw plenty–and we ignore it because the *rules* say ignore it. Is that professional? Is that how to cure a patient?"

Little Blaine said frostily, "If I may say so, Dr. Semmelweiss, there have been a great many cures made without the necessity of departing from the rules. I myself, in fact–"

"You yourself!" mimicked Semmelweiss. "You yourself never handled a patient alone in your life. When you going to get out of a group, Blaine?"

Blaine said furiously, "Dr. Fairless, I don't think I have to stand for this sort of personal attack. Just because Semmelweiss has seniority and a couple of private patients one day a week, he thinks–"

"Gentlemen," said Fairless mildly. "Please, let's get on with the work. Mr. Fry has come to us for help, not to listen to us losing our tempers."

"Sorry," said Semmelweiss curtly. "All the same, I appeal from the arbitrary and mechanistic ruling of the chair."

Fairless inclined his head. "All in favor of the ruling of the chair? Nine, I count. That leaves only you opposed, Dr. Semmelweiss. We'll proceed with the psychodrama, if the recorder will read us the notes and comments of the last session."

The recorder, a pudgy, low-ranking youngster named Sprogue, flipped back the pages of his notebook and read in a chanting voice, "Session of twenty-fourth May, subject, Morey Fry; in attendance, Doctors Fairless, Bileck, Semmelweiss, Carrado, Weber–"

Fairless interrupted kindly, "Just the last page, if you please, Dr. Sprogue."

"Um–oh, yes. After a ten-minute recess for additional Rorschachs and an electro-encephalogram, the group convened and conducted rapid-fire word association. Results were tabulated and compared with standard deviation patterns, and it was determined that subject's major traumas derived from, respectively–"

Morey found his attention waning. Therapy was *good;* everybody knew that, but every once in a while he found it a little dull. If it weren't for therapy, though, there was no telling what might happen. Certainly, Morey told himself, he had been helped considerably–at least he hadn't set fire to his house and shrieked at the fire-robots, like Newell down the block when his eldest daughter divorced her husband and came back to live with him, bringing her ration quota along, of course. Morey hadn't even been *tempted* to do anything as outrageously, frighteningly immoral as *destroy* things or *waste* them–well, he admitted to himself honestly, perhaps a little tempted, once in a great while. But never anything important enough to worry about; he was sound, perfectly sound.

He looked up, startled. All the doctors were staring at him. "Mr. Fry," Fairless repeated, "will you take your place?"

"Certainly," Morey said hastily. "Uh–where?"

Semmelweiss guffawed. *"Told* you. Never mind, Morey; you didn't miss much. We're going to run through one of the big scenes in your life, the one you told us about last time. Remember? You were fourteen years old, you said. Christmas time. Your mother had made you a promise."

Morey swallowed. "I remember," he said unhappily. "Well, all right. Where do I stand?"

"Right here," said Fairless. "You're you, Carrado is your mother, I'm your father. Will the doctors not participating mind moving back? Fine. Now, Morey, here we are on Christmas morning. Merry Christmas, Morey!"

"Merry Christmas," Morey said half-heartedly. "Uh–Father dear, where's my–uh–my puppy that Mother promised me?"

"Puppy!" said Fairless heartily. "Your mother and I have something much better than a puppy for you. Just take a look under the tree there—it's a *robot!* Yes, Morey, your very own robot—a full-size thirty-eight-tube fully automatic companion robot for you! Go ahead, Morey, go right up and speak to it. Its name is Henry. Go on, boy."

Morey felt a sudden, incomprehensible tingle inside the bridge of his nose. He said shakily, "But I—I didn't *want* a robot."

"Of course you want a robot," Carrado interrupted. "Go on, child, play with your nice robot."

Morey said violently, "I *hate* robots!" He looked around him at the doctors, at the gray-paneled consulting room. He added defiantly, "You hear me, all of you? I *still* hate robots!"

There was a second's pause; then the questions began.

It was half an hour before the receptionist came in and announced that time was up.

In that half hour, Morey had got over his trembling and lost his wild, momentary passion, but he had remembered what for thirteen years he had forgotten.

He hated robots.

The surprising thing was not that young Morey had hated robots. It was that the Robot Riots, the ultimate violent outbreak of flesh against metal, the battle to the death between mankind and its machine heirs . . . never happened. A little boy hated robots, but the man he became worked with them hand in hand.

And yet, always and always before, the new worker, the competitor for the job, was at once and inevitably outside the law. The waves swelled in—the Irish, the Negroes, the Jews, the Italians. They were squeezed into their ghettoes, where they encysted, seethed and struck out, until the burgeoning generations became indistinguishable.

For the robots, that genetic relief was not in sight. And still the conflict never came. The feed-back circuits aimed the anti-aircraft guns and, reshaped and newly planned, found a place in a new sort of machine—together with a miraculous trail of cams and levers, an indestructible and potent power source and a hundred thousand parts and sub-assemblies.

And the first robot clanked off the bench.

Its mission was its own destruction; but from the scavenged wreck of its pilot body, a hundred better robots drew their inspiration. And the hundred went to work, and hundreds more, until there were millions upon untold millions.

And still the riots never happened.

For the robots came bearing a gift and the name of it was "Plenty."

And by the time the gift had shown its own unguessed ills the time for a Robot Riot was past. Plenty is a habit-forming drug. You do not cut the dosage down. You kick it if you can; you stop the dose entirely. But the convulsions that follow may wreck the body once and for all.

The addict craves the grainy white powder; he doesn't hate it, or the runner who sells it to him. And if Morey as a little boy could hate the robot that had deprived him of his pup, Morey the man was perfectly aware that the robots were his servants and his friends.

But the little Morey inside the man—*he* had never been convinced.

Morey ordinarily looked forward to his work. The one day a week at which he *did* anything was a wonderful change from the dreary consume, consume, consume grind. He entered the bright-lit drafting room of the Bradmoor Amusements Company with a feeling of uplift.

But as he was changing from street garb to his drafting smock, Howland from Procurement came over with a knowing look. "Wainwright's been looking for you," Howland whispered. "Better get right in there."

Morey nervously thanked him and got. Wainwright's office was the size of a phone booth and as bare as Antarctic ice. Every time Morey saw it, he felt his insides churn with envy. Think of a desk with nothing on it but work surface—no calendar-clock, no twelve-color pen rack, no dictating machines!

He squeezed himself in and sat down while Wainwright finished a phone call. He mentally reviewed the possible reasons why Wainwright would want to talk to him in person instead of over the phone, or by dropping a word to him as he passed through the drafting room.

Very few of them were good.

Wainwright put down the phone and Morey straightened up. "You sent for me?" he asked.

Wainwright in a chubby world was aristocratically lean. As General Superintendent of the Design & Development Section of the Bradmoor Amusements Company, he ranked high in the upper section of the well-to-do. He rasped, "I certainly did. Fry, just what the hell do you think you're up to now?"

"I don't know what you m-mean, Mr. Wainwright," Morey stammered, crossing off the list of possible reasons for the interview all of the good ones.

Wainwright snorted. "I guess you don't. Not because you weren't told, but because you don't want to know. Think back a whole week. What did I have you on the carpet for then?"

Morey said sickly, "My ration book. Look, Mr. Wainwright, I know I'm running a little bit behind, but–"

"But nothing! How do you think it looks to the Committee, Fry? They got a complaint from the Ration Board about you. Naturally they passed it on to me. And naturally I'm going to pass it right along to you. The question is, what are you going to do about it? Good God, man, look at these figures–textiles, fifty-one per cent; food, sixty-seven per cent; amusements and entertainment, *thirty* per cent! You haven't come up to your ration in anything for months!"

Morey stared at the card miserably. "We–that is, my wife and I–just had a long talk about that last night, Mr. Wainwright. And, believe me, we're going to do better. We're going to buckle right down and get to work and–uh–do better," he finished weakly.

Wainwright nodded, and for the first time there was a note of sympathy in his voice. "Your wife. Judge Elon's daughter, isn't she? Good family. I've met the Judge many times." Then, gruffly, "Well, nevertheless, Fry, I'm warning you. I don't care how you straighten this out, but *don't let the Committee mention this to me again.*"

"No, sir."

"All right. Finished with the schematics on the new K-50?"

Morey brightened. "Just about, sir! I'm putting the first section on tape today. I'm very pleased with it, Mr. Wainwright, honestly I am. I've got more than eighteen thousand moving parts in it now, and that's without–"

"Good. Good." Wainwright glanced down at his desk. "Get back to it. And straighten out this other thing. You can do it, Fry. Consuming is everybody's duty. Just keep that in mind."

Howland followed Morey out of the drafting room, down to the spotless shops. "Bad time?" he inquired solicitously. Morey grunted. It was none of Howland's business.

Howland looked over his shoulder as he was setting up the programing panel. Morey studied the matrices silently, then got busy reading the summary tapes, checking them back against the schematics, setting up the instructions on the programing board. Howland kept quiet as Morey completed the setup and ran off a test tape. It checked perfectly; Morey stepped back to light a cigarette in celebration before pushing the *start* button.

Howland said, "Go on, run it. I can't go until you put it in the works."

Morey grinned and pushed the button. The board lighted up;

within it, a tiny metronomic beep began to pulse. That was all. At the other end of the quarter-mile shed, Morey knew, the automatic sorters and conveyers were fingering through the copper reels and steel ingots, measuring hoppers of plastic powder and colors, setting up an intricate weaving path for the thousands of individual components that would make up Bradmoor's new K-50 Spin-a-Game. But from where they stood, in the elaborately muraled programing room, nothing showed. Bradmoor was an ultra-modernized plant; in the manufacturing end, even robots had been dispensed with in favor of machines that guided themselves.

Morey glanced at his watch and logged in the starting time while Howland quickly counter-checked Morey's raw-material flow program.

"Checks out," Howland said solemnly, slapping him on the back. "Calls for a celebration. Anyway, it's your first design, isn't it?"

"Yes. First all by myself, at any rate."

Howland was already fishing in his private locker for the bottle he kept against emergency needs. He poured with a flourish. "To Morey Fry," he said, "our most favorite designer, in whom we are much pleased."

Morey drank. It went down easily enough. Morey had conscientiously used his liquor rations for years, but he had never gone beyond the minimum, so that although liquor was no new experience to him, the single drink immediately warmed him. It warmed his mouth, his throat, the hollows of his chest; and it settled down with a warm glow inside him. Howland, exerting himself to be nice, complimented Morey fatuously on the design and poured another drink. Morey didn't utter any protest at all.

Howland drained his glass. "You may wonder," he said formally, "why I am so pleased with you, Morey Fry. I will tell you why this is."

Morey grinned. "Please do."

Howland nodded. "I will. It's because I am pleased with the world, Morey. My wife left me last night."

Morey was as shocked as only a recent bridegroom can be by the news of a crumbling marriage. "That's too ba–I mean is that a fact?"

"Yes, she left my beds and board and five robots, and I'm happy to see her go." He poured another drink for both of them. "Women. Can't live with them and can't live without them. First you sigh and pant and chase after 'em–you like poetry?" he demanded suddenly.

Morey said cautiously, "Some poetry."

Howland quoted: "'How long, my love, shall I behold this wall between our gardens—yours the rose, and mine the swooning lily.' Like it? I wrote it for Jocelyn—that's my wife—when we were first going together."

"It's beautiful," said Morey.

"She wouldn't talk to me for two days." Howland drained his drink. "Lots of spirit, that girl. Anyway, I hunted her like a tiger. And then I caught her. *Wow!*"

Morey took a deep drink from his own glass. "What do you mean, *wow?*" he asked.

"Wow." Howland pointed his finger at Morey. *"Wow,* that's what I mean. We got married and I took her home to the dive I was living in, and *wow* we had a kid, and *wow* I got in a little trouble with the Ration Board—nothing serious, of course, but there was a mixup—and *wow* fights.

"Everything was a fight," he explained. "She'd start with a little nagging, and naturally I'd say something or other back, and *bang* we were off. Budget, budget, budget; I hope to die if I ever hear the word 'budget' again. Morey, you're a married man; you know what it's like. Tell me the truth, weren't you just about ready to blow your top the first time you caught your wife cheating on the budget?"

"Cheating on the budget?" Morey was startled. "Cheating how?"

"Oh, lots of ways. Making your portions bigger than hers. Sneaking extra shirts for you on her clothing ration. You know."

"Damn it, I do *not* know!" cried Morey. "Cherry wouldn't do anything like that!"

Howland looked at him opaquely for a long second. "Of course not," he said at last. "Let's have another drink."

Ruffled, Morey held out his glass. Cherry wasn't the type of girl to *cheat*. Of course she wasn't. A fine, loving girl like her—a pretty girl, of a good family; she wouldn't know how to begin.

Howland was saying, in a sort of chant, "No more budget. No more fights. No more 'Daddy never treated me like this.' No more nagging. No more extra rations for household allowance. No more—Morey, what do you say we go out and have a few drinks? I know a place where—"

"Sorry, Howland," Morey said. "I've got to get back to the office, you know."

Howland guffawed. He held out his wristwatch. As Morey, a little unsteadily, bent over it, it tinkled out the hour. It was a matter of minutes before the office closed for the day.

"Oh," said Morey. "I didn't realize—Well, anyway, Howland, thanks, but I can't. My wife will be expecting me."

"She certainly will," Howland sniggered. "Won't catch *her* eating up your rations and hers tonight."

Morey said tightly, "Howland!"

"Oh, sorry, sorry." Howland waved an arm. "Don't mean to say anything against *your* wife, of course. Guess maybe Jocelyn soured me on women. But honest, Morey, you'd like this place. Name of Uncle Piggotty's, down in the Old Town. Crazy bunch hangs out there. You'd like them. Couple nights last week they had–I mean, you understand, Morey, I don't go there as often as all that, but I just happened to drop in and–"

Morey interrupted firmly. "Thank you, Howland. Must go home. Wife expects it. Decent of you to offer. Good night. Be seeing you."

He walked out, turned at the door to bow politely, and in turning back cracked the side of his face against the door jamb. A sort of pleasant numbness had taken possession of his entire skin surface, though, and it wasn't until he perceived Henry chattering at him sympathetically that he noticed a trickle of blood running down the side of his face.

"Mere flesh wound," he said with dignity. "Nothing to cause you *least* conshter–consternation, Henry. Now kindly shut your ugly face. Want to think."

And he slept in the car all the way home.

It was worse than a hangover. The name is "holdover." You've had some drinks; you've started to sober up by catching a little sleep. Then you are required to be awake and to function. The consequent state has the worst features of hangover and intoxication; your head thumps and your mouth tastes like the floor of a bear-pit, but you are nowhere near sober.

There is one cure. Morey said thickly, "Let's have a cocktail, dear."

Cherry was delighted to share a cocktail with him before dinner. Cherry, Morey thought lovingly, was a wonderful, wonderful, wonderful–

He found his head nodding in time to his thoughts and the motion made him wince.

Cherry flew to his side and touched his temple. "Is it bothering you, darling?" she asked solicitously. "Where you ran into the door, I mean?"

Morey looked at her sharply, but her expression was open and adoring. He said bravely, "Just a little. Nothing to it, really."

The butler brought the cocktails and retired. Cherry lifted her glass. Morey raised his, caught a whiff of the liquor and nearly dropped it.

He bit down hard on his churning insides and forced himself to swallow.

He was surprised but grateful: It stayed down. In a moment, the curious phenomenon of warmth began to repeat itself. He swallowed the rest of the drink and held out his glass for a refill. He even tried a smile. Oddly enough, his face didn't fall off.

One more drink did it. Morey felt happy and relaxed, but by no means drunk. They went in to dinner in fine spirits. They chatted cheerfully with each other and Henry, and Morey found time to feel sentimentally sorry for poor Howland, who couldn't make a go of his marriage, when marriage was obviously such an easy relationship, so beneficial to both sides, so warm and relaxing . . .

Startled, he said, "What?"

Cherry repeated, "It's the cleverest scheme I ever heard of. Such a funny little man, dear. All kind of *nervous,* if you know what I mean. He kept looking at the door as if he was expecting someone, but of course that was silly. None of his friends would have come to *our* house to see him."

Morey said tensely, "Cherry, *please!* What was that you said about ration stamps?"

"But I told you, darling! It was just after you left this morning. This funny little man came to the door; the butler said he wouldn't give any name. Anyway, I talked to him. I thought he might be a neighbor and I certainly would *never* be rude to any neighbor who might come to call, even if the neighborhood was—"

"The ration stamps!" Morey begged. "Did I hear you say he was peddling phony ration stamps?"

Cherry said uncertainly, "Well, I suppose that in a *way* they're phony. The way he explained it, they weren't the regular official kind. But it was four for one, dear—four of his stamps for one of ours. So I just took out our household book and steamed off a couple of weeks' stamps and—"

"How many?" Morey bellowed.

Cherry blinked. "About—about two weeks' quota," she said faintly. "Was that wrong, dear?"

Morey closed his eyes dizzily. "A couple of weeks' stamps," he repeated. "Four for one—you didn't even get the regular rate."

Cherry wailed, "How was I supposed to know? I never had anything like this when I was *home!* We didn't have food riots and slums and all these horrible robots and filthy little revolting men coming to the door!"

Morey stared at her woodenly. She was crying again, but it made no impression on the case-hardened armor that was suddenly thrown around his heart.

Henry made a tentative sound that, in a human, would have been a preparatory cough, but Morey froze him with a white-eyed look.

Morey said in a dreary monotone that barely penetrated the sound of Cherry's tears, "Let me tell you just what it was you did. Assuming, at best, that these stamps you got are at least average good counterfeits, and not so bad that the best thing to do with them is throw them away before we get caught with them in our possession, you have approximately a two-month supply of funny stamps. In case you didn't know it, those ration books are not merely ornamental. They have to be turned in every month to prove that we have completed our consuming quota for the month.

"When they are turned in, they are spot-checked. Every book is at least glanced at. A big chunk of them are gone over very carefully by the inspectors, and a certain percentage are tested by ultra-violet, infra-red, X-ray, radio-isotopes, bleaches, fumes, paper chromatography and every other damned test known to Man." His voice was rising to an uneven crescendo. "*If* we are lucky enough to get away with using any of these stamps at all, we daren't—we simply *dare* not —use more than one or two counterfeits to every dozen or more real stamps.

"That means, Cherry, that what you bought is not a two-month supply, but maybe a two-*year* supply—and since, as you no doubt have never noticed, the things have expiration dates on them, there is probably no chance in the world that we can ever hope to use more than half of them." He was bellowing by the time he pushed back his chair and towered over her. "Moreover," he went on, "right *now,* right as of this *minute,* we have to make up the stamps you gave away, which means that at the very best we are going to be on double rations for two weeks or so.

"And that says nothing about the one feature of this whole grisly mess that you seem to have thought of least, namely that counterfeit stamps are against the *law!* I'm poor, Cherry; I live in a slum, and I know it; I've got a long way to go before I'm as rich or respected or powerful as your father, about whom I am beginning to get considerably tired of hearing. But poor as I may be, I can tell you *this* for sure: Up until now, at any rate, I have been *honest.*"

Cherry's tears had stopped entirely and she was bowed white-faced and dry-eyed by the time Morey had finished. He had spent himself; there was no violence left in him.

He stared dismally at Cherry for a moment, then turned wordlessly and stamped out of the house.

Marriage! he thought as he left.

He walked for hours, blind to where he was going.

What brought him back to awareness was a sensation he had not felt in a dozen years. It was not, Morey abruptly realized, the dying traces of his hangover that made his stomach feel so queer. He was hungry—actually hungry.

He looked about him. He was in the Old Town, miles from home, jostled by crowds of lower-class people. The block he was on was as atrocious a slum as Morey had ever seen—Chinese pagodas stood next to rococo imitations of the chapels around Versailles; gingerbread marred every facade; no building was without its brilliant signs and flarelights.

He saw a blindingly overdecorated eating establishment called Billie's Budget Busy Bee and crossed the street toward it, dodging through the unending streams of traffic. It was a miserable excuse for a restaurant, but Morey was in no mood to care. He found a seat under a potted palm, as far from the tinkling fountains and robot string ensemble as he could manage, and ordered recklessly, paying no attention to the ration prices. As the waiter was gliding noiselessly away, Morey had a sickening realization: He'd come out without his ration book. He groaned out loud; it was too late to leave without causing a disturbance. But then, he thought rebelliously, what difference did one more unrationed meal make, anyhow?

Food made him feel a little better. He finished the last of his *profiterole au chocolat,* not even leaving on the plate the uneaten one-third that tradition permitted, and paid his check. The robot cashier reached automatically for his ration book. Morey had a moment of grandeur as he said simply, "No ration stamps."

Robot cashiers are not equipped to display surprise, but this one tried. The man behind Morey in line audibly caught his breath, and less audibly mumbled something about *slummers*. Morey took it as a compliment and strode outside feeling almost in good humor.

Good enough to go home to Cherry? Morey thought seriously of it for a second; but he wasn't going to pretend he was wrong and certainly Cherry wasn't going to be willing to admit that *she* was at fault.

Besides, Morey told himself grimly, she was undoubtedly asleep. That was an annoying thing about Cherry at best: she never had any trouble getting to sleep. Didn't even use her quota of sleeping tablets, though Morey had spoken to her about it more than once. Of course, he reminded himself, he had been so polite and tactful about it, as befits a newlywed, that very likely she hadn't even understood that it was a complaint. Well, *that* would stop!

Man's man Morey Fry, wearing no collar ruff but his own, strode determinedly down the streets of the Old Town.

"Hey, Joe, want a good time?"

Morey took one unbelieving look. "You again!" he roared.

The little man stared at him in genuine surprise. Then a faint glimmer of recognition crossed his face. "Oh, yeah," he said. "This morning, huh?" He clucked commiseratingly. "Too bad you wouldn't deal with me. Your wife was a lot smarter. Of course, you got me a little sore, Jack, so naturally I had to raise the price a little bit."

"You skunk, you cheated my poor wife blind! You and I are going to the local station house and talk this over."

The little man pursed his lips. "We are, huh?"

Morey nodded vigorously. "Damn right! And let me tell you—" He stopped in the middle of a threat as a large hand cupped around his shoulder.

The equally large man who owned the hand said, in a mild and cultured voice, "Is this gentleman disturbing you, Sam?"

"Not so far," the little man conceded. "He might want to, though, so don't go away."

Morey wrenched his shoulder away. "Don't think you can strong-arm me. I'm taking you to the police."

Sam shook his head unbelievingly. "You mean you're going to call the law in on this?"

"I certainly am!"

Sam sighed regretfully. "What do you think of that, Walter? Treating his wife like that. Such a nice lady, too."

"What are you talking about?" Morey demanded, stung on a peculiarly sensitive spot.

"I'm talking about your wife," Sam explained. "Of course, I'm not married myself. But it seems to me that if I was, I wouldn't call the police when my wife was engaged in some kind of criminal activity or other. No, sir, I'd try to settle it myself. Tell you what," he advised, "why don't you talk this over with her? Make her see the error of—"

"Wait a minute," Morey interrupted. "You mean you'd involve my wife in this thing?"

The man spread his hands helplessly. "It's not me that would involve her, Buster," he said. "She already involved her own self. It takes two to make a crime, you know. I sell, maybe; I won't deny it. But after all, I can't sell unless somebody buys, can I?"

Morey stared at him glumly. He glanced in quick speculation at the large-sized Walter; but Walter was just as big as he'd remembered, so that took care of that. Violence was out; the police were out; that left no really attractive way of capitalizing on the good luck of running into the man again.

Sam said, "Well, I'm glad to see that's off your mind. Now, returning to my original question, Mac, how would you like a good time? You look like a smart fellow to me; you look like you'd be kind of interested in a place I happen to know of down the block."

Morey said bitterly, "So you're a dive-steerer, too. A real talented man."

"I admit it," Sam agreed. "Stamp business is slow at night, in my experience. People have their minds more on a good time. And, believe me, a good time is what I can show 'em. Take this place I'm talking about, Uncle Piggotty's is the name of it, it's what I would call an unusual kind of place. Wouldn't you say so, Walter?"

"Oh, I agree with you entirely," Walter rumbled.

But Morey was hardly listening. He said, "Uncle Piggotty's, you say?"

"That's right," said Sam.

Morey frowned for a moment, digesting an idea. Uncle Piggotty's sounded like the place Howland had been talking about back at the plant; it might be interesting, at that.

While he was making up his mind, Sam slipped an arm through his on one side and Walter amiably wrapped a big hand around the other. Morey found himself walking.

"You'll like it," Sam promised comfortably. "No hard feelings about this morning, sport? Of course not. Once you get a look at Piggotty's, you'll get over your mad, anyhow. It's something special. I swear, on what they pay me for bringing in customers, I wouldn't do it unless I *believed* in it."

"Dance, Jack?" the hostess yelled over the noise at the bar. She stepped back, lifted her flounced skirts to ankle height and executed a tricky nine-step.

"My name is Morey," Morey yelled back. "And I don't want to dance, thanks."

The hostess shrugged, frowned meaningfully at Sam and danced away.

Sam flagged the bartender. "First round's on us," he explained to

Morey. "Then we won't bother you any more. Unless you want us to, of course. Like the place?" Morey hesitated, but Sam didn't wait. "Fine place," he yelled, and picked up the drink the bartender left him. "See you around."

He and the big man were gone. Morey stared after them uncertainly, then gave it up. He was here, anyhow; might as well at least have a drink. He ordered and looked around.

Uncle Piggotty's was a third-rate dive disguised to look, in parts of it at least, like one of the exclusive upper-class country clubs. The bar, for instance, was treated to resemble the clean lines of nailed wood; but underneath the surface treatment, Morey could detect the intricate laminations of plyplastic. What at first glance appeared to be burlap hangings were in actuality elaborately textured synthetics. And all through the bar the motif was carried out.

A floor show of sorts was going on, but nobody seemed to be paying much attention to it. Morey, straining briefly to hear the master of ceremonies, gathered that the wit was on a more than mildly vulgar level. There was a dispirited string of chorus beauties in long ruffled pantaloons and diaphanous tops; one of them, Morey was almost sure, was the hostess who had talked to him just a few moments before.

Next to him a man was declaiming to a middle-aged woman:

Smote I the monstrous rock, yahoo!
Smote I the turgid tube, Bully Boy!
Smote I the cankered hill—

"Why, Morey!" he interrupted himself. "What are you doing here?"

He turned farther around and Morey recognized him. "Hello, Howland," he said. "I—uh—I happened to be free tonight, so I thought—"

Howland sniggered. "Well, guess your wife is more liberal than mine was. Order a drink, boy."

"Thanks, I've got one," said Morey.

The woman, with a tigerish look at Morey, said, "Don't stop, Everett. That was one of your most beautiful things."

"Oh, Morey's heard my poetry," Howland said. "Morey, I'd like you to meet a very lovely and talented young lady, Tanaquil Bigelow. Morey works in the office with me, Tan."

"Obviously," said Tanaquil Bigelow in a frozen voice, and Morey hastily withdrew the hand he had begun to put out.

The conversation stuck there, impaled, the woman cold, Howland relaxed and abstracted, Morey wondering if, after all, this had been such a good idea. He caught the eye-cell of the robot bartender and ordered a round of drinks for the three of them, politely putting them on Howland's ration book. By the time the drinks had come and Morey had just got around to deciding that it wasn't a very good idea, the woman had all of a sudden become thawed.

She said abruptly, "You look like the kind of man who *thinks,* Morey, and I like to talk to that kind of man. Frankly, Morey, I just don't have any patience at all with the stupid, stodgy men who just work in their offices all day and eat all their dinners every night, and gad about and consume like mad and where does it all get them, anyhow? That's right, I can see you understand. Just one crazy rush of consume, consume from the day you're born *plop* to the day you're buried *pop!* And who's to blame if not the robots?"

Faintly, a tinge of worry began to appear on the surface of Howland's relaxed calm. "Tan," he chided, "Morey may not be very interested in politics."

Politics, Morey thought; well, at least that was a clue. He'd had the dizzying feeling, while the woman was talking, that he himself was the ball in the games machine he had designed for the shop earlier that day. Following the woman's conversation might, at that, give his next design some valuable pointers in swoops, curves and obstacles.

He said, with more than half truth, "No, please go on, Miss Bigelow. I'm very much interested."

She smiled; then abruptly her face changed to a frightening scowl. Morey flinched, but evidently the scowl wasn't meant for him. "Robots!" she hissed. "Supposed to work for us, aren't they? Hah! We're their slaves, slaves for every moment of every miserable day of our lives. Slaves! Wouldn't you like to join us and be free, Morey?"

Morey took cover in his drink. He made an expressive gesture with his free hand—expressive of exactly what, he didn't truly know, for he was lost. But it seemed to satisfy the woman.

She said accusingly, "Did you know that more than three-quarters of the people in this country have had a nervous breakdown in the past five years and four months? That more than half of them are under the constant care of psychiatrists for psychosis—not just plain ordinary neurosis like my husband's got and Howland here has got and you've got, but psychosis. Like I've got. Did you know that? Did you know that forty per cent of the population are essentially manic depressive, thirty-one per cent are schizoid, thirty-eight per cent have an assortment of other unfixed psychogenic disturbances and twenty-four—"

"Hold it a minute, Tan," Howland interrupted critically. "You've got too many per cents there. Start over again."

"Oh, the hell with it," the woman said moodily. "I wish my husband were here. He expresses it so much better than I do." She swallowed her drink. "Since you've wriggled off the hook," she said nastily to Morey, "how about setting up another round–on my ration book this time?"

Morey did; it was the simplest thing to do in his confusion. When that was gone, they had another on Howland's book.

As near as he could figure out, the woman, her husband and quite possibly Howland as well belonged to some kind of anti-robot group. Morey had heard of such things; they had a quasi-legal status, neither approved nor prohibited, but he had never come into contact with them before. Remembering the hatred he had so painfully relived at the psychodrama session, he thought anxiously that perhaps he belonged with them. But, question them though he might, he couldn't seem to get the principles of the organization firmly in mind.

The woman finally gave up trying to explain it, and went off to find her husband while Morey and Howland had another drink and listened to two drunks squabble over who bought the next round. They were at the Alphonse-Gaston stage of inebriation; they would regret it in the morning; for each was bending over backward to permit the other to pay the ration points. Morey wondered uneasily about his own points; Howland was certainly getting credit for a lot of Morey's drinking tonight. Served him right for forgetting his book, of course.

When the woman came back, it was with the large man Morey had encountered in the company of Sam, the counterfeiter, steerer and general man about Old Town.

"A remarkably small world, isn't it?" boomed Walter Bigelow, only slightly crushing Morey's hand in his. "Well, sir, my wife has told me how interested you are in the basic philosophical drives behind our movement, and I should like to discuss them further with you. To begin with, sir, have you considered the principle of Twoness?"

Morey said, "Why–"

"Very good," said Bigelow courteously. He cleared his throat and declaimed:

Han-headed Cathay saw it first,
Bright as brightest solar burst;
Whipped it into boy and girl,

The blinding spiral-sliced swirl:
Yang
And Yin.

He shrugged deprecatingly. "Just the first stanza," he said. "I don't know if you got much out of it."

"Well, no," Morey admitted.

"Second stanza," Bigelow said firmly:

Hegal saw it, saw it clear;
Jackal Marx drew near, drew near:
O'er his shoulder saw it plain,
Turned it upside down again:
Yang
And Yin.

There was an expectant pause. Morey said, "I–uh–"

"Wraps it all up, doesn't it?" Bigelow's wife demanded. "Oh, if only others could see it as clearly as you do! The robot peril *and* the robot savior. Starvation *and* surfeit. Always twoness, always!"

Bigelow patted Morey's shoulder. "The next stanza makes it even clearer," he said. "It's really very clever–I shouldn't say it, of course, but it's Howland's as much as it's mine. He helped me with the verses." Morey darted a glance at Howland, but Howland was carefully looking away. "Third stanza," said Bigelow. "This is a hard one, because it's long, so pay attention."

Justice, tip your sightless scales;
One pan rises, one pan falls.

"Howland," he interrupted himself, "are you *sure* about that rhyme? I always trip over it. Well, anyway:

Add to A and B grows less;
A's B's partner, nonetheless.
Next, the Twoness that there be
In even electricity.
Chart the current as it's found:
Sine the hot lead, line the ground.
The wild sine dances, soars and falls,
But only to figures the zero calls.
Sine wave, scales, all things that be
Share a reciprocity.
Male and female, light and dark:

Name the numbers of Noah's Ark!
Yang
And Yin!

"Dearest!" shrieked Bigelow's wife. "You've never done it better!" There was a spatter of applause, and Morey realized for the first time that half the bar had stopped its noisy revel to listen to them. Bigelow was evidently quite a well-known figure here.

Morey said weakly, "I've never heard anything like it."

He turned hesitantly to Howland, who promptly said, "Drink! What we all need right now is a drink."

They had a drink on Bigelow's book.

Morey got Howland aside and asked him, "Look, level with me. Are these people nuts?"

Howland showed pique. "No. Certainly not."

"Does that poem mean anything? Does this whole business of twoness mean anything?"

Howland shrugged. "If it means something to them, it means something. They're philosophers, Morey. They see deep into things. You don't know what a privilege it is for me to be allowed to associate with them."

They had another drink. On Howland's book, of course.

Morey eased Walter Bigelow over to a quiet spot. He said, "Leaving twoness out of it for the moment, what's this about the robots?"

Bigelow looked at him round-eyed. "Didn't you understand the poem?"

"Of course I did. But diagram it for me in simple terms so I can tell my wife."

Bigelow beamed. "It's about the dichotomy of robots," he explained. "Like the little salt mill that the boy wished for: it ground out salt and ground out salt and ground out salt. He had to have salt, but not *that* much salt. Whitehead explains it clearly—"

They had another drink on Bigelow's book.

Morey wavered over Tanaquil Bigelow. He said fuzzily, "Listen. Mrs. Walter Tanaquil Strongarm Bigelow. Listen."

She grinned smugly at him. "Brown hair," she said dreamily.

Morey shook his head vigorously. "Never mind hair," he ordered. "Never mind poem. Listen. In *pre-cise* and el-e-*men*-ta-ry terms, explain to me what is wrong with the world today."

"Not enough brown hair," she said promptly.

"Never mind hair!"

"All right," she said agreeably. "Too many robots. Too many robots make too much of everything."

"Ha! Got it!" Morey exclaimed triumphantly. "Get rid of robots!"

"Oh, no. No! No! No. We wouldn't eat. Everything is mechanized. Can't get rid of them, can't slow down production–slowing down is dying, stopping is quicker dying. Principle of twoness is the concept that clarifies all these–"

"No!" Morey said violently. "What should we *do?*"

"Do? I'll tell you what we should do, if that's what you want. I can tell you."

"Then tell me."

"What we should do is–" Tanaquil hiccupped with a look of refined consternation–"have another drink."

They had another drink. He gallantly let her pay, of course. She ungallantly argued with the bartender about the ration points due her.

Though not a two-fisted drinker, Morey tried. He really worked at it.

He paid the price, too. For some little time before his limbs stopped moving, his mind stopped functioning. Blackout. Almost a blackout, at any rate, for all he retained of the late evening was a kaleidoscope of people and places and things. Howland was there, drunk as a skunk, disgracefully drunk, Morey remembered thinking as he stared up at Howland from the floor. The Bigelows were there. His wife, Cherry, solicitous and amused, was there. And oddly enough, Henry was there.

It was very, very hard to reconstruct. Morey devoted a whole morning's hangover to the effort. It was *important* to reconstruct it, for some reason. But Morey couldn't even remember what the reason was; and finally he dismissed it, guessing that he had either solved the secret of twoness or whether Tanaquil Bigelow's remarkable figure was natural.

He did, however, know that the next morning he had waked in his own bed, with no recollection of getting there. No recollection of anything much, at least not of anything that fit into the proper chronological order or seemed to mesh with anything else, after the dozenth drink when he and Howland, arms around each other's shoulders, composed a new verse on twoness and, plagiarizing an old marching tune, howled it across the boisterous barroom:

A twoness on the scene much later
Rests in your refrigerator.
Heat your house and insulate it.
Next your food: Refrigerate it.
Frost will damp your Freon coils,
So flux in nichrome till it boils.
See the picture? Heat in cold
In heat in cold, the story's told!
Giant-writ the sacred scrawl:
Oh, the twoness of it all!
Yang
And Yin!

It had, at any rate, seemed to mean something at the time.

If alcohol opened Morey's eyes to the fact that there *was* a twoness, perhaps alcohol was what he needed. For there was.

Call it a dichotomy, if the word seems more couth. A kind of two-pronged struggle, the struggle of two unwearying runners in an immortal race. There is the refrigerator inside the house. The cold air, the bubble of heated air that is the house, the bubble of cooled air that is the refrigerator, the momentary bubble of heated air that defrosts it. Call the heat Yang, if you will. Call the cold Yin. Yang overtakes Yin. Then Yin passes Yang. Then Yang passes Yin. Then—

Give them other names. Call Yin a mouth; call Yang a hand.

If the hand rests, the mouth will starve. If the mouth stops, the hand will die. The hand, Yang, moves faster.

Yin may not lag behind.

Then call Yang a robot.

And remember that a pipeline has two ends.

Like any once-in-a-lifetime lush, Morey braced himself for the consequences—and found startledly that there were none.

Cherry was a surprise to him. "You were so funny," she giggled. "And, honestly, so *romantic.*"

He shakily swallowed his breakfast coffee.

The office staff roared and slapped him on the back. "Howland tells us you're living high, boy!" they bellowed more or less in the same words. "Hey, listen to what Morey did—went on the town for the night of a lifetime *and didn't even bring his ration book along to cash in!*"

They thought it was a wonderful joke.

But, then, everything was going well. Cherry, it seemed, had reformed out of recognition. True, she still hated to go out in the evening and Morey never saw her forcing herself to gorge on unwanted food or play undesired games. But, moping into the pantry one afternoon, he found to his incredulous delight that they were well ahead of their ration quotas. In some items, in fact, they were *out*—a month's supply and more was gone ahead of schedule!

Nor was it the counterfeit stamps, for he had found them tucked behind a bain-marie and quietly burned them. He cast about for ways of complimenting her, but caution prevailed. She was sensitive on the subject; leave it be.

And virtue had its reward.

Wainwright called him in, all smiles. "Morey, great news! We've all appreciated your work here and we've been able to show it in some more tangible way then compliments. I didn't want to say anything till it was definite, but—your status has been reviewed by Classification and the Ration Board. You're out of Class Four Minor, Morey!"

Morey said tremulously, hardly daring to hope, "I'm a full Class Four?"

"Class Five, Morey. *Class Five!* When we do something, we do it right. We asked for a special waiver and got it—you've skipped a whole class." He added honestly, "Not that it was just our backing that did it, of course. Your own recent splendid record of consumption helped a lot. I told you you could do it!"

Morey had to sit down. He missed the rest of what Wainwright had to say, but it couldn't have mattered. He escaped from the office, sidestepped the knot of fellow-employees waiting to congratulate him, and got to a phone.

Cherry was as ecstatic and inarticulate as he. "Oh, darling!" was all she could say.

"And I couldn't have done it without you," he babbled. "Wainwright as much as said so himself. Said if it wasn't for the way we—well, *you* have been keeping up with the rations, it never would have got by the Board. I've been meaning to say something to you about that, dear, but I just haven't known how. But I do appreciate it. I—Hello?" There was a curious silence at the other end of the phone. "Hello?" he repeated worriedly.

Cherry's voice was intense and low. "Morey Fry, I think you're mean. I wish you hadn't spoiled the good news." And she hung up.

Morey stared slack-jawed at the phone.

Howland appeared behind him, chuckling. "Women," he said. "Never try to figure them. Anyway, congratulations, Morey."

"Thanks," Morey mumbled.

Howland coughed and said, "Uh—by the way, Morey, now that you're one of the big shots, so to speak, you won't—uh—feel obliged to—well, say anything to Wainwright, for instance, about anything I may have said while we—"

"Excuse me," Morey said, unhearing, and pushed past him. He thought wildly of calling Cherry back, of racing home to see just what he'd said that was wrong. Not that there was much doubt, of course. He'd touched her on her sore point.

Anyhow, his wristwatch was chiming a reminder of the fact that his psychiatric appointment for the week was coming up.

Morey sighed. The day gives and the day takes away. Blessed is the day that gives only good things.

If any.

The session went badly. Many of the sessions had been going badly, Morey decided; there had been more and more whispering in knots of doctors from which he was excluded, poking and probing in the dark instead of the precise psychic surgery he was used to. Something was wrong, he thought.

Something was. Semmelweiss confirmed it when he adjourned the group session. After the other doctor had left, he sat Morey down for a private talk. On his own time, too—he didn't ask for his usual ration fee. That told Morey how important the problem was.

"Morey," said Semmelweiss, "you're holding back."

"I don't mean to, Doctor," Morey said earnestly.

"Who knows what you 'mean' to do? Part of you 'means' to. We've dug pretty deep and we've found some important things. Now there's something I can't put my finger on. Exploring the mind, Morey, is like sending scouts through cannibal territory. You can't see the cannibals—until it's too late. But if you send a scout through the jungle and he doesn't show up on the other side, it's a fair assumption that something obstructed his way. In that case, we would label the obstruction 'cannibals.' In the case of the human mind, we label the obstruction a 'trauma.' What the trauma is, or what its effects on behavior will be, we have to find out, once we know that it's there."

Morey nodded. All of this was familiar; he couldn't see what Semmelweiss was driving at.

Semmelweiss sighed. "The trouble with healing traumas and penetrating psychic blocks and releasing inhibitions—the trouble with everything we psychiatrists do, in fact, is that we can't afford to do it too well. An inhibited man is under a strain. We try to relieve the strain. But if we succeed completely, leaving him with no inhibitions at all, we have an outlaw, Morey. Inhibitions are often socially necessary. Suppose, for instance, that an average man were not inhibited against blatant waste. It could happen, you know. Suppose that instead of consuming his ration quota in an orderly and responsible way, he did such things as set fire to his house and everything in it or dumped his food allotment in the river.

"When only a few individuals are doing it, we treat the individuals. But if it were done on a mass scale, Morey, it would be the end of society as we know it. Think of the whole collection of anti-social actions that you see in every paper. Man beats wife; wife turns into a harpy; junior smashes up windows; husband starts a black-market stamp racket. And every one of them traces to a basic weakness in the mind's defenses against the most important single anti-social phenomenon–failure to consume."

Morey flared, "That's not fair, Doctor! That was weeks ago! We've certainly been on the ball lately. I was just commended by the Board, in fact–"

The doctor said mildly, "Why so violent, Morey? I only made a general remark."

"It's just natural to resent being accused."

The doctor shrugged. "First, foremost and above all, we do *not* accuse patients of things. We try to help you find things out." He lit his end-of-session cigarette. "Think about it, please. I'll see you next week."

Cherry was composed and unapproachable. She kissed him remotely when he came in. She said, "I called Mother and told her the good news. She and Dad promised to come over here to celebrate."

"Yeah," said Morey. "Darling, what did I say wrong on the phone?"

"They'll be here about six."

"Sure. But what did I say? Was it about the rations? If you're sensitive, I swear I'll never mention them again."

"I *am* sensitive, Morey."

He said despairingly, "I'm sorry. I just–"

He had a better idea. He kissed her.

Cherry was passive at first, but not for long. When he had finished kissing her, she pushed him away and actually giggled. "Let me get dressed for dinner."

"Certainly. Anyhow, I was just–"

She laid a finger on his lips.

He let her escape and, feeling much less tense, drifted into the library. The afternoon papers were waiting for him. Virtuously, he sat down and began going through them in order. Midway through the *World-Telegram-Sun-Post-and-News,* he rang for Henry.

Morey had read clear through to the drama section of the *Times-Herald-Tribune-Mirror* before the robot appeared. "Good evening," it said politely.

"What took you so long?" Morey demanded. "Where are all the robots?"

Robots do not stammer, but there was a distinct pause before Henry said, "Belowstairs, sir. Did you want them for something?"

"Well, no. I just haven't seen them around. Get me a drink."

It hesitated. "Scotch, sir?"

"*Before* dinner? Get me a Manhattan."

"We're all out of Vermouth, sir."

"All out? Would you mind telling me how?"

"It's all used up, sir."

"Now that's just ridiculous," Morey snapped. "We have never run out of liquor in our whole lives and you know it. Good heavens, we just got our allotment in the other day and I certainly—"

He checked himself. There was a sudden flicker of horror in his eyes as he stared at Henry.

"You certainly what, sir?" the robot prompted.

Morey swallowed. "Henry, did I—did I do something I shouldn't have?"

"I'm sure I wouldn't know, sir. It isn't up to me to say what you should and shouldn't do."

"Of course not," Morey agreed grayly.

He sat rigid, staring hopelessly into space, remembering. What he remembered was no pleasure to him at all.

"Henry," he said. "Come along, we're going belowstairs. Right now!"

It had been Tanaquil Bigelow's remark about the robots. *Too many robots—make too much of everything.*

That had implanted the idea; it germinated in Morey's home. More than a little drunk, less than ordinarily inhibited, he had found the problem clear and the answer obvious.

He stared around him in dismal worry. His own robots, following his own orders, given weeks before . . .

Henry said, "It's just what you *told* us to do, sir."

Morey groaned. He was watching a scene of unparalleled activity, and it sent shivers up and down his spine.

There was the butler-robot, hard at work, his copper face expressionless. Dressed in Morey's own sports knickers and golfing shoes, the robot solemnly hit a ball against the wall, picked it up and teed it, hit it again, over and again, with Morey's own clubs. Until the ball wore ragged and was replaced; and the shafts of the clubs leaned out of true; and the close-stitched seams in the clothing began to stretch and abrade.

"My God!" said Morey hollowly.

There were the maid-robots, exquisitely dressed in Cherry's best, walking up and down in the delicate, slim shoes, sitting and rising and bending and turning. The cook-robots and the serving-robots were preparing Dionysian meals.

Morey swallowed. "You–you've been doing this right along," he said to Henry. "That's why the quotas have been filled."

"Oh, yes, sir. Just as you told us."

Morey had to sit down. One of the serving-robots politely scurried over with a chair, brought from upstairs for their new chores.

Waste.

Morey tasted the word between his lips.

Waste.

You never wasted things. You *used* them. If necessary, you drove yourself to the edge of breakdown to use them; you made every breath a burden and every hour a torment to use them, until through diligent consuming and/or occupational merit, you were promoted to the next higher class, and were allowed to consume less frantically. But you didn't wantonly destroy or throw out. You *consumed*.

Morey thought fearfully: When the Board finds out about this . . .

Still, he reminded himself, the Board hadn't found out. It might take some time before they did, for humans, after all, never entered robot quarters. There was no law against it, not even a sacrosanct custom. But there was no reason to. When breaks occurred, which was infrequently, maintenance robots or repair squads came in and put them back in order. Usually the humans involved didn't even know it had happened, because the robots used their own TBR radio circuits and the process was next thing to automatic.

Morey said reprovingly, "Henry, you should have told–well, I mean reminded me about this."

"But, sir!" Henry protested. "'Don't tell a living soul,' you said. You made it a direct order."

"Umph. Well, keep it that way. I–uh–I have to go back upstairs. Better get the rest of the robots started on dinner."

Morey left, not comfortably.

The dinner to celebrate Morey's promotion was difficult. Morey liked Cherry's parents. Old Elon, after the pre-marriage inquisition that father must inevitably give to daughter's suitor, had buckled right down to the job of adjustment. The old folks were good about not interfering, good about keeping their superior social status to themselves, good about helping out on the budget—at least once a week, they could be relied on to come over for a hearty meal, and Mrs. Elon had more than once remade some of Cherry's new dresses to fit herself, even to the extent of wearing all the high-point ornamentation.

And they had been wonderful about the wedding gifts, when Morey and their daughter got married. The most any member of Morey's family had been willing to take was a silver set or a few crystal table pieces. The Elons had come through with a dazzling promise to accept a car, a bird-bath for their garden and a complete set of living-room furniture! Of course, they could afford it—they had to consume so little that it wasn't much strain for them even to take gifts of that magnitude. But without their help, Morey knew, the first few months of matrimony would have been even tougher consuming than they were.

But on this particular night it was hard for Morey to like anyone. He responded with monosyllables; he barely grunted when Elon proposed a toast to his promotion and his brilliant future. He was preoccupied.

Rightly so. Morey, in his deepest, bravest searching, could find no clue in his memory as to just what the punishment might be for what he had done. But he had a sick certainty that trouble lay ahead.

Morey went over his problem so many times that an anesthesia set in. By the time dinner was ended and he and his father-in-law were in the den with their brandy, he was more or less functioning again.

Elon, for the first time since Morey had known him, offered him one of *his* cigars. "You're Grade Five—can afford to smoke somebody else's now, hey?"

"Yeah," Morey said glumly.

There was a moment of silence. Then Elon, as punctilious as any companion-robot, coughed and tried again. "Remember being peaked till I hit Grade Five," he reminisced meaningfully. "Consuming keeps a man on the go, all right. Things piled up at the law office, couldn't be taken care of while ration points piled up, too. And consuming comes first, of course—that's a citizen's prime duty. Mother and I had our share of grief over that, but a couple that wants to make a go of marriage and citizenship just pitches in and does the job, hey?"

Morey repressed a shudder and managed to nod.

"Best thing about upgrading," Elon went on, as if he had elicited a satisfactory answer, "don't have to spend so much time consuming, give more attention to work. Greatest luxury in the world, work. Wish I had as much stamina as you young fellows. Five days a week in court are about all I can manage. Hit six for a while, relaxed first time in my life, but my doctor made me cut down. Said we can't overdo pleasures. You'll be working two days a week now, hey?"

Morey produced another nod.

Elon drew deeply on his cigar, his eyes bright as they watched Morey. He was visibly puzzled, and Morey, even in his half-daze, could recognize the exact moment at which Elon drew the wrong inference. "Ah, everything okay with you and Cherry?" he asked diplomatically.

"Fine!" Morey exclaimed. "Couldn't be better!"

"Good, good." Elon changed the subject with almost an audible wrench. "Speaking of court, had an interesting case the other day. Young fellow–year or two younger than you, I guess–came in with a Section Ninety-seven on him. Know what that is? Breaking and entering!"

"Breaking and entering," Morey repeated wonderingly, interested in spite of himself. "Breaking and entering what?"

"Houses. Old term; law's full of them. Originally applied to stealing things. Still does, I discovered."

"You mean he *stole* something?" Morey asked in bewilderment.

"Exactly! He *stole*. Strangest thing I ever came across. Talked it over with one of his bunch of lawyers later; new one on him, too. Seems this kid had a girl friend, nice kid but a little, you know, plump. She got interested in art."

"There's nothing wrong with that," Morey said.

"Nothing wrong with her, either. She didn't do anything. She didn't like him too much, though. Wouldn't marry him. Kid got to thinking about how he could get her to change her mind and–well, you know that big Mondrian in the Museum?"

"I've never been there," Morey said, somewhat embarrassed.

"Um. Ought to try it some day, boy. Anyway, comes closing time at the Museum the other day, this kid sneaks in. He steals the painting. That's right–*steals* it. Takes it to give to the girl."

Morey shook his head blankly. "I never heard of anything like that in my life."

"Not many have. Girl wouldn't take it, by the way. Got scared when he brought it to her. She must've tipped off the police, I guess.

Somebody did. Took 'em three hours to find it, even when they knew it was hanging on a wall. Pretty poor kid. Forty-two room house."

"And there was a *law* against it?" Morey asked. "I mean it's like making a law against breathing."

"Certainly was. Old law, of course. Kid got set back two grades. Would have been more but, my God, he was only a Grade Three as it was."

"Yeah," said Morey, wetting his lips. "Say, Dad—"

"Um?"

Morey cleared his throat. "Uh—I wonder—I mean what's the penalty, for instance, for things like—well, misusing rations or anything like that?"

Elon's eyebrows went high. "Misusing rations?"

"Say you had a liquor ration, it might be, and instead of drinking it, you—well, flushed it down the drain or something . . ."

His voice trailed off. Elon was frowning. He said, "Funny thing, seems I'm not as broadminded as I thought I was. For some reason, I don't find that amusing."

"Sorry," Morey croaked.

And he certainly was.

It might be dishonest, but it was doing him a lot of good, for days went by and no one seemed to have penetrated his secret. Cherry was happy. Wainwright found occasion after occasion to pat Morey's back. The wages of sin were turning out to be prosperity and happiness.

There was a bad moment when Morey came home to find Cherry in the middle of supervising a team of packing-robots; the new house, suitable to his higher grade, was ready, and they were expected to move in the next day. But Cherry hadn't been belowstairs, and Morey had his household robots clean up the evidences of what they had been doing before the packers got that far.

The new house was, by Morey's standards, pure luxury.

It was only fifteen rooms. Morey had shrewdly retained one more robot than was required for a Class Five, and had been allowed a compensating deduction in the size of his house.

The robot quarters were less secluded than in the old house, though, and that was a disadvantage. More than once Cherry had snuggled up to him in the delightful intimacy of their one bed in their single bedroom and said, with faint curiosity, "I wish they'd stop that noise." And Morey had promised to speak to Henry about it in the morning. But there was nothing he could say to Henry, of course, unless he ordered Henry to stop the tireless consuming through each of the day's twenty-four hours that kept them always ahead, but never quite far enough ahead, of the inexorable weekly increment of ration quotas.

But, though Cherry might once in a while have a moment's curiosity about what the robots were doing, she was not likely to be able to guess at the facts. Her upbringing was, for once, on Morey's side—she knew so little of the grind, grind, grind of consuming that was the lot of the lower classes that she scarcely noticed that there was less of it.

Morey almost, sometimes, relaxed.

He thought of many ingenious chores for robots, and the robots politely and emotionlessly obeyed.

Morey was a success.

It wasn't all gravy. There was a nervous moment for Morey when the quarterly survey report came in the mail. As the day for the Ration Board to check over the degree of wear on the turned-in discards came due, Morey began to sweat. The clothing and furniture and household goods the robots had consumed for him were very nearly in shreds. It had to look plausible, that was the big thing—no normal person would wear a hole completely through the knee of a pair of pants, as Henry had done with his dress suit before Morey stopped him. Would the Board question it?

Worse, was there something about the *way* the robots consumed the stuff that would give the whole show away? Some special wear point in the robot anatomy, for instance, that would rub a hole where no human's body could, or stretch a seam that should normally be under no strain at all?

It was worrisome. But the worry was needless. When the report of survey came, Morey let out a long-held breath. *Not a single item disallowed!*

Morey was a success—and so was his scheme!

To the successful man come the rewards of success. Morey arrived home one evening after a hard day's work at the office and was alarmed to find another car parked in his drive. It was a tiny two-seater, the sort affected by top officials and the very well-to-do.

Right then and there Morey learned the first half of the embezzler's lesson: Anything different is dangerous. He came uneasily into his own home, fearful that some high officer of the Ration Board had come to ask questions.

But Cherry was glowing. "Mr. Porfirio is a newspaper feature writer and he wants to write you up for their 'Consumers of Distinction' page! Morey, I *couldn't* be more proud!"

"Thanks," said Morey glumly. "Hello."

Mr. Porfirio shook Morey's hand warmly. "I'm not exactly from a newspaper," he corrected. "Trans-video Press is what it is, actually. We're a news wire service; we supply forty-seven hundred papers with news and feature material. Every one of them," he added complacently, "on the required consumption list of Grades One through Six inclusive. We have a Sunday supplement self-help feature on consuming problems and we like to—well, give credit where credit is due. You've established an enviable record, Mr. Fry. We'd like to tell our readers about it."

"Um," said Morey. "Let's go in the drawing room."

"Oh, no!" Cherry said firmly. "I want to hear this. He's so modest, Mr. Porfirio, you'd really never know what kind of a man he is just to listen to him talk. Why, my goodness, I'm his wife and I swear *I* don't know how he does all the consuming he does. He simply—"

"Have a drink, Mr. Porfirio," Morey said, against all etiquette. "Rye? Scotch? Bourbon? Gin-and-tonic? Brandy Alexander? Dry Manha—I mean what would you like?" He became conscious that he was babbling like a fool.

"Anything," said the newsman. "Rye is fine. Now, Mr. Fry, I notice you've fixed up your place very attractively here and your wife says that your country home is just as nice. As soon as I came in, I said to myself, 'Beautiful home. Hardly a stick of furniture that isn't absolutely necessary. Might be a Grade Six or Seven.' And Mrs. Fry says the other place is even barer."

"She does, does she?" Morey challenged sharply. "Well, let me tell you, Mr. Porfirio, that every last scrap of my furniture allowance is accounted for! I don't know what you're getting at, but—"

"Oh, I certainly didn't mean to imply anything like *that!* I just want to get some information from you that I can pass on to our readers. You know, to sort of help them do as well as yourself. How *do* you do it?"

Morey swallowed. "We—uh—well, we just keep after it. Hard work, that's all."

Porfirio nodded admiringly. "Hard work," he repeated, and fished a triple-folded sheet of paper out of his pocket to make notes on. "Would you say," he went on, "that anyone could do as well as you simply by devoting himself to it—setting a regular schedule, for example, and keeping to it very strictly?"

"Oh, yes," said Morey.

"In other words, it's only a matter of doing what you have to do every day?"

"That's it exactly. I handle the budget in my house–more experience than my wife, you see–but no reason a woman can't do it."

"Budgeting," Porfirio recorded approvingly. "That's our policy, too."

The interview was not the terror it had seemed, not even when Porfirio tactfully called attention to Cherry's slim waistline ("So many housewives, Mrs. Fry, find it difficult to keep from being–well, a little plump") and Morey had to invent endless hours on the exercise machines, while Cherry looked faintly perplexed, but did not interrupt.

From the interview, however, Morey learned the second half of the embezzler's lesson. After Porfirio had gone, he leaped in and spoke more than a little firmly to Cherry. "That business of exercise, dear. We really have to start doing it. I don't know if you've noticed it, but you *are* beginning to get just a trifle heavier and we don't want that to happen, do we?"

In the following grim and unnecessary sessions on the mechanical horses, Morey had plenty of time to reflect on the lesson. Stolen treasures are less sweet than one would like, when one dare not enjoy them in the open.

But some of Morey's treasures were fairly earned.

The new Bradmoor K-50 Spin-a-Game, for instance, was his very own. His job was design and creation, and he was a fortunate man in that his efforts were permitted to be expended along the line of greatest social utility–namely, to increase consumption.

The Spin-a-Game was a well-nigh perfect machine for the purpose. "Brilliant," said Wainwright, beaming, when the pilot machine had been put through its first tests. "Guess they don't call me the Talent-picker for nothing. I knew you could do it, boy!"

Even Howland was lavish in his praise. He sat munching on a plate of petits-fours (he was still only a Grade Three) while the tests were going on, and when they were over, he said enthusiastically, "It's a beauty, Morey. That series-corrupter–sensational! Never saw a prettier piece of machinery."

Morey flushed gratefully.

Wainwright left, exuding praise, and Morey patted his pilot model affectionately and admired its polychrome gleam. The looks of the machine, as Wainwright had lectured many a time, were as important as its function: "You have to make them *want* to play it, boy! They won't play it if they don't *see* it!" And consequently the whole K series was distinguished by flashing rainbows of light, provocative strains of music, haunting scents that drifted into the nostrils of the passerby with compelling effect.

Morey had drawn heavily on all the old masterpieces of design—the one-arm bandit, the pinball machine, the juke box. You put your ration book in the hopper. You spun the wheels until you selected the game you wanted to play against the machine. You punched buttons or spun dials or, in any of 325 different ways, you pitted your human skill against the magnetic-taped skills of the machine.

And you lost. You had a chance to win, but the inexorable statistics of the machine's setting made sure that if you played long enough, you had to lose.

That is to say, if you risked a ten-point ration stamp—showing, perhaps, that you had consumed three six-course meals—your statistic return was eight points. You might hit the jackpot and get a thousand points back, and thus be exempt from a whole freezerful of steaks and joints and prepared vegetables; but it seldom happened. Most likely you lost and got nothing.

Got nothing, that is, in the way of your hazarded ration stamps. But the beauty of the machine, which was Morey's main contribution, was that, win or lose, you *always* found a pellet of vitamin-drenched, sugar-coated antibiotic hormone gum in the hopper. You played your game, won or lost your stake, popped your hormone gum into your mouth and played another. By the time that game was ended, the gum was used up, the coating dissolved; you discarded it and started another.

"That's what the man from the NRB liked," Howland told Morey confidentially. "He took a set of schematics back with him; they might install it on *all* new machines. Oh, you're the fair-haired boy, all right!"

It was the first Morey had heard about a man from the National Ration Board. It was good news. He excused himself and hurried to phone Cherry the story of his latest successes. He reached her at her mother's, where she was spending the evening, and she was properly impressed and affectionate. He came back to Howland in a glowing humor.

"Drink?" said Howland diffidently.

"Sure," said Morey. He could afford, he thought, to drink as much of Howland's liquor as he liked; poor guy, sunk in the consuming quicksands of Class Three. Only fair for somebody a little more successful to give him a hand once in a while.

And when Howland, learning that Cherry had left Morey a bachelor for the evening, proposed Uncle Piggotty's again, Morey hardly hesitated at all.

The Bigelows were delighted to see him. Morey wondered briefly if they *had* a home; certainly they didn't seem to spend much time in it.

It turned out they did, because when Morey indicated virtuously that he'd only stopped in at Piggotty's for a single drink before dinner, and Howland revealed that he was free for the evening, they captured Morey and bore him off to their house.

Tanaquil Bigelow was haughtily apologetic. "I don't suppose this is the kind of place Mr. Fry is used to," she observed to her husband, right across Morey, who was standing between them. "Still, we call it home."

Morey made an appropriately polite remark. Actually, the place nearly turned his stomach. It was an enormous glaringly new mansion, bigger even than Morey's former house, stuffed to bursting with bulging sofas and pianos and massive mahogany chairs and tri-D sets and bedrooms and drawing rooms and breakfast rooms and nurseries.

The nurseries were a shock to Morey; it had never occurred to him that the Bigelows had children. But they did and, though the children were only five and eight, they were still up, under the care of a brace of robot nursemaids, doggedly playing with their overstuffed animals and miniature trains.

"You don't know what a comfort Tony and Dick are," Tanaquil Bigelow told Morey. "They consume *so* much more than their rations. Walter says that every family ought to have at least two or three children to, you know, help out. Walter's so intelligent about these things, it's a pleasure to hear him talk. Have you heard his poem, Morey? The one he calls *The Twoness of–*"

Morey hastily admitted that he had. He reconciled himself to a glum evening. The Bigelows had been eccentric but fun back at Uncle Piggotty's. On their own ground, they seemed just as eccentric, but painfully dull.

They had a round of cocktails, and another, and then the Bigelows no longer seemed so dull. Dinner was ghastly, of course; Morey was nouveau-riche enough to be a snob about his relatively Spartan table. But he minded his manners and sampled, with grim concentration, each successive course of chunky protein and rich marinades. With the help of the endless succession of table wines and liqueurs, dinner ended without destroying his evening or his strained digestive system.

And afterward, they were a pleasant company in the Bigelow's ornate drawing room. Tanaquil Bigelow, in consultation with the children, checked over their ration books and came up with the announcement that they would have a brief recital by a pair of robot dancers, followed by string music by a robot quartet. Morey prepared himself for the worst, but found before the dancers were through that he was enjoying himself. Strange lesson for Morey: When you didn't *have* to watch them, the robot entertainers were fun!

"Good night, dears," Tanaquil Bigelow said firmly to the children when the dancers were done. The boys rebelled, naturally, but they went. It was only a matter of minutes, though, before one of them was back, clutching at Morey's sleeve with a pudgy hand.

Morey looked at the boy uneasily, having little experience with children. He said, "Uh–what is it, Tony?"

"Dick, you mean," the boy said. "Gimme your autograph." He poked an engraved pad and a vulgarly jeweled pencil at Morey.

Morey dazedly signed and the child ran off, Morey staring after him. Tanaquil Bigelow laughed and explained, "He saw your name in Porfirio's column. Dick *loves* Porfirio, reads him every day. He's such an intellectual kid, really. He'd always have his nose in a book if I didn't keep after him to play with his trains and watch tri-D."

"That was quite a nice write-up," Walter Bigelow commented–a little enviously, Morey thought. "Bet you make Consumer of the Year. I wish," he sighed, "that we could get a little ahead on the quotas the way you did. But it just never seems to work out. We eat and play and consume like crazy, and somehow at the end of the month we're always a little behind in something–everything keeps piling up–and then the Board sends us a warning, and they call me down and, first thing you know, I've got a couple of hundred added penalty points and we're worse off than before."

"Never you mind," Tanaquil replied staunchly. "Consuming isn't everything in life. You have your work."

Bigelow nodded judiciously and offered Morey another drink. Another drink, however, was not what Morey needed. He was sitting in a rosy glow, less of alcohol than of sheer contentment with the world.

He said suddenly, "Listen."

Bigelow looked up from his own drink. "Eh?"

"If I tell you something that's a *secret,* will you keep it that way?"

Bigelow rumbled, "Why, I guess so, Morey."

But his wife cut in sharply, "Certainly we will, Morey. Of course! What is it?" There was a gleam in her eye, Morey noticed. It puzzled him, but he decided to ignore it.

He said, "About that write-up. I–I'm not such a hot-shot consumer, really, you know. In fact—" All of a sudden, everyone's eyes seemed to be on him. For a tortured moment, Morey wondered if he was doing the right thing. A secret that two people know is compromised, and a secret known to three people is no secret. Still—

"It's like this," he said firmly. "You remember what we were talking about at Uncle Piggotty's that night? Well, when I went home I went down to the robot quarters, and I—"

He went on from there.

Tanaquil Bigelow said triumphantly, "I *knew* it!"

Walter Bigelow gave his wife a mild, reproving look. He declared soberly, "You've done a big thing, Morey. A mighty big thing. God willing, you've pronounced the death sentence on our society as we know it. Future generations will revere the name of Morey Fry." He solemnly shook Morey's hand.

Morey said dazedly, "I *what?*"

Walter nodded. It was a valedictory. He turned to his wife. "Tanaquil, we'll have to call an emergency meeting."

"Of course, Walter," she said devotedly.

"And Morey will have to be there. Yes, you'll have to, Morey; no excuses. We want the Brotherhood to meet you. Right, Howland?"

Howland coughed uneasily. He nodded noncommittally and took another drink.

Morey demanded desperately, "What are you talking about? Howland, you tell me!"

Howland fiddled with his drink. "Well," he said, "it's like Tan was telling you that night. A few of us, well, politically mature persons have formed a little group. We—"

"*Little* group!" Tanaquil Bigelow said scornfully. "Howland, sometimes I wonder if you really catch the spirit of the thing at all! It's everybody, Morey, everybody in the world. Why, there are eighteen of us right here in Old Town! There are *scores more* all over the world! I knew you were up to something like this, Morey. I told Walter so the morning after we met you. I said, 'Walter, mark my words, that man Morey is up to something.' But I must say," she admitted worshipfully, "I didn't know it would have the *scope* of what you're proposing now! Imagine—a whole world of consumers, rising as one man, shouting the name of Morey Fry, fighting the Ration Board with the Board's own weapon—the robots. What poetic justice!"

Bigelow nodded enthusiastically. "Call Uncle Piggotty's, dear," he ordered. "See if you can round up a quorum right now! Meanwhile, Morey and I are going belowstairs. Let's go, Morey—let's get the new world started!"

Morey sat there open-mouthed. He closed it with a snap. "Bigelow," he whispered, "do you mean to say that you're going to spread this idea around through some kind of subversive organization?"

"Subversive?" Bigelow repeated stiffly. "My dear man, *all* creative minds are subversive, whether they operate singly or in such a group as the Brotherhood of Freemen. I scarcely like–"

"Never mind what you like," Morey insisted. "You're going to call a meeting of this Brotherhood and you want *me* to tell them what I just told you. Is that right?"

"Well–yes."

Morey got up. "I wish I could say it's been nice, but it hasn't. Good night!"

And he stormed out before they could stop him.

Out on the street, though, his resolution deserted him. He hailed a robot cab and ordered the driver to take him on the traditional time-killing ride through the park while he made up his mind.

The fact that he had left, of course, was not going to keep Bigelow from going through with his announced intention. Morey remembered, now, fragments of conversation from Bigelow and his wife at Uncle Piggotty's, and cursed himself. They had, it was perfectly true, said and hinted enough about politics and purposes to put him on his guard. All that nonsense about twoness had diverted him from what should have been perfectly clear: They were subversives indeed.

He glanced at his watch. Late, but not too late; Cherry would still be at her parents' home.

He leaned forward and gave the driver their address. It was like beginning the first of a hundred-shot series of injections: you know it's going to cure you, but it hurts just the same.

Morey said manfully: "And that's it, sir. I know I've been a fool. I'm willing to take the consequences."

Old Elon rubbed his jaw thoughtfully. "Um," he said.

Cherry and her mother had long passed the point where they could say anything at all; they were seated side by side on a couch across the room, listening with expressions of strain and incredulity.

Elon said abruptly, "Excuse me. Phone call to make." He left the room to make a brief call and returned. He said over his shoulder to his wife, "Coffee. We'll need it. Got a problem here."

Morey said, "Do you think–I mean what should I do?"

Elon shrugged, then, surprisingly, grinned. "What can you do?" he demanded cheerfully. "Done plenty already, I'd say. Drink some coffee. Call I made," he explained, "was to Jim, my law clerk. He'll be here in a minute. Get some dope from Jim, then we'll know better."

Cherry came over to Morey and sat beside him. All she said was, "Don't worry," but to Morey it conveyed all the meaning in the world. He returned the pressure of her hand with a feeling of deepest relief. Hell, he said to himself, why *should* I worry? Worst they can do to me is drop me a couple of grades and what's so bad about that?

He grimaced involuntarily. He had remembered his own early struggles as a Class One and what *was* so bad about that.

The law clerk arrived, a smallish robot with a battered stainless-steel hide and dull coppery features. Elon took the robot aside for a terse conversation before he came back to Morey.

"As I thought," he said in satisfaction. "No precedent. No laws prohibiting. Therefore no crime."

"Thank heaven!" Morey said in ecstatic relief.

Elon shook his head. "They'll probably give you a reconditioning and you can't expect to keep your Grade Five. Probably call it anti-social behavior. Is, isn't it?"

Dashed, Morey said, "Oh." He frowned briefly, then looked up. "All right, Dad, if I've got it coming to me, I'll take my medicine."

"Way to talk," Elon said approvingly. "Now go home. Get a good night's sleep. First thing in the morning, go to the Ration Board. Tell 'em the whole story, beginning to end. They'll be easy on you." Elon hesitated. "Well, fairly easy," he amended. "I hope."

The condemned man ate a hearty breakfast.

He had to. That morning, as Morey awoke, he had the sick certainty that he was going to be consuming triple rations for a long, long time to come.

He kissed Cherry good-by and took the long ride to the Ration Board in silence. He even left Henry behind.

At the Board, he stammered at a series of receptionist robots and was finally brought into the presence of a mildly supercilious young man named Hachette.

"My name," he started, "is Morey Fry. I–I've come to–talk over something I've been doing with–"

"Certainly, Mr. Fry," said Hachette. "I'll take you in to Mr. Newman right away."

"Don't you want to know what I did?" demanded Morey.

Hachette smiled. "What makes you think we don't know?" he said, and left.

That was Surprise Number One.

Newman explained it. He grinned at Morey and ruefully shook his head. "All the time we get this," he complained. "People just don't take the trouble to learn anything about the world around them. Son," he demanded, "what do you think a robot is?"

Morey said, "Huh?"

"I mean how do you think it operates? Do you think it's just a kind of a man with a tin skin and wire nerves?"

"Why, no. It's a machine, of course. It isn't *human.*"

Newman beamed. "Fine!" he said. "It's a machine. It hasn't got flesh or blood or intestines–or a brain. Oh–" he held up a hand–"robots are *smart* enough. I don't mean that. But an electronic thinking machine, Mr. Fry, takes about as much space as the house you're living in. It has to. Robots don't carry brains around with them; brains are too heavy and much too bulky."

"Then how do they think?"

"With their brains, of course."

"But you just said–"

"I said they didn't *carry* them. Each robot is in constant radio communication with the Master Control on its TBR circuit–the 'Talk Between Robots' radio. Master Control gives the answer, the robot acts."

"I see," said Morey. "Well, that's very interesting, but–"

"But you still don't see," said Newman. "Figure it out. If the robot gets information from Master Control, do you see that Master Control in return necessarily gets information from the robot?"

"Oh," said Morey. Then, louder, "Oh! You mean that all my robots have been–" The words wouldn't come.

Newman nodded in satisfaction. "Every bit of information of that sort comes to us as a matter of course. Why, Mr. Fry, if you hadn't come in today, we would have been sending for you within a very short time."

That was the second surprise. Morey bore up under it bravely. After all, it changed nothing, he reminded himself.

He said, "Well, be that as it may, sir, here I am. I came in of my own free will. I've been using my robots to consume my ration quotas–"

"Indeed you have," said Newman.

"–and I'm willing to sign a statement to that effect any time you like. I don't know what the penalty is, but I'll take it. I'm guilty; I admit my guilt."

Newman's eyes were wide. "Guilty?" he repeated. "Penalty?"

Morey was startled. "Why, yes," he said. "I'm not denying anything."

"Penalties," repeated Newman musingly. Then he began to laugh. He laughed, Morey thought, to considerable excess; Morey saw nothing he could laugh at, himself, in the situation. But the situation, Morey was forced to admit, was rapidly getting completely incomprehensible.

"Sorry," said Newman at last, wiping his eyes, "but I couldn't help it. Penalties! Well, Mr. Fry, let me set your mind at rest. I wouldn't worry about the penalties if I were you. As soon as the reports began coming through on what you had done with your robots, we naturally assigned a special team to keep observing you, and we forwarded a report to the national headquarters. We made certain—ah—recommendations in it and—well, to make a long story short, the answers came back yesterday.

"Mr. Fry, the National Ration Board is delighted to know of your contribution toward improving our distribution problem. Pending a further study, a tentative program has been adopted for setting up consuming-robot units all over the country based on your scheme. Penalties? Mr. Fry, you're a *hero!*"

A hero has responsibilities. Morey's were quickly made clear to him. He was allowed time for a brief reassuring visit to Cherry, a triumphal tour of his old office, and then he was rushed off to Washington to be quizzed. He found the National Ration Board in a frenzy of work.

"The most important job we've ever done," one of the high officers told him. "I wouldn't be surprised if it's the last one we ever have! Yes, sir, we're trying to put ourselves out of business for good and we don't want a single thing to go wrong."

"Anything I can do to help—" Morey began diffidently.

"You've done fine, Mr. Fry. Gave us just the push we've been needing. It was there all the time for us to see, but we were too close to the forest to see the trees, if you get what I mean. Look, I'm not much on rhetoric and this is the biggest step mankind has taken in centuries and I can't put it into words. Let me show you what we've been doing."

He and a delegation of other officials of the Ration Board and men whose names Morey had repeatedly seen in the newspapers took Morey on an inspection tour of the entire plant.

"It's a closed cycle, you see," he was told, as they looked over a chamber of industriously plodding consumer-robots working off a shipment of shoes. "Nothing is permanently lost. If you want a car, you get one of the newest and best. If not, your car gets driven by a robot until it's ready to be turned in and a new one gets built for next year. We don't lose the metals—they can be salvaged. All we lose is a little power and labor. And the Sun and the atom give us all the power we need, and the robots give us more labor than we can use. Same thing applies, of course, to all products."

"But what's in it for the robots?" Morey asked.

"I beg your pardon?" one of the biggest men in the country said uncomprehendingly.

Morey had a difficult moment. His analysis had conditioned him against waste and this decidedly was sheer destruction of goods, no matter how scientific the jargon might be.

"If the consumer is just using up things for the sake of using them up," he said doggedly, realizing the danger he was inviting, "we could use wear-and-tear machines instead of robots. After all why waste *them?*"

They looked at each other worriedly.

"But that's what *you* were doing," one pointed out with a faint note of threat.

"Oh, no!" Morey quickly objected. "I built in satisfaction circuits —my training in design, you know. Adjustable circuits, of course."

"Satisfaction circuits?" he was asked. "Adjustable?"

"Well, sure. If the robot gets no satisfaction out of using up things—"

"Don't talk nonsense," growled the Ration Board official. "Robots aren't human. How do you make them feel satisfaction? And adjustable satisfaction at that!"

Morey explained. It was a highly technical explanation, involving the use of great sheets of paper and elaborate diagrams. But there were trained men in the group and they became even more excited than before.

"Beautiful!" one cried in scientific rapture. "Why, it takes care of every possible moral, legal and psychological argument!"

"What does?" the Ration Board official demanded. "How?"

"You tell him, Mr. Fry."

Morey tried and couldn't. But he could *show* how his principle operated. The Ration Board lab was turned over to him, complete with more assistants than he knew how to give orders to, and they built satisfaction circuits for a squad of robots working in a hat factory.

Then Morey gave his demonstration. The robots manufactured hats of all sorts. He adjusted the circuits at the end of the day and the robots began trying on the hats, squabbling over them, each coming away triumphantly with a huge and diverse selection. Their metallic features were incapable of showing pride or pleasure, but both were evident in the way they wore their hats, their fierce possessiveness . . . and their faster, neater, more intensive, more *dedicated* work to produce a still greater quantity of hats . . . which they also were allowed to own.

"You see?" an engineer exclaimed delightedly. "They can be adjusted to *want* hats, to wear them lovingly, to wear the hats to pieces. And not just for the sake of wearing them out–the hats are an incentive for them!"

"But how can we go on producing just hats and more hats?" the Ration Board man asked puzzledly. "Civilization does not live by hats alone."

"That," said Morey modestly, "is the beauty of it. Look."

He set the adjustment of the satisfaction circuit as porter robots brought in skids of gloves. The hat-manufacturing robots fought over the gloves with the same mechanical passion as they had for hats.

"And that can apply to anything we–or the robots–produce," Morey added. "Everything from pins to yachts. But the point is that they get satisfaction from possession, and the craving can be regulated according to the glut in various industries, and the robots show their appreciation by working harder." He hesitated. "That's what I did for my servant-robots. It's a feedback, you see. Satisfaction leads to more work–and *better* work–and that means more goods, which they can be made to want, which means incentive to work, and so on, all around."

"Closed cycle," whispered the Ration Board man in awe. "A *real* closed cycle this time!"

And so the inexorable laws of supply and demand were irrevocably repealed. No longer was mankind hampered by inadequate supply or drowned by overproduction. What mankind needed was there. What the race did not require passed into the insatiable–and adjustable–robot maw. Nothing was wasted.

For a pipeline has two ends.

Morey was thanked, complimented, rewarded, given a ticker-tape parade through the city, and put on a plane back home. By that time, the Ration Board had liquidated itself.

Cherry met him at the airport. They jabbered excitedly at each other all the way to the house.

In their own living room, they finished the kiss they had greeted each other with. At last Cherry broke away, laughing.

Morey said, "Did I tell you I'm through with Bradmoor? From

now on I work for the Board as civilian consultant. *And,*" he added impressively, "starting right away, I'm a Class Eight!"

"My!" gasped Cherry, so worshipfully that Morey felt a twinge of conscience.

He said honestly, "Of course, if what they were saying in Washington is so, the classes aren't going to mean much pretty soon. Still, it's quite an honor."

"It certainly is," Cherry said staunchly. "Why, Dad's only a Class Eight himself and he's been a judge for I don't know *how* many years."

Morey pursed his lips. "We can't all be fortunate," he said generously. "Of course, the classes still will count for *something*—that is, a Class One will have so much to consume in a year, a Class Two will have a little less, and so on. But each person in each class will have robot help, you see, to do the actual consuming. The way it's going to be, special facsimile robots will—"

Cherry flagged him down. "I know, dear. Each family gets a robot duplicate of every person in the family."

"Oh," said Morey, slightly annoyed. "How did you know?"

"Ours came yesterday," she explained. "The man from the Board said we were the first in the area—because it was your idea, of course. They haven't even been activated yet. I've still got them in the Green Room. Want to see them?"

"Sure," said Morey buoyantly. He dashed ahead of Cherry to inspect the results of his own brainstorm. There they were, standing statue-still against the wall, waiting to be energized to begin their endless tasks.

"Yours is real pretty," Morey said gallantly. "But—say, is that thing supposed to look like me?" He inspected the chromium face of the man-robot disapprovingly.

"Only roughly, the man said." Cherry was right behind him. "Notice anything else?"

Morey leaned closer, inspecting the features of the facsimile robot at a close range. "Well, no," he said. "It's got a kind of squint that I don't like, but—Oh, you mean *that!*" He bent over to examine a smaller robot, half hidden between the other pair. It was less than two feet high, big-headed, pudgy-limbed, thick-bellied. In fact, Morey thought wonderingly, it looked almost like—

"My God!" Morey spun around, staring wide-eyed at his wife. "You mean—"

"I mean," said Cherry, blushing slightly.

Morey reached out to grab her in his arms.

"Darling!" he cried. "Why didn't you *tell* me?"

The Snowmen

TANDY said, "Not tonight, Howard. Why, I'm practically in bed already, see?" And she flipped the vision switch just for a second; long enough so I could get a glimpse of a sheer negligee and feathered slippers and, well, naturally, I couldn't quite believe that she *really* wanted me to stay away. Nobody made her flip that switch.

I said, "Just for a minute, Tandy. One drink. A little music, perhaps a dance—"

"Howard, you're *terrible.*"

"No, dearest," I said, fast and soft and close to the phone, "I'm not terrible, I'm only very much in love. Don't say no. Don't say a word. Just close your eyes, and in ten minutes I'll be there, and—"

And then, confound them, they had to start that yapping. *Bleep-bleep* on the phone, and then: "Attention all citizens! Stand by for orders! Your world federal government has proclaimed a state of unlimited emergency. All heatpump power generators in excess of eight horsepower per—"

I slammed down the phone in disgust. Leave it to them! Yack-yack on the phone lines at all hours of the day and night, no consideration for anybody. I was disgusted, and then, when I got to thinking, not so disgusted. Why not go right over? She hadn't said no; she hadn't had a chance.

So I got the Bug out, locked the doors and set the thermostats, and I set out.

It isn't two miles to Tandy's place. Five years ago, even, I could make it in three or four minutes; now it takes ten. I call it a damned shame, though no one else seems to care. But I've always been more adventurous than most, and more social-minded. Jeffrey Otis wouldn't care about things like that. Ittel du Bois wouldn't even know—his idea is to bury his nose in a drama-tape when he goes out of the house, and let the Bug drive itself. But not me. I like to drive, even if you can't see anything and the autopilot is perfectly reliable. Life is for *living,* I say. *Live* it.

I don't pretend to understand this scientific stuff either—leave science to the people who like it, is another thing I say. But you know how when you're in your Bug and you've set the direction-finder for somebody's place, there's this *beepbeepbeepbeep* when you're going right and a *beep*SQUAWK or a SQUAWK*beep* when you go off the track? It has something to do with radio, only not radio—that's out of the question now, they say—but with sort of telephoned messages through the magma of the Earth's core. Well, that's what it says in the manual, and I know because one day I glanced through it. Anyway. Excuse me for getting technical. But I was going along toward Tandy's place, my mind full of warm pleasures and anticipating, and suddenly the *beepbeepbeep* stopped, and there was a sort of crystal chime and then a voice: "Attention! Operation of private vehicles is forbidden! Return to your home and listen to telephoned orders every hour on the hour!" And then the *beepbeepbeep* again. Why, they'd even learned how to jam the direction-finder with their confounded yapping! It was very annoying, and angrily I snapped the DF off. Daring? Yes, but I have to say that I'm an excellent driver, wonderful sense of direction, hardly need the direction-finder in the first place. And anyway we were close; the thermal pointers in the nose had already picked up Tandy's termperature gradient.

Tandy opened the locks herself. "Howard," she said in soft surprise, clutching the black film of negligee. "You really came. Oh, naughty Howard!"

"My darling!" I breathed, reaching out for her. But she dodged.

"No, Howard," she said severely, "you mustn't do that. Sit down for a moment. Have one little drink. And then I'm going to have to be terribly stubborn and send you right home, dear."

"Of course," I said, because that was, after all, the rules of the game. "Just one drink, certainly." But, damn it, she seemed to mean it! She wasn't a bit hospitable—I mean, not *really* hospitable. She seemed friendly enough and she talked sweetly enough, but. . . . Well, for example, she sat in the positively-not chair. I can tell you a lot about the way Tandy furnished her place. There's the wing chair by the fire, and that's a bad sign because the arms are slippery and there's only room for one actually sitting in it. There's the love seat—speaks for itself, doesn't it? And there's the big sofa and, best of all, the bearskin rug. But way at the other end of the scale is this perfectly straight, armless cane-bottomed thing, with a Ming vase on one side of it and a shrub of some kind or other rooted in a bowl on the other, and that's where she sat.

I grumbled, "I shouldn't have come at all."

"What, Howard?"

"I said, uh, I couldn't come any, uh, faster. I mean, I came as fast as I could."

"I know you did, you brute," she said roguishly, and stopped the Martini-mixer. It poured us each a drink. "Now don't dawdle," she said primly. "I've got to get some sleep."

"To love," I said, and sipped the top off the Martini.

"Don't do that," she warned. I got up from the floor at her feet and went back to another chair. "You," she said, "are a hard man to handle, Howard, dear." But she giggled.

Well, you can't win them all. I finished my drink and, I don't know, I think I would have hung around about five minutes just to show who was boss and then got back in the Bug and gone home. Frankly, I was a little sleepy. It had been a wearing day, hours and hours with the orchids and then listening to all nine Beethoven symphonies in a row while I played solitaire.

But I heard the annunciator bell tinkle.

I stared at Tandy.

"My," she said prettily, "I wonder who that can be?"

"Tandy!"

"Probably someone dull," she shrugged. "I won't answer. Now, do be a good boy and–"

"Tandy! How *could* you?" My mind raced; there was only one conclusion. "Tandy, do you have Ittel du Bois coming here tonight? Don't lie to me!"

"Howard, what a *terrible* thing to say. Ittel was *last* year."

"Tell me the truth!"

"I do not!" And she was angry. I'd hurt her, no doubt of it.

"Then it must be Jeffrey. I won't stand for it. I won the toss fair and square. Why can't we wait until next year? It isn't *decent*. I–"

She stood up, her blue eyes smoldering. "Howard McGuiness, you'd better go before you say something I won't be able to forgive."

I stood my ground. "Then who is it?"

"Oh, darn it," she said, and kicked viciously at the shrub by her left foot, "see for yourself. Answer the door."

So I did.

Now, I know Ittel du Bois's Bug–it's a Buick–and I know Jeff Otis's. It wasn't either one of them. The vehicle outside Tandy's door parked next to mine was a very strange looking Bug indeed. For one thing, it was only about eight feet long.

A bank of infrared lamps glowed on, bathing it in heat; the caked ice that forms in the dead spots along the hull, behind the treads and so on, melted, plopped off, turned into water and ran into the drain grille. You know how a Bug will crack and twang when it's being warmed up? They all do.

This one didn't.

It didn't make a sound. It was so silent that I could hear the snip-snip of Tandy's automatic load adjuster, throwing another heatpump into circuit to meet the drain of the infrared lamps. But no sound from the Bug outside. Also it didn't have caterpillar treads. Also it had—well, you can believe this or not—it had windows.

"You see?" said Tandy, in a voice colder than the four miles of ice overhead. "Now would you like to apologize to me?"

"I apologize," I said in a voice that hardly got past my lips. "I—" I stopped and swallowed. I begged, "Please, Tandy, what is it?"

She lit a cigarette unsteadily. "Well, I don't rightly know. I'm kind of glad you're here, Howard," she confessed. "Maybe I shouldn't have tried to get rid of you."

"Tell me!"

She glanced at the Bug. "All right. I'll make it fast. I got a call from this, uh, fellow. I couldn't understand him very well. But. . . ."

She looked at me sidewise.

"I understand," I said. "You thought he might be a mark."

She nodded.

"And you wouldn't cut me in!" I cried angrily. "Tandy, that's mean! When I found old Buchmayr dead, didn't I cut you in on looting his place? Didn't I give you first pick of everything you wanted—except heatpumps and machine patterns, of course."

"I know, dear," she said miserably, "but—hush! He's coming out."

She was looking out the window. I looked too.

And then we looked at each other. That fellow out of the strange Bug, he was as strange as his vehicle. He might be a mark or he might not; but of one thing I was pretty sure, and that was that he wasn't human.

No. Not with huge white eyes and a serpentine frill of orange tendrils instead of hair.

At once all my lethargy and weariness vanished.

"Tandy," I cried, "he isn't human!"

"I know," she whispered.

"But don't you know what this means? He's an alien! He must

come from another planet—perhaps from another star. Tandy, this is the most important thing that ever happened to us." I thought fast. "Tell you what," I said, "you let him in while I get around the side shaft—it's defrosted, isn't it? Good." I hurried. At the side door I stopped and looked at her affectionately. "Dear Tandy," I said. "And you thought this was just an ordinary mark. You see? You *need* me." And I was off, leaving her that thought to chew on as she welcomed her visitor.

I took a good long time in the stranger's Bug. Human or monster, I could rely on Tandy to keep him occupied, so I was very thorough and didn't rush, and came out with a splendid supply of what seemed to be storage batteries. I couldn't quite make them out, but I was sure that power was in them somehow or other; and if there was power, the heatpump would find a way to suck it out. Those I took the opportunity of tucking away in my own Bug before I went back in Tandy's place. No use bothering her about them.

She was sitting in the wing chair, and the stranger was nowhere in sight. I raised my brows. She nodded. "Well," I said, "he was your guest. I won't interfere."

Tandy was looking quiet, relaxed and happy. "What about the Bug?"

"Oh, lots of things," I said. "Plenty of metal! And food—a lot of food, Tandy. Of course, we'll have to go easy on it, till we find out if we can digest it, but it smells *delicious*. And—"

"Pumps?" she demanded.

"Funny," I said. "They don't seem to use them." She scowled. "Honestly, dearest! You can see for yourself—everything I found is piled right outside the door."

"What isn't in your Bug, you mean."

"Tandy!"

She glowered a moment longer, then smiled like the sun bursting through clouds on an old video tape. "No matter, Howard," she said tenderly, "we've got plenty. Let's have another Martini, shall we?"

"Of course." I waited and took the glass. "To love," I toasted. "And to crime. By the way, did you talk to him first?"

"Oh, for *hours,*" she said crossly. "Yap, yap. He's as bad as the feds."

I got up and idly walked across the room to the light switch. "Did he say anything interesting?"

"Not very. He spoke a very poor grade of English, to begin with.

Said he learned it off old radio broadcasts, of all things. They float around forever out in space, it seems."

I switched off the lights. "That better?"

She nodded drowsily, got up to refill her glass, and sat down again in the love seat. "He was awfully interested in the heatpumps," she said drowsily.

I put a tape on the player–Tchaikovsky. Tandy is a fool for violins. "He liked them?"

"Oh, in a way. He thought they were clever. But dangerous, he said."

"Him and the feds," I murmured, sitting down next to her. Click-click, and our individual body armor went on stand-by alert. At the first hostile move it would block us off, set up a force field–well, I *think* it's called a force field. "The feds are always yapping about the pumps too. Did I tell you? They're even cutting in on the RDF channels now."

"Oh, Howard! That's *too* much." She sat up and got another drink –and sat, this time, on the wide, low sofa. She giggled.

"What's the matter, dear?" I asked, coming over beside her.

"He was so *funny*. Ya-ta-ta-ta, ya-ta-ta-ta, all about how the heat-pumps were ruining the world."

"Just like the feds." Click-click some more, as I put my arm around her shoulders.

"Just like," she agreed. "He said it was evidently extremely high technology that produced a device that took heat out of its surrounding ambient environment, but had we ever thought of what would happen when *all* the heat was gone?"

"Crazy," I murmured into the base of her throat.

"Absolutely. As though all the heat could ever be gone! Absolute zero, he called it; said we're only eight or ten degrees from it now. That's why the snow, he said." I made a sound of polite disgust. "Yes, that's what he said. He said it wasn't just snow, it was frozen air– oxygen and nitrogen and all those things. We've frozen the Earth solid, he says, and now it's so shiny that its libido is nearly perfect."

I sat up sharply, then relaxed. "Oh. Not libido, dear. Albedo. That means it's shiny."

"That's what he said. He said the feds were right. . . . Howard. Howard, dear. Listen to me."

"Ssh," I murmured. "Did he say anything else?"

"But Howard! Please. You're–"

"Ssh."

She relaxed, and then in a moment giggled again. "Howard, wait. I forgot to tell you the funniest part."

It was irritating, but I could afford to be patient. "What was that, dearest?"

"He didn't have any personal armor!"

I sat up. I couldn't help it. "What?"

"None at all! Naked as a baby. So that proves he isn't human, doesn't it? I mean, if he can't take the simplest *care* of himself, he's only a kind of animal, right?"

I thought. "Well, I suppose so," I said. Really, the concept was hard to swallow.

"Good," she said, "because he's, well, in the freezer. I didn't want to *waste* him, Howard. And it isn't as if he was human."

I thought for a second. Well, why not? You get tired of rabbits and mice, and since there hasn't been any open sky for pasturing for nearly fifty years, that's about all there is. Now that I thought back on it, he was kind of plump and appetizing at that.

And, in any case, that was a problem for later on. I reached out idly and touched the button that controlled the last light in the room, the electric fireplace itself. "Oh," I said, pausing. "Where did he come from?"

"Sorry," her muffled voice came. "I forgot to ask."

I reached out thoughtfully and found my glass. There was a little bit left; I drained it off. Funny that the creature should bother to come down. In the old days, yes; back when Earth was open to the sky, you might expect aliens to come skyrocketing down from the stars and all that. But he'd come all the way from—well, from wherever—and for what? Just to make a little soup for the pot, to donate a little metal and power. It was funny, in a way. I couldn't help thinking that the feds would have liked to have met him. Not only because he agreed with them about the pumps and so on, but because they're interested in things like that. They're very earnest types, that's why they're always issuing warnings and so on. Of course, nobody pays any attention.

Still. . . .

Well, there was no sense bothering my small brain about that sort of stuff, was there? If the heatpumps were dangerous, nobody would have bothered to invent them, would they?

I set down my glass and switched off the fireplace. Tandy was still and warm beside me; motionless but, believe me, by no means asleep.

How to Count on Your Fingers

EVERYONE knows that the decimal system of counting, which is based on the ten digits 0 through 9, has driven out all other systems and has become universal, by virtue of being simplest and best. Like a good many things that "everyone knows," there is one thing wrong with that statement. It isn't so.

True, it is not that any of the predecessors of the decimal system is likely to make a comeback. There is, for instance, vanishingly little chance that we will return to the Babylonian sexagesimal (to the base 60) system—though that is a tough old bird and will not be finally dead as long as we count 60 minutes to the hour, and 360 degrees to the circle. There are traces of systems to other bases surviving in such terms as "score" and the French word for 80, *"quatre-vingt,"* suggesting an extinct system to the base 20; and in terms like "dozen," "gross," and so on, which appear to derive from a system to the base 12.

In science fiction most of the speculation on numbering systems of the future has dwelt on this base 12 ("duodecimal") system, but it is hard to understand why. It is argued that a 12-digit system simplifies writing "decimal" equivalents of such fractions as ⅓ and ⅙, but that seems a small reward for the enormous task of conversion. Setting aside the merits or demerits of the duodecimal system itself, think of the cost of such a change. For a starter, our decimal system of coinage either goes down the drain, to be replaced by a new one, or lingers on as a clumsy anachronism like the British £/s/d. And that cost is only the bare beginning. Science is measurement and interpretation; without measurement, interpretation is foggy soul-searching; and measurement is number. Change our system of writing numbers, and you must translate nearly the entire recorded body of human knowledge—lab reports and tax returns, cost estimates and time studies, knowledge about the behavior of *nu* mesons, and knowledge about transactions on the New York Stock Exchange.

The project of converting the world's essential records from one system of numbering to another staggers the mind. Its cost is measurable not merely in millions of dollars, but in perhaps millions of man-years.

That being so, why is this enormous project now in process?

The answer is, simply, that machines aren't any smarter than Russian peasants.

This is not meant to run down the Russians, but only to observe that UNIVAC and Ivan have a lot of things in common–and one of these things is a lack of skill in performing decimal multiplication and division.

Let's take a simple sum–say, 87 × 93–and see how it would be done by us, by Ivan, and by UNIVAC. You and I, having completed at least a couple of years of grade school, write down a compact little operation like this:

$$\begin{array}{r} 87 \\ \times 93 \\ \hline 261 \\ 783 \\ \hline 8091 \end{array}$$

That wasn't hard to do. If we had to, we probably could have done it in our heads.

However, Ivan would find that pretty hard, because he didn't happen to go to grade school. (And neither did UNIVAC.) What Ivan would do in a similar case is a process called "Russian multiplication"–or sometimes "mediation and duplication." (Which is to say, "halving and doubling.") It consists merely of writing down two columns of figures, side by side. The first column starts with one of your original figures, which is successively halved until there is nothing left to halve. Ivan didn't understand fractions very well, so he simply threw them away–he would write half of 25, for instance, as 12.

The second column starts with the other number, which is successively doubled as many times as the first number was halved. As follows:

87	93
43	186
21	372

10	744
5	1488
2	2976
1	5952

Having gotten this far, Ivan examines the left-hand, or halved, column for even numbers. He finds two of them—the fourth number, 10, and the sixth, 2. He strikes out the numbers next to them in the right-hand (or doubled) column—that is, 744 and 2976. He then adds up the remaining numbers in the right-hand column:

$$\begin{array}{r} 93 \\ 186 \\ 372 \\ 1488 \\ 5952 \\ \hline 8091 \end{array}$$

Having gone all around Robin Hood's barn to do it, as it appears, he was wound up with the same answer we got.

That may not seem like much of an accomplishment, at first glimpse, until you stop to think of Ivan's innocence of the multiplication table, and then it becomes pretty ingenious indeed. Ivan turns out to be a clever fellow.

Yet he was not so clever, all the same, but what he would have laughed in your face if you had accused him of seeking help from the binary system of numbering.

But that is what he did, and that, of course, is what UNIVAC and its electronic brothers do today.

To see *how* UNIVAC does this, let's take some numbers apart and see what is inside them.

Our own decimal numbers—87, for example—are simply a shorthand, "positional" way of saying (in this case) 8×10^2 plus 7×10^0. The larger the number the shorter the shorthand becomes. 1956, for instance, is shorthand for one-times-ten-cubed, plus nine-times-ten-squared, plus five-times-ten, plus six-times-one. Or:

$$\begin{array}{rcr} 1 \times 10^3 & = & 1000 \\ 9 \times 10^2 & = & 900 \\ 5 \times 10^1 & = & 50 \\ 6 \times 10^0 & = & 6 \\ \hline & & 1956 \end{array}$$

(In case it has been a long time since you went to high school, 10^1 just means 10; 10^0 means ten divided by ten, or 1. No matter how long it has been since you went to high school, you ought to remember that 10^2 means ten times ten, or a hundred, and so on.)

It has been said in many science-fiction stories (and not very often anywhere else) that this is homo sapiens' "natural" system of counting, because, look, don't we have ten fingers on our hands? As a theory, let's not worry ourselves about this too much; if true, it will have plenty of chance to prove itself when our exploring rockets turn up some 12-digited and duodecimal extraterrestrials. (Or, alternatively, when our archaeologists discover that the Babylonians had six times as many fingers as the rest of us.) Still, if we assume the fable is true, we can conveniently "explain" UNIVAC by saying that the computer, not having ten fingers to count on, has to use a simpler system. The name of this simpler system is the "binary" or "dyadic" system, and it is this system that most of the world's numbers are being translated into now, in order to be taped and fed into computers.

The binary system obeys all the laws of the decimal. It is positional; it can represent any finite number; it can be used for addition, subtraction, multiplication, division, exponential functions, and any other arithmetical process known to man or to UNIVAC. The only difference is that it is to the base 2 instead of the base 10. It lops off eight of the ten basic decimal digits—0, 1, 2, 3, 4, 5, 6, 7, 8, and 9—retaining only 0 and 1.

You can count with it, of course. 1 is one; 10 is two; 11 is three; 100 is four; 101 is five; 110 is six; 111 is seven; 1000 is eight; 1001 is nine; 1011 is ten, and so on. You can subtract or add with it:

Four	100
Plus three	11
Is seven	111

You can multiply or divide with it:

Six	110
Divided by three	11
Is two	10

And you can do all of these things rather simply, without the necessity of memorizing multiplication tables, thus freeing your preadolescent evenings for baseball and doorbell-ringing.

Look back at Ivan's system of Russian multiplication; let us do it over again in a slightly different way. Let's halve both columns, the right as well as the left. And instead of striking out any number, let us write a "1" next to the odd numbers and a "0" next to the even ones. As follows:

87	1	93	1
43	1	46	0
21	1	23	1
10	0	11	1
5	1	5	1
2	0	2	0
1	1	1	1

Now, you might not know what you have just accomplished—and Ivan certainly wouldn't—but you have translated two decimal numbers into their binary equivalents. Reading from bottom to top, 1010111 is binary for 87; 1011101 is binary for 93.

To see what these mean, remember how we dissected a decimal number. A binary number comes apart in the same sort of pieces; the only difference is that the pieces are multiples of powers of 2, not of powers of 10. 1010111, then, is a shorthand way of saying:

$$\begin{array}{r} 1 \times 2^6 = 64 \\ 0 \times 2^5 = 0 \\ 1 \times 2^4 = 16 \\ 0 \times 2^3 = 0 \\ 1 \times 2^2 = 4 \\ 1 \times 2^1 = 2 \\ 1 \times 2^0 = 1 \\ \hline 87 \end{array}$$

which is what we said it was in the first place.

When you feed numbers like 87 and 93 into UNIVAC, its digestion gets upset—in fact, it won't accept them until they are predigested. So you must convert them into binary digits ("bidgets" or "bits"), just as we did above. Such binary numbers as 1010111 and 1011101

UNIVAC handles very well indeed. Multiply them? No trouble at all. UNIVAC, in its electronic way, does something like this:

```
      1010111
     ×1011101
     --------
      1010111
           0
    1010111
   1010111
  1010111
        0
 1010111
-------------
1111110011011
```

That may look frightening, because it is unfamiliar; but it is still the same old product of 87 × 93; it is shorthand for:

1×2^{12}	4096
1×2^{11}	2048
1×2^{10}	1024
1×2^{9}	512
1×2^{8}	256
1×2^{7}	128
0×2^{6}	0
0×2^{5}	0
1×2^{4}	16
1×2^{3}	8
0×2^{2}	0
1×2^{1}	2
1×2^{0}	1
	8091

Observe the simplicity! True, the number is long; but see how simple manipulating it becomes. Addition, for instance, is reduced to simple counting. (Binary counting, of course—1, 10, 11, 100, and so on. You can call it "one," "ten," "eleven," and "one hundred," and so on, if you like, with no great harm.) To add a column of figures, like

```
  101
  100
  110
  111
-----
10110
```

you simply count the ones in the right-hand column (1, 10; write down 0 and 1 to carry); then count the ones in the middle column, starting, of course, with the one you carried (1, 10, 11; write down 1 and 1 to carry); then count the ones in the left-hand column, again remembering the one you carried (1, 10, 11, 100, 101; write down 1 and 10 to carry; write down the 10).

That is, I submit, about as simple as an arithmetical operation can get, and multiplication is nearly as much so. Multiplication becomes merely a matter of writing down the number, moved an appropriate number of places to the left, or not writing down the number at all (depending on whether the digit you are multiplying by is "1" or "0"). Thereafter it is addition, and addition, as we have seen, is merely counting. No multiplication tables! No tedious memorizing! No wonder UNIVAC and Ivan like it!

If binary arithmetic has a fault, it is that it is so excessively easy that it becomes boring.

But the world's work is full of boring operations that get done anyhow. We have found two good ways to handle them—either to turn them over to machines (like UNIVAC), which do not have the capacity for boredom, or to learn to do them as a matter of mechanical routine.

My wife observes (as most wives sometimes observe) that it doesn't much matter what sort of change she suggests, I can usually find a dozen splendid reasons for keeping things just as they are. Since the human animal is conservative, most of us can find objections to any sort of change. ("Better the devil you know.") Since the human animal is also educable, we often, however, overcome our objections when the change promises rewards.

Let us see what the drawbacks and rewards of changeover to binary notation may be. Not that the case is really arguable, since the silent vote of the computers constitutes a carrying majority over our human veto, but let us see if there are any advantages for us borable, error-prone humans.

The drawbacks stand out immediately, starting with the sheer physical size of a binary number as contrasted with its decimal equivalent. Still, a binary number isn't so *very* much longer than a decimal (about three times) as to be *ipso facto* out of the question. As a matter of fact, really large numbers are hopelessly unwieldy in any notation at all. In the prevailing decimal system scientific people express large numbers either as approximations (3×10^{47}, for instance) or in terms of their prime factors and exponents ($19^3 \times 641^5 \times 1861$) or in other factored or shorthand ways. Even the headlines in our daily papers are more likely to read $6.5 billion than $6,500,000,000.

For "household-sized" numbers–oh, up to a million, let's say–it doesn't seem as though the mere matter of length ought to be a prevailing count against binary notation. You might use 20 binary digits to write a number that big (as against seven in decimal notation) and a number such as–to take one at random–101001111001011000010 is pretty hideous. But is 1372866, its decimal equivalent, utterly lovely?

Perhaps the number itself isn't so bad; perhaps the way we are reading it could stand some improvement. Look at the number 1111110011011, for instance. You just came across it a couple of pages ago (our old friend, the product of 87 and 93), and yet you almost certainly failed to recognize it. Is it because its recognition value is intrinsically low? Or because we lack practice in reading (and in establishing conventions of writing) that sort of number?

In decimal notation, remember, we simplify the reading of such large numbers by setting off groups of three. 5000000000000 is pretty hard to read by itself, though 5,000,000,000,000 reveals itself to be five trillion rather conveniently. Why should we not adopt a similar convention for binary numbers? There is no reason to stick to groups of three; let's make it groups of five, and thus write the expression for the product of 87 × 93–that is, 8091–as follows: 111,-11100,11011.

Well, that's a help, but as is often the case, a little progress in one direction merely brightens the light on a related problem still unsolved. The related problem here is the problem of subvocalization. All of us are lip readers; even if the motion of the lip muscles is so thoroughly suppressed as to be invisible to the naked eye, the larynx is still forming the sounds of everything we read–or think, for that matter. And groups like oneoneone comma oneoneoneohoh comma oneoneohoneone simply do not pronounce well.

But being able to state a problem is progressing far toward solving it. It is apparent that there is no difficulty involved in assigning more pronounceable phonetic values to the parts of binary notation.

One such system is, in fact, already widely in use. If you walk into the Bank of Ireland Bar in Chelsea on a noisy night, you may come across a couple of Merchant Marine officers having a relaxed and private conversation which is not subject to either eavesdropping or interference, regardless of the surrounding noise. If you do, they are probably radiomen, and they are talking to each other in code. For the dots and dashes of Morse there is a well-established pronouncing convention: "Dit" is a dot, "Dah" is a dash. If we merely appropriate this convention for our binary numbers, we may sacrifice some efficiency—no doubt an even more compact and clear system could be worked out from basic phonetic principles. But it offers a very special advantage: It works. We don't have to test it or doubt it; we know it works; it has worked all over the world for countless radio operators for a period of decades.

Let us then pronounce "1" as "dit" and "0" as "dah." 111,11100,-11011 then becomes dididit didididahdah dididahdidit—

And we notice something odd. We already conceded that the binary system had an intrinsic drawback in that its terms were by definition *always* less compact than the decimal.

Yet if we wish to transmit the decimal number 8091 in Morse code, it must be expressed like this: dahdahdahdidit dahdahdahdahdah dahdahdahdahdit didahdahdahdah. That is, four groups, each comprising five "bits," or 20 "bits" in all.

But its binary equivalent needs only three groups totalling 13 "bits," as we have just seen.

Our concession was evidently premature. In this one special case, at least—and it is far from an unimportant one—the binary system can be made *more* compact than the decimal.

Having found one such case, let us be encouraged enough to look for more.

When I was around ten, we kids used to kill time on long auto rides by playing a game of counting. We would pick a common phenomenon—cows or Fords or "For Sale" signs on farms—and see who, in a given period, had spotted the most. It almost always kept us quiet and out of the driver's hair for the first mile or two—and almost never beyond that.

The trouble was that we counted on our fingers. That worked beautifully for numbers up to ten, of course. It worked passably for numbers up to 20, or even to 30—it wasn't much of a trick to remember that we were on the second or third go-around of finger-counting. But when we got to numbers much above that, we began to rely pretty heavily on our individually differing memories of just how many times we had counted up to ten, and that's when the fights would start.

Naturally, we were counting by the decimal system.

Could we have done better with the binary?

Spread out the ten fingers on your two hands before you (don't let's get into semantic arguments about whether or not a "thumb" is a "finger"—you know what I mean), and let's see what can be done with them.

We start by establishing a convention. An extended finger is a "1." A retracted finger is a "0."

Clench your fists and begin to count:

Extend the right little finger. That is 1–in both binary and decimal notation.

Retract the little finger and extend the right ring finger. Read it as 10 (or, in decimal notation, two).

Keep the ring finger out and extend the little finger beside it. Read: 11 (Decimal notation, three.)

Retract both those fingers and extend the middle finger of the right hand. Read 100 (binary) or four (decimal).

And so on. You may find that waggling your fingers like this requires practice or natural flexibility–unless, of course, you make it easy on yourself by resting the fingers against the edge of a table.

Your fingers are now indeed "digits," and you are using them in positional notation. Observe that you can represent any number from 00000,00000 (both hands clenched) to 11111,11111 (both hands extended). Next time you want to count a reasonably large number –say, the number of cars ahead of you in a tunnel jam, or the number of hits against a Met pitcher–you might try this system. It's good anywhere from 0 to 1023. Indeed, by a few obvious extensions–for instance, by adding on successively extended or retracted positions of the wrists, elbows, and so on–you can soon reach numbers beyond which you are never likely to count.

Moreover, your running total is available to you at any time (as it is not in the decimal system of finger counting, for instance, where you must count the fingers themselves to get such a total); you merely read it off. Suppose, for instance, you are out hiking with a companion (having lost your pedometer, let us say), and your friend wants to know how many paces you can go in a given period of time. You keep count on your fingers, and at the end of the time you see you have the little finger, index finger, and thumb of the left hand, and the thumb and ring finger of the right hand extended. Reading off your hands according to our established convention, you find you have come 10011,10010 paces, and you pass on the information to him according to the pronouncing convention: "didahdahdidit didahdahdidah."

Of course, your friend may be a square who still uses the old stick-in-the-mud decimal system, so you may want to translate for him. That's easy enough if you remember the decimal equivalents of each of the fingers:

Left Hand

Little finger:	$2^9 =$	512
Ring finger:	$2^8 =$	256
Middle finger:	$2^7 =$	128
Index finger:	$2^6 =$	64
Thumb:	$2^5 =$	32

Right Hand

Thumb:	$2^4 =$	16
Index finger:	$2^3 =$	8
Middle finger:	$2^2 =$	4
Ring finger:	$2^1 =$	2
Little finger:	$2^0 =$	1

Accordingly, to convert your finger count into decimal figures, just add up the finger equivalents given above; for the aforementioned 10011,10010, read:

Left little finger:	512
Left index finger:	64
Left thumb:	32
Right thumb:	16
Right ring finger:	2
	626

And inform your friend you have come 626 paces.

As promised, we have found another case where an ingenious use of binary notation is actually more compact than decimal—*by a factor of* 100, as it turns out. Let us turn, then, away from the demolished "drawbacks" of binary notation in order to take a quick look at some of its more attractive features.

We recall that it has already been demonstrated that binary arithmetic is about as simple as arithmetic can get. That is what makes it so uniquely right for UNIVAC, but even on a less complicated level of computer design, it presents lovely aspects. Think, for example, of the beautifully compact desk adding machine that might be designed for binary numbers. No wheels and gear trains—therefore, at least for normal-sized calculations, no necessity for a power source to drive them. To handle addition or subtraction of, say, ten-place numbers (and multiplication and division are only slightly more demanding) you need only a row of ten levers with an up ("1") and down ("0") position. Of course, you wouldn't have to spend much money on a calculator as simple as that. You could build it yourself. Or alternatively, you could merely use the built-in ten-place binary computer we've just been talking about, the one that grows out of the ends of your arms.

For instance: You're remodeling your house; you have 13 4×8 panels of sheetrock on hand, and you discover that you have 650 square feet of wall to cover. Question: How many additional panels of sheetrock will you have to go out and buy?

That's not the most difficult problem in the world, true, but let's run through it once in binary arithmetic, using our fingers as computers. First we need to convert to binary numbers–*but only because we chose to start out with decimal ones;* it isn't fair to include conversion time as part of the time required for solving the problem.

In binary numbers you have 1101 100×1000 panels on hand, and 10100,01010 square feet of wall to cover.

1101×100×1000, obviously, is merely a matter of pointing off places; you represent 01101 on your left hand, and 00000 on your right hand; that's how many square feet of sheetrock you have–uh, on hand, so to speak. Then the subtraction* is merely a matter of considering the successive digits, reading from the right, subtracting the digit shown on your finger from the corresponding digit in the written number you are subtracting from, *and carrying "borrowed" numbers.* (Are you able to remember how much trouble you had with "carrying" when you first learned the principles of decimal subtraction? Then don't give up on binary subtraction if it takes you a few minutes to get the hang of "carrying" here.)

The result you "write," one digit at a time, on your fingers. That is, by the time you are subtracting your right-thumb digit from the written figure, the remaining fingers on your right hand are already indicating the last four digits of the answer. When you're done, you read the answer off.

As already shown, the number of square feet of sheetrock you need to buy is 111,01010 (we padded the left-hand group out with zeroes to indicate all five finger positions in writing the subtraction). There are 1,00000 square feet in a panel; 111,01010 divided by

---

* 10100,01010 sq/ft wall to cover
−01101,00000 sq/ft sheetrock on hand

00111,01010 sq/ft needed

1,00000 is obviously 111 and a fraction. But you can't buy part of a panel so you add 1 to the 111 and get 1000. Answer: You need to buy 1000 panels. (Or, in decimal numbers, 8.)

Look hard? Once again, consider it from the perspective of *relative* difficulty. After all, this is probably your first binary problem. Make up a few more; by the time you've done six, it won't be hard at all; by the time you've done a hundred, it will be semi-automatic; by the time you've done a thousand–

Well, hold on for a moment before you do your thousand; perhaps it will cheer you up to know that there are some special cases of binary arithmetic which aren't *ever* hard, not even the first time.

For example: Multiplication (or division) by powers of 2 is an obvious case; you simply point off and add zeroes. True, the decimal system has a similar situation in regard to powers of 10. But you still have to give the verdict to binary on this point, simply because in any finite series there are more powers of 2 than powers of 10.

But if you want to see something really *easy,* consider the strange case of the problem 1023-*n*.

Let's arbitrarily take *n* as 626 (because we happen to have a binary equivalent conveniently to hand–any other number less than 1023 would do as well, of course). Do this one on your fingers. First show yourself the binary representation of 1023:

11111,11111

Then cancel that and represent on your fingers the binary equivalent of 626:

10011,10010

Don't bother about subtracting; you've already done it! Just reverse your convention for reading finger representations; read an extended finger as "0," a retracted finger as "1," and you get:

$$
\begin{array}{r}
11111,11111 \\
-10011,10010 \\
\hline
01100,01101
\end{array}
$$

In other words, any number *n* in binary notation is always the "reverse" of the number 1023-*n*. Not only that, but the same sort of rule can be made for the cases 511-*n,* 255-*n,* 127-*n,* etc.–for any number whose binary representation is "all ones," as you may already have realized. Try it and see.

It may be objected that such special cases are comparatively rare. This is true enough, but in the decimal system they are not only rare; they do not exist at all. And we have not, by any means, exhausted binary's bag of tricks. It is, in fact, hardly possible that any reader can spend as much as a single evening trying out experiments in binary arithmetic without discovering additional shortcuts to this one.

Decimal system?

That clumsy, sprawly, quaint old thing!

Grandy Devil

MAHLON begat Timothy, and Timothy begat Nathan, and Nathan begat Roger, and the days of their years were long on the Earth. But then Roger begat Orville, and Orville was a heller. He begat Augustus, Wayne, Walter, Benjamin and Carl, who was my father, and I guess that was going too far, because that was when Gideon Upshur stepped in to take a hand.

I was kissing Lucille in the parlor when the doorbell rang and she didn't take kindly to the interruption. He was a big old man with a burned-brown face. He stamped the snow off his feet and stared at me out of crackling blue eyes and demanded, "Orvie?"

I said, "My name is George."

"Wipe the lipstick off your face, George," he said, and walked right in.

Lucille sat up in a hurry and began tucking the ends of her hair in place. He looked at her once and calmly took off his coat and hung it over the back of a chair by the fire and sat down.

"My name is Upshur," he said. "Gideon Upshur. Where's Orville Dexter?"

I had been thinking about throwing him out up until then, but that made me stop thinking about it. It was the first time anybody had come around looking for Orville Dexter in almost a year and we had just begun breathing easily again.

I said, "That's my grandfather, Mr. Upshur. What's he done now?"

He looked at me. "You're his *grandson?* And you ask me what he's *done?*" He shook his head. "Where is he?"

I told him the truth: "We haven't seen Grandy Orville in five years."

"And you don't know where he is?"

"No, I don't, Mr. Upshur. He never tells anybody where he's going. Sometimes he doesn't even tell us after he comes back."

The old man pursed his lips. He leaned forward, across Lucille, and poured himself a drink from the Scotch on the side table.

"I swear," he said, in a high, shrill, old voice, "these Dexters are a caution. Go home."

He was talking to Lucille. She looked at him sulkily and opened her mouth, but I cut in.

"This is my fiancee," I said.

"Hah," he said. "No doubt. Well, there's nothing to do but have it out with Orvie. Is the bed made up in the guest room?"

I protested, "Mr. Upshur, it isn't that we aren't glad to see any friend of Grandy's, but Lord knows when he'll be home. It might be tomorrow, it might be six months from now or years."

"I'll wait," he said over his shoulder, climbing the stairs.

Having him there wasn't so bad after the first couple of weeks. I phoned Uncle Wayne about it, and he sounded quite excited.

"Tall, heavy-set old man?" he asked. "Very dark complexion?"

"That's the one," I said. "He seemed to know his way around the house pretty well, too."

"Well, why wouldn't he?" Uncle Wayne didn't say anything for a second. "Tell you what, George. You get your brothers together and——"

"I can't, Uncle Wayne," I said. "Harold's in the Army. I don't know *where* William's got to."

He didn't say anything for another second. "Well, don't worry. I'll give you a call as soon as I get back."

"Are you going somewhere, Uncle Wayne?" I wanted to know.

"I certainly am, George," he said, and hung up.

So there I was, alone in the house with Mr. Upshur. That's the trouble with being the youngest.

Lucille wouldn't come to the house any more, either. I went out to her place a couple of times, but it was too cold to drive the Jaguar and William had taken the big sedan with him when he left, and Lucille refused to go anywhere with me in the jeep. So all we could do was sit in *her* parlor, and her mother sat right there with us, knitting and making little remarks about Grandy Orvie and that girl in Eatontown.

So, all in all, I was pretty glad when the kitchen door opened and Grandy Orvie walked in.

"Grandy!" I cried. "I'm glad to see you! There's a man——"

"Hush, George," he said. "Where is he?"

"Upstairs. He usually takes a nap after I bring him his dinner on a tray."

"*You* take his dinner up? What's the matter with the servants?"

I coughed. "Well, Grandy, after that trouble in Eatontown, they—"

"Never mind," he said hastily. "Go ahead with what you're doing."

I finished scraping the dishes into the garbage-disposer and stacked them in the washer, while he sat there in his overcoat watching me.

"George," he said at last, "I'm an old man. A very old man."

"Yes, Grandy," I answered.

"My grandfather's older than I am. And *his* grandfather is older than that."

"Well, sure," I said reasonably. "I never met them, did I, Grandy?"

"No, George. At least, I don't believe they've been home much these last few years. Grandy Timothy was here in '86, but I don't believe you were born yet. Come to think of it, even your dad wasn't born by then."

"Dad's sixty," I told him. "I'm twenty-one."

"Certainly you are, George. And your dad thinks a lot of you. He mentioned you just a couple of months ago. He said that you were getting to an age where you ought to be told about us Dexters."

"Told what, Grandy Orville?" I asked.

"Confound it, George, that's what I'm coming to! Can't you see that I'm trying to tell you something? It's hard to put into words, that's all."

"Can I help?" said Gideon Upshur from the door.

Grandy Orville stood up straight and frosty. "I'll thank you, Gideon Upshur, to stay the be-dickens out of a family discussion!"

"It's my family, too, young man," said Gideon Upshur. "And that's why I'm here. I warned Cousin Mahlon, but he wouldn't listen. I warned Timothy, but he ran off to America—and look what *he* started!"

"A man's got a right to pass on his name," Grandy Orville said pridefully.

"Once, yes! I never said a man couldn't have a son—though you know I've never had one, Orvie. Where would the world be if all of us had children three and four at a time, the way you Dexters have been doing? Four now—sixteen when the kids grow up—sixty-four when *their* kids grow up. Why, in four or five hundred years, there'd be trillions of us, Orvie. The whole world would be covered six layers deep with immortals, squirming and fidgeting and I—"

"Hush, man!" howled Grandy Orville. "Not in front of the boy!"

Gideon Upshur stood up and yelled right back at him. "It's time he found out! I'm warning you, Orville Dexter, either you mend your ways or I'll mend them for you. I didn't come here to talk; I'm prepared to take sterner measures if I have to!"

"Why, you reeking pustoon," Grandy Orville started, but then he caught sight of me. "Out of here, George! Go up to your room till I call you. And as for you, you old idiot, I'm as prepared as you are, if it comes to that——"

I went. It looked like trouble and I hated to leave Grandy Orville alone, but orders were orders; Dad had taught me that. The noises from the kitchen were terrible for a while, but by and by they died down.

It was quiet for a long, long time. After a couple of hours, I began to get worried and I went back downstairs quietly and pushed the kitchen door open a crack.

Grandy Orville was sitting at the kitchen table, staring into space. I didn't see Mr. Upshur at all.

Grandy Orville looked up and said in a tired voice, "Come in, George. I was just catching my breath."

"Where did Mr. Upshur go?" I asked.

"It was self-defense," he said quickly. "He'd outlived his usefulness, anyway."

I stared at him. "Did something happen to Mr. Upshur?" I asked.

He sighed. "George, sometimes I think the old blood is running thin. Now don't bother me with any more questions right now, till I rest up a bit."

Orders were orders, as I say. I noticed that the garbage-disposal unit was whirring and I walked over to shut it off.

"Funny," I said. "I forgot I left it running."

Grandy Orville said nervously, "Don't give it a thought. Say, George, they haven't installed sewer lines while I was away, have they?"

"No, they haven't, Grandy," I told him. "Same old dry well and septic tank."

"That's too bad," he grumbled. "Well, I don't suppose it matters."

I wasn't listening too closely; I had noticed that the floor was slick and shiny.

"Grandy," I said, "you didn't have to mop the floor for me. I can manage, even if all the servants did quit when——"

"Oh, shut up about the servants," he snapped testily. "George, I've been thinking. There's a lot that needs to be explained to you, but this isn't the best time for it and maybe your dad ought to do the explaining. He knows you better than I do. Frankly, George, I just don't know how to put things so you'll understand. Didn't you ever notice that there was anything different about us Dexters?"

"Well, we're pretty rich."

"I don't mean that. For instance, that time you were run over by the truck when you were a kid. Didn't that make you suspect anything–how soon you mended, I mean?"

"Why, I don't think so, Grandy," I said, thinking back. "Dad told me that all the Dexters always healed fast." I bent down and looked under the table Grandy Orville was sitting at. "Why, that looks like old clothes down there. Isn't that the same kind of suit Mr. Upshur was wearing?"

Grandy Orville shrugged tiredly. "He left it for you," he explained. "Now don't ask me any more questions, because I've got to go away for a while and I'm late now. If your Uncle Wayne comes back, tell him thanks for letting me know Mr. Upshur was here. I'll give your regards to your dad if we happen to meet."

Well, that was last winter. I wish Grandy would come back so I could stop worrying about the problem he left me.

Lucille never did get over her peeve, so I married Alice along about the middle of February. I'd have liked having some of the family there at the wedding, but none of them was in town just then–or since, for that matter–and it wasn't really necessary because I was of legal age.

I was happy with Alice right from the start, but even more important, it explained what Grandy and Mr. Upshur had been trying to tell me. About what us Dexters are, that is.

Alice is a very attractive girl and a good housekeeper, which is a good thing–we haven't been able to get any of the servants back. But that's good, too, in a way, because it keeps her inside the house a lot.

It's getting on toward nice weather, though, and I'm having a tough time keeping her away from the third terrace, where the dry well and septic tank are. And if she goes down there, she's bound to hear the noises.

I don't know. Maybe the best thing I could do would be to roll the stone off the top of the septic tank and let what's struggling around in there come out.

But I'm afraid he's pretty mad.

Speed Trap

MY reservation was for a window seat, up front, because on this particular flight they serve from the front back; but on the seat next to mine, I saw a reservation tag for Gordie MacKenzie. I kept right on going until the hostess hailed me. "Why, Dr. Grew, nice to have you with us again . . ."

I stood blocking the aisle. "Can I switch to a seat back here somewhere, Clara?"

"Why, I think—let me see . . ."

"How about that one?" I didn't see a tag on it.

"Well, it's not a window seat . . ."

"But it's free?"

"Well, let's look." She flipped the seating chart out of her clipboard. "Certainly. May I take your bag?"

"Uh-uh. Work to do." And I did have work to do, too; that was why I didn't want to sit next to MacKenzie. I slouched down in the seat, scowling at the man next to me to indicate that I didn't want to strike up a conversation; he scowled back to show that that suited him fine. I saw MacKenzie come aboard, but he didn't see me.

Just before we took off, I saw Clara bend over him to check his seat belt; and in the same motion, she palmed the reservation card with my name on it. Smart girl. I decided to buy her a drink the next time I found myself in the motel where her crew stayed between flights.

I don't want to give you the idea that I'm a jet-set type who's on first-name terms with every airline stewardess around. The only ones I see enough of at all are a couple on the New York-L.A. run, and a few operating out of O'Hare, and maybe a couple that I see now and then between Huntsville and the Cape—oh, and one Air France girl I've flown with once or twice out of Orly, but only because she gave me a lift in her Citroën one time when there was a *métro* strike and no cabs to be found. Still, come to think of it, well—all right—yes, I guess I do get around a lot. Those are the hazards of the trade. Although my degree's in atmospheric physics, my specialty is signatures—you know, the instrument readings or optical observations that we interpret to mean such-and-such pressure, temperature, chemical composition and so on—and that's a pretty sexy field right now, and I get invited to a lot of conferences. I said "invited." I don't mean in the sense that I can say no. Not if I want to keep enough status in the department to have freedom to do my work. And it's all plushy and kind of fun, at least when I have time to have fun; and really, I've got pretty good at locating a decent restaurant in Cleveland or Albuquerque (try the Mexican food at the airport) and vetoing an inferior wine.

That's funny, too, because I didn't expect it to be this way—not when I was a kid reading Willy Ley's articles and going out to hunt ginseng in the woods around Potsdam (I mean the New York one) so I could earn money and go to MIT and build spaceships. I thought I would be a lean, hungry-eyed scientist in shabby clothes. I thought probably I would never get out of the laboratory (I guess I thought spaceships were designed in laboratories) and I'd waste my health on long night hours over the slide rule. And, as it turns out, what I'm wasting my health on is *truite amandine* and time-zone disorientation.

But I think I know what to do about that.

That's why I didn't want to spend the four and a half hours yakking with Gordie MacKenzie, because, by God, I maybe *do* know what to do about that.

It's not really my field, but I've talked it over with some systems people and they didn't get that polite look people get when you're trying to tell them about their own subject. I'll see if I can explain it. See, there are like twenty conferences and symposia and colloquia a month in any decent-sized field, and you're out of it unless you make a few of them. Not counting workshops and planning sessions and get-the-hell-down-here-Charley-or-we-lose-the-grant meetings. And they do have a way of being all over the place. I haven't slept in my own home all seven nights of any week since Christmas before last, when I had the flu.

Now, question is, what do all the meetings accomplish? I had a theory once that the whole *Gestalt* was planned—I mean, global scatter, jet travel and all. A sort of psychic energizer, designed to keep us all pumped up all the time—after all, if you're going somewhere in a jet at 600 miles an hour, you know you've got to be doing something important, or else you wouldn't be doing it so fast. But who would plan something like that?

So I gave up that idea and concentrated on ways of doing it better. You know, there really is no more stupid way of communicating information than flying 3000 miles to sit on a gilt chair in a hotel ballroom and listen to twenty-five people read papers at you. Twenty-three of the papers you don't care about anyway, and the twenty-fourth you can't understand because the speaker has a bad accent and, anyway, he's rushing it because he's under time pressure to catch his plane to the next conference, and that one single twenty-fifth paper has cost you four days, including travel time, when you could have read it in your own office in fifteen minutes. And got more out of it, too. Of course, there's the interplay when you find yourself sitting in the coffee shop next to somebody who can explain the latest instrumentation to you because his company's doing the telemetry; you can't get that from reading. But I've noticed there's less and less time for that. And less and less interest, too, maybe, because you get pretty tired of making new friends after about the three hundredth; and you begin to think about what's waiting for you on your desk when you get back, and you remember the time when you got stuck with that damn loudmouthed Egyptian at the I.A.U. in Brussels and had to fight the Suez war for an hour and a half.

All right, you can see what I mean. Waste of time and valuable kerosene jet fuel, right?

Because the pity of it is that electronic information handling is so cheap and easy. I don't know if you've ever seen the Bell Labs' demo of their picture phone–they had it at a couple of meetings–but it's *nearly* like face to face. Better than the telephone. You get all the signatures, except maybe the smell of whiskey on the breath or something like that. And that's only one gadget: there's facsimile, telemetry, remote-access computation, teletype–well, there it is, we've got them, why don't we use them? And go farther, too. You know about how they can strip down a taped voice message–leave out the unnecessary parts of speech, edit out the pauses, even drop some of the useless syllables? And you can still understand it perfectly, only at about four hundred words a minute instead of maybe sixty or seventy. (And about half of them repetitions or "What I mean to say.")

Well, that's the systems part; and, as I say, it's not my field. But it's there for the taking–expert opinion, not mine. A couple of the fellows were real hot, and we're going to get together on it as soon as we can find the time.

Maybe you wonder what I have to contribute. I do have something, I think. For example, how about problem-solving approaches to discussions? I've seen some papers that suggest a way of simplifying and pointing up a conference so you could really *confer*. I've even got a pet idea of my own. I call it the Quantum of Debate, the irreducible minimum of argument which each participant in a discussion can use to make one single point and get that understood (or argued or refuted) before he goes on to the next.

Why, if half of what I think is so, then people like me can get things done in–oh, be conservative–a quarter of the time we spend now.

Leaving three quarters of our time for–what? Why, for work! For doing the things that we know we ought to do but can't find the time for. I mean this literally and really and seriously. I honestly think that we can do four times as much work as we do. And I honestly think that this means we can land on Mars in five years instead of twenty, cure leukemia in twelve years instead of fifty, and so on.

Well, that's the picture, and that's why I didn't want to waste the time talking with Gordie MacKenzie. I'd brought all my notes in my briefcase, and four and a half hours was just about enough time to try to pull them all together and make some sort of presentation to show my systems friends and a few others who were interested.

So as soon as we were airborne, I had the little table down and I was sorting out little stacks of paper.

Only it didn't work out.

It's funny how often it doesn't work out–I mean, when you've got something you want to do and you look ahead and see where the time's going to be to do it, and then, all of a sudden, the time's gone and you didn't do it. What it was was that Clara worked her way back with the cocktails–she knew mine, an extra-dry martini with a twist of lemon–and I moved the papers out of her way out of politeness, and then she showed up with the hors d'oeuvres and I put them back in my bag out of hunger, and then I had to decide how I wanted my *tournedos,* and it took almost two hours for dinner, including the wine and the B & B; and although I didn't really want to watch the movie, there's something about seeing all those screens ahead of you, with the hero just making his bombing run on your own screen but shot up and falling in flames on the ones you can see out of the corner of your eye in the forward seats–and back in the briefing room, or even in the pub the night before on the screens in the other row that the film gets to after it gets to yours–all sort of like a cross section of instants of time, a plural "now." Disconcerting. It polarized my attention; of course, the liquor helped; and, anyway, by the time the movie was over, it was time for the second round of coffee and mints, and then the seat-belt sign was on and we were over the big aluminum dome on Mount Wilson, coming in, and I never had found the time to do my sorting. Well, I was used to that. I'd never found any ginseng back in Potsdam, either. I had to get through school on a scholarship.

I checked in, washed my face and went down to the meeting room just in time for a very dull tutorial on clear-air turbulence in planetary atmospheres. There was quite a good turnout, maybe seventy or eighty people in the room; but what they thought they were getting out of it, I cannot imagine, so I picked up a program and ducked out.

Somebody by the coffee machine called to me. "Hi, Chip."

I went over and shook his hand, a young fellow named Resnik from the little college where I'd got my bachelor's, looking bored and angry. He was with someone I didn't know, tall and gray-haired and bankerish. "Dr. Ramos, this is Chesley Grew. Chip, Dr. Ramos. He's with NASA–I think it's NASA?"

"No, I'm with a foundation," he said. "It's a pleasure to meet you, Dr. Grew. I've followed your work."

"Thank you. Thank you very much." I would have liked a cup of coffee, but I didn't particularly want to stand there talking to them while I drank it, so I said, "Well, I'd better get checked in, so if you'll excuse me . . ."

"Come off it, Chip," said Larry Resnik. "I saw you check in half an hour ago. You just want to go up to your room and work."

That was embarrassing, a little. I didn't mind it with Resnik, but I didn't know the other fellow. He grinned and said, "Larry tells me you're like that. Matter of fact, when you went by, he said you'd be back out in thirty seconds, and you were."

"Well. Clear-air turbulence isn't my subject, really . . ."

"Oh, nobody's blaming you. God knows not. Care for some coffee?"

The only thing to do was to be gracious about it, so I said, "Yes, please. Thanks." I watched him take a cup and fill it from the big silver urn. He looked vaguely familiar, but I couldn't place him. "Did we meet at the Dallas Double-A S sessions?"

"I'm afraid not. Sugar? No, I've actually been to very few of these meetings, but I've read some of your papers."

I stirred my coffee. "Thank you, Dr. Ramos." One of the things I've learned to do is repeat a name as often as I can so I won't forget it. About half the time I forget it anyway, of course. "I'll be speaking tomorrow morning, Dr. Ramos. 'A Photometric Technique for

Deriving Slopes from Planetary Fly-bys.' Nothing much that doesn't follow from what they've done at Langley, I'm afraid."

"Yes, I saw the abstract."

"But you'll get your brownie points for reading it, eh?" said Larry. He was breathing heavily. "How many does that make this year?"

"Well, a lot." I tried to drink my coffee both rapidly and inconspicuously. Larry seemed in an unhappy mood.

"That's what we were talking about when you came in," he said. "Thirty papers a year and committee reports between times. When was the last time you spent a solid month at your desk? I know, in my own department . . ."

I could feel myself growing interested and I didn't want to be, I wanted to get back to my notes. I took another gulp of my coffee.

"You know what Fred Hoyle said?"

"I don't think so, Larry."

"He said the minute a man does anything, anything at all, the whole world enters into a conspiracy to keep him from ever doing it again. Program chairmen invite him to read papers. Trustees put him onto committees. Newspaper reporters call him up to interview him. Television shows ask him to appear with a comic, a bandleader and a girl singer, to talk about whether there's life on Mars."

"And people who sympathize with him buttonhole him on his way out of meetings," said Dr. Ramos. He chuckled. "Really, Dr. Grew. We'll understand if you just keep on going."

"I'm not even sure it's this world," said Larry.

He was not only irritable, he was hardly making sense. "For that matter," he added, "I haven't even really done anything yet. Not like you, Chip. But I can, someday."

"Don't be modest," said Dr. Ramos. "And look, we're making a lot of noise here. Why don't we find some place to sit down and talk —unless you really do want to get back to your work, Dr. Grew?"

But you see, I was already more than half convinced that this *was* my work, to talk to Larry and Dr. Ramos; and what we finally did was go up to my room and then up to Larry's where he had a Rand Corporation report in his bag with some notes I'd sent him once, and we never did get back to the meeting room. Along about ten we had dinner sent up, and that was where we stayed, drinking cold coffee off the set-up table and sparingly drinking bourbon out of a bottle Larry had brought along, and I told them everything I'd ever thought about a systems approach to the transmission of technological information. And what it implied. And Dr. Ramos was with it at every step, the best listener either of us had ever had, though most of what he said was, "Yes, of course," and "I see." There really was a lot in it. I'd believed it, sitting by myself and computing, like a child anticipating Christmas, how much *work* I could get done for a couple K a year in amortization of systems and overhead. And with the two of them, I was sure of it. It was a giddy kind of evening. Toward the end, we even began to figure out how quickly we could colonize Mars and launch a fleet of interstellar space liners, with all the working time of the existing people spent *working;* and then there was a pause and Larry got up and threw back the glass French window and we looked out on his balcony. Twenty stories up, and Los Angeles out in front of us and a thunderstorm brewing over the southern hills. The fresh air cleared my head for a moment and then made me realize, first, that I was sleepy and, second, that I had to read that damned paper in about seven hours.

"We'd better call it a day," said Dr. Ramos.

Larry started to object, then grinned. "All right for you old fellows," he said. "Anyway, I want to look at those notes of yours by myself, Chip, if you don't mind."

"Just so you don't lose them," I said, and turned to go back to my room and get into my bed and lie with my eyes wide open, smiling to myself, before I fell asleep to dream about fifty weeks a year working at my trade.

Even so, I woke easily the moment the hotel clock buzzed by my head. We'd fixed it to have breakfast in Larry's room so I could reclaim my notes and maybe chat for a moment before the morning session began; and when I got to his floor, I saw Dr. Ramos padding toward me. "Morning," he said. "I just woke up two honeymooners who didn't appreciate it. Wasn't Larry's room 2051?"

"It's 2052. The other way." He grinned and fell into step and told me a fast and quite funny honeymooner joke, timing the punch line just as we reached Larry's door.

He didn't answer my knock. Still laughing, I said, "You try." But there was no answer to Dr. Ramos's knock, either.

I stopped laughing. "He couldn't have forgotten we were coming, could he?"

"Try the door, why don't you?"

And I did and it opened easily.

But Larry wasn't in the room. The door to the bath was standing open and so was the balcony window, and no Larry. His bed was rumpled but empty.

"I don't think he's gone out," said Dr. Ramos. "Look, his shoes are still there."

The balcony wasn't big enough to hide on, but I walked over and looked at it. Rain-slick and narrow, all that was on it were a couple of soaked deck chairs and some cigarette butts.

"Looks like he was out here," I said; and then, feeling melodramatic, I leaned over the rail and looked down; and it wasn't actually melodramatic after all, because there in the curve of the hotel's sweeping front, on the rim of a fountain, something was sprawled, and a man was standing by it, shouting at the doorman. It was too early for much noise, and I could hear his voice faintly coming up the two hundred vertical feet between us and what was left of Larry.

They canceled the morning session but decided to go ahead in the afternoon, and I got into a long, bruising fight with Gordie MacKenzie because he wanted to give his paper when it was scheduled, at three in the afternoon, and I'd been reshuffled into that time and I just wasn't feeling cheerful enough to let him get away with anything. Not after spending two hours with the coroner's men and the hotel staff, trying to help them figure out why Larry would have jumped or slipped off the balcony, and especially not after finding out that he had had all my notes in his hand when he jumped and they were now in sticky, sloppy clusters all over Los Angeles County.

So I was about fed up. I once heard Krafft Ehricke give what I would figure to be a twelve-minute paper in three minutes and forty-five seconds, and I tried to beat his record and pretty nearly made it. Then I threw everything I owned into my suitcase and checked out, figuring to head right out to the airport and get on the first plane going home.

But the clerk said, "I have a message for you, Mr. Grew. Dr. Ramos asked you not to leave without seeing him."

"Thanks," I said, after a moment of debating whether to do anything about it or not; but as it turned out, I didn't have to make the decision. Ramos came hurrying toward me across the lobby, his friendly face concerned.

"I thought you'd be leaving," he said. "Give me twenty minutes of your time first."

I hesitated and he snapped a finger at a bellboy. "Here. Let him take care of your bag and let's go down and have a cup of coffee." So I let him lead me to the outdoor patio by the coffee shop, warm and clean now after the rain. I wondered if he recognized the place where Larry had hit, but I'm not sensitive about that sort of thing and apparently neither was he. He really had a commanding presence when he wanted to. He had a waitress beside us before we had quite slid our chairs closer to the table, sent her after coffee and sandwiches without consulting me and started in on me without a pause. "Chip," he said, "don't blow it. I'm sorry about your notes. But I don't want to see you give up."

I leaned back in my chair, feeling very weary. "Oh, that I won't do, Dr. Ramos . . ."

"Call me Laszlo."

"That I won't do, Laszlo. As a matter of fact, I've been thinking about it already."

"I knew you would be."

"I figure that by cutting out a couple of meetings next week–I can use Larry's death as an excuse, some way; I'll use anything, actually –I can reconstruct most of them from memory. Well, maybe not in a week, come to think of it. I'll have to send for copies of some of the reports. But sooner or later . . ."

"Right. That's what I want to talk to you about." The girl brought the coffee and sandwiches and he waved her away briskly as soon as she'd set them down. "You see, you're the man I came here to see."

I looked at him. "You're interested in photometry?"

"No. Not your paper–your idea. What we were talking about all night, for God's sake. I didn't know it was you I wanted until Resnik mentioned you yesterday. But after last night, I was sure."

"I already have a job, Dr.–Laszlo."

"And I'm not offering you a job."

"Then, what . . ."

"I'm offering you a chance to make your idea work. I've got money, Chip, foundation money looking for something to be spent on. Not space research or cancer research or higher mathematics–they're funded well enough now. My foundation is looking for projects that don't fit into the usual patterns. Big ones. Like yours."

Well, of course I was excited. It was so good to be taken that seriously.

"I called the board secretary in Washington first thing–I mean, as soon as they were open there. Of course, I couldn't give him enough over the phone for a formal commitment. But he's on the hook, Chip. And the board will go along. There's a meeting next week and I want you there."

"In Washington? I suppose . . ."

"Well, no. The foundation's international, Chip, and this meeting's at Lake Como. But we'll pick up the tab, of course, and you can get a lot more done there, where your office isn't going to call you . . ."

"But, I mean, I'm not sure . . ."

"We'll back you. Everything you need. A staff. A headquarters. We've got the beginnings of a facility in Ames, Iowa; you'll have to go out there, of course. But it shouldn't be more than, oh, say, a couple days a month. And"—he grinned, a little apologetically—"I know it won't mean anything to you. After you've got one medal on your chest, the rest aren't too exciting. But it'll look nice in your *Who's Who* entry; and, anyway, the secretary has already authorized me to tell you that you're invited to accept appointment to a trusteeship."

I began to need the coffee and I took a long swallow. "You're moving too fast for me, Laszlo," I said.

"The trustees meet in Flagstaff; they've got a country-club deal there. You'll like it. Of course, it's only six times a year. But it's worth it, Chip. I mean, we have our politics like everything else; and if you're a trustee, you swing a lot of weight."

And he prattled on, and I sat there listening, and it was all coming true, everything I'd hoped for; and the next week in Italy, in a great shiny room with an enormous window looking out over Lake Como, I found myself a full-fledged project director, with status as a trustee, honorary membership on the priorities committee and a staff of forty-one.

Next week we dedicate the Lawrence Resnik Memorial Building in Ames—the name was my idea, but everybody agreed—and although it's been a hell of a year, I can see where we'll really make progress now. It still seems a little incongruous that I should be putting in so much time on managerial work and conferences. But when I mentioned it to Laszlo the other day in Montreal, he gave me the grin and an approving look. "I wondered how long it would take you to think of that," he chuckled. "But it's best to make haste slowly, and you can see for yourself it's paying off. Have I told you what a good impression your lecture tour made?"

"Thanks. Yes, as a matter of fact, you did. Anyway, once we get the Resnik installation going, there'll be a little more time."

"Damn right! And don't say I told you"—he winked—"but remember what I told you about a possible appointment to the President's Commission on Interdisciplinary Affairs? Well, it's not official. But it's definite. We've already taken a suite at the Shoreham for you.

You'll be using it a lot. We've even fitted up a room as an office; you can keep your notes and things there between trips."

Well, I told him, of course, that if he meant the notes I had been trying to reconstruct, they didn't require all that much room. Not by quite a lot, since I haven't in all truth got very far.

I think I would have, somehow or other, with a little luck. But I haven't actually been very lucky. Poor Honeyman, for instance–I'd already written him for another copy of the report he'd made up for me when I heard that his yawl had capsized in a storm. They didn't even find his body for a week. And nobody seems to know where he kept his copy of the report, if he ever made one. And . . .

Well, there was that funny thing Resnik said the day he died, about how the world conspired against anybody who'd ever done anything. And then he said, "I'm not even sure it's this world."

I figured out what the joke was–that is, if it was a joke. I mean, just for a hypothesis, suppose Somebody didn't want us to get ahead as fast as we could, Somebody from another world . . .

That's silly. That is, I think it's silly.

But if that line of thinking isn't silly, then it must be something quite the opposite of silly; by which I mean it must be dangerous. Just recently, I've almost been run over twice by crazy drivers in front of my own house. And then there's the air taxi I missed and saw crash on take-off before my eyes.

Just for the fun of it, there are two things I'd like to know. One is where the foundation gets its money and why. The other–and I just might see if I can get an answer to this one, next time I'm in L. A.–is whether there really were a pair of honeymooners in room 2051 that morning, to be accidentally awakened by Laszlo Ramos just about the time that Larry was on his way down twenty flights.

The Richest Man in Levittown

MARGERY tried putting the phone back on the hook, but it immediately rang again. She kicked the stand, picked up the phone and said: "Hang up, will you? We don't want any!" She slammed the phone down to break the connection and took it off the hook again.

The doorbell rang.

"My turn," I said, and put down the paper—it looked as though I never would find out what the National League standings were. It was Patrolman Gamelsfelder.

"Man to see you, Mr. Binns. Says it's important." He was sweating—you could see the black patches on his blue shirt. I knew what he was thinking: We had air conditioning and money, and he was risking his life day after day for a lousy policeman's pay, and what kind of a country was this anyhow? He'd said as much that afternoon.

"It might be important to him, but I don't want to see anybody. Sorry, officer." I closed the door.

Margery said: "Are you or are you not going to help me change the baby?"

I said cheerfully: "I'll be glad to, dear." And it was true—besides being good policy to say that, since she was pretty close to exploding. It was true because I wanted something to do myself. I wanted some nice, simple, demanding task like holding a one-year-old down with my knee in the middle of his chest, while one hand held his feet and the other one pinned the diaper. I mean, it was nice of Uncle Otto to leave me the money, but did they have to put it in the paper?

The doorbell rang again as I was finishing. Margery was upstairs with Gwennie, who took a lot of calming down because she'd had an exciting day, and because she always did, so I stood the baby on his fat little feet and answered the door myself. It was the policeman again. "Some telegrams for you, Mr. Binns. I wooden let the boy deliver them."

"Thanks." I tossed them in the drawer of the telephone stand. What was the use of opening them? They were from people who had heard about Uncle Otto and the money, and who wanted to sell me something.

"That fellow's still here," Patrolman Gamelsfelder said sourly. "I think he's sick."

"Too bad." I tried to close the door.

"Anyway, he says to tell Cuddles that Tinker is here."

I grabbed the door. "Tell Cud . . ."

"That's what he said." Gamelsfelder saw that that hit me, and it pleased him. For the first time he smiled.

"What–what's his name?"

"Winston McNeely McGhee," said Officer Gamelsfelder happily, "or anyway that's what he told me, Mr. Binns."

I said, "Send the son of a– Send the fellow in," I said, and jumped to get the baby away from the ashtray where Margery had left a cigarette burning. Winnie McGhee–it was all I needed to finish off my day.

He came in holding his head as though it weighed a thousand pounds. He was never what you'd call healthy-looking, even when Margery stood me up at the altar in order to elope with him. It was his frail, poetic charm, and maybe he still had that, and maybe he didn't, but the way he looked to me, he was sick, all right. He looked like he weighed a fast hundred pounds not counting the head; the head looked like a balloon. He moaned, "Hello, Harlan, age thirty-one, five-eleven, one seventy-three. You got an acetylsalicylic acid tablet?"

I said, "What?" But he didn't get a chance to answer right away because there was a flutter and a scurry from the expansion attic and Margery appeared at the head of the stairs. "I thought–" she began wildly, and then she saw that her wildest thought was true. "You!" She betrayed pure panic–fussing with her hair with one hand and smoothing her Bermuda shorts with the other, simultaneously trying to wiggle, no-hands, out of the sloppy old kitchen apron that had been good enough for *me*.

McGhee said pallidly, "Hello. Please, don't you have an acetylsalicylic acid tablet?"

"I don't know what it is," I said simply.

Margery chuckled ruefully. "Ah, Harlan, Harlan," she said with fond tolerance, beaming lovingly at me as she came down the stairs. It was enough to turn the stomach of a cat.

"You forget, Winnie. Harlan doesn't know much chemistry. Won't you find him an aspirin, Harlan? That's all he wants."

"Thanks," said Winnie with a grateful sigh, massaging his temples.

I went and got him an aspirin. I thought of adding a little mixer to the glass of water that went with it, but there wasn't anything in the medicine chest that looked right, and besides it's against the law. I don't mind admitting it, I never liked Winnie McGhee, and it isn't just because he swiped my bride from me. Well, she smartened up after six months, and then, when she turned up with an annulment and sincere repentance–well, I've never regretted marrying her. Or anyway, not much. But you can't expect me to like McGhee. My heavens, if I'd never *seen* the man before I'd hate his little purple guts on first contact, because he looks like a poet and talks like a scientist and acts like a jerk.

I started back to the living room and yelled: "The baby!"

Margery turned away from simpering at her former husband and sprang for the puppy's dish. She got it away from the baby, but not quite full. There was a good baby-sized mouthful of mixed milk and dog-biscuit that she had to excavate for, and naturally the baby had his way of counter-attacking for *that*.

"No bite!" she yelled, pulling her finger out of his mouth and putting it in hers. Then she smiled sweetly. "Isn't he a darling, Winnie? He's got his daddy's nose, of course. But don't you think he has my eyes?"

"He'll have your fingers too, if you don't keep them out of his mouth," I told her.

Winnie said: "That's normal. After all, with twenty-four paired chromosomes forming the gamete, it is perfectly obvious that the probability of inheriting none of his traits from one parent–that is, being exactly like the other–is one chance in 8,388,608. Ooh, my head."

Margery gave him a small frown. "What?"

He was like a wound-up phonograph. "That's without allowance for spontaneous mutation," he added. *"Or* induced. And considering the environmental factors *in utero*–that is, broad-spectrum antibiotics, tripling of the background radiation count due to nuclear weapons, dietary influences, *et cetera*–yes, I should put the probability of induced mutation rather high. Yes. Perhaps of the order of–"

I interrupted. "Here's your aspirin. Now, what do you want?"

"Harlan!" Margery said warningly.

"I mean–well, what *do* you want?"

He leaned his head on his hands. "I want you to help me conquer the world," he said.

Crash-splash. "Go get a mop!" Margery ordered; the baby had just spilled the puppy's water. She glared at me and smiled at Winnie. "Go ahead," she coaxed. "Take your nice aspirin, and we'll talk about your trip around the world later."

But that hadn't been what he had said.

Conquer the world. I heard it plain as day. I went to fetch the mop, because that was as good a way as any to think over what to do about Winston McNeely McGhee. I mean, what did I want with the world? Uncle Otto had already *bequeathed* me the world, or anyway as much of it as I ever hoped to own.

When I came back Winnie was tottering around the room, followed at a respectful distance by my wife holding the baby. She was saying to the prospective conqueror of all the world:

"How did you hear about Harlan's good lu– About the tragic loss of his dear uncle, I mean?"

He groaned, "I read it in the paper." He fiddled aimlessly with the phone.

"It's all for the best, I say," said Margery in a philosophic tone, carving damp graham-cracker crumbs out of the baby's ear. "Dear Otto lived a rich and full life. Think of all those years in Yemen! And the enormous satisfaction it must have given him to be personally responsible for the installation of the largest petroleum-cracking still west of the Suez!"

"*East,* my dear. East. The Mutawakelite Kingdom lies just south of Saudi Arabia."

She looked at him thoughtfully, but all she said was, "Winnie, you've changed."

And so he had; but for that matter so had she. It was not like Margery to be a hypocrite. Simpering over her ex-husband I could understand–it wasn't so bad; she was merely showing the poor guy how very much better off she was than she ever would have been with him. But the tragic loss of my dear uncle had never occasioned a moment's regret in her–*or* in me; the plain fact of the matter is that until the man from the Associated Press called up she didn't even know I had an Uncle Otto. And I had pretty nearly forgotten it myself. Otto was the brother that my mother's family didn't talk about. How were they to know that he was laying up treasures of oil and gold on the Arabian Peninsula?

The phone rang; Winnie had thoughtlessly put it back on the

hook. "No!" Margery cried into it, hardly listening, "We don't want any uranium stock! We've got *closets* full!"

I said, taking advantage of the fact that her attention was diverted: "Winnie. I'm a busy man. How about you telling me what you want?"

He sat down with his head on his hands and made a great effort.

"It's—difficult," he said, speaking very slowly. Each word came out by itself, as though he had to choose and sort painfully among all the words that were rushing to his mouth. "I—invented something. You understand? And when I heard about you inheriting money—"

"You thought you could get some of it away from me," I sneered.

"No!" He sat up sharply—and winced and clutched his head. "I want to *make* money for you."

"We've got closets full," I said gently.

He said in a desperate tone, "But I can give you the world, Harlan. Trust me!"

"I never have—"

"Trust me now! You don't understand, Harlan. We can own the world, the two of us, if you'll just give me a little financial help. I've invented a drug that gives me total recall."

"How nice for you," I said, reaching for the knob of the door.

But then I began to think.

"Total recall?" I asked.

He said, sputtering with eagerness, "The upwelling of the unconscious! The ability to remember everything—the eidetic memory of an idiot savant and the indexing system of a quiz winner. You want to know the first six kings of England? Egbert, Ethelwulf, Ethelbald, Ethelbert, Ethelred and Alfred. You want to know the mating call of a ruff-necked grouse?" He demonstrated the call of the ruff-necked grouse.

"Oh," said Margery, coming back into the room with the freshly diapered baby. "Bird imitations."

"And more!" cried Winnie. "Do you know about the time the United States had two presidents?"

"No, but—"

"March the third," he said. "Eighteen seventy-seven. Rutherford B. Hayes—I'd better say Rutherford *Birchard* Hayes—was about to succeed Grant, and he was sworn in a day early. I ought to explain that—"

"No," I said. "Don't explain."

"Well, how about this? Want me to name the A.B.C. bowling champions from 1931 to date? Clack, Nitschke, Hewitt, Vidro, Brokaw, Gagliardi, Anderson—oh, wait a minute. I forgot 1936. That's Warren. *Then* Gagliardi, Anderson, Danek—"

"Winnie," I said, "cut it out, will you? This has been a tough day."

"But this is the key to conquering the world!"

"Hah," I said. "You're going to bore everybody to death by naming bowling champions?"

"Knowledge is power, Harlan." He rested his head on his palms briefly. "But it does make my head ache."

I took my hand off the knob of the door.

I said grudgingly, "Sit down, Winnie. I admit you've got me interested. I can't wait to hear what the swindle is."

"Harlan!" warned Margery.

Winnie said: "There's no swindle, I promise you. But think what it can mean! Knowledge is power, Harlan, as I say. Why, with my super-brain we can outwit the rulers of any country anywhere. We can own the world! And—money, you say? Knowledge is money too. For instance—" he winked—"worried about taxes? I can tell you the minority opinion in U. S. Govt. *v.* Oosterhagen, 486 Alabama 3309. There's a loophole there you could drive an armored truck through!"

Margery sat down with a cigarette in the long, long holder I'd bought her to square a beef the year after we were married. She looked at me and then at the cigarette; and it penetrated, and I raced over with a match.

"Thank you, darling," she said throatily.

She had changed herself as well as the baby. She now wore something more suitable for a co-heiress of a big fat hunk of money entertaining an ex-husband. It was a gold lamé housecoat, and she had bought it, within an hour of the time the Associated Press man had called, on a charge account we'd never owned until the early editions of the papers hit the stores around Levittown.

And that reminded me. Money. Who needed money? What was the use of inheriting all that loot from Uncle Otto if I couldn't throw Winnie out on his ear?

Politeness made me temporize: "All this is very interesting, Winnie, but—"

"Harlan, the baby!" Margery yelled. "Get him out of the pretzels!"

I did, while Winnie said faintly behind me: "The shape of a pretzel represents children's arms folded in prayer—or so it was thought in the seventh century. A good pretzel bender can bend more than thirty-five a minute. Of course, machines are faster."

I said, "Winnie—"

"Like to know the etymology of the word 'navvy'? Most people think it has something to do with sailors."

"Winnie, listen to me–"

"It doesn't, though. It comes from the laborers on the Inland Navigation Canals–eighteenth-century England, you know. Well, the laborers–"

I said firmly, "Winnie, go away."

"Harlan!"

"You stay out of this, Margery," I told her. "Winnie's after my dough, that's all. Well, I haven't had it long enough to want to throw it away. Besides, who wants to rule the world?"

"Well . . ." Margery said thoughtfully.

"With all our money?" I cried. "Who needs it?"

Winnie clutched his head. "Oh," he moaned. "Wait, Harlan. All I need is a stake. I've got the long-term cycles of every stock on the Exchange down in my head–splits and dividends and earnings records since nineteen ought four! I know the private brokers' hand signals on the Curb–wave up for buy, wave down for sell; look, see how my fingers are bent? That means the spread between bid and asked is three-eighths of a point. Give me a million dollars, Harlan!"

"No."

"Just a million, that's all. You can spare it! And I'll double it in a week, quadruple it in a month–in a year we'll have a billion. A billion dollars!"

I shook my head. "The taxes–"

"Remember U. S. Govt. *v.* Oosterhagen!" he cried. "And that's a bare beginning. Ever think what a billion dollars could do in the hands of a super-genius?" He was talking faster and faster, a perfect diarrhoea of words, as though he couldn't control the spouting. "Here!" he yelled, clutching at his temple with one hand, pulling something out of his pocket with the other. "Look at this, Harlan! It's yours for a million dollars–no, for a hundred thousand. Yes, a hundred thousand dollars and you can have it! I'll sell it for that, and then I won't split with you–we'll *both* be super-geniuses. Eh? Fair enough?"

I was trapped by my own curiosity. "What is it?" I asked. He waved it at me–a squat little bottle, half-filled with pale capsules.

"Mine," he said proudly. "My hormone. It's a synapse-relaxer. One of these and the blocks between adjoining cells in your brain are weakened for an hour. Three of them, for every twenty pounds of body weight, and you're a super-genius for life. You'll never forget! You'll remember things you think have passed out of your recollection years ago! You'll recall the post-partum slap that started you breathing, you'll remember the name of the nurse who carried you to the door of your father's Maxwell. Oh, Harlan, there is simply no limit to—"

"Go away," I said, and pushed him.

Patrolman Gamelsfelder appeared like a genie from a lamp.

"Thought so," he said somberly, advancing on Winnie McGhee. "Extortion's your game, is it? Can't say I blame you, brother, but it's a trip to the station house and a talk with the sergeant for you."

"Just get rid of him," I said, and closed the door as Winnie was challenging the cop to name an opera by Krenek, other than *Johnny Spielt Auf*.

Margery put the baby down, breathing hard.

She said: "*Scuffling* and pushing people *around* and bad *manners*. You weren't like this when we were married, Harlan. There's something come over you since you inherited that money!"

I said, "Help me pick these things up, will you?" I hadn't pushed him hard, but all the same those pills had gone flying.

Margery stamped her foot and burst into tears. "I *know* how you feel about poor Winnie," she sobbed, "but it's just that I'm *sorry* for him. "Couldn't you at least be polite? Couldn't you at least have given him a couple of lousy hundred thousand dollars?"

"Watch the baby," I warned her. At the head of the stairs Gwennie appeared, attracted by the noise, rubbing her eyes with her fists and beginning to cry.

Margery glared at me, started to speak, was speechless, turned her back and hurried up to comfort Gwennie.

I began to feel the least little bit ashamed of myself.

I stood up, patting the baby absent-mindedly on the head, looking up the stairs at the female half of our household. I had been, when you stopped to think of it, something of a clunk.

Item: I had been rough on poor old Winnie. Suppose it had been I who discovered the hormone, and needed a few lousy hundred thousand, as Margery put it so well, as a stake in order to grasp undreamed-of wealth and power? Well, why not? Why shouldn't I have given it to him? The poor fellow was evidently suffering the effects of the hormone wearing off as much as from any hangover. I could have been more kind, yes.

And, item: Margery did have a tough time with the kids and all, and on this day of all days she was likely to be excited.

And, item: I had just inherited a bloody mint!

Why wasn't I—the thought came to me with sudden appalling clarity—using some of Uncle Otto's money to make life easier for all of us?

I galloped up the steps two at a time. "Margery," I cried. "Margery, I'm sorry!"

"I think you should—" she began and then looked up from Gwennie and saw my face.

I said: "Look, honey. Let's start over. I'm sorry about poor Winnie, but forget him, huh? We're rich. Let's start living as though we were rich! Let's go out, just the two of us—it's early yet! We'll grab a cab and go into New York—all the way by cab, why not? We'll eat at the Colony, and see *My Fair Lady* from the fifth row on the aisle—you can get quite good seats, they tell me, for a hundred bucks or so. Why not?"

Margery looked up at me, and suddenly smiled. "But—" she patted Gwennie's head. "The kids. What about them?"

"Get a baby-sitter," I cried. "Mrs. Schroop'll be glad of the work."

"But it's such short notice—"

"Margery," I said, "we don't inherit a fortune *every* night. Call her up."

Margery stood up, holding Gwennie, beginning to smile. "Why," she said, "that sounds like fun, Harlan! Why not, as you say? Only—do you remember Mrs. Schroop's number?"

"It's written down," I told her.

"No, that was on the old directory." She frowned. "You've told it to me a thousand times. It isn't listed in her own name—it's her son-in-law. Oh, what *is* that number . . ."

A thin voice from down the stairs said: "Ovington Eight Zero Zero Fourteen. It's listed under Sturgis, Arthur R., number Forty-one Universe Avenue."

Margery looked at me, and I looked at Margery.

I said sharply: "Who the devil said that?"

"I did, Daddy," said the owner of the voice, all of twenty-eight inches tall, appearing at the foot of the steps. He had to use one hand to steady himself, because he didn't walk so very well; in the other hand he held the squat glass bottle that Winnie McGhee had dropped.

The bottle was empty.

Well, we don't live in Levittown any more—of course.

Margery and Gwennie and I have tried everything—changing our name, dyeing our hair, even plastic surgery once. It didn't work, so we had the same surgeon change us back.

People keep recognizing us.

What we mostly do now is cruise up and down the coast of the U.S.J.I. in our yacht, inside the twelve-mile limit. When we need supplies we send some of the crew in with the motor launch. That's risky, yes. But it isn't as risky as landing in any other country would be; and we just don't want to go back to J.I.–as they've taken to calling it these days. You can't blame us. How would *you* like it?

I wish he'd leave us alone.

The way it goes, we just cruise up and down, and every once in a while he remembers us and calls up on the ship-to-shore. He called yesterday, matter of fact. He said: "You can't stay out there forever, Daddy. Your main engines are due for a refit after eleven months, seven days of running and you've been gone ten months, six. What are you using for dairy products? The load you shipped in Jacksonville must have run out last Thursday week. There isn't any point in your starving yourself. Besides, it's not fair to Gwennie and Mom. Come home. We'll make a place for you in the government."

"Thanks," I said. "But no thanks."

"You'll be sorry," he warned, pleasantly enough. And he hung up.

Well, we should have kept him out of those pills.

I guess it was my fault. I should have listened when old Winnie–heaven rest his soul, wherever he is–said that the lifetime dose was three tablets for every twenty pounds of body weight. The baby only weighed twenty-four pounds then–last time we'd taken him to the pediatrician; naturally, we couldn't take him again after he swallowed the pills. And he must've swallowed at least a dozen.

But I guess Winnie was right.

At the very least, the world is well on its way to being conquered now. The United States fell to Juvens Imperator, as he calls himself (and I blame Margery for that–*I* never used Latin in front of the kid) in eighteen months, after his sensational coup on the $256,000 Question, and his later success in cornering soybean futures and the common stock of United States Steel. The rest of the world is just a matter of time. And not very much time, at that. And don't they just know it, though; that's why we daren't land abroad.

But who would have thought it?

I mean, I watched his inauguration last October, on the television. The country has had some pretty peculiar people running it, no doubt. But did you ever think you'd live to see the oath of office administered to my little boy, with one hand upraised and the thumb of the other in his mouth?

The Day the Icicle Works Closed

I

THE wind was cold, pink snow was falling and Milo Pulcher had holes in his shoes. He trudged through the pink-gray slush across the square from the courthouse to the jail. The turnkey was drinking coffee out of a vinyl container. "Expecting you," he grunted. "Which one you want to see first?"

Pulcher sat down, grateful for the warmth. "It doesn't matter. Say, what kind of kids are they?"

The turnkey shrugged.

"I mean, do they give you any trouble?"

"How could they give me trouble? If they don't clean their cells they don't eat. What else they do makes no difference to me."

Pulcher took the letter from Judge Pegrim out of his pocket, and examined the list of his new clients. Avery Foltis, Walter Hopgood, Jimmy Lasser, Sam Schlesterman, Bourke Smith, Madeleine Gaultry. None of the names meant anything to him. "I'll take Foltis," he guessed, and followed the turnkey to a cell.

The Foltis boy was homely, pimply and belligerent. "Cripes," he growled shrilly, "are you the best they can do for me?"

Pulcher took his time answering. The boy was not very lovable; but, he reminded himself, there was a fifty-dollar retainer from the county for each one of these defendants, and conditions being what they were Pulcher could easily grow to love three hundred dollars. "Don't give me a hard time," he said amiably. "I may not be the best lawyer in the Galaxy, but I'm the one you've got."

"Cripes."

"All right, all right. Tell me what happened, will you? All I know is that you're accused of conspiracy to commit a felony, specifically an act of kidnaping a minor child."

"Yeah, that's it," the boy agreed. "You want to know what happened?" He bounced to his feet, then began acting out his story. "We were starving to death, see?" Arms clutched pathetically around his belly. "The Icicle Works closed down. Cripes, I walked the streets nearly a year, looking for something to do. Anything." Marching in place. "I even rented out for a while, but–that didn't work out." He scowled and fingered his pimply face. Pulcher nodded. Even a body-renter had to have some qualifications. The most important one was a good-looking, disease-free, strong and agile physique. "So we got together and decided, the hell, there was money to be made hooking old Swinburne's son. So–I guess we talked too much. They caught us." He gripped his wrists, like manacles.

Pulcher asked a few more questions, and then interviewed two of the other boys. He learned nothing he hadn't already known. The six youngsters had planned a reasonably competent kidnaping, and talked about it where they could be heard, and if there was any hope of getting them off it did not make itself visible to their court-appointed attorney.

Pulcher left the jail abruptly and went up the street to see Charley Dickon.

The committeeman was watching a three-way wrestling match on a flickery old TV set. "How'd it go, Milo," he greeted the lawyer, keeping his eyes on the wrestling.

Pulcher said, "I'm not going to get them off, Charley."

"Oh? Too bad." Dickon looked away from the set for the first time. "Why not?"

"They admitted the whole thing. Handwriting made the Hopgood boy on the ransom note. They all had fingerprints and cell-types all over the place. And besides, they talked too much."

Dickon said with a spark of interest, "What about Tim Lasser's son?"

"Sorry." The committeeman looked thoughtful. "I can't help it, Charley," the lawyer protested. The kids hadn't been even routinely careful. When they planned to kidnap the son of the mayor they had talked it over, quite loudly, in a juke joint. The waitress habitually taped everything that went on in her booths. Pulcher suspected a thriving blackmail business, but that didn't change the fact that there was enough on tape to show premeditation. They had picked the mayor's son up at school. He had come with them perfectly willingly–the girl, Madeleine Gaultry, had been a babysitter for him. The boy was only three years old, but he couldn't miss an easy identification like that. And there was more: the ransom note had been sent special delivery, and young Foltis had asked the post-office clerk to put the postage on instead of using the automatic meter. The clerk remembered the pimply face very well indeed.

The committeeman sat politely while Pulcher explained, though it was obvious that most of his attention was on the snowy TV screen. "Well, Milo, that's the way it goes. Anyway, you got a fast three hundred, hey? And that reminds me."

Pulcher's guard went up.

"Here," said the committeeman, rummaging through his desk. He brought out a couple of pale green tickets. "You ought to get out and meet some more people. The Party's having its annual Chester A. Arthur Day Dinner next week. Bring your girl."

"I don't have a girl."

"Oh, you'll find one. Fifteen dollars per," explained the committeeman, handing over the tickets. Pulcher sighed and paid. Well, that was what kept the wheels oiled. And Dickon had suggested his name to Judge Pegrim. Thirty dollars out of three hundred still left him a better week's pay than he had had since the Icicle Works folded.

The committeeman carefully folded the bills into his pocket, Pulcher watching gloomily. Dickon was looking prosperous, all right. There was easily a couple of thousand in that wad. Pulcher supposed that Dickon had been caught along with everybody else on the planet when the Icicle Works folded. Nearly everybody owned stock in it, and certainly Charley Dickon, whose politician brain got him a piece of nearly every major enterprise on Altair Nine—a big clump of stock in the Tourist Agency, a sizable share of the Mining Syndicate—certainly he would have had at least a few thousand in the Icicle Works. But it hadn't hurt him much. He said, "None of my business, but why don't you take that girl?"

"Madeleine Gaultry? She's in jail."

"Get her out. Here." He tossed over a bondsman's card. Pulcher pocketed it with a scowl. That would cost another forty bucks anyway, he estimated; the bondsman would naturally be one of Dickon's club members.

Pulcher noticed that Dickon was looking strangely puzzled. "What's the matter?"

"Like I say, it's none of my business. But I don't get it. You and the girl have a fight?"

"Fight? I don't even know her."

"She said you did."

"Me? No. I don't know any Madeleine Gaultry– Wait a minute! Is that her married name? Did she used to be at the Icicle Works?"

Dickon nodded. "Didn't you see her?"

"I didn't get to the women's wing. I–" Pulcher stood up, oddly flustered. "Say, I'd better run along, Charley. This bondsman, he's open now? Well–" He stopped babbling and left.

Madeleine Gaultry! Only her name had been Madeleine Cossett. It was funny that she should turn up now–in jail and, Pulcher abruptly realized, likely to stay there indefinitely. But he put that thought out of his mind; first he wanted to see her.

The snow was turning lavender now.

Pink snow, green snow, lavender snow–any color of the pastel rainbow. It was nothing unusual. That was what had made Altair Nine worth colonizing in the first place.

Now, of course, it was only a way of getting your feet wet.

Pulcher waited impatiently at the turnkey's office while he shambled over to the women's wing and, slowly, returned with the girl. They looked at each other. She didn't speak. Pulcher opened his mouth, closed it, and silently took her by the elbow. He steered her out of the jail and hailed a cab. That was an extravagance, but he didn't care.

Madeleine shrank into a corner of the cab, looking at him out of blue eyes that were large and shadowed. She wasn't hostile, she wasn't afraid. She was only remote.

"Hungry?" She nodded. Pulcher gave the cab driver the name of a restaurant. Another extravagance, but he didn't mind the prospect of cutting down on lunches for a few weeks. He had had enough practice at it.

A year before this girl had been the prettiest secretary in the pool at the Icicle Works. He dated her half a dozen times. There was a company rule against it, but the first time it was a kind of schoolboy's prank, breaking the headmaster's regulations, and the other times it was a driving need. Then–

Then came the Gumpert Process.

That was the killer, the Gumpert Process. Whoever Gumpert was. All anybody at the Icicle Works knew was that someone named Gumpert (back on Earth, one rumor said; another said he was a colonist in the Sirian system) had come up with a cheap, practical method of synthesizing the rainbow antibiotic molds that floated free in Altair Nine's air, coloring its precipitation and, more important, providing a priceless export commodity. A whole Galaxy had depended on those rainbow molds, shipped in frozen suspensions to every inhabited planet by Altamycin, Inc.–the proper name for what everyone on Altair Nine called the Icicle Works.

When the Gumpert Process came along, suddenly the demand vanished.

Worse, the jobs vanished. Pulcher had been on the corporation's legal staff, with an office of his own and a faint hint of a vice-presidency, some day. He was out. The stenos in the pool, all but two or three of the five hundred who once had got out the correspondence and the bills, they were out. The shipping clerks in the warehouse were out, the pumphands at the settling tanks were out, the freezer attendants were out. Everyone was out. The plant closed down. There were more than fifty tons of frozen antibiotics in storage and, though there might still be a faint trickle of orders from old-fashioned die-hards around the Galaxy (backwoods country doctors who didn't believe in the new-fangled synthetics, experimenters who wanted to run comparative tests), the shipments already en route would much more than satisfy them. Fifty tons? Once the Icicle Works had shipped three hundred tons a day–physical transport, electronic rockets that took years to cover the distance between stars. The boom was over. And of course, on a one-industry planet, everything else was over too.

Pulcher took the girl by the arm and swept her into the restaurant. "Eat," he ordered. "I know what jail food is like." He sat down, firmly determined to say nothing until she had finished.

But he couldn't.

Long before she was ready for coffee he burst out, "Why, Madeleine? Why would you get into something like this?"

She looked at him but did not answer.

"What about your husband?" He didn't want to ask it, but he had to. That had been the biggest blow of all the unpleasant blows that had struck him after the Icicle Works closed. Just as he was getting a law practice going–not on any big scale but, through Charley Dickon and the Party, a small, steady handout of political favors that would make it possible for him to pretend he was still an attorney–the gossip reached him that Madeleine Cossett had married.

The girl pushed her plate away. "He emigrated."

Pulcher digested that slowly. Emigrated? That was the dream of every Niner since the Works closed down, of course. But it was only a dream. Physical transport between the stars was ungodly expensive. More, it was ungodly slow. Ten years would get you to Dell, the thin-aired planet of a chilly little red dwarf. The nearest *good* planet was thirty years away.

What it all added up to was that emigrating was almost like dying. If one member of a married couple emigrated, it meant the end of the marriage. . . . "We got a divorce," said Madeleine, nodding. "There wasn't enough money for both of us to go, and Jon was unhappier here than I was."

She took out a cigarette and let him light it. "You don't want to ask me about Jon, do you? But you want to know. All right. Jon was an artist. He was in the advertising department at the Works, but that was just temporary. He was going to do something big. Then the bottom dropped out for him, just as it did for all of us. Well, Milo, I didn't hear from you."

Pulcher protested, "It wouldn't have been *fair* for me to see you when I didn't have a job or anything."

"Of course you'd think that. It's wrong. But I couldn't find you to tell you it was wrong, and then Jon was very persistent. He was tall, curly-haired, he has a baby's face–do you know, he only shaved twice a week. Well, I married him. It lasted three months. Then he just had to get away." She leaned forward earnestly. "Don't think he was just a bum, Milo! He really was quite a good artist. But we didn't have enough money for paints, even, and then it seems that the colors are all wrong here. Jon explained it. In order to paint landscapes that sell you have to be on a planet with Earth-type colors; they're all the vogue. And there's too much altamycin in the clouds here."

Pulcher said stiffly, "I see." But he didn't, really. There was at least one unexplained part. If there hadn't been enough money for paint, then where had the money come from for a starship ticket, physical transport? It meant at least ten thousand dollars. There just was no way to raise ten thousand dollars on Altair Nine, not without taking a rather extreme step. . . .

The girl wasn't looking at him.

Her eyes were fixed on a table across the restaurant, a table with a loud, drunken party. It was only lunch time, but they had a three-o'clock-in-the-morning air about them. They were *stinking.* There were four of them, two men and two women; and their physical bodies were those of young, healthy, quite good-looking, perfectly normal Niners. The appearance of the physical bodies was entirely irrelevant, though, because they were tourists. Around the neck of each of them was a bright golden choker with a glowing red signal-jewel in the middle. It was the mark of the tourist Agency; the sign that the bodies were rented.

Milo Pulcher looked away quickly. His eyes stopped on the white face of the girl, and abruptly he knew how she had raised the money to send Jon to another star.

II

Pulcher found the girl a room and left her there. It was not what he wanted. What he wanted was to spend the evening with her and to go on spending time with her, until time came to an end: but there was the matter of her trial.

Twenty-four hours ago he had got the letter notifying him that the court had appointed him attorney for six suspected kidnapers and looked on it as a fast fee, no work to speak of, no hope for success. He would lose the case, certainly. Well, what of it?

But now he wanted to win!

It meant some fast, hard work if he was to have even a chance—and at best, he admitted to himself, the chance would not be good. Still, he wasn't going to give up without a try.

The snow stopped as he located the home of Jimmy Lasser's parents. It was a sporting-goods shop, not far from the main Tourist Agency; it had a window full of guns and boots and scuba gear. He walked in, tinkling a bell as he opened the door.

"Mr. Lasser?" A plump little man, leaning back in a chair by the door, got slowly up, looking him over.

"In back," he said shortly.

He led Pulcher behind the store, to a three-room apartment. The living room was comfortable enough, but for some reason it seemed unbalanced. One side was somehow heavier than the other. He noticed the nap of the rug, still flattened out where something heavy had been, something rectangular and large, about the size of a Tri-V electronic entertainment unit. "Repossessed," said Lasser shortly. "Sit down. Dickon called you a minute ago."

"Oh?" It had to be something important. Dickon wouldn't have tracked him down for any trivial matter.

"Don't know what he wanted, but he said you weren't to leave till he called back. Sit down. May'll bring you a cup of tea."

Pulcher chatted with them for a minute, while the woman fussed over a teapot and a plate of soft cookies. He was trying to get the feel of the home. He could understand Madeleine Gaultry's desperation, he could understand the Foltis boy, a misfit in society anywhere. What about Jimmy Lasser?

The elder Lassers were both pushing sixty. They were first-generation Niners, off an Earth colonizing ship. They hadn't been born on Earth, of course—the trip took nearly a hundred years, physical transport. They had been born in transit, had married on the ship. As the ship had reached maximum population level shortly after they were born, they were allowed to have no children until they landed. At that time they were all of forty. May Lasser said suddenly, "Please help our boy, Mr. Pulcher! It isn't Jimmy's fault. He got in with a bad crowd. You know how it is: no work, nothing for a boy to do."

"I'll do my best." But it was funny, Pulcher thought, how it was always "the crowd" that was bad. It was never Jimmy—and never Avery, never Sam, never Walter. Pulcher sorted out the five boys and remembered Jimmy: nineteen years old, quite colorless, polite, not very interested. What had struck the lawyer about him was only surprise that this rabbity boy should have had the enterprise to get into a criminal conspiracy in the first place.

"He's a good boy," said May Lasser pathetically. "That trouble with the parked cars two years ago wasn't his fault. He got a fine job right after that, you know. Ask his probation officer. Then the Icicle Works closed. . . ." She poured more tea, slopping it over the side of the cup. "Oh, sorry! But— But when he went to the unemployment office, Mr. Pulcher, do you know what they said to him?"

"I know."

"They asked him would he take a job if offered," she hurried on, unheeding. "A *job*. As if I didn't know what they meant by a 'job!' They meant *renting*." She plumped the teapot down on the table and began to weep. "Mr. Pulcher, I wouldn't let him rent if I died for it! There isn't anything in the Bible that says you can let someone else use your body and not be responsible for what it does! You know what tourists do! 'If thy right hand offend thee, cut it off.' It doesn't say, unless somebody else is using it. Mr. Pulcher, renting is a *sin!*"

"May." Mr. Lasser put his teacup down and looked directly at Pulcher. "What about it, Pulcher? Can you get Jimmy off?"

The attorney reflected. He hadn't known about Jimmy Lasser's probation before, and that was a bad sign. If the county prosecutor was holding out on information of that sort, it meant he wasn't willing to cooperate. Probably he would be trying for a conviction with maximum sentence. Of course, he didn't have to tell a defense attorney anything about the previous criminal records of his clients. But in a juvenile case, where all parties were usually willing to go easy on the defendants, it was customary. . . . "I don't know, Mr. Lasser. I'll do the best I can."

"Damn right you will!" barked Lasser. "Dickon tell you who I am?

I was committeeman here before him, you know. So get busy. Pull strings. Dickon will back you, or I'll know why!"

Pulcher managed to control himself. "I'll do the best I can. I already told you that. If you want strings pulled, you'd better talk to Dickon yourself. I only know law. I don't know anything about politics."

The atmosphere was becoming unpleasant. Pulcher was glad to hear the ringing of the phone in the store outside. May Lasser answered it and said: "For you, Mr. Pulcher. Charley Dickon."

Pulcher gratefully picked up the phone. Dickon's rich, political voice said sorrowfully, "Milo? Listen, I been talking to Judge Pegrim's secretary. He isn't gonna let the kids off with a slap on the wrist. There's a lot of heat from the mayor's office."

Pulcher protested desperately: "But the Swinburne kid wasn't hurt! He got better care with Madeleine than he was getting at home."

"I know, Milo," the committeeman agreed, "but that's the way she lies. So what I wanted to say to you, Milo, is don't knock yourself out on this one because you aren't going to win it."

"But—" Pulcher suddenly became aware of the Lassers just behind him. "But I think I can get an acquittal," he said, entirely out of hope, knowing that it wasn't true.

Dickon chuckled. "You got Lasser breathing down your neck? Sure, Milo. But you want my advice you'll take a quick hearing, let them get sentenced and then try for executive clemency in a couple months. I'll help you get it. And that's another five hundred or so for you, see?" The committeeman was being persuasive; it was a habit of his. "Don't worry about Lasser. I guess he's been telling you what a power he is in politics here. Forget it. And, say, tell him I notice he hasn't got his tickets for the Chester A. Arthur Day Dinner yet. You pick up the dough from him, will you? I'll mail him the tickets. No —hold on, don't ask him. Just tell him what I said." The connection went dead.

Pulcher stood holding a dead phone, conscious of Lasser standing right behind him. "So long, Charley," he said, paused, nodded into space and said, "So long," again.

Then the attorney turned about to deliver the committeeman's message about that most important subject, the tickets to the Chester A. Arthur Day Dinner. Lasser grumbled, "Damn Dickon, he's into you for one thing after another. Where's he think I'm going to get thirty bucks?"

"Tim. Please." His wife touched his arm.

Lasser hesitated. "Oh, all right. But you better get Jimmy off, hear?"

Pulcher got away at last and hurried out into the cold, slushy street.

At the corner he caught a glimpse of something palely glowing overhead and stopped, transfixed. A huge skytrout was swimming purposefully down the avenue. It was a monster, twelve feet long at least and more than two feet thick at the middle; it would easily go eighteen, nineteen ounces, the sort of lunker that sportsmen hiked clear across the Dismal Hills to bag. Pulcher had never in his life seen one that size. In fact, he could only remember seeing one or two fingerlings swim over inhabited areas.

It gave him a cold, worried feeling.

The skyfish were about the only tourist attraction Altair Nine had left to offer. From all over the Galaxy sportsmen came to shoot them, with their great porous flesh filled with bubbles of hydrogen, real biological Zeppelins that did not fly in the air but swam it. Before human colonists arrived, they had been Altair Nine's highest form of life. They were so easy to destroy with gunfire that they had almost been exterminated in the inhabited sections; only in the high, cold hills had a few survived. And now. . . .

Were even the fish aware that Altair Nine was becoming a ghost planet?

The next morning Pulcher phoned Madeleine but didn't have breakfast with her, though he wanted to very much.

He put in the whole day working on the case. In the morning he visited the families and friends of the accused boys; in the afternoon he followed a few hunches.

From the families he learned nothing. The stories were all about the same. The youngest boy was Foltis, only seventeen; the oldest was Hopgood at twenty-six. They all had lost their jobs, most of them at the Icicle Works, saw no future, and wanted off-planet. Well, physical transport meant a minimum of ten thousand dollars, and not one of them had a chance in the worlds of getting that much money in any legitimate way.

Mayor Swinburne was a rich man, and his three-year-old son was the apple of his eye. It must have been an irresistible temptation to try to collect ransom money, Pulcher realized. The mayor could certainly afford it, and once the money was collected and they were aboard a starship it would be almost impossible for the law to pursue them.

Pulcher managed to piece together the way the thing had started.

The boys all lived in the same neighborhood, the neighborhood where Madeleine and Jon Gaultry had had a little apartment. They had seen Madeleine walking with the mayor's son—she had had a part-time job, now and then, taking care of him. The only part of the thing that was hard to believe was that Madeleine had been willing to take part in the scheme, once the boys approached her.

But Milo, remembering the expression on the girl's face as she looked at the tourists, decided that wasn't so strange after all.

For Madeleine had rented.

Physical transport was expensive and eternally slow.

But there was a faster way for a man to travel from planet to planet—practically instantaneous, from one end of the Galaxy to the other. The pattern of the mind is electronic in nature. It can be taped, and it can be broadcast on an electromagnetic frequency. What was more, like any electromagnetic signal, it could be used to modulate an ultrawave carrier. The result: Instantaneous transmission of personality, anywhere in the civilized Galaxy.

The only problem was that there had to be a receiver.

The naked ghost of a man, stripped of flesh and juices, was no more than the countless radio and TV waves that passed through everyone all the time. The transmitted personality had to be given form. There were mechanical receivers, of course—computerlike affairs with mercury memory cells where a man's intelligence could be received, and could be made to activate robot bodies. But that wasn't *fun*. The tourist trade was built on *fun*. Live bodies were needed to satisfy the customers. No one wanted to spend the price of a fishing broadcast to Altair Nine in order to find himself pursuing the quarry in some clanking tractor with photocell eyes and solenoid muscles. A body was wanted, even a rather attractive body; a body which would be firm where the tourist's own, perhaps, was flabby, healthy where the tourist's own had wheezed. Having such a body, there were other sports to enjoy than fishing.

Oh, the laws were strict about misuse of rented bodies.

But the tourist trade was the only flourishing industry left on Altair Nine. The laws remained strict, but they remained unenforced.

Pulcher checked in with Charley Dickon. "I found out why Madeleine got into this thing. She rented. Signed a long-term lease with the Tourist Agency and got a big advance on her earnings."

Dickon shook his head sadly. "What people will do for money," he commented.

"It wasn't for her! She gave it to her husband, so he could get a ticket to someplace off-world." Pulcher got up, turned around and kicked his chair as hard as he could. Renting was bad enough for a man. For a woman it was–

"Take it easy," Dickon suggested, grinning. "So she figured she could buy her way out of the contract with the money from Swinburne?"

"Wouldn't you do the same?"

"Oh, I don't know, Milo. Renting's not so bad."

"The hell it isn't!"

"All right. The hell it isn't. But you ought to realize, Milo," the committeeman said stiffly, "that if it wasn't for the tourist trade we'd all be in trouble. Don't knock the Tourist Agency. They're doing a perfectly decent job."

"Then why won't they let me see the records?"

The committeeman's eyes narrowed and he sat up straighter.

"I tried," said Pulcher. "I got them to show me Madeleine's lease agreement, but I had to threaten them with a court order. Why? Then I tried to find out a little more about the Agency itself–incorporation papers, names of shareholders and so on. They wouldn't give me a thing. Why?"

Dickon said, after a second, "I could ask you that too, Milo. Why did you want to know?"

Pulcher said seriously, "I have to make a case any way I can, Charley. They're all dead on the evidence. They're guilty. But every one of them went into this kidnaping stunt in order to stay away from renting. Maybe I can't get Judge Pegrim to listen to that kind of evidence, but maybe I can. It's my only chance. If I can show that renting is a form of cruel and unusual punishment–if I can find something wrong in it, something that isn't allowed in its charter, then I have a chance. Not a good chance. But a chance. And there's got to be something wrong, Charley, because otherwise why would they be so secretive?"

Dickon said heavily, "You're getting in pretty deep, Milo. . . . Ever occur to you you're going about this the wrong way?"

"Wrong how?"

"What can the incorporation papers show you? You want to find out what renting's like. It seems to me the only way that makes sense is to try it yourself."

"Rent? Me?" Pulcher was shocked.

The committeeman shrugged. "Well, I got a lot to do," he said, and escorted Pulcher to the door.

The lawyer walked sullenly away. Rent? Him? But he had to admit that it made a certain amount of sense. . . .

He made a private decision. He would do what he could to get Madeleine and the others out of trouble. *Completely* out of trouble. But if, in the course of trying the case, he couldn't magic up some way of getting her out of the lease agreement as well as getting an acquittal, he would make damn sure that he didn't get the acquittal.

Jail wasn't so bad; renting, for Madeleine Gaultry, was considerably worse.

III

Pulcher marched into the unemployment office the next morning with an air of determination far exceeding what he really felt. Talk about loyalty to a client! But he had spent the whole night brooding about it, and Dickon had been right.

The clerk blinked at him and wheezed: "Gee, you're Mr. Pulcher, aren't you? I never thought I'd see *you* here. Things pretty slow?"

Pulcher's uncertainty made him belligerent. "I want to rent my body," he barked. "Am I in the right place or not?"

"Well, sure, Mr. Pulcher. I mean, you're not, if it's voluntary, but it's been so long since they had a voluntary that it don't make much difference, you know. I mean, I can handle it for you. Wait a minute." He turned away, hesitated, glanced at Pulcher and said, "I better use the other phone."

He was gone only a minute. He came back with a look of determined embarrassment. "Mr. Pulcher. Look. I thought I better call Charley Dickon. He isn't in his office. Why don't you wait until I can clear it with him?"

Pulcher said grimly, "It's already cleared with him."

The clerk hesitated. "But– Oh. All right," he said miserably, scribbling on a pad. "Right across the street. Oh, and tell them you're a volunteer. I don't know if that will make them leave the cuffs off you, but at least it'll give them a laugh." He chuckled.

Pulcher took the slip of paper and walked sternly across the street to the Tourist Rental Agency, Procurement Office, observing without pleasure that there were bars on the windows. A husky guard at the door straightened up as he approached and said genially, "All right, sonny. It isn't going to be as bad as you think. Just gimme your wrists a minute."

"Wait," said Pulcher quickly, putting his hands behind him. "You won't need the handcuffs for me. I'm a volunteer."

The guard said dangerously, "Don't kid with me, sonny." Then he took a closer look. "Hey, I know you. You're the lawyer. I saw you at the Primary Dance." He scratched his ear. He said doubtfully, "Well, maybe you are a volunteer. Go on in." But as Pulcher strutted past he felt a heavy hand on his shoulder and, click, click, his wrists were circled with steel. He whirled furiously. "No hard feelings," boomed the guard cheerfully. "It costs a lot of dough to get you ready, that's all. They don't want you changing your mind when they give you the squeeze, see?"

"The squeeze–? All right," said Pulcher, and turned away again. The squeeze. It didn't sound so good, at that. But he had a little too much pride left to ask the guard for details. Anyway, it couldn't be *too* bad, he was sure. Wasn't he? After all, it wasn't the same as being executed. . . .

An hour and a half later he wasn't so sure.

They had stripped him, weighed him, fluorographed him, taken samples of his blood, saliva, urine and spinal fluid; they had thumped his chest and listened to the strangled pounding of the arteries in his arm.

"All right, you pass," said a fortyish blonde in a stained nurse's uniform. "You're lucky today, openings all over. You can take your pick–mining, sailing, anything you like. What'll it be?"

"What?"

"While you're *renting*. What's the matter with you? You got to be doing something while your body's rented, you know. Of course, you can have the tank if you want to. But they mostly don't like that. You're conscious the whole time, you know."

Pulcher said honestly: "I don't know what you're talking about." But then he remembered. While a person's body was rented out there was the problem of what to do with his own mind and personality. It couldn't stay in the body. It had to go somewhere else. "The tank" was a storage device, only that and nothing more; the displaced mind was held in a sort of pickling vat of transistors and cells until its own body could be returned to it. He remembered a client of his boss's, while he was still clerking, who had spent eight weeks in the tank and had then come out to commit a murder. No. Not the tank. He said, coughing, "What else is there?"

The nurse said impatiently, "Golly, whatever you want, I guess. They've got a big call for miners operating the deep gas generators right now, if you want that. It's pretty hot, is all. They burn the coal into gas, and of course you're right in the middle of it. But I don't think you feel much. Not *too* much. I don't know about sailing or rocketing, because you have to have some experience for that. There might be something with the taxi company, but I ought to tell you usually the renters don't want that, because the live drivers don't like seeing the machines running cabs. Sometimes if they see a machine-cab they tip it over. Naturally, if there's any damage to the host machine it's risky for you."

Pulcher said faintly, "I'll try mining."

He went out of the room in a daze, a small bleached towel around his middle his only garment and hardly aware of that. His own clothes had been whisked away and checked long ago. The tourist who would shortly wear his body would pick his own clothes; the haberdashery was one of the more profitable subsidiaries of the Tourist Agency.

Then he snapped out of his daze as he discovered what was meant by "the squeeze."

A pair of husky experts lifted him onto a slab, whisked away the towel, unlocked and tossed away the handcuffs. While one pinned him down firmly at the shoulders, the other began to turn viselike wheels that moved molded forms down upon him. It was like a sectional sarcophagus closing in on him. Pulcher had an instant childhood recollection of some story or other–the walls closing in, the victim inexorably squeezed to death. He yelled, "Hey, hold it! What are you doing?"

The man at his head, bored, said, "Oh, don't worry. This your first time? We got to keep you still, you know. Scanning's close work."

"But—"

"Now shut up and relax," the man said reasonably. "If you wiggle when the tracer's scanning you you could get your whole personality messed up. Not only that, we might damage the body an' then the Agency'd have a suit on its hands, see? Tourists don't like damaged bodies. . . . Come on, Vince. Get the legs lined up so I can do the head."

"But–" said Pulcher again, and then, with effort, relaxed. It was only for twenty-four hours, after all. He could stand anything for twenty-four hours, and he had been careful to sign up for only that long. "Go ahead," he said. "It's only for twenty-four hours."

"What? Oh, sure, friend. Lights out, now; have a pleasant dream."

And something soft but quite firm came down over his face.

He heard a muffled sound of voices. Then there was a quick ripping feeling, as though he had been plucked out of some sticky surrounding medium.

Then it *hurt*.

Pulcher screamed. It didn't accomplish anything, he no longer had a voice to scream with.

Funny, he had always thought of mining as something that was carried on underground. He was under *water*. There wasn't any doubt of it. He could see vagrant eddies of sand moving in a current; he could see real fish, not the hydrogen Zeppelins of the air; he could see bubbles, arising from some source of the sand at his feet– No! Not at his feet. He didn't have feet. He had tracks.

A great steel bug swam up in front of him and said raspingly, "All right, you there, let's go." Funny again. He didn't hear the voice with ears–he didn't have ears, and there was no stereophonic sense–but he did, somehow, hear. It seemed to be speaking inside his brain. Radio? Sonar? "Come on!" growled the bug.

Experimentally Pulcher tried to talk. "Watch it!" squeaked a thin little voice, and a tiny, many-treaded steel beetle squirmed out from under his tracks. It paused to rear back and look at him. "Dope!" it chattered scathingly. A bright flame erupted from its snout as it squirmed away.

The big bug rasped, "Go on, follow the burner, Mac." Pulcher thought of walking, rather desperately. Yes. Something was happening. He lurched and moved. "Oh, God," sighed the steel bug, hanging beside him, watching with critical attention. "This your first time? I figured. They *always* give me the new ones to break in. Look, that burner–the little thing that just went down the cline, Mac! That's a burner. It's going to burn the hard rock out of a new shaft. You follow it and pull the sludge out. With your *buckets,* Mac."

Pulcher gamely started his treads and lurchingly followed the little burner. All around him, visible through the churned, silty water, he caught glimpses of other machines working. There were big ones and little ones, some with great elephantine flexible steel trunks that sucked silt and mud away, some with wasp's stingers that planted charges of explosive, some like himself with buckets for hauling and scooping out pits. The mine, whatever sort of mine it was to be, was only a bare scratched-out beginning on the sea floor as yet. It took him–an hour? a minute? he had no means of telling time–to learn the rudiments of operating his new steel body.

Then it became boring.

Also it became painful. The first few scoops of sandy grime he carried out of the new pit made his buckets tingle. The tingle became a pain, the pain an ache, the ache a blazing agony. He stopped. Something was wrong. They couldn't expect him to go on like this! "Hey, Mac. Get busy, will you?"

"But it *hurts.*"

"Goddamighty, Mac, it's *supposed* to hurt. How else would you be able to feel when you hit something hard? You want to break your buckets on me, Mac?" Pulcher gritted his–not-teeth, squared his–not-shoulders, and went back to digging. Ultimately the pain became, through habit, bearable. It didn't become less. It just became bearable.

It was boring, except when once he did strike a harder rock than his phospher-bronze buckets could handle, and had to slither back out of the way while the burner chopped it up for him. But that was the only break in the monotony. Otherwise the work was strictly routine. It gave him plenty of time to think.

This was not altogether a boon.

I wonder, he thought with a drowned clash of buckets, I wonder what my body is doing now.

Perhaps the tenant who now occupied his body was a businessman, Pulcher thought prayerfully. A man who had had to come to Altair Nine quickly, on urgent business–get a contract signed, make a trading deal, arrange an interstellar loan. That wouldn't be so bad! A businessman would not damage a rented property. No. At the worst, a businessman might drink one or two cocktails too many, perhaps eat an indigestible lunch. All right. So when–in surely only a few hours now–Pulcher resumed his body, the worst he could expect would be a hangover or dyspepsia. Well, what of that? An aspirin. A dash of bicarb.

But maybe the tourist would not be a businessman.

Pulcher flailed the coarse sand with his buckets and thought apprehensively: He might be a sportsman. Still, even that wouldn't be so bad. The tourist might walk his body up and down a few dozen mountains, perhaps even sleep it out in the open overnight. There might be a cold, possibly even pneumonia. Of course, there might also be an accident–tourists did fall off the Dismal Hills; there could be a broken leg. But that was not *too* bad, it was only a matter of a few days rest, a little medical attention.

But maybe, Pulcher thought grayly, ignoring the teeming agony of his buckets, maybe the tenant will be something worse.

He had heard queer, smutty stories about female tenants who rented male bodies. It was against the law. But you kept hearing the stories. He had heard of men who wanted to experiment with drugs, with drink, with–with a thousand secret, sordid lusts of the flesh. All of them were unpleasant. And yet in a rented body, where the ultimate price of dissipation would be borne by someone else, who might not try one of them? For there was no physical consequence to the practitioner. If Mrs. Lasser was right, perhaps there was not even a consequence in the hereafter.

Twenty-four hours had never passed so slowly.

The suction hoses squabbled with the burners. The scoops quarreled with the dynamiters. All the animate submarine mining machines constantly irritably snapped at each other. But the work was getting done.

It seemed to be a lot of work to accomplish in one twenty-four hour day, Pulcher thought seriously. The pit was down two hundred yards now, and braced. New wet-setting concrete pourers were already laying a floor. Shimmery little spiderlike machines whose limbs held chemical testing equipment were sniffing every load of sludge that came out now for richness of ore. The mine was nearly ready to start producing.

After a time Pulcher began to understand the short tempers of the machines. None of the minds in these machines were able to forget that, up topside, their bodies were going about unknown errands, risking unguessed dangers. At any given moment that concrete pourer's body, for instance, might be dying . . . might be acquiring a disease . . . might be stretched out in narcotic stupor, or might gayly be risking dismemberment in a violent sport. Naturally tempers were touchy.

There was no such thing as rest, as coffee-breaks or sleep for the machines; they kept going. Pulcher, when finally he remembered that he had had a purpose in coming here, it was not merely some punishment that had come blindly to him for a forgotten sin, began to try to analyse his own feelings and to guess at the feelings of the others.

The whole thing seemed unnecessarily *mean.* Pulcher understood quite clearly why anyone who had had the experience of renting would never want to do it again. But why did it have to be so unpleasant? Surely, at least, conditions for the renter-mind in a machine-body could be made more bearable; the tactile sensations could be reduced from pain to some more supportable feeling without enough loss of sensation to jeopardize the desired ends.

He wondered wistfully if Madeleine had once occupied this particular machine.

Then he wondered how many of the dynamiters and diggers were female, how many male. It seemed somehow wrong that their gleaming stainless-steel or phosphor-bronze exteriors should give no hint of age or sex. There ought to be some lighter work for women, he thought idly, and then realized that the thought was nonsense. What difference did it make? You could work your buckets off, and when you got back topside you'd be healthy and rested—

And then he had a quick, dizzying qualm, as he realized that that thought would be the thought in the mind of the tourist now occupying his own body.

Pulcher licked his—not-lips and attacked the sand with his buckets more viciously than before.

"All right, Mac."

The familiar steel bug was back beside him. "Come on, back to the barn," it scolded. "You think I want to have to haul you back? Time's up. Get the tracks back in the parking lot."

Never was an order so gladly obeyed.

But the overseer had cut it rather fine. Pulcher had just reached the parking space, had not quite turned his clanking steel frame around when, *rip,* the tearing and the pain hit him. . . .

And he found himself struggling against the enfolded soft shroud that they called "the squeeze."

"Relax, friend," soothed a distant voice. Abruptly the pressure was removed from his face and the voice came nearer. "There you are. Have a nice dream?"

Pulcher kicked the rubbery material off his legs. He sat up.

"Ouch!" he said suddenly, and rubbed his eye.

The man by his head looked down at him and grinned. "Some shiner. Must've been a good party." He was stripping the sections of rubbery gripping material off him as he talked. "You're lucky. I've seen them come back in here with legs broken, teeth out, even bullet holes. Friend, you wouldn't believe me if I told you. 'Specially the girls." He handed Pulcher another bleached towel. "All right, you're through here. Don't worry about the eye, friend. That's easy two, three days old already. Another day or two and you won't even notice it."

"Hey!" Pulcher cried suddenly. "What do you mean, two or three days? How long was I down there?"

The man glanced boredly at the green-tabbed card on Pulcher's wrist. "Let's see, this is Thursday. Six days."

"But I only signed up for twenty-four hours!"

"Sure you did. *Plus* emergency overcalls, naturally. What do you think, friend, the Agency's going to evict some big-spending tourist just because you want your body back in twenty-four hours? Can't do it. You can see that. The Agency'd lose a fortune that way." Unceremoniously Pulcher was hoisted to his feet and escorted to the door. "If only these jokers would read the fine print," the first man was saying mournfully to his helper as Pulcher left. "Oh, well. If they had any brains they wouldn't rent in the first place—then what would me and you do for jobs?"

The closing door swallowed their laughter.

Six days! Pulcher raced through medical check-out, clothes redemption, payoff at the cashier's window. "Hurry, please," he kept saying, "can't you please hurry?" He couldn't wait to get to a phone.

But he had a pretty good idea already what the phone call would tell him. Five extra days! No wonder it had seemed so long down there, while up in the city time had passed along.

He found a phone at last and quickly dialed the private number of Judge Pegrim's office. The judge wouldn't be there, but that was the way Pulcher wanted it. He got Pegrim's secretary. "Miss Kish? This is Milo Pulcher."

Her voice was cold. "So *there* you are. Where have you been? The judge was *furious.*"

"I—" He despaired of explaining it to her; he could hardly explain it to himself. "I'll tell you later, Miss Kish. Please. Where does the kidnap case stand now?"

"Why, the hearing was yesterday. Since we couldn't locate you, the judge had to appoint another attorney. Naturally. After all, Mr. Pulcher, an attorney is supposed to be in court when his clients are——"

"I know that, Miss Kish. What happened?"

"It was open and shut. They all pleaded *non vult*—it was over in twenty minutes. It was the only thing to do on the evidence, you see. They'll be sentenced this afternoon—around three o'clock, I'd say. *If* you're interested."

IV

It was snowing again, blue this time.

Pulcher paid the cab driver and ran up the steps of the courthouse. As he reached for the door he caught sight of three airfish solemnly swimming around the corner of the building toward him. Even in his hurry he paused to glance at them.

It was past three, but the judge had not yet entered the courtroom. There were no spectators, but the six defendants were already in their seats, a bailiff lounging next to them. Counsel's table was occupied by–Pulcher squinted–oh, by Donley. Pulcher knew the other lawyer slightly. He was a youngster, with good political connections–that explained the court's appointing him for the fee when Pulcher didn't show up–but without much to recommend him otherwise.

Madeleine Gaultry looked up as Pulcher approached, then looked away. One of the boys caught sight of him, scowled, whispered to the others. Their collective expressions were enough to sear his spirit.

Pulcher sat at the table beside Donley. "Hello. Mind if I join you?"

Donley twisted his head. "Oh, hello, Charley. Sure. I didn't expect to see you here." He laughed. "Say, that eye's pretty bad. I guess–"

He stopped.

Something happened in Donley's face. The young baby-fat cheeks became harder, older, more worried-looking. Donley clamped his lips shut.

Pulcher was puzzled. "What's the matter? Are you wondering where I was?"

Donley said stiffly, "Well, you can't blame me for that."

"I couldn't help it, Donley. I was renting. I was trying to gather evidence–not that that helps much now. I found one thing out, though. Even a lawyer can goof in reading a contract. Did you know the Tourist Agency has the right to retain a body for up to forty-five days, regardless of the original agreement? It's in their contract. I was lucky, I guess. They only kept me five."

Donley's face did not relax. "That's interesting," he said noncommittally.

The man's attitude was most peculiar. Pulcher could understand being needled by Donley–could even understand this coldness if it had been from someone else–but it wasn't like Donley to take mere negligence so seriously.

But before he could try to pin down exactly what was wrong the other lawyer stood up. "On your feet, Pulcher," he said in a stage whisper. "Here comes the judge!"

Pulcher jumped up.

He could feel Judge Pegrim's eyes rake over him. They scratched like diamond-tipped drills. In an ordinarily political, reasonably corrupt community, Judge Pegrim was one man who took his job seriously and expected the same from those around him. "Mr. Pulcher," he purred. "We're honored to have you with us."

Pulcher began an explanation but the judge waved it away. "Mr. Pulcher, you know that an attorney is an officer of the court? And, as such, is expected to know his duties–and to fulfill them?"

"Well, Your Honor. I thought I was fulfilling them. I—"

"I'll discuss it with you at another time, Mr. Pulcher," the judge said. "Right now we have a rather disagreeable task to get through. Bailiff! Let's get started."

It was all over in ten minutes. Donley made a couple of routine motions, but there was no question about what would happen. It happened. Each of the defendants drew a ten-year sentence. The judge pronounced it distastefully, adjourned the court and left. He did not look at Milo Pulcher.

Pulcher tried for a moment to catch Madeleine's eye. Then he succeeded. Shaken, he turned away, bumping into Donley. "I don't understand it," he mumbled.

"What don't you understand?"

"Well, don't you think that's a pretty stiff sentence?"

Donley shrugged. He wasn't very interested. Pulcher scanned the masklike young face. There was no sympathy there. It was funny, in a way. This was a face of flint; the plight of six young people, doomed to spend a decade each of their lives in prison, did not move him at all. Pulcher said dispiritedly, "I think I'll go see Charley Dickon."

"Do that," said Donley curtly, and turned away.

But Pulcher couldn't find Charley Dickon.

He wasn't at his office, wasn't at the club. "Nope," said the garrulous retired police lieutenant who was the club president–and who used the club headquarters as a checker salon. "I haven't seen Charley in a couple of days. Be at the dinner tonight, though. You'll see him there." It wasn't a question, whether Pulcher would be at the dinner or not; Pop Craig knew he would. After all, Charley had passed the word out. *Everybody* would be there.

Pulcher went back to his apartment.

It was the first time he had surveyed his body since reclaiming it. The bathroom mirror told him that he had a gorgeous shiner indeed. Also certain twinges made him strip and examine his back. It looked, he thought gloomily, staring over his shoulder into the mirror, as though whoever had rented his body had had a perfectly marvelous time. He made a mental note to get a complete checkup some day soon, just in case. Then he showered, shaved, talcumed around the black eye without much success, and dressed.

He sat down, poured himself a drink and promptly forgot it was there. He was thinking. Something was trying to reach the surface of his mind. Something perfectly obvious, which he all the same couldn't quite put his finger on. It was rather annoying.

He found himself drowsily thinking of airfish.

Damn, he thought grouchily, his body's late tenant hadn't even troubled to give it a decent night's sleep! But he didn't want to sleep, not now. It was still only early evening. He supposed the Chester A. Arthur Day Dinner was still a must, but there were hours yet before that. . . .

He got up, poured the untasted drink into the sink and set out. There was one thing he could try to help Madeleine. It probably wouldn't work. But nothing else would either, so that was no reason for not trying it.

The mayor's mansion was ablaze with light; something was going on.

Pulcher trudged up the long, circling driveway in slush that kept splattering his ankles. He tapped gingerly on the door.

The butler took his name doubtfully, and isolated Pulcher in a contagion-free sitting room while he went off to see if the mayor would care to admit such a person. He came back looking incredulous. The mayor would.

Mayor Swinburne was a healthy, lean man of medium height, showing only by his thinning hair that he was in his middle forties. Pulcher said, "Mr. Mayor, I guess you know who I am. I represent the six kids who were accused of kidnaping your son."

"Not accused, Mr. Pulcher. Convicted. And I didn't know you still represented them."

"I see you know the score. All right. Maybe, in a legal sense, I don't represent them any more. But I'd like to make some representations on their behalf to you tonight—entirely unofficially." He gave the mayor a crisply worded, brief outline of what had happened in the case, how he had rented, what he had found as a renter, why he had missed the hearing. "You see, sir, the Tourist Agency doesn't give its renters even ordinary courtesy. They're just bodies, nothing else. I can't blame those kids. Now that I've rented myself, I'll have to say that I wouldn't blame anybody who did *anything* to avoid it."

The mayor said dangerously, "Mr. Pulcher, I don't have to remind you that what's left of our economy depends heavily on the Tourist Agency for income. Also that some of our finest citizens are among its shareholders."

"Including yourself, Mr. Mayor. Right." Pulcher nodded. "But the management may not be reflecting your wishes. I'll go farther. I think, sir, that every contract the Tourist Agency holds with a renter ought to be voided as against public policy. Renting out your body for a purpose which well may be in violation of law—which, going by experience, nine times out of ten *does* involved a violation of law—is the same thing as contracting to perform any other illegal act. The contract simply cannot be enforced. The common law gives us a great many precedents on this point, and——"

"Please, Mr. Pulcher. I'm not a judge. If you feel so strongly, why not take it to court?"

Pulcher sank back into his chair, deflated. "There isn't time," he admitted. "And besides, it's too late for that to help the six persons I'm interested in. They've already been driven into an even more illegal act, in order to escape renting. I'm only trying to explain it to you, sir, because you are their only hope. You can pardon them."

The mayor's face turned beet red. "Executive clemency, from *me?* For *them?*"

"They didn't hurt your boy."

"No, they did not," the mayor agreed. "And I'm sure that Mrs. Gaultry, at least, would not willingly have done so. But can you say the same of the others? Could she have prevented it?" He stood up. "I'm sorry, Mr. Pulcher. The answer is no. Now you must excuse me."

Pulcher hesitated, then accepted the dismissal. There wasn't anything else to do.

He walked somberly down the hall toward the entrance, hardly noticing that guests were beginning to arrive. Apparently the mayor was offering cocktails to a select few. He recognized some of the faces—Lew Yoder, the County Tax Assessor, for one; probably the mayor was having some of the whiter-collared politicians in for drinks before making the obligatory appearance at Dickon's fund-raising dinner. Pulcher looked up long enough to nod grayly at Yoder and walked on.

"Charley Dickon! What the devil are you doing here like that?"

Pulcher jerked upright. Dickon here? He looked around.

But Dickon was not in sight. Only Yoder was coming down the corridor toward him; oddly, Yoder was looking straight at him! And it had been Yoder's voice.

Yoder's face froze.

The expression on Yoder's face was an odd one but not unfamiliar to Milo Pulcher. He had seen it once before that day. It was the identical expression he had seen on the face of that young punk who had replaced him in court, Donley.

Yoder said awkwardly, "Oh, Milo, it's you. Hello. I, uh, thought you were Charley Dickon."

Pulcher felt the hairs at the back of his neck tingle. Something was odd here. Very odd. "It's a perfectly natural mistake," he said. "I'm six feet tall and Charley's five feet three. I'm thirty-one years old. He's fifty. I'm dark and he's almost bald. I don't know how anybody ever tells us apart anyway."

"What the devil are you talking about?" Yoder blustered.

Pulcher looked at him thoughtfully for a second.

"You're lucky," he admitted. "I'm not sure I know. But I hope to find out."

V

Some things never change. Across the entrance to The New Metropolitan Cafe & Men's Grille a long scarlet banner carried the words:

VOTE THE STRAIGHT TICKET

Big poster portraits of the mayor and Committeeman Dickon flanked the door itself. A squat little soundtruck parked outside the door blared ancient marches of the sort that political conventions had suffered through for more than two centuries back on Earth. It was an absolutely conventional political fund-raising dinner; it would have the absolutely conventional embalmed roast beef, the one conventionally free watery Manhattan at each place, and the conventionally boring after-dinner speeches. (Except for one.) Milo Pulcher, stamping about in the slush outside the entrance, looked up at the constellations visible from Altair Nine and wondered if those same stars were looking down on just such another thousand dinners all over the Galaxy. Politics went on, wherever you were. The constellations would be different, of course; the Squirrel and the Nut were all local stars and would have no shape at all from any other system. But—

He caught sight of the tall thin figure he was waiting for and stepped out into the stream of small-time political workers, ignoring their greetings. "Judge, I'm glad you came."

Judge Pegrim said frostily, "I gave you my word, Milo. But you've got a lot to answer to me for if this is a false alarm. I don't ordinarily attend partisan political affairs."

"It isn't an ordinary affair, Judge." Pulcher conducted him into the room and sat him at the table he had prepared. Once it had held place cards for four election-board workers from the warehouse district, who now buzzed from table to table angrily; Pulcher had filched their cards. The judge was grumbling:

"It doesn't comport well with the bench to attend this sort of thing, Milo. I don't like it."

"I know, Judge. You're an honest man. That's why I wanted you here."

"Mmm." Pulcher left him before the *Mmm* could develop into a question. He had fended off enough questions since the thoughtful half hour he had spent pacing back and forth in front of the mayor's mansion. He didn't want to fend off any more. As he skirted the tables, heading for the private room where he had left his special guests, Charley Dickon caught his arm.

"Hey, Milo! I see you got the judge out. Good boy! He's just what we needed to make this dinner complete."

"You have no idea how complete," said Pulcher pleasantly, and walked away. He didn't look back. There was another fine potential question-source; and the committeeman's would be even more difficult to answer than the judge's. Besides, he wanted to see Madeleine.

The girl and her five accomplices were where he had left them. The private bar where they were sitting was never used for affairs like this. You couldn't see the floor from it. Still, you could hear well enough, and that was more important.

The boys were showing nervousness in their separate ways. Although they had been convicted hardly more than a day, had been sentenced only a few hours, they had fallen quickly into the convict habit. Being out on bail so abruptly was a surprise. They hadn't expected it. It made them nervous. Young Foltis was jittering about, muttering to himself. The Hopgood boy was slumped despondently in a corner, blowing smoke rings. Jimmy Lasser was making a castle out of sugar cubes.

Only Madeleine was relaxed.

As Pulcher came in she looked up calmly. "Is everything all right?" He crossed his fingers and nodded. "Don't worry," she said. Pulcher blinked. *Don't worry*. It should have been he who was saying that to her, not the other way around. It came to him that there was only one possible reason for her calm confidence.

She trusted him.

But he couldn't stay. The ballroom was full now, and irritable banquet waiters were crashing plates down in front of the loyal Party workers. He had a couple of last-minute things to attend to. He carefully avoided the eye of Judge Pegrim, militantly alone at the table by the speaker's dais, and walked quickly across the room to Jimmy

Lasser's father. He said without preamble: "Do you want to help your son?"

Tim Lasser snarled, "You cheap shyster! You wouldn't even show up for the trial! Where do you get the nerve to ask me a question like that?"

"Shut up. I asked you something."

Lasser hesitated, then read something in Pulcher's eyes. "Well, of course I do," he grumbled.

"Then tell me something. It won't sound important. But it is. How many rifles did you sell in the past year?"

Lasser looked puzzled, but he said, "Not many. Maybe half a dozen. Business is lousy all over, you know, since the Icicle Works closed."

"And in a normal year?"

"Oh, three or four hundred. It's a big tourist item. You see, they need cold-shot rifles for hunting the fish. A regular bullet'll set them on fire–touches off the hydrogen. I'm the only sporting-goods merchant in town that carries them, and–say, what does that have to do with Jimmy?"

Pulcher took a deep breath. "Stick around and you'll find out. Meanwhile, think about what you just told me. If rifles are a tourist item, why did closing the Icicle Works hurt your sales?" He left.

But not quickly enough. Charley Dickon scuttled over and clutched his arm, his face furious. "Hey, Milo, what the hell! I just heard from Sam Apfel–the bondsman–that you got that whole bunch out of jail again on bail. How come?"

"They're my clients, Charley."

"Don't give me that! How'd you get them out when they're convicted, anyway?"

"I'm going to appeal the case," Pulcher said gently.

"You don't have a leg to stand on. Why would Pegrim grant bail anyhow?"

Pulcher pointed to Judge Pegrim's solitary table. "Ask him," he invited, and broke away.

He was burning a great many bridges behind him, he knew. It was an exhilarating feeling. Chancy but tingly; he decided he liked it. There was just one job to do. As soon as he was clear of the scowling but stopped committeeman, he walked by a circular route to the dais. Dickon was walking back to his table, turned away from the dais; Pulcher's chance would never be better. "Hello, Pop," he said.

Pop Craig looked up over his glasses. "Oh, Milo. I've been going over the list. You think I got everybody? Charley wanted me to introduce all the block captains and anybody else important. You know anybody important that ain't on this list?"

"That's what I wanted to tell you, Pop. Charley said for you to give me a few minutes. I want to say a few words."

Craig said agitatedly, "Aw, Milo, if you make a speech they're all gonna want to make speeches! What do you want to make a speech for? You're no candidate."

Pulcher winked mysteriously. "What about next year?" he asked archly, with a lying inference.

"Oh. Oh-*ho.*" Pop Craig nodded and returned to his list, mumbling. "Well. In *that* case, I guess I can fit you in after the block captains, or maybe after the man from the sheriff's office—" But Pulcher wasn't listening. Pulcher was already on his way back to the little private bar.

Man had conquered all of space within nearly fifty light years of dull, yellow old Sol, but out in that main ballroom political hacks were talking of long-dead presidents of almost forgotten countries centuries in the past. Pulcher was content to listen—to allow the sounds to vibrate his eardrums, at least, for the words made little sense to him. If, indeed, there was any content of sense to a political speech in the first place. But they were soothing.

Also they kept his six fledglings from bothering him with questions. Madeleine sat quietly by his shoulder, quite relaxed still and smelling faintly, pleasantly, of some floral aroma. It was, all in all, as pleasant a place to be as Pulcher could remember in his recent past. It was too bad that he would have to go out of it soon. . . .

Very soon.

The featured guest had droned through his platitudes. The visiting celebrities had said their few words each. Pop Craig's voluminous old voice took over again. "And now I wanta introduce some of the fine Party workers from our local districts. There's Keith Ciccarelli from the Hillside area. Keith, stand up and take a bow!" Dutiful applause. "And here's Mary Beth Whitehurst, head of the Women's Club from Riverview!" Dutiful applause—and a whistle. Surely the whistle was sardonic; Mary Beth was fat and would never again see fifty. There were more names.

Pulcher felt it coming the moment before Pop Craig reached his own name. He was on his way to the dais even before Craig droned out: "That fine young attorney and loyal Party man—the kind of young fellow our Party needs—Milo Pulcher!"

Dutiful applause again. That was habit, but Pulcher felt the whispering question that fluttered around the room.

He didn't give the question a chance to grow. He glanced once at the five hundred loyal Party faces staring up at him and began to speak. "Mr. President. Mr. Mayor. Justice Pegrim. Honored guests. Ladies and gentlemen." That was protocol. He paused. "What I have to say to you tonight is in the way of a compliment. It's a surprise for an old friend, sitting right here. That old friend is–Charley Dickon." He threw the name at them. It was a special political sort of delivery; a tone of voice that commanded: *Clap now*. They clapped. That was important, because it made it difficult for Charley to think of an excuse to interrupt him–as soon as Charley realized he ought to, which would be shortly.

"Way out here, on the bleak frontier of interstellar space, we live isolated lives, ladies and gentlemen." There were whispers, he could hear them. The words were more or less right, but he didn't have the right political accent; the audience knew there was something wrong. The true politician would have said: *This fine, growing frontier in the midst of interstellar space's greatest constellations.* He couldn't help it; he would have to rely on velocity now to get him through. "How isolated, we sometimes need to reflect. We have trade relations through the Icicle Works–now closed. We have tourists in both directions, through the Tourist Agency. We have ultrawave messages–also through the Tourist Agency. And that's about all.

"That's a very thin link, ladies and gentlemen. *Very* thin. And I'm here to tell you tonight that it would be even thinner if it weren't for my old friend there–yes, Committeeman Charley Dickon!" He punched the name again, and got the applause–but it was puzzled and died away early.

"The fact of the matter, ladies and gentlemen, is that just about every tourist that's come to Altair Nine this past year is the personal responsibility of Charley Dickon. Who have these tourists been? They haven't been businessmen–there's no business. They haven't been hunters. Ask Phil Lasser, over there; he hasn't sold enough fishing equipment to put in your eye. Ask yourselves, for that matter. How many of you have seen airfish right over the city? Do you know why? Because they aren't being hunted any more! There aren't any tourists to hunt them."

The time had come to give it to them straight. "The fact of the matter, ladies and gentlemen, is that the tourists we've had haven't been tourists at all. They've been natives, from right here on Altair Nine. Some of them are right in this room! I know that, because I rented myself for a few days–and do you know who took my body? Why, Charley did. Charley himself!" He was watching Lew Yoder out of the corner of his eye. The assessor's face turned gray; he seemed to shrink. Pulcher enjoyed the sight, though. After all, he had a certain debt to Lew Yoder; it was Yoder's slip of the tongue that had finally started him thinking on the right track. He went on hastily: "And what it all adds up to, ladies and gentlemen, is that Charley Dickon, and a handful of his friends in high places–most of them right here in this room–have cut off communication between Altair Nine and the rest of the Galaxy!"

That did it.

There were yells, and the loudest yell came from Charley Dickon. "Throw him out! Arrest him! Craig, get the sergeant-at-arms! I say I don't have to sit here and listen to this maniac!"

"And I say you do," boomed the cold courtroom voice of Judge Pegrim. The judge stood up. "Go on, Pulcher!" he ordered. "I came here tonight to hear what you have to say. It may be wrong. It may be right. I propose to hear all of it before I make up my mind."

Thank heaven for the cold old judge! Pulcher cut right in before Dickon could find a new point of attack; there wasn't much left to say anyway. "The story is simple, ladies and gentlemen. The Icicle Works was the most profitable corporation in the Galaxy. We all know that. Probably everybody in this room had a couple of shares of stock. Dickon had plenty.

"But he wanted more. And he didn't want to pay for them. So he used his connection with the Tourist Agency to cut off communication between Nine and the rest of the Galaxy. He spread the word that Altamycin was worthless now because some fictitious character had invented a cheap new substitute. He closed down the Icicle Works. And for the last twelve months he's been picking up stock for a penny on the dollar, while the rest of us starve and the Altamycin the rest of the Galaxy needs stays right here on Altair Nine and–"

He stopped, not because he had run out of words but because no one could hear them any longer. The noises the crowd was making were no longer puzzled; they were ferocious. It figured. Apart from Dickon's immediate gang of manipulators, there was hardly a man in the room who hadn't taken a serious loss in the past year.

It was time for the police to come rushing in, as per the phone call Judge Pegrim had made, protestingly, when Pulcher urged him to the dinner. They did–just barely in time. They weren't needed to arrest Dickon so much; but they were indispensable for keeping him from being lynched.

Hours later, escorting Madeleine home, Milo was still bubbling over. "I was worried about the Mayor! I couldn't make up my mind whether he was in it with Charley or not. I'm glad he wasn't, because he said he owed me a favor, and I told him how he could pay it. Executive clemency. The six of you will be free in the morning."

Madeleine said sleepily, "I'm free enough now."

"And the Tourist Agency won't be able to enforce those contracts any more. I talked it over with Judge Pegrim. He wouldn't give me an official statement, but he said–Madeleine, you're not listening."

She yawned. "It's been an exhausting day, Milo," she apologized. "Anyway, you can tell me all about that later. We'll have plenty of time."

"Years and years," he promised. "Years and–" They stopped talking. The mechanical cab-driver, sneaking around through back streets to avoid the resentment of displaced live drivers, glanced over its condenser cells at them and chuckled, making tiny sparks in the night.

The Hated

THE bar didn't have a name; all it said on the outside was:

Café
EAT
Cocktails

which doesn't make a lot of sense. But it was a bar. It had a big TV set going ya-ta-ta ya-ta-ta in three glorious colors, and a jukebox that tried to drown out the TV with that lousy music they play. Anyway, it wasn't a kid hangout. I kind of like it. But I wasn't supposed to be there at all–it's in the contract. I was supposed to stay in New York and the New England states.

Café-EAT-*Cocktails* was right across the river. I think the name of the place was Hoboken, I'm not sure. It all had a kind of dreamy feeling to it. I was. . . . Well, I couldn't even remember going there. I remembered one minute I was downtown New York, looking across the river. I did that a lot. And then I was there. I don't remember crossing the river at all.

I was drunk, you know.

You know how it is? Double bourbons and keep them coming. And after a while the bartender stops bringing me the ginger ale because gradually I forget to mix them. I got pretty loaded long before I left New York, I realize that. I guess I had to get pretty loaded to risk the pension and all.

Used to be I didn't drink much, but now, I don't know, when I have one drink I get to thinking about Sam and Wally and Chowderhead and Gilvey and the captain. If I don't drink I think about them too, and then I take a drink. And that leads to another drink, and it all comes out to the same thing. Well, I guess I said it already. I drink a pretty good amount, but you can't blame me.

There was a girl.

I always get a girl someplace. Usually they aren't much, and this one wasn't either. I mean, she was probably somebody's mother. She was around thirty-five and not so bad, though she had a long scar from under her ear down along her throat to the little round spot where her larynx was. It wasn't ugly. She smelled nice–while I could still smell, you know–and she didn't talk much. I liked that. Only––

Well, did you ever meet somebody with a nervous cough? Like when you say something funny, a little funny, not a big yock, they don't laugh and they don't stop with just smiling, but they sort of cough? She did that. I began to itch; I couldn't help it. I asked her to stop it.

She spilled her drink and looked at me almost as though she was scared–and I'd tried to say it quietly, too. "Sorry," she said, a little angry, a little scared. "*Sorry*. But you don't have to–"

"Forget it."

"Sure. But you asked me to sit down here with you, remember? If you're going to–"

"Forget it!" I nodded at the bartender and held up two fingers. "You need another drink," I said. "The thing is," I said, "Gilvey used to do that."

"What?"

"That cough."

She looked puzzled. "You mean like–"

"God damn it, stop it!" Even the bartender looked over at me that time. Now she was really mad, but I didn't want her to go away. I said, "Gilvey was a fellow who went to Mars with me. Pat Gilvey."

"Oh." She sat down again and leaned across the table, low. *"Mars."*

The bartender brought our drinks and looked at me suspiciously. I said, "Say, Mac. Would you mind turning down the air-conditioning?"

"My name isn't Mac. No."

"Oh, have a heart. It's too cold in here."

"Sorry." He didn't sound sorry. But I was cold. I mean, that kind of weather, it's always cold in those places. You know around New York in August? It hits eighty, eighty-five, ninety. All the places have air-conditioning and what they really want is for you to wear a shirt and tie. But I like to walk a lot. You would too, you know. And you can't walk around much in long pants and a suit coat and all that stuff. Not around there. Not in August. And so then when I went into a bar it'd have one of those built-in freezers for the used-car salesmen with their dates, or maybe their wives, all dressed up. For what? But I froze.

"Mars," the girl breathed. *"Mars."*

I began to itch again. "Want to dance?"

"They don't have a license," she said. "Byron, *I* didn't know you'd been to *Mars!* Please *tell* me about it."

"It was all right," I said. That was a lie.

She was interested. She forgot to smile. It made her look nicer. She said, "I knew a man—my brother-in-law—he was my husband's brother—I mean my ex-husband—"

"I know."

"He worked for General Atomic. In Rockford, Illinois. You know where that is?"

"Sure." I couldn't go there, but I knew where Illinois was.

"He worked on the first Mars ship. Oh, fifteen years ago, wasn't it? He always wanted to go himself, but he couldn't pass the tests." She stopped and looked at me. I knew what she was thinking. But I didn't always look this way, you know. Not that there's anything wrong with me now, I mean, but I couldn't pass the tests any more. Nobody can. That's why we're all one-trippers.

I said, "The only reason I'm shaking like this is because I'm cold."

It wasn't true, of course. It was that cough of Gilvey's. I didn't like to think about Gilvey, or Sam or Chowderhead or Wally or the captain. I didn't like to think about any of them. It made me shake. You see, we couldn't kill each other. They wouldn't let us do that. Before we took off they did something to our minds to make sure. What they did, it doesn't last forever. It lasts for two years, and then it wears off. That's long enough, you see, because that gets you to Mars and back; and it's plenty long enough, in another way, because it's like a strait jacket. You know how to make a baby cry? Hold his hands. It's the most basic thing there is. What they did to us so we couldn't kill each other, it was like being tied up, like being in a strait jacket, like having our hands held so we couldn't get free. Well. But two years was long enough. Too long.

The bartender came over and said, "Pal, I'm sorry. Look, I turned the air-conditioning down. You all right? You look so—"

I said, "Sure, I'm all right." He sounded worried. I hadn't even heard him come back. The girl was looking worried too, I guess because I was shaking so hard I was spilling my drink. I put some money on the table without even counting it. "It's all right," I said. "We were just going."

"We were?" She looked confused. But she came along with me; they always do. Once they find out you've been to Mars.

In the next place she said, between trips to the powder room:

"It must take a lot of courage to sign up for something like that. Were you scientifically inclined in school? Don't you have to know an awful lot to be a spaceflyer? Did you ever see any of those little monkey characters they say live on Mars? I read an article about how they lived in little cities of puptents or something like that—only they didn't make them, they grew them. Funny! Ever see those? That trip must have been a real drag, I bet. What is it, nine months? You couldn't have a baby! Excuse me. . . . Say, tell me. All that time, how'd you, well, manage things? I mean, didn't you ever have to go to the you-know, or anything?"

"We managed," I said. She giggled, and that reminded her, so she went to the powder room again. I thought about getting up and leaving while she was gone, but what was the use of that? I'd only pick up somebody else.

It was nearly midnight. A couple of minutes wouldn't hurt. I reached in my pocket for the little box of pills they give us—it isn't refillable, but we get a new prescription in the mail every month, along with the pension check. The label on the box said:

> Caution
>
> Use only as directed by physician. Not to be taken by persons suffering heart condition, digestive upset or circulatory disease. Not to be used in conjunction with alcoholic beverages.

I took three of them. I don't like to start them before midnight, but anyway I stopped shaking.

I closed my eyes, and then I was on the ship again. The noise in the bar became the noise of the rockets and the air washers and the sludge sluicers. I began to sweat, although this place was air-conditioned too. I could hear Wally whistling to himself the way he did, the sound muffled by his oxygen mask and drowned in the rocket noise, only still perfectly audible. The tune was *Sophisticated Lady*. Sometimes it was *Easy to Love* and sometimes *Chasing Shadows,* but mostly *Sophisticated Lady*. He was from Juilliard. Somebody sneezed, and it sounded just like Chowderhead sneezing. You know how everybody sneezes according to his own individual style? Chowderhead had a ladylike little sneeze—it went *hutta,* real quick, all through the mouth, no nose involved. The captain went *Hrasssh!* Wally was Ashoo, ashoo, *ashoo.* Gilvey was *Hutch*-uh. Sam didn't sneeze much, but he sort of coughed and sprayed, and that was worse. Sometimes I used to think about killing Sam by tying him down and having Wally and the captain sneeze him to death. But that was a kind of a joke, naturally, when I was feeling good. Or pretty good. Usually I thought about a knife for Sam. For Chowderhead it was a gun, right in the belly, one shot. For Wally it was a tommy gun–just stitching him up and down, you know, back and forth. The captain was putting him in a cage with hungry lions, and Gilvey was strangling with my bare hands. That was probably because of the cough, I guess.

She was back. "Please tell me about it," she begged. "I'm *so* curious."

I opened my eyes.

"You want me to tell you about it?"

"Oh, please!"

"About what it's like to fly to Mars on a rocket?"

"Yes!"

"All right," I said. It's wonderful what three little white pills will do. I wasn't even shaking. "There's six men, see? In a space the size of a Buick, and that's all the room there is. Two of us in the bunks all the time, four of us on watch. Maybe you want to stay in the sack an extra ten minutes–because it's the only place on the ship where you can stretch out, you know, the only place where you can rest without somebody's elbow in your side. But you can't. Because by then it's the next man's turn. And maybe you don't have elbows in your side while it's your turn off watch, but in the starboard bunk there's the air regenerator master valve–I bet I could still show you the business, right around my kidneys–and in the port bunk there's the emergency escape hatch handle. That gets you right in the temple, if you turn your head too fast. And you can't really sleep–I mean not soundly–because of the noise. That is, when the rockets are going. When they aren't going, then you're in free-fall, and that's bad too, because you dream about falling. But when they're going, I don't know, I think it's worse. It's pretty loud. And even if it weren't for the noise, if you sleep too soundly you might roll over on your oxygen line. Then you dream about drowning. Ever do that? You're struggling and choking and you can't get any air? It isn't dangerous, I guess. Anyway, it always woke me up in time. Though I heard about a fellow in a flight six years ago–

"Well. So you've always got this oxygen mask on, all the time, except if you take it off for a second to talk to somebody. You don't do that very often, because what is there to say? Oh, maybe the first couple of weeks, sure—everybody's friends then. You don't even need the mask, for that matter. Or not very much. Everybody's still pretty clean. The place smells—oh, let's see—about like the locker room in a gym. You know? You can stand it. That's if nobody's got space sickness, of course. We were lucky that way. I heard about a flight where two of the crew got space sickness on the first course correction, and chucked up all over the place the second day out. Man! But that's about the way it's going to get anyway, you know. Outside the masks it's soup. It isn't that you smell it so much. You kind of *taste* it, in the back of your mouth, and your eyes sting. That's after the first two or three months. Later on it gets worse. And with the mask on, of course, the oxygen mixture is coming in under pressure. That's funny if you're not used to it. Your lungs have to work a little bit harder to get rid of it, especially after you're asleep, so after a while the muscles get sore. And then they get sorer. And then—

"Well.

"Before we take off, the psych people give us a long doo-da that keeps us from killing each other. But they can't stop you from thinking about it. And afterwards, after we're back on Earth—this is what you won't read about in the articles—they keep us apart. You know how they work it? We get a pension, naturally. I mean, there's got to be a pension, otherwise there isn't enough money in the world to make anybody go. But in the contract it says to get the pension we have to stay in our own area. The whole country's marked off. Six sections. Each has one big city in it, at least. I was lucky, I got a lot of them. They try to keep it so every man's home town is in his own section, but—Well, like with us, Chowderhead and the captain both happened to come from Santa Monica. I think it was Chowderhead that got California, Nevada, all that southwest stuff. It was the luck of the draw. God knows what the captain got.

"Maybe New Jersey," I said, and took another white pill.

We went on to another place.

She said suddenly: "I figured something out. The way you keep looking around."

"What did you figure out?"

"Well, part of it was what you said about the other fellow getting New Jersey. This is New Jersey. You don't belong in this section, right?"

"Right," I said after a minute.

"So why are you here? I know why. You're here because you're looking for somebody."

I said, "That's right."

She said triumphantly, "You want to find that other fellow from your crew! You want to fight him!"

I couldn't help shaking, white pills or no white pills. But I had to correct her.

"No. I want to kill him."

"How do you know he's here? He's got a lot of states to roam around in too, hasn't he?"

"Six. New Jersey, Pennsylvania, Delaware, Maryland—the way down to Washington."

"Then how do you know—"

"He'll be here." I didn't have to tell her how I knew. But I knew.

I wasn't the only one who spent his time at the border of his assigned area, looking across the river or staring across a state line, knowing that somebody was on the other side. I knew. You fight a war and you don't have to guess that the enemy might have his troops a thousand miles away from the battle line. You know where his troops will be. You know he wants to fight too.

Hutta, Hutta.

I spilled my drink.

I looked at her. "You—you didn't—"

She looked definitely frightened. "What's the matter?"

"Did you just sneeze?"

"Sneeze? Me? Did I—"

I said something quick and nasty, I don't know what. No! It hadn't been her. I knew it.

It was Chowderhead's sneeze.

Chowderhead.

Marvin T. Roebuck, his name was. Five feet eight inches tall. Dark complected, with a cast in one eye. Spoke with a midwest kind of accent, even though he came from California—"shrick" for "shriek," "hawror" for "horror," like that. It drove me crazy after a while. Maybe that gives you an idea what he talked about mostly. A skunk. A thorough-going, deep-rooted, mother-murdering skunk.

I kicked over my chair and roared: "Roebuck! Where are you, damn you?"

The bar was suddenly silent. Only the jukebox kept going.

"I know you're here," I screamed. "Come out and get it, curse you!

You louse, I told you I'd get you for calling me a liar the day Wally ripped his mask!"

Silence, everybody looking at me.

Then the door of the men's room opened.

He came out.

He looked *lousy*. Eyes all red-rimmed and his hair falling out—the poor bastard couldn't have been over twenty-nine. He shrieked: "You!" He called me a million names. He said: "Thieving rat, I'll teach you to try to cheat me out of my candy ration!"

He had a knife.

I didn't care. I didn't have anything and that was stupid, but it didn't matter. I got a bottle of beer from the next table and smashed it against the back of a chair. It made a good weapon, you know; I'd take that against a knife any time. I did. I ran toward him, and he came all staggering and lurching toward me, looking crazy and desperate, mumbling and raving—I could hardly hear him, because I was talking too. Nobody tried to stop us. Somebody went out the door and I figured it was to call the cops, but that was all right. Once I took care of him I didn't care what the cops did.

I went for the face.

He cut me first. I felt the knife slide up along my left arm but, you know, it didn't even hurt—only kind of stung a little. I didn't care about that. I got him in the face, and the bottle came away, and it was all like gray and white jelly, and then blood began to spring out. He screamed. Oh, that scream! I never heard anything like that scream; it was what I had been waiting for all my life. I kicked him as he staggered back, and he fell. And I was on top of him, with the bottle, and I was careful to stay away from the heart or the throat, because that was too quick—but I worked over the face, and I felt his knife get me a couple times more, and——

And——

And I woke up, you know. And there was Dr. Santly over me with a hypodermic needle that he'd just taken out of my arm, and four male nurses in fatigues holding me down. And I was drenched with sweat.

For a minute I didn't know where I was. It was a horrible queasy falling sensation, as though the bar and the fight and the world were all dissolving into smoke around me.

Then I knew where I was.

It was almost worse.

I stopped yelling and just lay there, looking up at them.

Dr. Santly said, trying to keep his face friendly and noncommittal, he said: "You're doing much better, Byron, boy. *Much* better."

I didn't say anything.

He said: "You worked through the whole thing in two hours and eight minutes. Remember the first time? You were sixteen hours killing him. Captain Van Wyck it was that time, remember? Who was it this time?"

"Chowderhead." I looked at the male nurses. Doubtfully they let go of my arms and legs.

"Chowderhead," said Dr. Santly. "Oh–Roebuck. That boy," he said mournfully, his expression saddened, "he's not coming along nearly as well as you. *Nearly*. He can't run through a cycle in less than five hours. And, that's funny, it's usually you he. . . . Well, I better not say that, shall I? No sense setting up a counterimpression when your pores are all open, so to speak." He smiled at me, but he was a little worried in back of the smile.

I sat up. "Anybody got a cigarette?"

"Give him a cigarette, Johnson," the doctor ordered the male nurse by my right foot. Johnson did. I fired up. "You're coming along *splendidly,*" Dr. Santly said. He was one of these psych guys that thinks if you say it's so it makes it so. You know the kind? "We'll have you down under an hour before the end of the week. That's *marvelous* progress. Then we can work on the conscious level! Boy, you're doing extremely well, whether you know it or not. Why, in six months–say in eight months, because I like to be conservative–" he twinkled at me–"we'll have you out of here! You'll be the first of your crew to be discharged, you know that?"

"That's nice," I said. "The others aren't doing so well?"

"No. Not at all well, most of them. Particularly Dr. Gilvey, the run-throughs leave him in terrible shape. I don't mind admitting I'm worried about him."

"That's nice," I said, and this time I meant it.

He looked at me thoughtfully, but all he did was say to the male nurses: "He's all right, now. Help him off the table."

It was hard standing up. I had to hold onto the rail around the table for a minute. I said my set little speech: "Dr. Santly, I want to tell you again how grateful I am for this. I was reconciled to living the rest of my life confined to one part of the country, the way the other crews always did. But this is much better. I appreciate it. I'm sure the others do, too."

"Of course, boy. Of course." He took out a fountain pen and made a note on my chart; I couldn't see what it was, but he looked gratified.

"It's only what you have coming, Byron," he said. "I'm grateful that I could be the one to make it come to pass."

He glanced conspiratorially at the male nurses. "You know how important this is to me. It's the triumph of a whole new approach to psychic rehabilitation. I mean to say, our heroes of space travel are entitled to freedom when they come back to Earth, aren't they?"

"Definitely," I said, scrubbing some of the sweat off my face onto my sleeve.

"So we've got to end this system of designated areas. We can't avoid the tensions incident to space travel, no. But if we can help you work off the tensions through a few run-throughs, why, it's not too high a price to pay, is it?"

"Not a bit."

"I mean to say," he said, warming up, "you can look forward to the time when you'll be able to mingle with your old friends from the rocket, free and easy, without any need for restraint. That's a lot to look forward to, isn't it?"

"It is," I said. "I look forward to it very much," I said. "And I know exactly what I'm going to do the first time I meet one—I mean, without any restraints, as you say," I said. And it was true; I did. Only it wouldn't be a busted beer bottle that I would do it with.

I had much more elaborate ideas than that.

The Martian in the Attic

DUNLOP was short and pudgy; his eyelashes were blond and his hair was gone. He looked like the sort of man you see sitting way off at the end of the stadium at the Big Game, clutching a hot dog and a pennant and sitting with his wife, who would be making him explain every play. Also he stuttered.

The girl at the reception desk of LaFitte Enterprises was a blue-eyed former model. She had Dunlop catalogued. She looked up slowly. She said bleakly: "Yes?"

"I want to see Mr. LaF-F-F–" said Dunlop, and paused to clear his throat. "I want to see Mr. La*Fitte.*"

The ex-model was startled enough to blink. *Nobody* saw Mr. LaFitte! Oh, John D. the Sixth might. Or President Brockenheimer might drop by, after phoning first. Nobody else. Mr. LaFitte was a very great man who had invented most of America's finest gadgets and sold them for some of America's finest money, and he was not available to casual callers. Particularly nobodies with suits that had come right off a rack.

The ex-model was, however, a girl with a sympathetic heart–as was known only to her mother, her employer and the fourteen men who, one after another, had broken it. She was sorry for Dunlop. She decided to let the poor jerk down easy and said: "Who shall I say is calling, sir? Mr. Dunlop? Is that with an 'O,' sir? One moment." And she picked up the phone, trying to smile.

The reception room was carpeted in real Oriental wool–none of your flimsy nylon or even LaFitton!–and all about it were the symbols of LaFitte's power and genius. In a floodlighted nook, stood an acrylic model of the LaFitte Solar Transformer, transparently gleaming. On a scarlet pedestal in the center of the room was the LaFitte Ion-Exchange Self-Powered Water Still, in the small or forty-gallon-a-second model. (Two of the larger size provided all of London with sparkling clear water from the muddy, silty, smelly Thames.)

Dunlop said hoarsely: "Hold it a second. Tell him that he won't know my name, but we have a mutual friend."

The ex-model hesitated, struggling with the new fact. That changed things. Even Mr. LaFitte might have a friend who might by chance be acquainted with a little blond nobody whose shoes needed shining. It wasn't likely, but it was a possibility. Especially when you consider that Mr. LaFitte himself sprang from quite humble origins: at one time he had taught at a university.

"Yes, sir," she said, much more warmly. "May I have the friend's name?"

"I d-don't know his name."

"Oh!"

"But Mr. LaFitte will know who I m-mean. Just say the friend is a M– is a M– is a M-Martian."

The soft blue eyes turned bleak. The smooth, pure face shriveled into the hard *Vogue* lines that it had possessed before an unbearable interest in chocolate nougats had taken her from before the fashion cameras and put her behind this desk.

"Get out!" she said. "That isn't a bit funny!"

The chubby little man said cheerfully: "Don't forget the name, Dunlop. And I'm at 449 West 19th Street. It's a rooming house." And he left. She wouldn't give anyone the message, he knew, but he knew, comfortably, that it didn't matter. He'd seen the little goldplated microphone at the corner of her desk. The LaFitte Auto-Sec it was hooked up to would unfailingly remember, analyze and pass along every word.

"Ho-hum," said Dunlop to the elevator operator, "they make you fellows work too hard in this kind of weather. I'll see that they put in air-conditioning."

The operator looked at Dunlop as though he was some kind of a creep, but Dunlop didn't mind. Why should he? He *was* a creep. But he would soon be a very rich one.

Hector Dunlop trotted out into the heat of Fifth Avenue, wheezing because of his asthma. But he was quite pleased with himself.

He paused at the corner to turn and look up at the LaFitte Building, all copper and glass bands in the quaint period architecture that La-Fitte liked. Let him enjoy it, thought Dunlop generously. It looks awful, but let LaFitte have his pleasures; it was only fair that LaFitte have the kind of building he wanted. Dunlop's own taste went to more modern lines, but there would be nothing to stop him from putting up a hundred-and-fifty-*two*-story building across the street if he liked. LaFitte was entitled to everything he wanted–as long as he was willing to share with Hector Dunlop. As he certainly would be, and probably that very day.

Musing cheerfully about the inevitable generosity of LaFitte, Dunlop dawdled down Fifth Avenue in the fierce, but unfelt, heat. He had plenty of time. It would take a little while for anything to happen.

Of course, he thought patiently, it was possible that nothing would happen at all today. Whatever human the Auto-Sec reported to might forget. Anything might go wrong. But still he had time. All he had to do was try again, and try still more after that if necessary. Sooner or later the magic words would reach LaFitte. After eight years of getting ready for this moment it didn't much matter if it took an extra day or two.

Dunlop caught his breath.

A girl in needle-pointed heels came clicking by, the hot breeze plastering her skirt against her legs. She glanced casually at the volume of space which Hector Dunlop thought he was occupying and found it empty. Dunlop snarled out of habit; she was not the only hormone-pumping girl who had seen nothing where he stood. But he regained his calm. To hell with you, my dear, he said good-humoredly to himself. I will have you later if I like. I will have twenty like you, or twenty a day if I wish–starting very soon.

He sprinted across Forty-second Street, and there was the gray familiar old-fashioned bulk of the Library.

On a sentimental impulse he climbed the steps and went inside. The elevator operator nodded. "Good afternoon, Mr. Dunlop. Three?"

"That's right, Charley. As usual." They all liked him here. It was the only place in the world where that was true, he realized, but then he had spent more time here than anywhere else in the world.

Dunlop got out of the slow elevator as it creaked to an approximate halt on the third floor. He walked reminiscently down the wide, warm hall between the rows of exhibits. Just beyond the drinking fountain there–that was the door to the Fortescue Collection. Flanking it were the glass cabinets that housed some of Fortescue's own Martian photographs, along with the unexplained relics of a previous race that had built the canals.

Dunlop looked at the prints and could hardly keep from giggling. The Martians were seedy, slime-skinned creatures with snaky arms and no heads at all. Worse, according to Updyke's *The Martian Adventure,* Fortescue's own *First to Land* and Wilbert, Shevelsen and Buchbinder's *Survey of Indigenous Martian Semi-Fauna* (in the *Proceedings of the Astro-Biological Institute* for Winter, 2011), they smelled like rotting fish. Their mean intelligence was given by Fortescue, Burlutski and Stanko as roughly equivalent to the *Felidae* (though Gaffney placed it higher, say about that of the lower primates). They possessed no language. They did not have the use of fire. Their most advanced tool was a hand-axe. In short, the Martians were the dopes of the Solar System, and it was not surprising that LaFitte's receptionist had viewed describing a Martian as her employer's friend as a gross insult.

"Why, it's Mr. Dunlop," called the librarian, peering out through the wire grating on the door. She got up and came toward him to unlock the door to the Fortescue Collection.

"No, thanks," he said hastily. "I'm not coming in today, Miss Reidy. Warm weather, isn't it? Well, I must be getting along."

When hell freezes over I'll come in, he added to himself as he turned away, although Miss Reidy had been extremely helpful to him for eight years; she had turned the Library's archives over to him, not only in the extraterrestrial collections but wherever his researching nose led him. Without her, he would have found it much more difficult to establish what he now knew about LaFitte. On the other hand, she wore glasses. Her skin was sallow. One of her front teeth was chipped. Dunlop would see only TV stars and the society debutantes, he vowed solemnly, and decided that even those he would treat like dirt.

The Library was pressing down on him; it was too much a reminder of the eight grub-like years that were now past. He left it and took a bus home.

Less than two hours had elapsed since leaving LaFitte's office.

That wasn't enough. Not even the great LaFitte's organization would have been quite sure to deliver and act on the message yet, and Dunlop was suddenly wildly anxious to spend no time waiting in his rooming house. He stopped in front of a cheap restaurant, paused, smiled broadly and walked across the street to a small, cozy, expensive place with potted palms in the window. It would just about clean out what cash he had left, but what of it?

Dunlop ate the best lunch he had had in ten years, taking his time. When some fumbling chemical message told him that enough minutes had elapsed, he walked down the block to his rooming house, and the men were already there.

The landlady peered out of her window from behind a curtain, looking frightened.

Dunlop laughed out loud and waved to her as they closed in. They were two tall men with featureless faces. The heavier one smelled of chlorophyll chewing gum. The leaner one smelled of death.

Dunlop linked arms with them, grinning broadly, and turned his back on his landlady. "What did you tell her you w-were, boys? Internal Revenue? The F.B.I?"

They didn't answer, but it didn't matter. Let her think what she liked; he would never, never, never see her again. She was welcome to the few pitiful possessions in his cheap suitcase. Very soon now Hector Dunlop would have only the best.

"You don't know your boss's secret, eh?" Dunlop prodded the men during the car ride. "But I do. It took me eight years to find it out. Treat me with a little respect or I m-might have you fired."

"Shut up," said chlorophyll-breath pleasantly, and Dunlop politely obeyed. It didn't matter, like everything else that happened now. In a short time he would see LaFitte and then–

"Don't p-p-push!" he said irritably, staggering before them out of the car.

They caught him, one at each elbow, Chlorophyll opening the iron gate at the end of the walk and Death pushing him through. Dunlop's glasses came off one ear and he grabbed for them.

They were well out of the city, having crossed the Hudson. Dunlop had only the haziest sense of geography, having devoted all his last eight years to more profitable pursuits, but he guessed they were somewhere in the hills back of Kingston. They went into a great stone house and saw no one. It was a Frankenstein house, but it cheered Dunlop greatly, for it was just the sort of house he had imagined LaFitte would need to keep his secret.

They shoved Dunlop through a door into a room with a fireplace. In a leather chair before a fire (though the day was hot) was a man who had to be Quincy LaFitte.

"Hello," said Dunlop with poise, strutting toward him. "I suppose y-you know why I– Hey! What are you d-doing?"

Chlorophyll was putting one gray glove on one hand. He walked to a desk, opened it, took out something–a gun! In his gloved hand he raised it and fired at the wall. *Splat.* It was a small flat sound, but a great chip of plaster flew.

"Hey!" said Dunlop again.

Mr. LaFitte watched him with polite interest. Chlorophyll walked briskly toward him, and abruptly Death reached for–for–

Chlorophyll handed Dunlop the gun he had fired. Dunlop instinctively grasped it, while Death took out another, larger, more dangerous-looking one.

Dunlop abruptly jumped, dropped the gun, beginning to understand. "Wait!" he cried in sudden panic. "I've g-g–" He swallowed and dropped to his knees. "Don't shoot! I've g-got everything written d-down in my luh–in my luh–"

LaFitte said softly: "Just a moment, boys."

Chlorophyll just stopped where he was and waited. Death held his gun competently on Dunlop and waited.

Dunlop managed to stammer: "In my *lawyer's* office. I've got the whole th-thing written down. If anything happens to me he ruh–he ruh–he *reads* it."

LaFitte sighed. "Well," he said mildly, "that was the chance we took. All right, boys. Leave us alone." Chlorophyll and Death took their scent and their menace out the door.

Dunlop was breathing very hard. He had just come very close to dying, he realized; one man handed him the gun, and the other was about to shoot him dead. Then they would call the police to deliver the body of an unsuccessful assassin. Too bad, officer, but he certainly fooled us! Look, there's where the bullet went. I only tried to wing the poor nut, but. . . . A shrug.

Dunlop swallowed. "Too bad," he said in a cracked voice. "But naturally I had to take p-precautions. Say. Can I have a drink?"

Mr. LaFitte pointed to a tray. He had all the time there was. He merely waited, with patience and very little concern. He was a tall old man with a very bald head, but he moved quickly when he wanted to, Dunlop noticed. Funny, he hadn't expected LaFitte to be bald.

But everything else was going strictly according to plan!

He poured himself a stiff shot of twelve-year-old bourbon and downed it from a glass that was Steuben's best hand-etched crystal.

He said: "I've got you, LaFitte! You know it, don't you?"

LaFitte gave him a warm, forgiving look.

"Oh, that's the boy," Dunlop enthused. "B-Be a good loser. But you know I've found out what your fortune is based on." He swallowed another quick one and felt the burning tingle spread. "Well. To b-begin with, eight years ago I was an undergrad at the university you taught at. I came across a reference to a thesis called *Certain Observations on the Ontogenesis of the Martian P-Paraprimates*. By somebody named Quincy A. W. L-LaFitte, B.S."

LaFitte nodded faintly, still smiling. His eyes were tricky, Dunlop decided; they were the eyes of a man who had grown quite accustomed to success. You couldn't read much into eyes like those. You had to watch yourself.

Still, he reassured himself, he had all the cards. "So I l-looked for the paper and I couldn't f-find it. But I guess you know that!" Couldn't find it? No, not in the stacks, not in the Dean's file, not even in the archives. It was very fortunate that Dunlop was a persistent man. He had found the printer who had done the thesis in the first place, and there it was, still attached to the old dusty bill.

"I remember the w-words," Dunlop said, and quoted from the conclusion. He didn't stutter at all:

"'It is therefore to be inferred that the Martian paraprimates at one time possessed a mature culture comparable to the most sophisticated *milieux* of our own planet. The artifacts and structural remains were not created by another race. Perhaps there is a correlation with the so-called Shternweiser Anomaly, when conjecturally an explosion of planetary proportions depleted the Martian water supply.'"

LaFitte interrupted: "Shternweiser! You know, I had forgotten his name. It's been a long time. But Shternweiser's paper suggested that Mars might have lost its water in our own historical times–and then the rest was easy!"

Dunlop finished his quotation:

"'In conjunction, these factors inescapably suggest a pattern. The Martian paraprimates require an aqueous phase for development from grub to imago, as in many terrestrial invertebrates. Yet there has not been sufficient free water on the surface of Mars since the time of the Shternweiser explosion theory. It seems likely, therefore, that the present examples surviving are mere sexed grubs and that the adult Martian paraprimate does not exist *in vivo,* though its historical existence is attested by the remarkable examples left of their work.'"

"And then," finished Dunlop, "you b-began to realize what you had here. And you d-destroyed all the copies. All, th-that is, b-but one."

It was working! It was all working the way it should!

LaFitte would have thrown him out long ago, of course, if he had dared. He didn't dare. He knew that Dunlop had followed the long, crooked trail of evidence to its end.

Every invention that bore the name LaFitte had come from a Martian mind.

The fact that the paper was suppressed was the first clue. Why suppress it? The name attached to the paper was the second–though it had taken an effort of the imagination to connect a puny B.S. with the head of LaFitte Enterprises.

And all the other clues had come painfully and laboriously along the trail that led past Miss Reidy's room at the Library, the Space Exploration wing of the Smithsonian, the Hall of Extraterrestrial Zooforms at the Museum of Natural History, and a thousand dusty chambers of learning all over the country.

LaFitte sighed. "And so you know it all, Mr. Dunlop. You've come a long way."

He poured himself a gentlemanly film of brandy in a large inhaler and warmed it with his breath. He said meditatively: "You did a lot of work, but, of course, I did more. I had to go to Mars, for one thing."

"The *S-Solar Argosy,"* Dunlop supplied promptly.

LaFitte raised his eyebrows. *"That* thorough? I suppose you realize, then, that the crash of the *Solar Argosy* was not an accident. I had to cover up the fact that I was bringing a young Martian back to Earth. It wasn't easy. And even so, once I had him here, that was only half the battle. It is quite difficult to raise an exogenous life-form on Earth."

He sipped a drop of the brandy and leaned forward earnestly. "I had to let a Martian develop. It meant giving him an aqueous environment, as close as I could manage to what must have been the conditions on Mars before the Shternweiser event. All guesswork, Mr. Dunlop! I can only say that luck was with me. And even then—why, think of yourself as a baby. Suppose your mother had abandoned you, kicking and wetting your diaper, on Jupiter. And suppose that some curious-shaped creature that resembled Mommy about as much as your mother resembled a tree then took over your raising."

He shook his head solemnly. "Spock was no help at all. The problem of discipline! The toilet training! And then I had nothing but a naked mind, so to speak. The Martian adult mind is great, but it needs to be filled with knowledge before it can create, and that, Mr. Dunlop, in itself took me six difficult years."

He stood up. "Well," he said, "suppose you tell me what you want."

Dunlop, caught off base, stammered terribly: "I w-w-want half of the tuh—of the tuh—"

"You want half of the take?"

"That's ruh—that's—"

"I understand. In order to keep my secret, you want me to give you half of everything I earn from my Martian's inventions. And if I don't agree?"

Dunlop said, suddenly panicked: "But you *must!* If I t-t-tell your secret, anyone can do the same!"

LaFitte said reasonably: "But I already have my money, Mr. Dunlop. No, that's not enough of an inducement . . . But," he said after a moment, "I doubt that such a consideration will persuade you to keep still. And, in fact, I do want this matter kept confidential. After all, six men died in the crash of the *Solar Argosy,* and on that sort of thing there is no statute of limitations."

He politely touched Dunlop's arm. "Come along. You deduced there was a Martian in this house? Let me show you how right you were."

All the way down a long carpeted corridor, Dunlop kept hearing little clicks and rustles that seemed to come from the wall. "Are those your b-bodyguards, LaFitte? Don't try any tricks!"

LaFitte shrugged. "Come on out, boys," he said without raising his voice; and a few feet ahead of them a panel opened and Death and Chlorophyll stepped through.

"Sorry about that other business, Mr. Dunlop," said Chlorophyll.

"No hard f-feelings," said Dunlop.

LaFitte stopped before a door with double locks. He spun the tumblers and the door opened into a dark, dank room.

"V-r-r-roooom, v-r-r-room." It sounded like a huge deep rumble from inside the room.

Dunlop's pupils slowly expanded to admit more light, and he began to recognize shapes.

In the room was a sort of palisade of steel bars. Behind them, chained to a stake, was—

A Martian!

Chained?

Yes, it was chained and cuffed. What could only be the key hung where the Martian would be able to see it always but reach it never. Dunlop swallowed, staring. The Martians in Fortescue's photographs were slimy, ropy, ugly creatures like thinned-out sea anemones, man-tall and headless. The chained creature that thundered at him now was like those Martians only as a frog is like a tadpole. It possessed a head, round-domed, with staring eyes. It possessed a mouth that clacked open and shut on great square teeth.

"V-r-r-room," it roared, and then Dunlop listened more closely. It was not a wordless lion's bellow. It was English! The creature was talking to them; it was only the Earth's thick atmosphere that made it boom. "Who are you?" it croaked in a slobbery-drunk Chaliapin's boom.

Dunlop said faintly: "God b-bless." Inside that hideous skull was the brain that had created for LaFitte the Solar Transformer, the Ion-Exchange Self-Powered Water Still, the LaFitte Negative-Impedance

Transducer, and a thousand other great inventions. It was not a Martian Dunlop was looking at; it was a magic lamp that would bring him endless fortune. But it was an ugly nightmare.

"So," said LaFitte. "And what do you think now, Mr. Dunlop? Don't you think I did something great? Perhaps the Still and the Transducer were his invention, not mine. But I invented *him.*"

Dunlop pulled himself together. "Y-yes," he said, bobbing his head. He had a concept of LaFitte as a sort of storybook blackmail victim, who needed only a leer, a whisper and the Papers to start disgorging billions. It had not occurred to him that LaFitte would take honest pride in what he had done. Now, knowing it, Dunlop saw, or thought he saw, a better tactic.

He said instantly: "Great? N-No, LaFitte, it's more than that. I am simply amazed that you brought him up without, say, r-rickets. Or juvenile delinquency. Or whatever Martians might get, lacking proper care."

LaFitte looked pleased. "Well, let's get down to business. You want to become an equal partner in LaFitte Enterprises; is that what you're asking for?"

Dunlop shrugged. He didn't have to answer. That was fortunate; in a situation as tense as this one, he couldn't have spoken at all.

LaFitte said cheerfully: "Why not? Who needs all this? Besides, some new blood in the firm might perk things up." He gazed benevolently at the Martian, who quailed. "Our friend here has been lethargic lately. All right, I'll make you work for it, but you can have half."

"Th–Th–Thank–"

"You're welcome, Dunlop. How shall we do it? I don't suppose you'd care to take my word–"

Dunlop smiled.

LaFitte was not offended. "Very well, we'll put it in writing. I'll have my attorneys draw something up. I suppose you have a lawyer for them to get in touch with?" He snapped his fingers. Death stepped brightly forward with a silver pencil and Chlorophyll with a pad.

"G-G-Good," said Dunlop, terribly eager. "My l-lawyer is P. George Metzger, and he's in the Empire State Building, forty-first fl–"

"Fool!" roared the Martian with terrible glee. LaFitte wrote quickly and folded the paper into a neat square. He handed it to the man who smelled of chlorophyll chewing gum.

Dunlop said desperately: "That's not the s-same lawyer."

LaFitte waited politely. "Not what lawyer?"

"My *other* lawyer is the one that has the p-p-papers."

LaFitte shook his head and smiled.

Dunlop sobbed. He couldn't help it. Before his eyes a billion dollars had vanished, and the premium on his life-insurance policy had run out. They had Metzger's name. They knew where to find the fat manila envelope that contained the sum of eight years' work.

Chlorophyll, or Death, or any of LaFitte's hundreds of confidential helpers, would go to Metzger's office, and perhaps present phony court orders or bull a way through, a handkerchief over the face and a gun in the hand. One way or another they would find the papers. The sort of organization that LaFitte owned would surely not be baffled by the office safe of a recent ex-law clerk, now in his first practice.

Dunlop sobbed again, wishing he had not economized on lawyers; but it really made no difference. LaFitte knew where the papers were kept and he would get them. It remained only for him to erase the last copy of the information—that is, the copy in the head of Hector Dunlop.

Chlorophyll tucked the note in his pocket and left. Death patted the bulge under his arm and looked at LaFitte.

"Not here," said LaFitte.

Dunlop took a deep breath.

"G-Good-bye, Martian," he said sadly, and turned toward the door. Behind him the thick, hateful voice laughed.

"You're taking this very well," LaFitte said in surprise.

Dunlop shrugged and stepped aside to let LaFitte precede him through the doorway.

"What else can I d-do?" he said. "You have me cold. Only—" The Death man was through the door, and so was LaFitte, half-turned politely to listen to Dunlop. Dunlop caught the edge of the door, hesitated, smiled and leaped back, slamming it. He found a lock and turned it. "Only you have to c-catch me first!" he yelled through the door.

Behind him the Martian laughed like a wounded whale.

"You were very good," complimented the thick, tolling voice.

"It was a matter of s-simple s-self-defense," said Dunlop.

He could hear noises in the corridor, but there was time. "N-Now! Come, Martian! We're going to get away from LaFitte. You're coming w-with me, because he won't dare shoot you and—and certainly you, with your great mind, can find a way for us both to escape."

The Martian said in a thick sulky voice: "I've tried."

"But I can help! Isn't that the k-k-key?"

He clawed the bright bit of metal off the wall. There was a lock on the door of steel bars, but the key opened it. The Martian was just inside, ropy arms waving.

"V-r-r-room," it rumbled, eyes like snake's eyes staring at Dunlop.

"Speak more c-clearly," Dunlop requested impatiently, twisting the key out of the lock.

"I said," repeated the thick drawl, "I've been waiting for you."

"Of course. What a t-terrible life you've led!"

Crash went the door behind him; Dunlop didn't dare look. And this key insisted on sticking in its lock! But he freed it and leaped to the Martian's side–at least there they would not dare fire, for fear of destroying their meal-ticket!

"You c-can get us out of here," Dunlop panted, fumbling for the lock on the Martian's ankle cuff and gagging. (It was true. They did smell like rotting fish.) "B-but you must be strong! LaFitte has been a father to you, but what a f-false f-father! Feel no loyalty to him, Martian. He made you his slave, even if he d-did keep you healthy and s-sane."

And behind him LaFitte cleared his throat. "But I didn't," he observed. "I didn't keep him sane."

"No," rumbled the thick, slow Martian voice. "No, he didn't."

The ropes that smelled like rotting fish closed lovingly and lethally around Dunlop.

The Census Takers

IT GETS TO BE A MADHOUSE around here along about the end of the first week. Thank heaven we only do this once a year, that's what I say! Six weeks on, and forty-six weeks off–that's pretty good hours, most people think. But they don't know what those six weeks are like.

It's bad enough for the field crews, but when you get to be an Area Boss like me it's frantic. You work your way up through the ranks, and then they give you a whole C.A. of your own; and you think you've got it made. Fifty three-man crews go out, covering the whole Census Area; a hundred and fifty men in the field, and twenty or thirty more in Area Command–and you boss them all. And everything looks great, until Census Period starts and you've got to work those hundred and fifty men; and six weeks is too unbearably long to live through, and too impossibly short to get the work done; and you begin living on black coffee and thiamin shots and dreaming about the vacation hostel on Point Loma.

Anybody can panic, when the pressure is on like that. Your best field men begin to crack up. But you can't afford to, because you're the Area Boss. . . .

Take Witeck. We were Enumerators together, and he was as good a man as you ever saw, absolutely nerveless when it came to processing the Overs. I counted on that man the way I counted on my own right arm; I always bracketed him with the greenest, shakiest new cadet Enumerators, and he never gave me a moment's trouble for years. Maybe it was too good to last; maybe I should have figured he would crack.

I set up my Area Command in a plush penthouse apartment. The people who lived there were pretty well off, you know, and they naturally raised the dickens about being shoved out. "Blow it," I told them. "Get out of here in five minutes, and we'll count you first." Well, that took care of *that;* they were practically kissing my feet on the way out. Of course, it wasn't strictly by the book, but you have to be a little flexible; that's why some men become Area Bosses, and others stay Enumerators.

Like Witeck.

Along about Day Eight things were really hotting up. I was up to my neck in hurry-ups from Regional Control–we were running a little slow–when Witeck called up. "Chief," he said, "I've got an In."

I grabbed the rotary file with one hand and a pencil with the other. "Blue card number?" I asked.

Witeck sounded funny over the phone. "Well, Chief," he said, "he doesn't have a blue card. He says–"

"No blue card?" I couldn't believe it. Come in to a strange C.A. without a card from your own Area Boss, and you're one In that's a cinch to be an Over. "What kind of a crazy C.A. does he come from, without a blue card?"

Witeck said, "He don't come from any C.A., Chief. He says–"

"You mean he isn't from this country?"

"That's right, Chief. He–"

"Hold it!" I pushed away the rotary file and grabbed the immigration roster. There were only a couple of dozen names on it, of course –we have enough trouble with our own Overs, without taking on a lot of foreigners, but still there were a handful every year who managed to get on the quotas. "I.D. number?" I demanded.

"Well, Chief," Witeck began, "he doesn't have an I.D. number. The way it looks to me–"

Well, you can fool around with these irregulars for a month, if you want to, but it's no way to get the work done. I said: "Over him!" and hung up. I was a little surprised, though; Witeck knew the ropes, and it wasn't like him to buck an irregular on to me. In the old days, when we were both starting out, I'd seen him Over a whole family just because the spelling of their names on their registry cards was different from the spelling on the checklist.

But we get older. I made a note to talk to Witeck as soon as the rush was past. We were old friends; I wouldn't have to threaten him with being Overed himself, or anything like that. He'd know, and maybe that would be all he would need to snap him back. I certainly would talk to him, I promised myself, as soon as the rush was over, or anyway as soon as I got back from Point Loma.

I had to run up to Regional Control to take a little talking-to myself just then, but I proved to them that we were catching up and they were only medium nasty. When I got back Witeck was on the phone again. "Chief," he said, real unhappy, "this In is giving me a headache. I–"

"Witeck," I snapped at him, "are you bothering me with another In? Can't you handle anything by yourself?"

He said, "It's the same one, Chief. He says he's a kind of ambassador, and–"

"Oh," I said. "Well, why the devil don't you get your facts straight in the first place? Give me his name and I'll check his legation."

"Well, Chief," he began again, "he, uh, doesn't have any legation. He says he's from the–" he swallowed– "from the middle of the earth."

"You're crazy." I'd seen it happen before, good men breaking under the strain of census taking. They say in cadets that by the time you process your first five hundred Overs you've had it; either you take a voluntary Over yourself, or you split wide open and they carry you off to a giggle farm. And Witeck was past the five hundred mark, way past.

There was a lot of yelling and crying from the filter center, which I'd put out by the elevators, and it looked like Jumpers. I stabbed the transfer button on the phone and called to Carias, my number-two man: "Witeck's flipped or something. Handle it!"

And then I forgot about it, while Carias talked to Witeck on the phone; because it was Jumpers, all right, a whole family of them.

There was a father and a mother and five kids–*five* of them. Aren't some people disgusting? The field Enumerator turned them over to the guards–they were moaning and crying–and came up and gave me the story. It was bad.

"You're the head of the household?" I demanded of the man.

He nodded, looking at me like a sick dog. "We–we weren't Jumping," he whined. "Honest to heaven, mister–you've got to believe me. We were–"

I cut in, "You were packed and on the doorstep when the field crew came by. Right?" He started to say something, but I had him dead to rights. "That's plenty, friend," I told him. "That's Jumping, under the law: Packing, with intent to move, while a census Enumeration crew is operating in your locale. Got anything to say?"

Well, he had plenty to say, but none of it made any sense. He turned my stomach, listening to him. I tried to keep my temper–you're not supposed to think of individuals, no matter how worthless and useless and generally unfit they are; that's against the whole principle of the Census–but I couldn't help telling him: "I've met your kind before, mister. Five kids! If it wasn't for people like you we wouldn't *have* any Overs, did you ever think of that? Sure you didn't –you people never think of anything but yourself! Five kids, and then when Census comes around you think you can get smart and Jump." I tell you, I was shaking. "You keep your little beady eyes peeled, sneaking around, watching the Enumerators, trying to count how many it takes to make an Over; and then you wait until they get close to you, so you can Jump. Ever stop to think what trouble that makes for us?" I demanded. "Census is supposed to be fair and square, everybody an even chance—and how can we make it that way unless everybody stands still to be counted?" I patted Old Betsy, on my hip. "I haven't Overed anybody myself in five years," I told him, "but I swear, I'd like to handle you personally!"

He didn't say a word once I got started on him. He just stood there, taking it. I had to force myself to stop, finally; I could have gone on for a long time, because if there's one thing I hate it's these lousy, stinking breeders who try to Jump when they think one of them is going to be an Over in the count-off. Regular Jumpers are bad enough, but when it's the people who make the mess in the first place—

Anyway, time was wasting. I took a deep breath and thought things over. Actually, we weren't too badly off; we'd started off Overing every two-hundred-and-fiftieth person, and it was beginning to look as though our preliminary estimate was high; we'd just cut back to Overing every three-hundredth. So we had a little margin to play with.

I told the man, dead serious: "You know I could Over the lot of you on charges, don't you?" He nodded sickly. "All right, I'll give you a chance. I don't want to bother with the red tape; if you'll take a voluntary Over for yourself, we'll start the new count with your wife."

Call me soft, if you want to; but I still say that it was a lot better than fussing around with charges and a hearing. You get into a hearing like that and it can drag on for half an hour or more; and then Regional Control is on your tail because you're falling behind.

It never hurts to give a man a break, even a Jumper, I always say—as long as it doesn't slow down your Census.

Carias was waiting at my desk when I got back; he looked worried about something, but I brushed him off while I initialed the Overage report on the man we'd just processed. He'd been an In, I found out when I canceled his blue card. I can't say I was surprised. He'd come from Denver, and you know how they keep exceeding their Census figures; no doubt he thought he'd have a better chance in my C.A. than anywhere else. And no doubt he was right, because we certainly don't encourage breeders like him—actually, if he hadn't tried to Jump it was odds-on that the whole damned family would get by without an Over for years.

Carias was hovering right behind me as I finished. "I hate these voluntaries," I told him, basketing the canceled card. "I'm going to talk to Regional Control about it; there's no reason why they can't be processed like any other Over, instead of making me okay each one individually. Now, what's the matter?"

He rubbed his jaw. "Chief," he said, "it's Witeck."

"Now what? Another In?"

Carias glanced at me, then away. "Uh, no, Chief. It's the same one. He claims he comes from, uh, the center of the earth."

I swore out loud. "So he has to turn up in my C.A.!" I complained bitterly. "He gets out of the nuthouse, and right away—"

Carias said, "Chief, he might not be crazy. He makes it sound pretty real."

I said: "Hold it, Carias. Nobody can live in the center of the earth. It's solid, like a potato."

"Sure, Chief," Carias nodded earnestly. "But he says it isn't. He says there's a what he calls neutronium shell, whatever that is, with dirt and rocks on both sides of it. We live on the outside. He lives on the inside. His people—"

"Carias!" I yelled. "You're as bad as Witeck. This guy turns up, no blue card, no I.D. number, no credentials of any kind. What's he going to say, 'Please sir, I'm an Over, please process me'? Naturally not! So he makes up a crazy story, and you fall for it!"

"I know, Chief," Carias said humbly.

"Neutronium shell!" I would have laughed out loud, if I'd had the time. "Neutronium my foot! Don't you know it's *hot* down there?"

"He says it's hot neutronium," Carias said eagerly. "I asked him that myself, Chief. He said it's just the shell that—"

"Get back to work!" I yelled at him. I picked up the phone and got Witeck on his wristphone. I tell you, I was boiling. As soon as Witeck answered I lit into him; I didn't give him a chance to get a word in. I gave it to him up and down and sidewise; and I finished off by giving him a direct order. "You Over that man," I told him, "or I'll personally Over you! You hear me?"

There was a pause. Then Witeck said, "Jerry? Will you listen to me?"

That stopped me. It was the first time in ten years, since I'd been promoted above him, that Witeck had dared call me by my first name. He said, "Jerry, listen. This is something big. This guy is really from the center of the earth, no kidding. He—"

"Witeck," I said, "you've cracked."

"No, Jerry, honest! And it worries me. He's right there in the next room, waiting for me. He says he had no idea things were like this on the surface; he's talking wild about cleaning us off and starting all over again; he says–"

"*I* say he's an Over!" I yelled. "No more talk, Witeck. You've got a direct order–now carry it out!"

So that was that.

We got through the Census Period, after all, but we had to do it shorthanded; and Witeck was hard to replace. I'm a sentimentalist, I guess, but I couldn't help remembering old times. We started even; he might have risen as far as I–but of course he made his choice when he got married and had a kid; you can't be a breeder and an officer of the Census both. If it hadn't been for his record he couldn't even have stayed on as an Enumerator.

I never said a word to anyone about his crackup. Carias might have talked, but after we found Witeck's body I took him aside. "Carias," I said reasonably, "we don't want any scandal, do we? Here's Witeck, with an honorable record; he cracks, and kills himself, and that's bad enough. We won't let loose talk make it worse, will we?"

Carias said uneasily, "Chief, where's the gun he killed himself with? His own processor wasn't even fired."

You can let a helper go just so far. I said sharply, "Carias, we still have at least a hundred Overs to process. You can be on one end of the processing–or you can be on the other. You understand me?"

He coughed. "Sure, Chief. I understand. We don't want any loose talk."

And that's how it is when you're an Area Boss. But I didn't ever get my vacation at Point Loma; the tsunami there washed out the whole town the last week of the Census. And when I tried Baja California, they were having that crazy volcanic business; and the Yellowstone Park bureau wouldn't even accept my reservation because of some trouble with the geysers, so I just stayed home. But the best vacation of all was just knowing that the Census was done for another year.

Carias was all for looking for this In that Witeck was talking about, but I turned him down. "Waste of time," I told him. "By now he's a dozen C.A.'s away. We'll never see him again, him or anybody like him–I'll bet my life on that."

The Children of Night

I

"WE MET before," I told Haber. "In 1988, when you were running the Des Moines office."

He beamed and held out his hand. "Why, darn it, so we did! I remember now, Odin."

"I don't like to be called Odin."

"No? All right. Mr. Gunnarsen–"

"Not 'Mr. Gunnarsen,' either. Just 'Gunner.' "

"That's right, Gunner; I'd almost forgotten."

I said, "No, you hadn't forgotten. You never knew my name in Des Moines. You didn't even know I was alive, because you were too busy losing the state for our client. I pulled you out of that one, just like I'm going to pull you out now."

The smile was a little cracked, but Haber had been with the company a long time, and he wasn't going to let me throw him. "What do you want me to say, Gunner? I'm grateful. Believe me, boy, I know I need help–"

"And I'm not your boy. Haber, you were a fat cat then, and you're a fat cat now. All I want from you is, first, a quick look around the shop here and, second, a conference of all department heads, including you, in thirty minutes. So tell your secretary to round them up, and let's get started on the sight-seeing."

Coming in to Belport on the scatjet, I had made a list of things to do. The top item was:

1. Fire Haber.

Still, in my experience that isn't always the best way to put out a fire. Some warts you remove; some you just let wither away in obscurity. I am not paid by M & B to perform cosmetic surgery on their Habers, only to see that the work the Habers should have done gets accomplished.

As a public relations branch manager he was a wart, but as a tourist guide he was fine, although he was perspiring. He led me all around the shop. He had taken a storefront on one of the main shopping malls—air-curtain door, windows draped tastefully in gray silk. It looked like the best of four funeral parlors in a run-down neightborhood. In gilt letters on the window was the name of the game:

MOULTRIE & BIGELOW
Public Relations
Northern Lake State Division
T. Wilson Haber
Division Manager

"Public relations," he informed me, "starts at home. They know we're here, eh, Gunner?"

"Reminds me of the Iowa office," I said, and he stumbled where there wasn't even a sill. That was the Presidential campaign of '88, where Haber had been trying to carry the state for the candidate who had retained us, and those twelve electoral votes came over at the last minute only because we sent Haber to Nassau to rest and I took over from him. I believe Haber's wife had owned stock in the company.

His Belport layout was pretty good, at that, though. Four pry booths, each with a Simplex 9090 and an operator-receptionist in the donor's waiting room. You can't tell from appearances, but the donors who were waiting for their interrogation looked like a good representative sample—a good mixture of sexes, ages, conditions of affluence—and with proper attention to weighing he should at least be getting a fair survey of opinions. Integration of the pry scores was in a readout station in back—I recognized one of the programmers and nodded to him: good man—along with telefax equipment to the major research sources, the Britannica, Library of Congress, news-wire services, and so on. From the integration room the readout operator could construct a speech, a 3-V commercial, a space ad, or anything else, with the research lines to feed him any data he needed and test its appeal on his subjects. In the front of the building was a taping booth and studio. Everything was small and semiportable, but good stuff. You could put together a 3-V interview or edit one as well here as you could on the lot in the home office.

"An A-number-one setup, right, Gunner?" said Haber. "Set it up myself to do the job."

I said, "Then why aren't you doing it?" He tightened up. The eyes looked smaller and more intelligent, but he didn't say anything directly. He took my elbow and turned me to the data-processing room.

"Want you to meet someone," he said, opened the door, led me inside, and left me.

A tall, slim girl looked up from a typer. "Why, hello, Gunner," she said. "It's been a long time."

I said, "Hello, Candace."

Apparently Haber was not quite such a fat cat as he had seemed, for he had clearly found out a little something about my personal life before I showed up in his office. The rest of the list I had scribbled down in the scatjet was:

2. Need "big lie."
3. Investigate Children.
4. Investigate opponents' proposition.
5. Marry Candace Harmon?

This was a relatively small job for Moultrie & Bigelow, but it was for a very, very big account. It was important to win it. The client was the Arcturan Confederacy.

In the shop the word was that they had been turned down by three or four other PR agencies before we took them on. Nobody said why, exactly, but the reason was perfectly clear. It was just because they were the Arcturan Confederacy. There is nothing in any way illegal or immoral about a public relations firm representing a foreign account. That is a matter of statute—as most people don't take the trouble to know: the Smith-Macchioni Act of '71. And the courts held that it applied to extra-planetary "foreigners" as well as to terrestrials in 1985, back when the only "intelligent aliens" were the mummies on Mars. Not that the mummies had ever hired anybody on Earth to do anything for them. But it was Moultrie & Bigelow's law department that sued for the declaratory judgment, as a matter of fact. Just on the off chance. That's how M & B operates.

Any public relations man takes on the color of his clients in the eyes of some people. That's the nature of the beast. The same people wouldn't think of blaming a surgeon because he dissolved a malignancy out of Public Enemy No. 1, or even a lawyer for defending him. But when you are in charge of a client's emotional image and that image isn't liked, some of the dislike rubs off on you.

At M & B there is enough in the pay check at the end of every month so that we don't mind that. M & B has a reputation for taking on the tough ones–the only surviving American cigarette manufacturer is ours. So is the exiled Castroite government of Cuba, that still thinks it might one day get the State Department to back up its claim for paying off on the bonds it printed for itself. However, for two reasons–as a simple matter of making things easy for ourselves and because it's better doctrine–we don't flaunt our connection with the unpopular clients. Especially when the job is going badly. One of the surest ways to get a bad public response to PR is to let the public know that some hotshot PR outfit is working on it.

So every last thing Haber had done was wrong.

In this town it was too late for pry booths and M/R.

I had just five minutes left before the conference, and I spent it in the pry-booth section, anyhow. I noticed a tri-D display of our client's home planet in the reception room, where donors were sitting and waiting their turn. It was very attractive: the wide, calm seas with the vertical air-mount islets jutting out at intervals.

I turned around and walked out fast, boiling mad.

A layman might not have seen just how many ways Haber had found to go wrong. The whole pry-booth project was probably a mistake, anyway. To begin with, to get any good out of pry booths you need depth interviews, way deep-down M/R stuff. And for that you need paid donors, lots of them. And to get them you have to have a panel to pick from.

That means advertising in the papers and on the nets and interviewing twenty people for every one you hire. To get a satisfactory sample in a town the size of Belport you need to hire maybe fifty donors. And that means talking to a thousand people, every one of whom will go home and talk to his wife or her mother or their neighbors.

In a city like Chicago or Saskatoon you can get away with it. With good technique the donor never really knows what he's being interviewed *for,* although, of course, a good newspaperman or private eye can interview a couple of donors and work backward from the sense-impulse stimuli with pretty fair accuracy. But not in Belport, not when we never had a branch here before, not when every living soul in town knew what we were doing because the rezoning ordinance was Topic One over every coffee table. In short, we had tipped our hand completely.

As I say, an amateur might not have spotted that. But Haber was not supposed to be an amateur.

I had just seen the trend charts, too. The referendum on granting rezoning privileges to our client was going to a vote in less than two weeks. When Haber had opened the branch, sampling showed that it would fail by a four-to-three vote. Now, a month and a half later, he had worsened the percentage to three to two and going downhill all the way.

Our client would be extremely unhappy—probably was unhappy already, if they had managed to puzzle out the queer terrestrial progress reports we had been sending them.

And this was the kind of client that a flackery didn't want to have unhappy. I mean, all the others were little-league stuff in comparison. The Arcturan Confederacy was a culture as wealthy and as powerful as all Earth governments combined, and as Arcturans don't bother with nonsense like national governments or private enterprise, at least not in any way that makes sense to us, this one client was—

As big as every other *possible* client combined.

They were the ones who decided they needed this base in Belport, and it was up to M & B—and specifically to me, Odin Gunnarsen—to see that they got it.

It was too bad that they had been fighting Earth six months earlier.

In fact, in a technical sense we were still at war. It was only armistice, not a peace, that had called off the H-bomb raids and the fleet engagements.

Like I say. M & B takes on the tough ones!

Besides Haber, four of the staff looked as though they knew which end was up. Candace Harmon, the pry-integration programmer, and two very junior T.A.s. I took the head chair at the conference table without waiting to see where Haber would want to sit and said, "We'll make this fast, because we're in trouble here and we don't have time to be polite. You're Percy?" That was the programmer; he nodded. "And I didn't catch your name?" I said, turning to the next along the table. It was the copy chief, a lanky shave-headed oldster named Tracy Spockman. His assistant, one of the T.A.s I had had my eye on, turned out to be named Manny Brock.

I had picked easy jobs for all the deadheads, reserving the smart ones for whatever might turn up, so I started with the copy chief. "Spockman, we're opening an Arcturan purchasing agency, and you're it. You should be able to handle this one; if I remember correctly, you ran the Duluth shop for a year."

He sucked on a cal pipe without expression. "Well, thanks, Mr. Gun—"

"Just Gunner."

"Well, thanks, but as copy chief—"

"Manny here should be able to take care of that. If I remember the way you ran the Duluth operation, you've probably got things set up so he can step right in." And so he probably did. At least, it surely would do no real harm to give somebody else a chance at lousing things up. I handed Spockman the "positions wanted" page from the paper I'd picked up at the scatport, and a scrawled list of notes I'd made up on the way in. "Hire these girls I've marked for your staff, rent an office, and get some letters out. You'll see what I want from the list. Letters to every real estate dealer in town, asking them if they can put together a five-thousand-acre parcel in the area covered by the zoning referendum. Letter to every general contractor, asking for bids on buildings. Make it separate bids on each—I think there'll be five buildings altogether. One exoclimatized—so get the air-conditioning, heating, and plumbing contractors to bid, too. Letter to every food wholesaler and major grocery outlet asking if they are interested in bidding on supplying Arcturans with food. Fax Chicago for what the Arcturans fancy; I don't remember—no meat, I think, but a lot of green vegetables—anyway, find out and include the data in the letters. Electronics manufacturers, office equipment dealers, car and truck agencies—well, the whole list is on that piece of paper. I want every businessman in Belport starting to figure out by tomorrow morning how much profit he might make on an Arcturan base. Got it?"

"I think so, Mr.—Gunner. I was thinking. How about stationery suppliers, attorneys, C.P.A.'s?"

"Don't ask—do it. Now, you down at the end there—"

"Henry Dane, Gunner."

"Henry, what about club outlets in Belport? I mean specialized groups. The Arcturans are hot for navigation, sailing, like that; see what you can do with the motorboat clubs and so on. I noticed in the paper that there's a flower show at the armory next Saturday. It's pretty late, but squeeze in a speaker on Arcturan fungi. We'll fly in a display. They tell me Arcturans are hot gardeners when they're home—love all the biological sciences—nice folks, like to dabble." I hesitated and looked at my notes. "I have something down here about veterans' groups, but I haven't got the handle for it. Still, if you can think of an angle, let me know—what's the matter?"

He was looking doubtful. "It's only that I don't want to conflict with Candy, Gunner."

And so, of course, I had to face up to things and turn to Candace Harmon. "What's that, honey?" I asked.

"I think Henry means my Arcturan-American Friendship League." It turned out that that had been one of Haber's proudest ideas. I wasn't surprised. After several weeks and about three thousand dollars it had worked up to a total of forty-one members. How many of those were employees of the M & B branch? "Well, all but eight," Candace admitted at once. She wasn't smiling, but she was amused.

"Don't worry about it," I advised Henry Dane. "We're folding the Arcturan-American Friendship League, anyway. Candace won't have time for it. She'll be working with me."

"Why, fine, Gunner," she said. "Doing what?"

I almost did marry Candace one time, and every once in a while since I have wished I hadn't backed away. A very good thing was Candace Harmon.

"Doing," I said, "what Gunner says for you to do. Let's see. First thing, I've got five hundred Arcturan domestic animals coming in tomorrow. I haven't seen them, but they tell me they're cute, look like kittens, are pretty durable. Figure out some way of getting them distributed fast—maybe a pet shop will sell them for fifty cents each."

Haber protested, "My dear Gunner! The freight alone—"

"Sure, Haber, they cost about forty dollars apiece just to get them here. Any other questions like that? No? That's good. I want one in each of five hundred homes by the end of the week, and if I had to pay a hundred dollars to each customer to take them, I'd pay. Next: I want somebody to find me a veteran, preferably disabled, preferably who was actually involved in the bombing of the home planet—"

I laid out a dozen more working lines—an art show of the Arcturan bas-relief stuff that was partly to look at but mostly to feel, a 3-V panel show on Arcturus that we could plant . . . the whole routine. None of it would do the job, but all of it would help until I got my bearings. Then I got down to business. "What's the name of this fellow who's running for councilman—Connick?"

"That's right," said Haber.

"What've you got on him?" I asked.

I turned to Candace, who said promptly, "Forty-one years old, Methodist, married, three kids of his own plus one of the casualties, ran for State Senate last year and lost, but he carried Belport, running opposed to the referendum this year, very big in Junior Chamber of Commerce and V.F.W.—"

"No. What've you got *on* him?" I persisted.

Candace said slowly, "Gunner, look. This is a nice guy."

"Why, I know that, honey. I read his piece in the paper today. So now tell me the dirt that he can't afford to have come out."

"It wouldn't be fair to destroy him for nothing!"

I brushed aside the "fair" business. "What do you mean, 'for nothing'?"

"We're not going to win this referendum, you know."

"Honey, I've got news for you. This is the biggest account anybody ever had, and I want it. We *will* win. What've you got on Connick?"

"Nothing. Really nothing," she said quietly.

"But you can get it."

Candace said, visibly upset, "Of course, there's probably some–"

"Of course. Get it. Today."

II

But I wasn't relying totally on anyone, not even Candace. Since Connick was the central figure of the opposition I caught a cab and went to see him.

It was already dark, a cold, clear night, and over the mushroom towers of the business district a quarter-moon was beginning to rise. I looked at it almost with affection; I had hated it so when I was there.

As I paid the cab, two kids in snowsuits came sidling out to inspect me. I said, "Hello. Is your Daddy home?"

One was about five, with freckles and bright blue eyes; the other was darker, brown-eyed, and he had a limp. The blue-eyed one said, "Daddy's down in the cellar. Mommy will let you in if you ring the doorbell. Just push that button."

"Oh, that's how those things work. Thanks." Connick's wife turned out to be a good-looking, skinny blonde in her thirties, and the kids must have raced around the back way and alerted the old man, because as she was taking my coat, he was already coming through the hall.

I shook his hand and said, "I can tell by the smells from your kitchen that it's dinnertime. I won't keep you. My name is Gunnarsen and–"

"And you're from Moultrie & Bigelow–here, sit down, Mr. Gunnarsen–and you want to know if I won't think it over and back the Arcturan base. No, Mr. Gunnarsen, I won't. But why don't you have a drink with me before dinner? And then why don't you have dinner?"

He was a genuine article, this Connick. I had to admit he had caught me off balance.

"Why, I don't mind if I do," I said after a moment. "I see you know why I'm here."

He was pouring drinks. "Well, not altogether, Mr. Gunnarsen. You don't really think you'll change my mind, do you?"

"I can't say that until I know why you oppose the base in the first place, Connick. That's what I want to find out."

He handed me a drink, sat down across from me, and took a thoughtful pull at his own. It was good Scotch. Then he looked to see if the kids were within earshot, and said: "The thing is this, Mr. Gunnarsen. If I could, I would kill every Arcturan alive, and if it meant I had to accept the death of a few million Earthmen to do it, that wouldn't be too high a price. I don't want the base here because I don't want anything to do with those murdering animals."

"Well, you're candid," I said, finished my drink, and added, "If you meant that invitation to dinner, I believe I will take you up on it."

I must say they were a nice family. I've worked elections before: Connick was a good candidate because he was a good man. The way his kids behaved around him proved it, and the way he behaved around me was the clincher. I didn't scare him a bit.

Of course, that was not altogether bad, from my point of view.

Connick kept the conversation off Topic A during dinner, which was all right with me, but as soon as it was over and we were alone, he said, "All right. You can make your pitch now, Mr. Gunnarsen. Although I don't know why you're here instead of with Tom Schlitz."

Schlitz was the man he was running against. I said, "You don't know this business, I guess. What do we need him for? He's already committed on our side."

"And I'm already committed against you, but I guess that's what you're hoping to change. Well, what's your offer?"

He was moving too fast for me. I pretended to misunderstand. "Really, Mr. Connick, I wouldn't insult you by offering a bribe—"

"No, I know you wouldn't. Because you're smart enough to know I wouldn't take money. So it isn't money. What is it, then? Moultrie & Bigelow working for me instead of Schlitz in the election? That's a pretty good offer, but the price is too high. I won't pay it."

"Well," I said, "as a matter of fact, we would be willing—"

"Yes, I thought so. No deal. Anyway, do you really think I need help to get elected?"

That was a good point, I was forced to admit. I conceded, "No, not if everything else were equal. You're way ahead right now, as your surveys and ours both show. But everything else isn't equal."

"By which you mean that you're going to help old Slits-and-fits. All right, that makes it a horse race."

I held up my glass, and he refilled it. I said, "Mr. Connick, I told you once you didn't know this business. You don't. It isn't a horse race because you can't win against us."

"I can sure give it a hell of a try, though. Anyway"–he finished his own drink thoughtfully–"you brainwashers are a little bit fat, I think. Everybody knows how powerful you are, and you haven't really had to show it much lately. I wonder if the emperor's really running around naked."

"Oh, no, Mr. Connick. Best-dressed emperor you ever saw, take my word for it."

He said, frowning a little bit, "I think I'll have to find out for myself. Anyway, frankly, I think people's minds are made up, and you can't change them."

"We don't have to," I said. "Don't you know why people vote the way they do, Connick? They don't vote their 'minds.' They vote attitudes and they vote impulses. Frankly, I'd rather work on your side than against you. Schlitz would be easy to beat. He's Jewish."

Connick said angrily, "There's none of that in Belport, man."

"Of anti-Semitism, you mean. Of course not. But if one candidate is Jewish and if it turns up that fifteen years ago he tried to square a parking ticket–and there's always something that turns up, Connick, believe me–then they'll vote against him for fixing parking tickets. That's what I mean by 'attitudes.' Your voter–oh, not all of them, but enough to swing any election–goes into the booth pulled this way and that. We don't have to change his mind. We just have to help him decide which part of it to operate on." I let him refill my glass and took a pull at it. I was aware that I was beginning to feel the effects. "Take you, Connick," I said. "Suppose you're a Democrat and you go in to cast your vote. We know how you're going to vote for President, right? You're going to vote for the Democratic candidate."

Connick said, not unbending much, "Not necessarily. But probably."

"Not necessarily, right. And why not necessarily? Because maybe you know this fellow who's running on the Democratic ticket–or maybe somebody you know has a grudge against him, couldn't get the postmaster's job he wanted, or ran against his delegates for the convention. Point is, you have something *against* him just because your first instinct is *for* him. So how do you vote? Whichever way happens to get dominance *at the moment of voting*. Not at any other moment. Not as a matter of principle. But right then. No, we don't have to change any minds . . . because most people don't have enough mind to change!"

He stood up and absentmindedly filled his own glass—I wasn't the only one who was beginning to feel the liquor. "I'd hate to be you," he said, half to himself.

"Oh, it's not bad."

He shook his head, then recollected himself and said, "Well, thanks for the lesson. I didn't know. But I'll tell you one thing you'll never do. You'll never get me to vote on the Arcturan side on *any* question."

I sneered, "There's an open mind for you! Leader of the people! Takes an objective look at every question!"

"All right, I'm not objective. They stink."

"Race prejudice, Connick?"

"Oh, don't be a fool."

"There is," I said, "an Arcturan aroma. They can't help it."

"I didn't say 'smell.' I said 'stink.' I don't want them in this town, and neither does anybody else. Not even Schlitz."

"You don't ever have to see them. They don't like Earth climate, you know. Too hot for them. Too much air. Why, Connick," I said, "I'll bet you a hundred bucks you won't set eyes on an Arcturan for at least a year, not until the base is built and staffed. And then I doubt they'll bother to—What's the matter?"

He was looking at me as though I were an idiot, and I almost began to think I was.

"Why," he said, again in that tone that was more to himself than to me, "I guess I've been overrating you. You think you're God, so I've been accepting your own valuation."

"What do you mean?"

"Inexcusably bad staff work, Mr. Gunnarsen," he said, nodding judgmatically. "It ought to make me feel good. But you know, it doesn't. It scares me. With the kind of power you throw around, you should always be right."

"Spit it out!"

"It's just that you lose your bet. Didn't you know there's an Arcturan in town right now?"

III

When I got back to the car, the phone was buzzing and the "Message Recorded" light blinked at me. The message was from Candace: "Gunner, a Truce Team has checked into the Statler-Bills to supervise the election, and get this. One of them's an Arcturan!"

The staff work wasn't so bad, after all, just unpardonably slow. But there wasn't much comfort in that.

I called the hotel and was connected with one of the Truce Team staff–the best the hotel would do for me. The staff man was a colonel who said, "Yes, Mr. Knafti is aware of your work here and specifically does not wish to see you. This is a Truce Team, Mr. Gunnarsen. Do you know what that means, exactly?"

And he hung up on me. Well, I did know what it meant–strictly hands-off, all the way–I simply hadn't known that they would interpret it that rigidly.

It was a kick in the eye, any way I looked at it. Because it made me look like a fool in front of Connick, when I kind of wanted him scared of me. Because Arcturans do, after all, stink–not good public relations at all when your product smells like well-rotted garlic buds a few hundred feet away. I didn't want the voters smelling them.

And most of all because of the inference that I was sure any red-blooded, stubborn-minded, confused voter would draw: Jeez, Sam, you hear about that Arcturan coming to spy on us? Yeah, Charlie, the damn bugs are practically accusing us of rigging the election. Damn right, Sam, and you know what else? They stink, Sam.

Half an hour later I got a direct call from Haber. "Gunner boy! Good God! Oh, this is the reeking end!"

I said, "It sounds to me like you've found out about the Arcturan on the Truce Team."

"You know? And you didn't tell *me?*"

Well, I had been about to ream him for not telling *me,* but obviously that wasn't going to do any good. I tried, anyway, but he fell back on his fat ignorance. "They didn't clue me in from Chicago. Can I help that? Be fair now, Gunner boy!"

Gunner boy very fairly hung up.

I was beginning to feel very sleepy. For a moment I debated taking a brisk-up pill, but the mild buzz Connick's liquor had left with me was pleasant enough, and besides, it was getting late. I went to the hotel suite Candace had reserved for me and crawled into bed.

It only took me a few minutes to fall asleep, but I was faintly aware of an odor. It was the same hotel the Truce Team was staying at.

I couldn't really be smelling this Arcturan, Knafti. It was just my imagination. That's what I told myself as I dialed for sleep and drifted off.

The pillow-phone hummed, and Candace's voice said out of it, "Wake up and get decent, Gunner. I'm coming up."

I managed to sit up, shook my head, and took a few whiffs of amphetamine. As always, it woke me right up, but at the usual price of feeling that I hadn't had quite enough sleep. Still, I got into a robe and was in the bathroom fixing breakfast when she knocked on the door. "It's open," I called. "Want some coffee?"

"Sure, Gunner." She came and stood in the doorway, watching me turn the Hilsch squirt to full boil and fill two cups. I spooned dry coffee into them and turned the squirt to cold. "Orange juice?" She took the coffee and shook her head, so I just mixed one glassful, swallowed it, tossed the glass in the disposal hamper, and took the coffee into the other room. The bed had stripped itself already; it was now a couch, and I leaned back on it, drinking my coffee. "All right, honey," I said, "what's the dirt on Connick?"

She hesitated, then opened her bag and took out a photofax and handed it to me. It was a reproduction of an old steel engraving headed, in antique script, *The Army of the United States,* and it said:

Be it known to all men that

DANIEL T. CONNICK

ASIN Aj-32880515

has this date been separated from the service of the United States for the convenience of the government; and

Be it further known to all men that the conditions of his discharge are

DISHONORABLE

"Well, what do you know!" I said. "You see, honey? There's always something."

Candace finished her coffee, set the cup down neatly on a windowsill, and took out a cigarette. That was like her: She always did one thing at a time, an orderly sort of mind that I couldn't match—and couldn't stand, either. Undoubtedly she knew what I was thinking because undoubtedly she was thinking it, too, but there wasn't any nostalgia in her voice when she said: "You went and saw him last night, didn't you? . . . And you're still going to knife him?"

I said, "I'm going to see that he is defeated in the election, yes. That's what they pay me for. Me and some others."

"No, Gunner," she said, "that's not what M & B pay *me* for, if that's what you mean, because there isn't that much money."

I got up and went over beside her. "More coffee? No? Well, I guess I don't want any, either. Honey—"

Candace stood up, crossed the room, and sat down in a straight-backed chair. "You wake up all of a sudden, don't you? Don't change the subject. We were talking about–"

"We were talking," I told her, "about a job that we're paid to do. All right, you've done one part of it for me–you got me what I wanted on Connick."

I stopped, because she was shaking her head. "I'm not so sure I did."

"How's that?"

"Well, it's not on the fax, but I know why he got his DD. 'Desertion of hazardous duty.' On the Moon, in the U.N. Space Force. The year was 1998."

I nodded, because I understood what she was talking about. Connick wasn't the only one. Half the Space Force had cracked up that year. November. A heavy Leonid strike of meteorites and a solar flare at the same time. The Space Force top brass had decided they had to crack down and asked the U.S. Army to court-martial every soldier who cut and ran for an underground shelter, and the Army had felt obliged to comply. "But most of them got Presidential clemency," I said. "He didn't?"

Candace shook her head. "He didn't apply."

"Um. Well, it's still on record." I dismissed the subject. "Something else. What about these Children?"

Candace put out her cigarette and stood up. "Why I'm here, Gunner. It was on your list. So–get dressed."

"For what?"

She grinned. "For my peace of mind, for one thing. Also for investigating the Children, like you say. I've made you an appointment at the hospital in fifty-five minutes."

You have to remember that I didn't know anything about the Children except rumors. Bless Haber, he hadn't thought it necessary to explain. And Candace only said, "Wait till we get to the hospital. You'll see for yourself."

Donnegan General was seven stories of cream-colored ceramic brick, air-controlled, wall-lighted throughout, tiny asepsis lamps sparkling blue where the ventilation ducts opened. Candace parked the car in an underground garage and led me to an elevator, then to a waiting room. She seemed to know her way around very well. She glanced at her watch, told me we were a couple of minutes early, and pointed to a routing map that was a mural with colored lights showing visitors the way to whatever might be their destination. It also showed, quite impressively, the size and scope of Donnegan General. The hospital had twenty-two fully equipped operating rooms, a specimen and transplant bank, X-ray and radiochemical departments, a cryogenics room, the most complete prosthesis installation on Earth, a geriatrics section, O.T. rooms beyond number . . .

And, of all things, a fully equipped and crowded pediatric wing.

I said, "I thought this was a V.A. facility."

"Exactly. Here comes our boy."

A Navy officer was coming in, hand and smile outstretched to Candace. "Hi, good to see you. And you must be Mr. Gunnarsen."

Candace introduced us as we shook hands. The fellow's name was Commander Whitling; she called him Tom. He said, "We'll have to move. Since I talked to you, there's been an all-hands evolution scheduled for eleven–some high brass inspection. I don't want to hurry you, but I'd like it if we were out of the way . . . this is a little irregular."

"Nice of you to arrange it," I said. "Lead on."

We went up a high-rise elevator and came out on the top floor of the building, into a corridor covered with murals of Disney and Mother Goose. From a sun deck came the tinkle of a music box. Three children, chasing each other down the hall, dodged past us, yelling. They made pretty good time, considering that two of them were on crutches. "What the hell are you doing here?" asked Commander Whitling sharply.

I looked twice, but he wasn't talking to me or the kids. He was talking to a man with a young face but a heavy black beard, who was standing behind a Donald Duck mobile, looking inconspicuous and guilty.

"Oh, hi, Mr. Whitling," the man said. "Jeez, I must've got lost again looking for the PX."

"Carhart," said the commander dangerously, "if I catch you in this wing again, you won't have to worry about the PX for a year. Hear me?"

"Well, jeez! All right, Mr. Whitling." As the man saluted and turned, his face wearing an expression of injury, I noticed that the left sleeve of his bathrobe was tucked, empty, into a pocket.

"You can't keep them out," said Whitling and spread his hands. "Well, all right, Mr. Gunnarsen, here it is. You're seeing the whole thing."

I looked carefully around. It was all children–limping children, stumbling children, pale children, weary children. "But what am I seeing, exactly?" I asked.

"Why, the Children, Mr. Gunnarsen. The ones we liberated. The ones the Arcturans captured on Mars."

And then I connected. I remembered about the capture of the colony on Mars.

Interstellar war is waged at the pace of a snail's crawl, because it takes so long to go from star to star. The main battles of our war with Arcturus had been fought no farther from Earth than the surface of Mars, and the fleet engagement around Orbit Saturn. Still, it had taken eleven years, first to last, from the surprise attack on the Martian colony to the armistice signed in Washington.

I remembered seeing a reconstructed tape of that Martian surprise attack. It was a summer's day–hot–at full noon, ice melted into water. The place was the colony around the Southern Springs. Out of the small descending sun a ship appeared.

It was a rocket. It was brilliant gold metal, and it came down with a halo of gold radiation around its splayed front, like the fleshy protuberance of a star-nosed mole. It landed with an electrical crackle on the fine-grained orange sand, and out of it came the Arcturans.

Of course, no one had known they were Arcturans then. They had swung around the sun in a long anecliptic orbit, watching and studying, and they had selected the small Martian outpost as the place to strike. In Mars gravity they were bipeds–two of their ropy limbs were enough to lift them off the ground–man tall, in golden pressure suits. The colonists came running out to meet them–and were killed. All of them. All of the adults.

The children, however, had not been killed, not that quickly or that easily, at least. Some had not been killed at all, and some of those were here in Donnegan General Hospital.

But not all.

Comprehension beginning to emerge in my small mind, I said, "Then these are the survivors."

Candace, standing very close to me, said "Most of them, Gunner. The ones that aren't well enough to be sent back into normal life."

"And the others?"

"Well, they mostly don't have families–having been killed, you see. So they've been adopted out into foster homes here in Belport. A hundred and eight of them–isn't that right, Tom? And now maybe you get some idea of what you're up against."

There were something like a hundred of the Children in that wing, and I didn't see all of them. Some of them were not to be seen.

Whitling just told me about but couldn't show me the blood-temperature room, where the very young and very bad cases lived. They had a gnotobiotic atmosphere, a little rich in oxygen, a little more humid than the ambient air, plus pressure to help their weak metabolism keep oxygen spread in their parts. On their right, a little farther along, were the small individual rooms belonging to the worst cases of all. The contagious. The incurables. The unfortunates whose very appearance was bad for the others. Whitling was good enough to open polarizing shutters and let me look in on some of those where they lay (or writhed or stood like sticks) in permanent solitary. One of the Arcturan efforts had been transplantation, and the project seemed to have been directed by a whimsical person. The youngest was about three; the oldest in the late teens.

They were a disturbing lot, and if I have glossed lightly over what I felt, it is because what I felt is all too obvious.

Kids in trouble! Of course, those who had been put back into population weren't put back shocking as these. But they would pull at the heartstrings–they even pulled at mine–and every time a foster parent or a foster parent's neighbor or a casual passer-by on the street felt that heartstring tug, he would feel, too, a single thought: The *Arcturans did this.*

For after killing the potentially dangerous adults, they had caged the tractable small ones as valuable research specimens.

And I had hoped to counteract this with five hundred Arcturan pets!

Whitling had been all this time taking me around the wing, and I could hear in his voice the sound of what I was up against, because he loved and pitied those kids. "Hi, Terry," he said on the sun deck, bending over a bed and patting its occupant on his snow-white hair. Terry smiled up at him. "Can't hear us, of course," said Whitling. "We grafted in new auditory nerves four weeks ago–I did it myself–but they're not surviving. Third try, too. And, of course, each attempt is a worse risk than the one before: antibodies."

I said, "He doesn't look more than five years old." Whitling nodded. "But the attack on the colony was–"

"Oh, I see what you mean," said Whitling. "The Arcturans were, of course, interested in reproduction too. Ellen–she left us a couple of weeks ago–was only thirteen, but she'd had six children. Now this is Nancy."

Nancy was perhaps twelve, but her gait and arm coordination were those of a toddler. She came stumbling in after a ball, stopped, and regarded me with dislike and suspicion. "Nancy's one of our cures," Whitling said proudly. He followed my eyes. "Oh, nothing wrong there," he said. "Mars-bred. She hasn't adjusted to Earth gravity, is all; she isn't slow–the ball's bouncing too fast. Here's Sam."

Sam was a near-teen-ager, giggling from his bed as he tried what was obviously the extremely wearing exercise of lifting his head off the mattress. A candy-striped practical nurse was counting time for him as he touched chin to chest, one and two, one and two. He did it five times, then slumped back, grinning. "Sam's central nervous system was almost gone," Whitling said fondly. "But we're making progress. Nervous tissue regeneration, though, is awfully–" I wasn't listening; I was looking at Sam's grin, which showed black and broken teeth. "Diet deficiency," said Whitling, following my look again.

"All right," I said, "I've seen enough; now I want to get out of here before they have me changing diapers. I thank you, Commander Whitling. I think I thank you. Which way is out?"

IV

I didn't want to go back to Haber's office. I was afraid of what the conversation might be like. But I had to get a fill-in on what had been happening with our work, and I had to eat.

So I took Candace back to my room and ordered lunch from room service.

I stood at the thermal window looking out at the city while Candace checked with the office. I didn't even listen, because Candace knew what I would want to know; I just watched Belport cycle through an average dull Monday at my feet. Belport was a radial town, with an urban center-cluster of the mushroom-shaped buildings that were popular twenty years ago. The hotel we were in was one, in fact, and from my window I could see three others looming above and below me, to right and left, and beyond them the cathedral spires of the apartment condominia of the residential districts. I could see a creeping serpent of gaily colored cars moving along one of the trafficways, pinpointed with sparks of our pro-referendum campaign parades. Or one of the opposition's. From four hundred feet it didn't seem to matter.

"You know, honey," I said as she clicked off the 3-V, "there isn't any sense to this. I admit the kids are sad cases, and who can resist kids in trouble? But they don't have one solitary damned thing to do with whether or not the Arcturans should have a telemetry and tracking station out on the lake."

Candace said, "Weren't you the man who told me that logic didn't have anything to do with public relations?" She came to the window beside me, turned, and half-sat on the ledge and read from her notes: "Survey index off another half-point. . . . Haber says be sure to tell you that's a victory—would have been off two points at least without the Arcats. Supplier letters out. Chicago approves budget overdraft. And that's all that matters."

"Thanks." The door chimed, and she left me to let the waiter in with our lunch. I watched her without much appetite, except maybe for the one thing that I knew wasn't on the menu: Candace herself. But I tried to eat.

Candace did not seem to be trying to help me eat. In fact, she did something that was quite out of character for her. All the way through lunch she kept talking, and the one subject she kept talking about was the kids. I heard about Nina, who was fifteen when she came to Donnegan General and had been through the occupation all the way—who wouldn't talk to anybody and weighed fifty-one pounds and screamed unless she was allowed to hide under the bed. "And after six months," said Candace, "they gave her a hand-puppet, and she finally talked through *that*."

"How'd you find all this out?" I asked.

"From Tom. And then there were the germ-free kids. . . ."

She told me about them, and about the series of injections and marrow transplants that they had needed to restore the body's immune reaction without killing the patient. And the ones with auditory and vocal nerves destroyed, apparently because the Arcturans were investigating the question of whether humans could think rationally in the absence of articulate words. The ones raised on chemically pure glucose for dietary studies. The induced bleeders. The kids with no sense of touch, and the kids with no developed musculature.

"Tom told you all this?"

"And lots more, Gunner. And remember, these are the survivors. Some of the kids who were deliberately—"

"How long have you known Tom?"

She put down her fork, sugared her coffee, and took a sip, looking at me over the cup. "Oh, since I've been here. Two years. Since before the kids came, of course."

"Pretty well, I judge."

"Oh, yes."

"He really likes those kids—I could see that. And so do you." I swallowed some more of my own coffee, which tasted like diluted pig swill, and reached for a cigarette and said, "I think maybe I waited too long about the situation here, wouldn't you say?"

"Why, yes, Gunner," she said carefully, "I think you maybe missed the boat."

"I tell you what else I think, honey. I think you're trying to tell me something, and it isn't all about Proposition Four on the ballot next week."

And she said, not irrelevantly, "As a matter of fact, Gunner, I'm going to marry Tom Whitling on Christmas Day."

I sent her back to the office and stretched out on my bed, smoking and watching the smoke being sucked into the wall vents. It was rather peaceful and quiet because I'd told the desk to hold all calls until further notice, and I wasn't feeling a thing.

Perfection is so rare that it is interesting to find a case in which one has been perfectly wrong all the way.

If I had taken out my little list, then I could have checked off all the points. One way or another. I hadn't fired Haber, and in fact, I really didn't want to anymore, because he wasn't much worse than I was at this particular job; the record showed it. I had investigated the Children, all right. A little late. I had investigated Connick, the number one opponent to the proposition, and what I had found would hurt Connick, all right, but I couldn't really see how it would help do our job. And I certainly wasn't going to marry Candace Harmon.

Come to think of it, I thought, lighting another cigarette from the stub of the old one, there had been a fifth item, and I had blown that one, too.

The classics of public relations clearly show how little reason has to do with M/R, and yet I had allowed myself to fall into that oldest and most imbecilic of traps set for flacks. Think of history's master strokes of flackery: "The Jews stabbed Germany in the back!" "Seventy-eight (or fifty-nine, or one hundred and three) card-carrying Communists in the State Department!" "I will go to Korea!" It is not enough for a theme to be rational; indeed it is *wrong* for a theme to be rational if you want to move men's glands, because, above all else, it must seem new and fresh and of such revolutionary simplicity that it illuminates an enormous, confused, and disagreeable problem in a fresh and hopeful light. Or so it must seem to the Average Man. And since he has spent any number of surly, worried hours groping for some personal salvation in the face of a bankrupt Germany or a threat of subversion or a war that is going nowhere, no *rational* solution can ever meet those strictures . . . since he has already considered all the rational solutions and found either that they are useless or that the cost is more than he wants to pay.

So what I should have concentrated on in Belport was the bright, irrational, distractive issue. The Big Lie, if you will. And I had hardly found even a Sly Insinuation.

It was interesting to consider in just how many ways I had done the wrong thing. Including maybe the wrongest of all: I had let Candace Harmon get away. And then in these thoughts, myself almost despising, haply the door chimed, and I opened it, and there was this fellow in Space Force olive-greens saying, "Come along, Mr. Gunnarsen, the Truce Team wants to talk to you."

For one frozen moment there, I was nineteen years old again. I was a Rocketman 3/c on the Moon, guarding the Aristarchus base against invaders from outer space. (We thought that to be a big joke at the time. Shows how unfunny a joke can turn.) This fellow was a colonel, and his name was Peyroles, and he took me down the corridor, to a private elevator I had never known was there, up to the flat dome of the mushroom and into a suite that made my suite look like the cellar under a dog run in Old Levittown. The reek was overpowering. By then I had gotten over my quick response to the brass, and I took out a ker-pak and held it to my nose. The colonel did not even look at me.

"Sit down!" barked the colonel, and left me in front of an unlighted fireplace. Something was going on; I could hear voices from another room, a lot of them:

"–burned one in effigy, and by God we'll burn a real one–"

"–smells like a skunk–"

"–turns my stomach!" And that last fellow, whoever he was, was pretty near right at that–although actually in the few seconds since I'd entered the suite I had almost forgotten the smell. It was funny how you got used to it. Like a ripe cheese: The first whiff knocked you sick, but pretty soon the olfactory nerves got the hang of the thing and built up a defense.

"–all right, the war's over and we have to get along with them, but a man's home town–"

Whatever it was that was going on in the other room, it was going on loudly. Tempers were always short when Arcturans were around, because the smell, of course, put everybody on edge. People don't like bad smells. They're not nice. They remind us of sweat and excrement, which we have buttressed our lives against admitting as real, personal facts. Then there was a loud military yell for order–I recognized the colonel, Peyroles–and then a voice that sounded queerly not-quite-human, although it spoke in English. An Arcturan? What was his name, Knafti? But I had understood they couldn't make human sounds.

Whoever it was, he put an end to the meeting. The door opened.

Through it I could see a couple of dozen hostile backs, leaving through another door, and coming toward me the Space Force colonel, a very young man with a pale angel's face and a dragging limp, in civilian clothes . . . and, yes, the Arcturan. It was the first one I had ever been with at so close range, in so small a group. He wobbled toward me on four or six of his coat-hanger limbs, breathing-thorax encased in a golden shell, his mantis face and bright black eyes staring at me.

Peyroles closed the door behind them.

He turned to me and said, "Mr. Gunnarsen . . . Knafti . . . Timmy Brown."

I hadn't the ghost of a clue whether to offer to shake, and if so, with what. Knafti, however, merely regarded me gravely. The boy nodded. I said: "I'm glad to meet you, gentlemen. As you perhaps know, I tried to set up an appointment before, but your people turned me down. I take it now the shoe is on the other foot."

Colonel Peyroles frowned toward the door he had just shut—there were still noises behind it—but said to me, "You're quite right. That was a meeting of a civic leaders' committee—"

The door interrupted him by opening, and a man leaned through and yelled: "Peyroles! Can that thing understand white man's talk? I hope so. I hope it hears me when I say that I'm going to make it my personal business to take it apart if it's still in Belport this time tomorrow. And if any human being, or so-called human being like you, gets in the way, I'll take him apart, too!" He slammed the door without waiting for an answer.

"You see?" said Peyroles gruffly, angrily. Things like that would never have happened with well-tempered troops. "That's what we want to talk to you about."

"I see," I said, and I did see, very clearly, because that fellow who had leaned through the door had been the Arcturan-property-sale standard bearer we had counted on, old—what had Connick called him?—old Slits-and-fits Schlitz, the man we were attempting to elect to get our proposition through.

Judging by the amount of noise I'd heard from the citizens' delegation, there was lynching in the atmosphere. I could understand why they would reverse themselves and ask for me, before things got totally out of control and wound up in murder, if you call killing an Arcturan murder—

—although, it occurred to me, lynching Knafti might not be the worst thing that could happen; public sentiment might bounce back—

I shoved that thought out of my mind and got down to business. "What, exactly?" I asked. "I gather you want me to do something about your image."

Knafti sat himself down, if that's what Arcturans do, on a twining-rack. The pale boy whispered something to him, then came to me. "Mr. Gunnar*sen,*" he said, "I am Knaf*ti.*" He spoke with a great precision of vowels and a stress at the end of each sentence, as though he had learned English out of a handbook. I had no trouble in understanding him. At least, not in understanding what it was he said. It did take me a moment to comprehend what he meant, and then Peyroles had to help.

"He means at this moment he's speaking for Knafti," said the colonel. "Interpreter. See?"

The boy moved his lips for a moment–shifting gears, it seemed–and said, "That is right, I am Timmy *Brown. Knafti's* translator and assis*tant.*"

"Then ask Knafti what he wants from me." I tried to say it the way he had–a sort of sneeze for the "K" and an indescribable whistle for the "f."

Timmy Brown moved his lips again and said, "I, Knafti, wish you to stop . . . to leave . . . to discontinue your operation in Bel*port.*"

From the twining-tree the Arcturan waved his ropy limbs and chittered like a squirrel. The boy chirped back and said: "I, Knafti, commend you on your effective work, but stop *it.*"

"By which," rumbled Colonel Peyroles, "he means knock it off."

"Go fight a space war, Peyroles. Timmy–I mean, Knafti, this is the job I'm paid to do. The Arcturan Confederacy itself hired us. I take my orders from Arthur S. Bigelow, Jr., and I carry them out whether Knafti likes it or not."

Chirp and chitter between Knafti and the pale, limping boy. The Arcturan left his twining-tree and moved to the window, looking out into the sky and the copter traffic. Timmy Brown said: "It does not matter what your orders may be. I, Knafti, tell you that your work is harm*ful.*" He hesitated, mumbling to himself. "We do not wish to obtain our base here at the cost of what is true, and–" he turned imploringly to the Arcturan–"it is apparent you are attempting to change the *truth.*"

He chirped at the Arcturan, who took his blind black eyes from the window and came toward us. Arcturans don't walk, exactly. They drag themselves on the lower part of the thorax. Their limbs are supple and thin, and what are not used for support are used for gestures. Knafti used a number of his now as he chirped one short series of sounds at the boy.

"Otherwise," Timmy Brown finished off, "I, Knafti, tell you we will have to fight this war over *again.*"

As soon as I was back in my room, I messaged Chicago for orders and clarification and got back the answer I expected:

Hold everything. Referring matter to ASB-jr. Await instructions.

So I awaited. The way I awaited was to call Candace at the office and get the latest sitrep. I told her about the near-riot in the Truce Team's suite and asked her what it was all about.

She shook her head. "We have their appointments schedule, Gunner. It just says, 'Meeting with civic leaders.' But one of the leaders has a secretary who goes to lunch with a girl from Records and Accounting here, and–"

"And you'll find out. All right, do that, and now what's the current picture?"

She began reading off briefing digests and field reports. They were mixed, but not altogether bad. Opinion sampling showed a small rise in favor of the Arcturans, in fact. It wasn't much, but it was the first plus change I had seen, and doubly puzzling because of Knafti's attitude and the brawl with the civic leaders.

I asked, "Why, honey?"

Candace's face in the screen was as puzzled as mine. "We're still digging."

"All right. Go on."

There were more pluses. The flower show had yielded surprisingly big profits in attitudes–among those who attended. Of course, they were only a tiny fraction of the population of Belport. The Arcats were showing a plus for us, too. Where we were down was in PTA meeting resolutions, in resignations from Candace's Arcturan-American Friendship League, in poor attendance at neighborhood *kaffeeklatsches.*

Now that I knew what to look for, I could see what the Children had done to us. In every family-situation sampling, the attitudes were measurably worse than when the subjects were interviewed in a non-family environment–at work, stopped on the street, in a theater.

The importance of that was just what I had told Connick. No man is a simple entity. He behaves one way when his self-image is as head of a family, another when he is at a cocktail party, another at work, another still when a pretty girl sits down beside him on a commuter-copter. Elementary truths. But it had taken the M/R boys half a century to learn how to use them.

In this case the use was clear: Play down family elements, play up play. I ordered more floats, torchlight parades, and a teen-age beauty contest. I canceled the 14 picnic rallies we had planned and ordered a hold on the kaffeeklatsches.

I was not exactly obeying Chicago's orders. But it didn't matter. All this could be canceled with a single word, and, anyway, it was only nit-picking detail. The One Big Weeny still escaped me.

I lit a cigarette, thought for a minute, and said, "Honey, get me some of the synoptic extracts of opinion sampling from heads of families and particularly families containing some of the Children. I don't want the integration or analysis. Just the raw interviews, but with the scutwork left out."

And as soon as she was off the line, the Chicago circuit came in with a message they'd been holding:

> Query from ASB-jr. Provided top is taken off budget and your hand is freed, can you guarantee, repeat guarantee, win on referendum question?

It was not the response I had expected from them.

Still, it was a legitimate question. I took a moment to think it over. Junior Bigelow had already given me a pretty free hand—as he always did; how else can a troubleshooter work? If he was now emphasizing that my hand was freed entirely, it would not be because he thought I hadn't understood him in the first place. Nor would it be because he suspected I might be cheese-paring secretarial salaries. He meant one thing: Win, no matter what.

Under those conditions, could I do it?

Well, of course I could win. Yes. Provided I found the One Big Weeny. You can always win an election, any election anywhere, provided you are willing to pay the right price.

It was finding the price to pay that was hard. Not just money. Sometimes the price you pay is a human being, in the role for which I had been lining up Connick. Throw a human sacrifice to the gods, and your prayer is granted. . . .

But was Connick the sacrifice the gods wanted? Would it help to defeat him, bearing in mind that his opponent was one of the men who had been screaming at Knafti in the Truce Team suite? And if so—had my knife enough edge to drain his blood?

Well, it always had had before. And if Connick wasn't the right man, I would find the man who was. I messaged back, short and sweet: Yes.

And in less than a minute, as though Junior had been standing by at the faxtape receiver, waiting for the word from me—and perhaps he had!—his reply came back:

Gunner, we've lost the Arcturan Confederacy account. Arc Con liaison man says all bets off. They're giving notice of cancellation our contract, suggestion they will cancel entire armistice treaty, too. I don't have to tell you we need them. Some possibility that showing strong results in Belport will get them back. That's what we have to play for. No holds barred, Gunner, win that election.

The office circuit chimed then. Probably it was Candace, but I didn't want to talk to her just then. I turned all the communication circuits to "hold," stripped down, climbed into the shower, set it for full needle spray, and let the water beat on me. It was not an aid to thought, it was a replacement for thought.

I didn't want to think anymore. I wanted time out.

I did not want to think about (a) whether the war would break out again, and, if so, in what degree I would have helped to bring that about; (b) what I was doing to Nice Guy Connick; (c) whether It Was All Worth It, or (d) how much I was going to dislike myself that coming Christmas Day. I only wanted to let the hot splash of scented foaming water anesthetize me. When my skin began to look pale and wrinkly, although I had not come to any conclusions or found any solutions, I came out, dressed, opened the communications circuits, and let them all begin blinking, ringing, and winking at once.

I took Candace first. She said, "Gunner! Dear Lord, have you heard about the Armistice Commission? They've just released a statement–"

"I heard. What else, honey?"

Good girl, she shifted gears without missing a beat. "Then there was that meeting of civic leaders in the Truce Team suite–"

"I saw. Feedback from the Armistice Commission's statement. What else?"

She glanced at the papers in her hand, hesitated, then said: "Nothing important. Uh–Gunner, that 3-V preempt for tonight–"

"Yeah, honey?"

"Do you want me to cancel it?"

I said, "No. You're right, we won't use the time for the Arcturan-American Friendship League or whatever we had scheduled, but you're wrong, we'll use the time some way. I don't know how right now."

"But Junior said–"

"Honey," I told her, "Junior says all sorts of things. Anybody looking to scalp me?"

"Well," she said, "there's Mr. Connick. I didn't think you'd want to see him."

"No, I'll see him. I'll see anybody."

"Anybody?" I had surprised her. She dove into her list again. "There's somebody from the Truce Team—"

"Make it everybody from the Truce Team."

"—and Commander Whitling from—"

"From the hospital. Sure, and tell him to bring some kids."

"—and . . ." She trailed off and looked at me. "Gunner, are you putting me on? You don't really want to see all these people."

I smiled and reached out and patted the viewphone. From her point of view it would look like an enormous cloudy hand closing in on her screen, but she would know what I meant. I said, "You could not be more wrong. I do. I want to see them all, the more the better, and the way I'd like to see them best is in my office all at once. So set it up, honey, because I'll be busy between now and then."

"Busy doing what, Gunner?"

"Busy trying to think of what I want to see them for." And I turned off the viewphone, got up, and walked out, leaving the others gobbling into emptiness behind me. What I needed was a long, long walk, and I took it.

When I was tired of walking, I went to the office and evicted Haber from his private quarters. I kept him standing by what had once been his own desk while I checked with Candace and found that she had made all my appointments for that evening; then I told him to get lost. "And thanks," I said.

He paused on his way to the door. "For what, Gunner?"

"For a very nice office to kill time in." I waved at the furnishings. "I wondered what you'd spent fifty grand on when I saw the invoices in the Chicago office, Haber, and I admit I thought there might have been a little padding. But I was wrong."

He said woundedly: "Gunner-boy! I wouldn't do anything like that."

"I believe you. Wait a minute." I thought for a second, then told him to send in some of the technical people and not to let anybody, repeat anybody, disturb me for any purpose whatever. I scared him good, too. He left, a shaken man, a little angry, a little admiring, a little excited inside, I think, at the prospect of seeing how the great man would get himself out of this one. Meanwhile the great man talked briefly to the technicians, took a ten-minute nap, drank the martinis out of his dinner tray, and pitched the rest of it in the dispos-all.

Then, as I had nearly an hour before the appointments Candace had set up for me, I scrounged around fat-cat Haber's office to see what entertainment it offered.

There were his files. I glanced at them and forgot them; there was nothing about the hoarded memoranda that interested me, not even for gossip. There were the books on his shelf. But I did not care to disturb the patina of dust that even the cleaning machines had not been able to touch. There was his private bar, and the collection of photographs in the end compartment of his desk drawer.

It looked like very dull times, waiting, until the studio men reported in that they had completed their arrangements at my request, and the 3-V tape-effects monitor could now be controlled by remote from my desk, and then I knew I had a pleasant way of killing any amount of time.

Have you ever played with the console of a 3-V monitor, backed by a library of tape-effects strips? It is very much like being God.

All that the machine does is take the stored videotapes that are in its files and play them back. But it also manipulates size and perspective or superimposes one over another . . . so that you can, as I, in fact, have done, put the living person of someone you don't like in a position embarrassing to him, and project it on a montage screen so that only a studio tech can find the dots on the pattern where the override betrays its presence.

Obviously, this is a way out of almost any propaganda difficulty, since it is child's play to make up any event you like and give it the seeming of reality.

Of course, everybody knows it can be done. So the evidence of one's own eyes is no longer quite enough, even for a voter. And the laws can cut you down. I had thought of whomping up some frightful frame around Connick, for example. But it wouldn't work; no matter when I did it, there would still be time for the other side to spread the word of an electoral fraud, and a hoax of this magnitude would make its own way onto the front pages. So I used the machine for something much more interesting to me. I used it as a toy.

I started by dialing the lunar base at Aristarchus for background, found a corps of Rocketmen marching off in the long lunar step, patched my own face onto one of the helmeted figures, and zoomed in and out with the imaginary camera, watching R3/c Odin Gunnarsen as a boy of nineteen, scared witless but doing his job. He was a pretty nice boy, I thought objectively, and wondered what had gone wrong with him later. I abandoned that and sought for other amusements. I found Candace's images on tape in the files and pleasured myself with her for a time. Her open, friendly face gave some dignity to the fantastic bodies of half a dozen 3-V strippers in the files, but I stopped that child's game.

I looked for a larger scope. I spread the whole panoply of the heavens across the screen of the tape machine. I sought out the crook of the Big Dipper's handle, traced its arc across half the heavens until I located orange Arcturus. Then I zoomed in on the star, as littler stars grew larger and hurtled out of range around it, sought its seven gray-green planets and located Number Five among them, the watery world that Knafti had spawned upon. I bade the computing mind inside the tape machine reconstruct the events of the orbit bombing for me and watched hell-bombs splash enormous mushrooms of poisonous foam into the Arcturan sky, whipping the island cities with tidal waves and drowning them in death.

Then I destroyed the whole planet. I turned Arcturus into a nova and watched the hot driven gases sphere out to embrace the planet, boil its seas, slag its cities . . . and found myself sweating. I ordered another drink from the dispenser and switched the machine off. And then I became aware that the pale blue light over the door to Haber's office was glowing insistently. It was time; my visitors had arrived.

Connick had brought his kids along, three of them; the lover from Donnegan General had brought two more; Knafti and Colonel Peyroles had Timmy Brown. "Welcome to Romper Room," I said. "They're making lynch mobs young this year."

They all yelled at me at once–or all but Knafti, whose tweeting chitter just didn't have the volume to compete. I listened, and when they showed signs of calming down, I reached into fat cat Haber's booze drawer and poured myself a stiff one and said, "All right, which of you creeps want first crack?" And they boiled up again while I drank my drink. All of them, except Candace Harmon, who only stood by the door and looked at me.

So I said, "All right, Connick, you first. Are you going to make me spread it all over the newscasts that you had a dishonorable discharge? . . . And by the way, maybe you'd like to meet my assistant blackmailer; Miss Harmon over there dug up the dirt on you."

Her boyfriend yelped, but Candace just went on looking. I didn't look back, but kept my eyes on Connick. He squinted his eyes, put his hands in his pockets, and said, with considerable self-restraint, "You know I was only seventeen years old when that happened."

"Oh, sure. I know more. You had a nervous breakdown the year after your discharge, space cafard, as they call it on the soapies. Yellow fever is what we called it on the Moon."

He glanced quickly at his kids, the two who were his own and the one who was not, and said rapidly: "You know I could have had that DD reversed–"

"But you didn't. The significant fact isn't that you deserted. The significant fact is that you were loopy. And, I'd say, still are."

Timmy Brown stuttered: "One mo*ment*. I, Knafti, have asked that you cease–"

But Connick brushed him aside. "Why, Gunnarsen?"

"Because I intend to win this election. I don't care what it costs–especially what it costs you."

"But, I, Knafti, have instructed–" That was Timmy Brown trying again.

"The Armistice Commission issued orders–" That was Peyroles.

"I don't know which is worse, you or the bugs!" And that was Candace's little friend from the hospital, and they all were talking at once again. Even Knafti came dragging toward me on his golden slug's belly, chirruping and hooting, and Timmy Brown was actually weeping as he tried to tell me I was wrong, I had to stop; the whole thing was against orders and why wouldn't I de*sist?*

I shouted: "Shut up, all of you!"

They didn't, but the volume level dropped minutely. I rode over it: "What the hell do I care what any of you want? I'm paid to do a job. My job is to make people act in a certain way. I do it. Maybe tomorrow I'll be paid to make them act the opposite way, and I'll do that, too. Anyway, who the hell are you to order me around? A stink-bug like you, Knafti? A GI quack like yourself, Whitling? Or you, Connick. A–"

"A candidate for public office," he said clearly. And I give him much mana–he didn't shout, but he talked right over me. "And as such I have an obligation–"

But I outyelled him, anyway. "Candidate! You're a candidate right up till the minute I tell the voters you're a nut, Connick. And then you're dead! And I will tell them, I promise, if–"

I didn't get a chance to finish that sentence, because all three of Connick's kids were diving at me, his own two and the other one. They sent papers flying off Haber's desk and smashed his sand-crystal decanter, but they didn't get to my throat, where they clearly were aimed, because Connick and Timmy Brown dragged them back. Not easily.

I allowed myself a sneer. "And what does that prove? Your kids like you, I admit—even the one from Mars. The one that Knafti's people used for vivisection—that Knafti himself worked over, likely as not. Nice picture, right? Your bug-buddy there, killing babies, destroying kids . . . or didn't you know that Knafti himself was one of the boss bugs on the baby-killing project?"

Timmy Brown shrieked wildly, "You don't know what you are do*ing*. It was not Knafti's fault at *all!*" His ashen face was haggard, his rotten teeth bared in a grimace. And he was weeping.

If you apply heat to a single molecule, it will take off like a tom with a spark under his tail, but you cannot say where it will go. If you heat a dozen molecules, they will fling out in all directions, but you still do not know which directions they will be. If, however, you heat a few billion, about as many as are in a thimble of dilute gas, you know where they will go: they will expand. Mass action. You can't tell what a single molecule may do—call it the molecule's free will if you like—but masses obey mass laws. Masses of anything, even so small a mass as the growling troop that confronted me in Haber's office. I let them yell, and all the yelling was at me. Even Candace was showing the frown and the darkening of the eyes and the working of the lips, although she watched me as silently and steadily as ever.

Connick brought it to a head. "All *right,* everybody," he yelled, "now listen to me! Let's get this thing straightened out!"

He stood up, a child gripped by each elbow, and the third, the youngest, trapped between him and the door. He looked at me with such loathing that I could feel it—and didn't like it, either, although it was no more than I had expected, and he said: "It's true. Sammy, here, was one of the kids from Mars. Maybe that has made me think things I shouldn't have thought—he's my kid now, and when I think of those stink bugs cutting—"

He stopped himself and turned to Knafti. "Well, I see something. A man who would do a thing like that would be a fiend. I'd cut his heart out with my bare hands. But you aren't a man."

Grimly he let go of the kids and strode toward Knafti. "I can't forgive you. God help me, it isn't possible. But I can't blame you—exactly—any more than I can blame lightning for striking my house. I think I was wrong. Maybe I'm wrong now. But—I don't know what you people do—I'd like to shake your hand. Or whatever the hell it is you've got there. I've been thinking of you as a perverted murderer and a filthy animal, but I'll tell you right now, I'd rather work together with you–for your base, for peace, for whatever we can get together on–than with some human beings in this room!"

I didn't stay to watch the tender scene that followed.

I didn't have to, since the cameras and tape recorders that the studio people had activated for me behind every one-way mirror in the room would be watching for me. I could only hope they had not missed a single word or scream, because I didn't think I could do that scene over again.

I opened the door quietly and left. And as I was going, I caught the littlest Connick kid sneaking past me, headed for the 3-V set in the waiting room, and snaked out an arm to stop him. "Stinker!" he hissed. "Rat fink!"

"You may be right," I told him, "but go back and keep your father company. You're in on living history today."

"Nuts! I always watch *Dr. Zhivago* on Monday nights, and it's on in five minutes, and–"

"Not tonight it isn't, son. You can hold that against me, too. We preempted the time for a different show entirely."

I escorted him back into the room, closed the door, picked up my coat, and left.

Candace was waiting for me with the car. She was driving it herself.

"Will I make the nine-thirty flight?" I asked.

"Sure, Gunner." She steered onto the autotraffic lane, put the car on servo, and dialed the scatport, then sat back and lit a cigarette for each of us. I took one and looked morosely out the window.

Down below us, on the slow-traffic level, we were passing a torchlight parade, with floats and glee clubs and free beer at the major pedestrian intersections. I opened the glove compartment and took out field glasses, looked through them–

"Oh, you don't have to check up, Gunner. I took care of it. They're all plugging the program."

"I see they are." Not only were the marchers carrying streamers that advertised our preempt show that was now already beginning to be on the air, but the floats carried projection screens and amplifiers. You couldn't look anywhere in the procession without seeing Knafti, huge and hideous in his gold carapace, clutching the children and protecting them against the attack of that monster from another planet, me. The studio people had done a splendid job of splicing in no time at all. The whole scene was there on camera, as real as I had just lived it.

"Want to listen?" Candace fished out and passed me a hyperboloid long-hearer, but I didn't need it. I remembered what the voices would be saying. There would be Connick denouncing me. Timmy Brown denouncing me. The kids denouncing me, all of them. Colonel Peyroles denouncing me, Commander Whitling denouncing me, even Knafti denouncing me. All that hate and only one target.

Me.

"Of course, Junior'll fire you. He'll have to, Gunner."

I said, "I need a vacation, anyway." It wouldn't matter. Sooner or later, when the pressure was off, Junior would find a way to hire me back. Once the lawsuits had been settled. Once the Armistice Commission could finish its work. Once I could be put on the payroll inconspicuously, at an inconspicuous job in an inconspicuous outpost of the firm. With an inconspicuous future.

We slid over the top of a spiraling ramp and down into the parking bays of the scatport. "So long, honey," I said, "and Merry Christmas to you both."

"Oh, Gunner! I wish–"

But I knew what she really wished, and I wouldn't let her finish. I said, "He's a nice fellow, Whitling. And you know? I'm not."

I didn't kiss her good-bye.

The scatjet was ready for boarding. I fed my ticket into the check-in slot, got the green light as the turnstile clicked open, entered the plane, and took a seat on the far side, by the window.

You can win any cause if you care to pay the price. All it takes is one human sacrifice.

By the time the scatjet began to roar, to quiver, and to turn on its axis away from the terminal, I had faced the fact that that price once and for all was paid. I saw Candace standing there on the roof of the loading dock, her skirts whipped by the back-blast. She didn't wave to me, but she didn't go away as long as I could see her standing on the platform.

Then, of course, she would go back to her job and ultimately on Christmas morning to that nice guy at the hospital. Haber would stay in charge of his no-longer-important branch office. Connick would win his campaign. Knafti would transact his incomprehensible business with Earth, and if any of them ever thought of me again, it would be with loathing, anger, and contempt. But that is the way to win an election. You have to pay the price. It was just the breaks of the game that the price of this one was me.

What the author has to say about all this
Afterword to THE BEST OF FREDERIK POHL

WHEN we first talked about a collection of the "best" of my stories I dove right into something close to catatonia. It isn't *easy* to pick out the best of your life's work. That is almost like asking me to pick which two of my four children were to appear in a "best of the family" household anthology. In fact, it is exactly like that because, although like most writers I try to maintain a pose of public professionalism, also like most writers I bleed and die with every story I write. The stories don't always turn out to be masterpieces. In fact, I have written stories that were awful. But in no case is that the story's fault. The fault is only mine; and I must admit that it gives me great pain to admit to anyone that a story–child of mine is in any way handicapped, however clearly I know it in my private mind. But, of course, saying which is "best" is only the other side of saying which is "worst."

So when Ballantine Books suggested that someone else make the selections for me, I was ecstatic with relief. And I could not have picked a better man than Lester del Rey, best of friends, most mortal of combatants, most trustworthy person I have ever known.

At my request, Lester limited his selection to stories published in the first half-century of my life. That's just smarts on my part. I am saving up for a second volume when I reach 100. (At the moment I have almost 46 years to go, and who knows what I'm going to write yet?) And at *his* request I am appending a few notes about some of the stories.

This is one of the few writers' vices I don't usually have. It seems to me that a story should say what it has to say internally. If something should be said about it that will affect its impact on a reader, then the only fair way for the author to behave would be to go around to every reader and tell him about it. As that isn't practical, or even desirable—how terrible it would be to listen to all those excuses and cries of pain!–I try as much as I can to make the stories speak for themselves.

But for some of these stories there are thanks I should give, or circumstances that I think are interesting enough to warrant departing from my rule . . . and so below are notes on some of the stories in this volume.

THE TUNNEL UNDER THE WORLD

In 1954 Lester del Rey and I were writing a novel in collaboration, and it was taking forever. Lester is a fine writer as well as an old and close friend, but we should never collaborate. He has his way of writing, and I have my own, wholly incompatible, way of writing, and neither of us is about to change one whim to accommodate the other.

So one day, when we were on the third draft of chapter six, or possibly the sixth draft of chapter three, I announced I needed a vacation, and I took a week off and wrote "The Tunnel Under the World." (I didn't call it that. I called it "The Ides of June," and I still like that title better, but it seems a little late, now, to change it back.)

Scientific American said of "The Tunnel Under the World" that it was a cautionary tale, representing what the advertising people would do to us if they had the power. One of the best things about writing is finding out, from time to time, that you are understood exactly. That's the statement I meant to make, and I believe that statement to be true.

THE MIDAS PLAGUE

The idea for "The Midas Plague" originally came from Horace Gold, editor of *Galaxy* Magazine. He said, "Fred, why don't you write a story about a world in which the problem is over-, rather than under-, production?" I said, "Because I don't for one second believe any such world could exist." So I turned him down; and I was not the only writer to do so by a long shot–I think he must have asked every regular in *Galaxy*'s pages to write that story. All of them turned him down, too. But he kept insisting for a year or so, until finally I noticed that my subconscious had been tinkering with the idea, trying permutations and complications on for size. Suddenly I realized I could, in fact, write the story after all.

So I did, and Horace published it, and it has been just about the most widely republished shorter-than-novel story I ever wrote; it turns up in economics texts and sociology courses, and I once listened to Robert Theobald lecturing on a possible alternative economic future for twenty minutes before it gradually dawned on me that he was telling the story of "The Midas Plague."

DAY MILLION

When I lecture at colleges, during the question period somebody usually asks how I know when a story is ready to be written, and how long it takes to write one. Those are harder questions than they seem. Let me answer them for "Day Million" to show why.

The parts of "Day Million" had been rattling around my head for a long time—the notion of gender being a matter of choice, the use of taped reproductions of people to replace the people (I first began to think of that as a story possibility when I first heard of Turing's Paradox), and so on. So in a sense I had been working on the story for about ten years. However, in terms of actual chained-to-the-typewriter time, I began to write the story at about four o'clock one morning (I work at night when I can, because there are fewer interruptions), finished the first draft at six, stopped for breakfast, put clean paper in the typewriter and had the story in the mail by nine. So the length of time it took me was five hours *or* ten years.

How did I know it was ready to write? I didn't. I simply wanted to write a story about the millionth day of the Christian era, and when I started to consider what that millionth day might be like, all the bits and pieces of "Day Million" began to fall into place.

Why did I want to write a story about the millionth day of the Christian era? I am a little embarrassed to say. The fact is I had had a notion for a tv series which I wanted to call *Day Million*—and the principal reason for writing the story, which had nothing at all to do with the series I had in mind, was to protect the title until I could get the series produced.

I never did get the series produced, and I see no reason to think I ever will—but I did write the story!

HAPPY BIRTHDAY, DEAR JESUS

The first book I ever had published was a novel written in collaboration with C. M. Kornbluth, *The Space Merchants.* It represents the major part of my perceptions about the advertising industry, but there were a few left over that I discovered long after *The Space Merchants* was in print. This is one.

How could I have left Christmas out of the saga of forcing things people don't need down their regurgitating throats? I don't know. Clearly here was an oversight of enormous proportions. It was too late for me to do anything about *The Space Merchants,* but when my first short-story collection came to be published, and the editor suggested I write one original for it, I leaped at the chance to write and include "Happy Birthday, Dear Jesus."

SPEED TRAP

In the mid-1960s, I received my first invitation to participate in an actual swear-to-God *scientific* meeting, on Planetology and Space Mission Planning, sponsored by the New York Academy of Sciences. I loved it. Later that year I wrote this story, using some of the color and background I had picked up—of course changing it around considerably. I invented a cast of characters named with names like Resnik, Grew and MacKenzie, and an unnamed Egyptian astronomer who had not gotten over the Suez war (the Six-Day War had not yet happened). While the story was going through the hatching process at *Playboy,* being illustrated and set and proofread and printed, I went to another such meeting, this one in Boston, and you'll never guess who sat down beside me at lunch? A man named McKenzie. And there was a man named Resnick on the roster, and also, I was told, there was quite an unpleasant scene in the bar one night with a Lebanese (not Egyptian) astronomer who was still thoroughly unreconciled to the Suez War.

That is enough to make a person wonder.

THE CENSUS TAKERS

From time to time I get into discussions with people on what good science fiction should be. One of the strictures often proposed is that sf should be relevant to contemporary problems. I don't believe this for one second. I think sf should not discuss what everyone else discusses. I think it should discuss what everyone *should* be discussing, but hasn't yet come to understand. When Carol Burnett signs off her TV program with "Don't pollute, folks!", ecology is no longer a fit subject for sf.

The point is that this twenty-year-old story is about overpopulation. I wouldn't write it now. But I'm glad I wrote it then.

PUNCH

I originally called this story "A Cure for Warts and Killing," but the editors of *Playboy* decided against that title when they printed it. They may have been right.

THE CHILDREN OF NIGHT

One thing I've noticed about science-fiction writers is that those who know a great deal about a particular subject seldom discuss that subject in their science-fiction stories. For example, Eric Temple Bell was both a first-rate mathematician and, under the name of John Taine, a first-rate sf writer some years ago. He never wrote about mathematics. Isaac Asimov, whose Ph.D. is in biochemistry, writes about all the sciences *except* biochemistry.

If there is an area of human endeavor in which I know a specialist's kind of knowledge, it is politics. I spent 20 years in political work, have written one book (*Practical Politics*) on the subject and a lot of shorter pieces, have ghost-written speeches, run campaigns—the lot.

At least a dozen times I've tried to write a science-fiction story about politics, and every time I've abandoned the effort—every time but one. "The Children of Night" is the one.

THE DAY THE MARTIANS CAME

One of my interests is war. My library of war books is as big as my library of scientific books, and I feel I know quite a lot about what war does to people. One of the things I have observed is that the reaction of people to war is never simple or holistic. If you have stock in an aircraft company, your reaction is quite unlike that of your neighbor, who is of draft age and deeply involved in his career. If your personal life is unrewarding, you are a lot more likely to be a damn-the-torpedoes hero than if you really like your job, wife and home. Etc.

It seemed to me at one time that it would be an interesting project to write a series of stories about what the discovery of intelligent life elsewhere in the universe would mean to a selected cast of lead characters—a fashion designer (*Martian prints the rage!*), a philologist, a diplomat, etc. I managed to get two of the stories written—"Sad Solarian Screenwriter Sam," about a screenwriter in this situation, was one; this is the other. I doubt I will ever write more—but someone still should!

It is not easy to stop there, when there are other stories in the volume to talk about, and I remember so well every birth pang, every cranky teething through the typewriter. But I have something else I want to say, and that is to acknowledge a very large debt that accumulated over nearly a quarter of a century to two people. I am not the only one who owes much to them. Every science-fiction writer and every reader is in their debt, for being the first with the courage and the sagacity to make sf a staple in the mass-market paperback field.

I personally owe them something more than that. I owe them friendship, courtesy, help beyond the call of duty . . . and love.

Their names are Betty and Ian Ballantine, and until the day I die they will both have a very special place in my heart.

—Frederik Pohl
1974